Ramah

Rob Munday

malcolm down

PUBLISHING

First published 2021 by Malcolm Down Publishing Ltd.
www.malcolmdown.co.uk

24 23 22 21   7 6 5 4 3 2 1

British Library Cataloguing in Publication Data
A catalogue record for this book is available from
the British Library.

ISBN 978-1-912863-90-7

Cover design by Esther Kotecha
Art direction by Sarah Grace

Printed in the UK

For Marcelinito.

You may never be able to read this book, or even hear or
understand the story.
But your smile inspired me.

Author's Note

I was brought up on, and enjoyed, the colourful stories of the Bible, and could repeat them faithfully, knowing all the supposedly important details. So, it was only when I taught my own children and their friends these same stories that I noticed little notes and nudges in the gospel texts that hinted at a life beyond the 15 minutes in real time that they occupy in Scripture.

Following up these leads led me not only to the heroes and villains of the Bible dramas, but also to the imagined characters in this book. They all, alike, spoke excitedly of a certain 'Yeshua', who I quickly realised was the person I knew as 'Jesus' from my English Bible. This emphasised for me the fact that these events occurred far away and long ago, in an eastern culture very different from mine.

Whilst it is important to have the Scriptures in modern language and even using familiar idioms, I realised that the dressing gowns and tea towels of nativity plays, together with the blond, blue-eyed, well-groomed Jesus of my childhood picture books, may have distorted and underplayed the reality of life in Bible times.

As this story has developed, I have tried to portray the background and detail of life in those days as realistically as I could. Whilst I have been to Palestine, travelling through the Judean desert, Galilee and Jerusalem, this was a only brief visit, so I have called on my experiences of another hot, arid country where our family lived among the poor and marginalised in a third-world culture under a harsh military regime that I imagine was not dissimilar to first-century Palestine. I may have made some false assumptions and possibly got some of the accounts muddled, but I have tried to faithfully retell their story using the fixed points that are mentioned in the gospels to give it some sense of authenticity.

Authors of fiction are usually careful to state that 'the characters portrayed in this book bear no relation to anyone living or dead', but those in this book are very real to me. I have relived their story with them as it played out over the last thirty years. They have become good friends with whom I have laughed and wept, sometimes pleading with them to take another course, but to no avail. If any disappoint you, then it will be because of failings in my characterisation of them rather than from any lack of colour in their lives. Like many people, now and down the ages the world over, they struggle to understand the big picture but nevertheless seek to live by the light revealed to them.

Many, then as now, find joy and comfort in singing the songs of the Bible. These are most often the Psalms, but there are other songs, too, especially the love song known as the 'Song of Songs' or sometimes the 'Song of Solomon'. Of course, in those days they would have sung in the local language and not having our modern translations, the version in this book is how they came to me. I have quoted them as they sang them in the story, but have included Bible links so that readers can look them up in a modern version and experience for themselves how the songs might speak to their hearts.

Rob Munday

Ramah

A sound of weeping heard in Ramah, Rachel weeping for her children.

Chapter 1

The door to the guardroom burst open with such ferocity that the men instinctively jerked into unobtrusive postures to avoid attracting the attention and wrath of the obviously furious centurion.

"Come on! Let's be having you! Sharp now!" yelled the officer. The men tumbled to order, hastily making themselves presentable, pocketing dice and pushing the jars of wine under the bench.

"What's got into him?" growled one soldier, adjusting his belt so that his wine paunch sat more comfortably over the top of it.

"Silence! Now get fell in like the brave soldiers that you pretend to be."

"Optio!" he barked to his second-in-command.

"Sir!"

"Lances and short swords, mounted and ready!"

He turned on his heel and strode up the short steps, flinging the door back so that it crashed against the wall, then disappeared into the darkness.

The men quickly gathered themselves together, grumbling under their breath but knowing the centurion was not to be messed with tonight. Several had drunk a skinful of wine and so they were grateful when they eased themselves into the saddle, glad to be sitting down and able to rely on the clearer minds of their Arab horses, who would instinctively follow the rest of the troop.

They were still milling around, adjusting reins and stirrups, when the centurion burst through from the officer's stable, breaking into a canter as he reached the gate. Anxious to keep up, the soldiers urged on their horses, jostling and wheeling while some of the more fuddle-headed lurched alarmingly, barely staying in their saddles. In a ragged line, they headed through the gate and into the night after the officer, the younger soldiers spurring their horses on to keep up with the centurion.

Short swords and lances! They were going into action! After weeks of hot dusty routine guard duty along the wide-open approaches to Jerusalem, the last few days had seen some real soldiering; searching the hills and valleys of the Judean desert for infiltrators from the East. And now there might be combat! A nighttime raid! Zealots maybe!

Once the optio had ensured that all the troops were in a vaguely respectable formation, he drew his horse alongside the centurion.

"Just routine patrol, sir?" he ventured.

The officer did not answer but stared on ahead, and the optio might have thought that he had not heard, except that he repeated through his clenched teeth, "Routine patrol ... routine patrol!" Suddenly, he barked, "Are your men drunk, optio?"

"We don't permit drinking on duty..." started the optio, but the centurion shouted him down.

"Liar! Your men are constantly drunk. May the gods help any that is sober tonight!" He reined his horse in and the troops came to a halt, the horses shaking their heads, blowing and shifting their feet after their brisk canter. The centurion sat for some time, looking at the lights of a peaceful Bethlehem settling down for the night on the hill opposite. He turned to the soldiers.

"This is the sort of night's work I am sure some of you have already excelled at."

"Women is it, sir?" quipped a voice from the dark, and a rumble of laughter passed through the ranks.

"No, soldier." The officer spoke quite calmly. "It's not the women... It's their babies." And then his voice raised in anger.

"Did you hear? Babies, I said! Baby boys! Every baby boy under two years old is to be killed… in case he has designs on the throne!" he spat out disgustedly. "Those are our brave orders!"

The optio cleared his throat.

"Now sir, some of us are old campaigners, and sometimes in the course of war we… Well, what I mean is…"

"Optio!" roared the officer. "If you've not got the stomach to face the babies, consider if you have the guts to face Herod in the morning for disobeying his orders! Do you understand?"

The soldiers hesitated for just a moment and then, in the mindlessness of soldiers down the ages who were 'just obeying orders', they launched themselves on the unsuspecting village in the ever-increasing frenzy of men committed to an evil senseless errand.

All over the village, innocent babies lay dying or lifeless in their distraught mothers' arms; numb fathers tore at their hair in helpless anger, frustration and disbelief; and brothers and sisters cowered in terrified confusion. At the barracks, the old soldiers drank themselves into oblivion, and the young recruits retched and vomited in the darkness. At the palace, a drained centurion delivered his report to a smug and callous king, who sipped his wine while the world turned sadly through yet another night of pitch black evil and waited for the light that would surely dawn one day.

Chapter 2

The mid-morning sun was warm after the coolness of the night, and Sarah basked in it as she rested at the roadside on the crest of the hill. It would be hot in a couple of hours, but the sun was so pleasant now. At her feet, her little boy, Issa, toddled around picking up stones and throwing them back on the path. They had been on the road now for several days, sleeping where they could – always cold, for Sarah had to carry Issa and didn't have the strength to carry much more than a thin blanket, a few clothes and some food. Still, tonight they would arrive back in Bethlehem and all that was familiar. But how would she be received? Would her aged aunt have her back in the house? She had left home a rather wilful and headstrong sixteen-year-old, and now she was coming home older and wiser.

And with a son.

As she sat musing in the sun, she heard footsteps approaching and she instinctively drew Issa to her side, but relaxed when a young Jewish couple with a donkey appeared up the other side of the hill, the man leading while the wife rode. Sarah would be pleased for some decent company, especially after having to fight off the attentions of the caravanners she had met at the various stops on the road, so she determined to try and strike up a conversation. Maybe they would stop for a while.

"Shalom," she ventured with a smile.

The man returned the Shalom rather half-heartedly, obviously tired after the climb and needing little encouragement to rest now. Sarah noticed a small boy riding with his mother and the change of rhythm woke him. The man tenderly lifted him to the ground, where he stood blinking sleepily while his father helped his mother down, spreading blankets on the ground for them to sit on as the donkey wandered away to sniff the dry stalks by the roadside.

The man remained silent, looking thoughtfully back down the road they had just come along while his wife sorted food from the bags. Their child sat, still sleepy, on the horse blankets.

Sarah tried again.

"This is the Bethlehem road, isn't it?" She knew very well that it was.

The young man turned after a few moments, as if noticing her for the first time. As the question registered, he replied in some confusion, "Yes. Yes, it is. I'm sorry, sister, we have travelled all night. I'm a little weary. You should get there before nightfall. It's a good road."

He went over to the donkey, tying it to the branch of a low thorn tree, brushing dust and burrs from its coat and adjusting the halter, obviously wanting no further conversation.

His wife smiled at Sarah.

"Forgive my husband. These are hard times for our men folk, especially good husbands who want to protect their families. We were happy in Bethlehem, but then…" She said no more, but put her arm round her son while giving him a cup of milk she poured from a skin.

Sarah felt her own little boy gripping her dress, as young children do when wanting to attract a parent's attention to a good thing they fear to ask for out loud. Sarah, too, would love some fresh milk. All they had was some dry bread. She looked away, trying to seem uninterested.

The small boy, sleepily holding the cup, became aware of the other child watching him. They eyed each other for a few moments and then, looking down at his cup and getting to his feet, he brought it over to Sarah's son and proffered it.

Issa looked at his mother, unsure, but when she nodded encouragingly, he took it somewhat ungraciously and drank it down with noisy relish.

He handed the cup back and returned to clutching his mother's dress.

Sarah was grateful for the generosity. She was bending to her son, encouraging him to show his thankfulness when she became aware of the other child holding out the cup with more milk for her. The milk was so inviting, but she felt she should refuse it. The child's mother laughed.

"Have it. Please. He loves to share, and anyway, we have more than we need. It will quickly turn once the sun is up."

Sarah laughed in confusion but accepted the cup and drank slowly. It was good.

"You have a lovely son," she said, handing the cup back.

"Thank you, sister." The child's mother looked at him lovingly as he took the cup and drank, watching Issa over the brim. "He is special... He's called Yeshua."

"My boy is Issa and I'm Sarah," replied Sarah hurriedly, wanting to keep the conversation going.

"Issa? then the boys have the same name!"

Sarah looked puzzled.

"Yeshua is the name in our language. Issa is the same in one of the other languages around, though I'm not sure which. My husband would know. But where are you from?"

"Issa was born in a village near Arabia," Sarah replied cautiously. "They spoke another language there," she added, hoping it would explain everything.

"Well, I'm Mary," said the other cheerfully, "and my husband's name is Joseph."

"Oh. Then why Yesh...?" Sarah tailed off, realising that she was being a bit too forward.

Mary smiled and seemed pleased to reply, "You could say it was his father's choice, it wasn't up to us."

Sarah looked up quickly at the odd reply. Mary was still smiling,

13

knowing she was being mysterious.

"But how about you? What are you doing on the road alone so far from Arabia?"

"I really come from Bethlehem. I've been away for a while and I'm going home," Sarah replied simply.

Mary nodded and said nothing. Innocently, she looked away to the children playing. Sarah, imagining an implied question and raised eyebrows, flared up defensively.

"No! I have no husband to care for me, but it wasn't like that!"

She had been rehearsing her defence for several days, knowing that she would have to face the elders of the village. It was always at the forefront of her mind. How could she ever explain?

She had been young and headstrong and readily flattered by the swarthy, proud, handsome young man who put up in her aunt's house while his parents and younger brothers and sisters stayed in the larger but crowded inn a few doors down. Bethlehem had been heaving with visitors. A town so blessed with sons and daughters who were proud to come from 'David's City' now found it hard accommodate them when, as all over the Roman empire, everyone was required to register in their hometown. Sarah had worked hard helping her aunt care for the demanding extra guests, who were angry at the cost and upheaval the census had caused.

She had been pleased when the young man came to seek her out after the house had settled down for the night while she cleaned the kitchen, a small separate wattle and daub building, where she slept to guard the food. Her aunt slept by the main door. They would talk into the night, close together, to avoid disturbing the house. It was cold and he soon gallantly wrapped his coat around both their shoulders, drawing her close to keep out the cold. Sarah was flattered and the 'romance' rushed on headlong. In all the confusion, no one noticed; the normal alarm bells

14

of gossip and disapproval failed to ring. He left her just before daylight, whispering promises that everything would be all right and he would sort out all the formalities when they got back to his village. It would be impossible here, with all the crowds and confusion of the census. She tried to talk about it to her aunt, but it developed into a row, so a few mornings later, she had stolen out of the house to join the tail of the caravan as it set out just before dawn. She had mingled with the crowd; his father not finding out about the relationship for several days. He was furious when he did, but it was too late to by then; they were far from the village and anyway, he had always given into his eldest son's whims.

They lived on the edge of Arabia. Although nominally Jewish, they had adopted many of their neighbours' customs, including the language. Wives were kept separate from the rest of the household, Sarah being installed in a small house in the extended family compound. She had tried to make a little home for them both and while at first he was very attentive to her, as the heir, he had to take his place among the men of the family. There had never been a wedding ceremony or any marriage certificate, and when she had spoken to him about it he had just laughed, saying she was as bad as the Romans with their paperwork. When she found she was pregnant, he had visited less and didn't come to see her for several days after the baby was born. She kept telling herself everything was all right, but she became increasingly lonely, and would have despaired but for her lovely baby boy to keep her occupied.

Then one day, overhearing talk of a wedding, an icy chill stole over her as she realised it was her supposed 'husband' Abbas who was soon to marry some important chief's daughter. In tears of despair, she pleaded with him; he explained it was a political marriage, but that she would always be his lover.

But how could he do this? She was his wife! He had promised! There could be no other!

He had left in a temper and didn't visit her again for several days, but she was numb and wouldn't let him near her. She realised now that the family regarded her as no more than a courtesan, rather an embarrassment. So, when he went to his proposed wife's family for an official visit of several days, she left with just a few belongings and a little money. At least they made no attempt to stop her taking the child. They were obviously pleased to see the last of them. By the time he returned, she would be far away.

But how to explain this to the elders of the village?

Had she been married? She believed before God that she had.

Did that count? Was her baby a…? No, she hated even the word.

She had suffered enough. If they won't understand, at least let it be between her and God.

As the thoughts she had gone over so many times came to her mind, she spoke these last out loud: "Don't jump to conclusions, you couldn't understand! You have a good husband. I have none. But the truth isn't that simple. Is it not enough that it's between me and God? Let him judge!"

Mary, looking down, smiled gently. Thoughtful. She brushed the dust off her sandals.

"Maybe I do understand… being misunderstood." And then, after a longer pause, "You see, I was pregnant before we were married."

Sarah was taken aback. Before she could stop herself, she looked up rather too rapidly to where Joseph was looking back down the valley. She realised too late that Mary was watching her, and she was covered with confusion.

"I mean… Well, it's just, I didn't…"

"Think he looked the type?" laughed Mary, finishing the line for her. "No. He's a wonderful husband to me and a devoted father to Yeshua, though he isn't Yeshua's father. But I can't explain. Let's just say it's between me and God. Just let another young girl carry the truth in her heart while the world jumps to harsh and hasty conclusions."

Mary

Chapter 3

Mary had been on this road several times before. The first journey was etched in her memory when, as a young girl, she had been forced by circumstances to leave her home near Hebron to travel to a new life in Nazareth. How she had missed her cousin Elizabeth and her priestly husband Zechariah! Having no children of their own, they indulged Mary as their own daughter, Zechariah even teaching Mary how to read. Rather than playing in the street with the other children, she would sit unnoticed in the shadows after supper, when the storytelling started, recounting the great victories of the heroes of long ago.

She loved the psalms they sang on the sabbath and, having a good voice, she learnt them by heart. The stories and music stirred up something deep within her, although it was clear that the rabbis relegated them to the exaggerated imagination of a less learned time, and expected life to run along more moderate and predictable lines. It may all have happened far away and long ago, but Mary was determined to enjoy the echoes that came down to her through history.

But when the fortunes of her family changed, she was sent to join the extended family in Nazareth. Life was tough in that Galilean village, and like all girls of her age in poor families, she had to earn her keep, collecting wood and water and gleaning in the fields. One day she would be married off. At least the synagogue in Nazareth had a woman's section behind a trellis where Mary would go each Sabbath, even calling in during the week whenever she could, to sit quietly and sing her simple songs of worship. If there were no men around, she would creep to the lectern and carefully read the scroll that was laid out for the day.

Joseph noticed her there one day when he was returning a bench he had repaired. She had not seen him coming and hurried away in confusion, but not before he realised she had been reading the scroll.

He noticed her again the next day as he worked at his bench in his carpenter's shop, which gave into the street. She had been collecting firewood from the hills and on impulse, he suggested that she might like to 'glean' the wood-shavings and off-cuts that were piled up and littered the floor of his shop. As it was easier to collect the shavings after sweeping them up, she took to bringing a palm frond from the street to use as a brush. Soon, collecting the shavings grew into sweeping the shop and if Joseph was out, she even took to tidying it.

When a friend remarked at how tidy his workplace looked with a woman's touch, and how he ought to find a wife, he began to think about marriage. His friend had made some suggestions of suitable girls, but as Joseph thought of the possibility, he began to imagine Mary as more than a girl who gleaned in his shop.

Though she was quite shy, she used to sing softly as she worked, and Joseph would find something quiet to do so that he could listen.

One day, as he worked on an intricate joint, she stopped to watch and suddenly started to talk, oblivious of the convention that girls should not speak to men outside of their family. He carried on his work, careful not to break the spell, enthralled by the cadences of her voice. She had the same soft Judean accent that he remembered from his mother. As she spoke of her life in Hebron and her family history, he suddenly realised that, like him, she too was descended from King David. He looked up with a start. The spell broke and she was suddenly overcome with confusion, but Joseph put his hand on her arm to stop her from turning away. Her skin was so soft to touch and instinctively he took her small hand.

"But then I am your kinsman," he said gently, "for I too am a descendant of David."

Being unsure of what to do next, he ran his fingers gently over the back of her hand just as he would when feeling the finish on a piece of his work. It was so delicate. He suddenly realised what he was doing and released her hand, which she quickly pulled away. Embarrassed, they both returned to their tasks, and when Joseph looked up she was gone. He coloured, cursing himself for a clumsy fool and rubbing his eyes and face in frustration. As he did so, he noted the faintest fragrance that must have been on her wrist. This startled him; he had assumed she was just a sensible hard-working girl and had been somehow unaware of her femininity.

He didn't notice her enter two days later until she was sweeping the shop and he could think of nothing to say. Though he was tongue-tied, he was desperate to take up the conversation he had so crassly curtailed but was struck dumb. He saw her make to leave with the bundle of offcuts and, in a final effort, called huskily after her, "Shalom, sister!"

She stopped and, slowly turning with eyes averted, replied, "My kinsman."

It was a respectful formalism, which would have been innocent enough, had she not then looked up smiling into his eyes for just half a second longer than necessary before hurrying off.

He turned back to his work, but his heart beat hard. She was not offended; she had continued where they had left off. But 'My kinsman?' Subconsciously, his mind replayed the words over and over, looking at them from every possible angle. Then he noticed she had left the large headscarf which she sometimes used to carry home a bundle of wood chips to use as kindling. She must have taken it off to use and then forgotten it. He picked it up, thinking of how often it reminded him of Ruth, the young widow of Israel's history and great-grandmother to

David, who had gleaned then, as her descendant Mary did now, filling her scarf with the grain from the stores of Boaz, a distant relative.

My kinsman! My kinsman... redeemer. The words Ruth spoke to Boaz.

Mary did not need a kinsman redeemer as Ruth had all those years ago. She was cared for by her family. But could that look in her eyes have spoken the same passion that Ruth put into those words?

My kinsman... friend?

My kinsman... lover, even?

My kinsman... husband?

Probably none of these had entered her head, but that smile! It was not coquettish; that was not like her. She was a serious, hard-working girl, earning her keep in the family home, caring for the younger children and doing the fetching and carrying. And yet so fascinating! He had taken to looking out for her at the synagogue as she listened to the teaching from behind the women's trellis early on the Sabbath. She might be a pauper with no dowry, but she was related to a respectable family... and she was quite beautiful... and she had that lovely voice... and suddenly, he was aware that he was holding her scarf up to his face, savouring that same delicate scent that had too quickly faded from his hand. Colouring, he put the scarf down, quickly looking around as he did so. What if someone caught him sniffing a girl's scarf and daydreaming? Even worse, what would Mary think if she came back right then to retrieve it?

He need not have worried. At the same time, Mary was covering her embarrassment at being caught by one of her nephews savouring the smell of the cedar wood chips that she now carried around in her apron pocket.

Chapter 4

News of Joseph and Mary's betrothal spread fast round the village. In general, the people were pleased for them both: Joseph was a hardworking, serious man, the sort any father would welcome as a son in law, and Mary, though still not well known, would obviously make him a good wife. Joseph ignored the raised eyebrows of his synagogue acquaintances, for whom women in general and wives in particular were drudges, and marriage was a tedious necessity which you made the best of by a big dowry or good family connections, neither of which made Mary a commendable choice. The patriarch of Mary's household was a brother-in-law. Joseph knew him from the synagogue as a pious and self-righteous Pharisee. Having long since assumed that Mary would continue to be a cheap servant to them, unless they could marry her off to some rich senile widower in exchange for his patronage, he haggled on every point when Joseph asked for her hand.

He questioned Joseph's pedigree: she was, after all, of royal blood.

So, he countered, was he.

They were poor. She could not be spared from her household duties to prepare for marriage.

Joseph readily agreed to pay for her keep while she lived with them between betrothal and marriage.

She had no dowry.

"Riches we inherit from parents, but a good wife is from the Lord," he had replied.

He was actually quoting a proverb of Solomon, but the brother-in-law was taken aback, thinking that Joseph knew about the small inheritance due to Mary, which he had taken charge of and craftily 'made over to the Lord' so that it was untouchable. Feeling cornered, he consented as quickly as he could while still saving face and before Joseph, though in reality entirely oblivious, could press the point.

Custom had it that there be a respectable time between the betrothal ceremony and the final marriage when the bride would be carried in joyful procession to her husband's house. During this time, the couple would prepare materially and spiritually for married life. Mary had little to bring from her side, though she did have her late mother's bridal veil; body-length sheer silk from the East, she had been told. There was also some jewellery: a gold chain, gold bangles and a bride's headpiece, which she had managed to keep secret from her bother-in-law, for they were obviously valuable.

Joseph, being a down-to-earth artisan, was not sure what spiritual preparation he should make, there being no male equivalent to the custom of the girls spending some time away with an elder married relative. Now that he had released Mary from having to glean, there was no excuse for her almost daily visits to collect wood chips. Though Joseph sorely missed these visits, he lovingly devoted himself to getting the house ready for the day his bride would come to stay forever.

The carpenter's shop, storerooms and back house could be easily converted into a married home. Joseph roofed the courtyard to make a kitchen and living area and cleared a section of the one large room to create a pleasant and secluded bed chamber for them.

So, it was a surprise to him when a month later, Mary came to the shop with one of her nephews. She sat watching the street for some time until the boy wandered off to fiddle among the tools of the carpenter's shop.

Seizing the opportunity, she turned to Joseph with wide eyes and, searching his face, blurted out, "There's going to be a baby…" And then, in more measured tones, she said slowly, "God has told me I will have a baby."

Joseph slowly put down the tool he was holding while he thought of the right reply. He had hoped, in fact rather assumed, that babies would not be far away once they were married. He well knew the facts and felt the powerful stirrings within him, but he had not counted on having to explain these to Mary, and certainly not here in his shop with the world going by.

"Of course you shall Mary, God willing. We trust he will bless us with children. It's what happens after you get married," he added with a self-conscious smile.

Clearly, something was troubling Mary. She took his hand and held it to her cheek. She was quiet for a few moments while the memories rushed through her head.

It had been so easy until the angel came. How had she known he was an angel? When you meet one, you just know! But in the old stories, angels didn't just come to pass the time of day. They came to bring news, big news! And often of the smiting kind. So when he had greeted her by name, her heart almost stopped.

But it was good news, he said: she was to have a baby. Right now! Good News?

She had protested that she was a virgin and had not 'known' any man. Though a bit short of the full details, she was well aware that lying naked in Joseph's arms was the sort of knowing she had in mind; she had read the Song of Solomon.

No, this baby was from the Lord. He would be conceived of the Holy Spirit and would be called the Son of God.

She was stunned! The angel had called her blessed, but she was not so sure her betrothed, beloved Joseph, would feel quite so blessed.

Could she have been mistaken? Was the angel a charlatan?

No. He had even told her his name, Gabriel – as if she could check up on his credentials.

But how do you do check on an angel?

No one, not even the pious in the synagogue, believed in angels now, let alone claimed to have met one.

But the events that immediately followed and the process it set in train were no imagination. That very night, the blind over the window of her little room blew gently to one side and her room was filled with a fragrant presence that engulfed her, while from head to toe, waves of what she could only describe as love flowed on and on till she felt she must burst with joy. There was no fear. Just perfect love. Whatever had happened, she had missed her next period and had been sick two days running in the morning. Her sister had joked about it the first morning, not realising how close to the truth she was, but Mary had managed to hide it on the second. But what could she do now? She couldn't hide it forever. Her sister wouldn't believe her, and poor Joseph clearly didn't understand that she was trying to tell him she was pregnant. How could he understand? But who would understand? Gabriel had mentioned another name. Elizabeth, her cousin. She too was pregnant, he had said.

Of course, that's who she could talk to!

"Elizabeth!" she spoke out loud and excitedly. "My Lord, I would like to go to my cousin Elizabeth." Smiling self-consciously, she added, "To talk about having babies."

"Your cousin Elizabeth? In Judea? But I didn't think she'd ever had children."

"No, but there's one on the way now. Please sir, give me leave. I'll take my niece Salome and maybe a nephew for protection. We'll be back soon."

Still not sure what it was all about, but pleased that Mary was going for guidance to such an apparently good woman as Elizabeth and relieved that he wouldn't have to do any more baby talk, he took her face in his hands, tenderly kissing her forehead.

"And when you return, we'll be married, and you'll come to live with me here!"

The journey to the Judean hills took several days and Mary had time to think. Elizabeth was a lot older than Mary and had never had children, but the same angel had told her that Elizabeth was now pregnant. There was obviously some link, and it was natural to visit her. She thought of the women throughout Israel's history who bore unexpected children – usually precious babies after long years of disappointment – Sarah, Rebekah, Rachel, Hannah and suddenly Elizabeth. And now here she was, also bearing an unexpected baby.

Would anyone rejoice with her?

Would anyone understand?

Would anyone believe her?

Her mood swung from bursts of exhilaration to shivers of fear. She rehearsed a little speech, trying to think how to explain it all to Elizabeth and Zechariah.

Would they think she had made it up? Would they be shocked?

But then a thrill would run through her as she strung together couplets from the psalms and other songs as music seemed to well up inside her.

As she turned into the familiar street of her childhood, her heart beat fast, both with the joy of the approaching reunion with Elizabeth and fear of her make-or-break reaction.

"If Elizabeth doesn't understand, I'm on my own," she whispered to herself.

And then suddenly there was Elizabeth, running to meet her, laughing, hugging Mary and Salome and clutching at her bulge, doubling up with happy cries as her own baby kicked and punched inside her womb.

"He knows!" she cried. "Mary, he knows! How wonderful that you have come to me!"

Female intuition, revelation or prophetic inspiration; Elizabeth's welcome made all explanations unnecessary and the song that had been growing in Mary's mind burst forth, the words forming and tumbling out to a deep and haunting melody:

I'm singing, I'm dancing, my spirit rejoices.
What God has done for this lowly girl will be sung of forever.
His mercy flows to those who fear him.
He has shown his strength and mighty deeds
and scattered the proud.
The mighty are fallen; the humble are raised.
The hungry are fed; the rich sent away empty.
He has remembered his servant Israel,
    just as he promised.

Zechariah stood in silence all the while, blinking uncomprehendingly at the women's antics. Not disapproval, Elizabeth explained later, rather that he had been struck dumb with disbelief on hearing the news of her own imminent pregnancy.

"Poor Zechariah," thought Mary. "Poor Joseph. We women just feel these things. They will try to work it all out!"

Chapter 5

Mary stayed three months in all, longer than she had intended. By then the sharp eyes of the women of the village noted the changes and there were knowing glances. While many women came to visit and a few tried to delve, respect for Elizabeth protected Mary from any hurtful comments. The men, of course, would not notice that she was pregnant for months yet, but Zechariah puzzled over what he had heard and discussed it with his old friend Simeon, but having to write everything down made this a slow process. They would sit together, each with his own thoughts, enjoying the happy company of the two girls from Nazareth; Zechariah swelling with pride as his wife swelled with child and Simeon watching indulgently the young Mary who had quite stolen his kind old heart and renewed his faith in young people. But even respect for Elizabeth and love for Mary did not prevent rumours about Mary circulating around the village and back up the road to Nazareth.

It's a long way from Hebron to Nazareth, and consequently the rumours arrived worn and distorted, but enough for people to fish for more. While Joseph may not have understood what lay behind the rather cold enquiries after Mary's health and other comments, he did hope she would soon be home.

It was not until the rumours were substantiated by a reliable witness in the form of a man who had actually been in the village where Zechariah and Elizabeth lived, that Nazareth became alive with the scandal. After the Sabbath synagogue meeting, the men confronted Joseph with the matter and awaited his reaction. It would be a cut and dried case if the rumours were true, and it now seemed they were; girl goes off for a few months then comes back pregnant. It could well result in a stoning, but each man was guarding his counsel on the matter. It was not that the girl herself mattered, but rather that each man had his network of family links. While they could easily fuel the righteous indignation of the village, each would only get involved if they could be sure there were no family recriminations that might affect their own relatives.

Would Joseph seek redress from her sister's family?

Would he seek to besmirch their good name?

Could it lead to a family feud?

Questioning the witness only reinforced his story, and by the end of the meeting a clearly shaken and pale Joseph left with, "We shall see when the girl returns."

The others were content with that. When Mary returned – if she returned – then the drama would really start, and each could work out his own strategy as it unfolded.

Joseph walked slowly back to his home, numb and desperate. He sat at his bench all day, thinking. He could not believe this of Mary! How could it have happened, if it had?

Did she love someone else?

Had she been seduced?

Had she been violated on the journey?

He must think calmly. Could the witness be mistaken, lying even?

He could be mistaken, but hardly intentionally; he had too much to lose. Such a serious accusation, if false, could result in the lynching of the malicious witness.

If Mary returned pregnant, the village would be ruthless. But if she wasn't pregnant, the witness might easily convince the village that she had destroyed the baby. After all, he was a man, and she just a young girl.

He had to know. He had to get to her first. Then, if she was pregnant, he must persuade her to stay with Zechariah and Elizabeth. However devastated he would be should it turn out to be true, he could not bear the thought of her being stoned to death. He would free her from her betrothal and leave her with her family in Judea, but she must not return to Nazareth.

And if it wasn't true, then he must first defend her reputation before bringing her home. Resolving that the next day he would set out for Judea, he lay back in his chair and closed his eyes as the evening closed in on his workshop.

Chapter 6

But events moved faster than Joseph had planned.

He woke with a start. He had been having a vivid dream and thought this must have awakened him, but then he realised that someone was banging on the door. He called out a groggy reply trying to focus his thoughts, but suddenly he was wide awake.

"The girl has returned," said the voice. "She is at her home."

His heart racing, he opened the door to the street. In the dark, he recognised two lads he sometimes engaged to help him move a heavy log from the fields to the workshop.

"Who? Who has come back? Where is she?" Joseph stuttered, trying to clear his head and think.

The boys were rather unsure of themselves at this muddled response and, not being sure what to say, looked back down the street the way they had come as if trying to reassure themselves that they had got it right.

"Umm, the girl... the woman... She's back... back at her sister's house," they said nervously.

"What woman? Do you mean Mary?"

"Hmm... Yeah, Mary... the girl who..."

"Just wait there," interjected Joseph, his heart pounding as he shut the door to the street and put the heavy bar over it.

He left by a side entrance, which he then barricaded in a particular way, hard to work out in the dark. These were the normal security arrangements in Nazareth. The lads were waiting in the darkened street and loyally fell in with him as he walked in the moonlight down through the village to Mary's sister's house. All the while his mind was racing, trying to focus his thoughts on what might be happening and still puzzling over the dream he had woken from so abruptly. The abrupt awakening had left it there in his mind, fixed, and like a backdrop to every other thought. Even though he knew he was going to a desperate situation, the backdrop wasn't black, but like the first glow of dawn.

They moved in silence through the darkened streets, walking down the middle of the road where the moonlight was brightest, out of the shadow of the trees and where there were likely to be fewer obstacles. A dog came and barked at them, alerting all the neighbours' animals, who bayed and growled menacingly as they passed. The young men would reach down as if to pick up a stone as just this gesture turned most dogs away, but occasionally they sent a stone spinning; a dog would yelp, scurrying out of range to continue its howling.

Mary's sister lived on the far side of the village, beyond a grove of trees which overshadowed the road. As they approached in the darkness, they could see the crowd around the door; no women were present. This was men's business. The young men hung back, but Joseph pushed into the crowd. Men turned angrily to see who was pushing but, recognising Joseph, parted to let him through, nudging those in front who then silently made way. A solitary voice was sounding off as he made his way through the crowd. Some faces he knew, others were unfamiliar, but there were no encouraging looks – just eyes that followed him as he made his way forward. They were all waiting to follow the crowd, waiting their cue to maybe take part in the macabre stoning that might follow.

At the front of the crowd were some of the up-and-coming would-be leaders, young men with wispy beards, all trying to look knowledgeable and all dangerously convinced of their own righteousness and of the need to make a mark for justice. He recognised the voice as that of Mary's brother-in-law and saw him standing and gesticulating.

"A disgrace to our house! Such shame and so brazen!" he declaimed to the village elders, the older ones stony-faced and guarding their counsel whilst some of the less experienced nodded knowledgeably, encouraging the pompous brother-in-law in his tirade. Joseph was now at the front of the crowd. In the dim lamp light, sitting on her bundle was a tired Mary, expressionless, looking at a spot on the floor, not meeting anyone's eyes. Salome squatted by her, fiddling with the corner of her cloak. Both girls were still in their journeying clothes, dusty and dishevelled, sitting just where they had arrived. They had waited till the end of the Sabbath before hurrying the last few miles home, hence their arrival after nightfall.

The crowd all around began to buzz as they recognised Joseph, whispering his name to those behind. Now the offended betrothed husband was here, things should liven up.

Someone spoke to the elders, who immediately looked around trying to locate him in the dim lamp light. All attention was now focussed on Joseph and, as a murmur swelled in the room, the brother-in-law dried up in mid-sentence. The crowd had long since grown tired of his self-righteous repetitions. Now they wanted some action.

His heart racing, Joseph knew he had to gain the high ground. He was not well-known but was nevertheless respected in the village. Being tall and strongly built, he commanded respect. He took a step forward, consciously standing erect, looking around slowly before addressing the elders.

"May I ask what is going on?"

The brother-in-law, so recently robbed of the stage, was anxious to regain it. Sweeping his arm to end up pointing at Mary, he cried dramatically, "This woman has been caught in sin… she is pregnant!"

The leading elder, who had been about to speak and was clearly irritated by the interruption, replied drily, "If procreation was a sin, then you would be guilty many times over."

It caused a ripple of laughter around the crowd and the brother-in-law reddened and sat down scowling.

The leading elder was impatient to get on, and so continued. "We have convened to hear an explanation of a serious irregularity. This woman stands accused, and on the face of it with justification, of the sin of fornication, of violation of her betrothal vows." He raised his voice emphatically, as the brother-in-law threatened to begin again his protestations of his family's good name. "And of bringing disgrace on her family…"

"And the house that took her in off the streets where she clearly is more at home," ranted the brother-in-law, unable to contain himself.

"We have not yet been able to question the girl," pressed on the elder, with a hard glance at the grumbling brother-in-law. "However, we suspect that you may be equally surprised to learn that this woman is with child. We fully expect, therefore, to tackle this matter according to our laws and see that a just solution is reached."

The last words he spoke with emphasis, deepening his voice with the gravity of his allusion.

"If you would therefore say the word, we will proceed, and you need not take further part in the matter."

A silence that seemed to last forever fell on the room, while everyone waited for Joseph to speak. Joseph waited a long moment till every eye was on him, the crowd in breathless silence, attentive for the words that would seal Mary's fate.

He moved towards Mary, but rather than thrusting out his hand in a condemning gesture, he placed it gently on her shoulder.

"I have come to take my wife home," he declared, firmly and resolutely.

There was a stunned gasp. Low voiced comments were quickly passed around the room and back into the crowd, swelling to a dull rumble like distant thunder as those at the back sought confirmation that they had heard correctly.

Joseph's hand was laid so gently on Mary's shoulder, yet it felt so strong and sure. The elders looked at each other, perplexed, and as the crowd fell silent again, addressed Joseph sternly.

"Are you saying that you are the father? That the child is yours?"

Another rumble from the crowd.

Joseph waited till he was sure of being heard and then a few seconds longer for effect.

"I am not the father," he declared in a clear voice, and as the rumble started again, he silenced it. "But… the child is mine!"

Now it took a long time for the crowd to settle. The elders looked at each other again and there were hastily whispered discussions. Eventually, the leader spoke up.

"You know then who is the father?"

Everyone waited on Joseph's next words.

"The child is of God," came the softer reply. Some did not catch the words, and those who thought they did passed it back, puzzled and uncertain of what Joseph could possibly mean, assuming they had heard correctly.

The elders were confused and returned to their consultations.

"Make the girl speak. Ask her whose the child is, if he will not say. Command her!" came the strangled cry from the brother-in law, bent on being proved right, but now not sure about what. All the while, Joseph's hand was on Mary's shoulder, the bonding growing with each second, every sensation heightened in the tension of the moment.

"Will you speak, woman?" demanded the leading elder harshly. "Who is the father?"

Mary did not answer but looked questioningly at Joseph.

"You may answer the question," said Joseph quietly but firmly, loud enough for others to hear. The looks, the words, did not escape the crowd.

"It is as my husband says," Mary replied, softly but clearly.

The balance shifted. The crowd no longer saw a forlorn girl without hope, but a resolute young couple; a determined husband protecting his wife and unborn child.

"Blasphemy! They are blaspheming!" the brother-in-law screamed. Aware of the changing dynamic of the situation, he tried to regain the moral high ground.

This appealed to some in the crowd, who were concerned that Joseph had offended an important principle which could lead to all sorts of trouble with women. Blasphemy was a usefully vague accusation when the situation needed to be redirected. While Mary might not now be alone, there was a real danger that the crowd could turn against them both.

Discussion broke out, some of it heated, and the crowd took a while to notice the oldest member of the council holding his hand up for silence. He was well respected and usually held his counsel till the end of the session and even then, often did not always express it if, as frequently happened, the proceedings were long and tedious and sleep had overtaken him. As the hush crept round the room he rose to speak, leaning on his stick.

"Blasphemy is a serious accusation to make and those who make it too readily should themselves be ready for the consequences of having to withdraw. Of course the child is of God, what child is not? Does not the psalm say 'children are a gift from the Lord'?" he paused, collecting his thoughts.

"Irregular?" He leaned on his stick and looked at the ground, grunting and nodding deep in thought. "Unexpected, maybe. But then these two young people are both from the royal line, in which a good deal of the unexpected happens."

Both Joseph and Mary were surprised that this old man should know anything about them. Why would he champion their cause? Whatever the reason, it was a relief that someone seemed to be on their side.

The old man warmed to his subject. "Are there not some unexpected mothers in the royal line? Tamar, who bore a child by her father-in-law, Judah. Rahab the prostitute, from Jericho. And was not King David the great-grandson of Ruth from Moab, a nation we as Israelites had been commanded not to marry into for the promiscuity that led many to die in the wilderness...? And yet, is Ruth not revered in our writings? And was not the royal line continued through Bathsheba? Let us not confuse God's ways and respectability.

"In each case, history has shown us a bigger picture that was not evident at the time. We may suppose that we are more enlightened than they were in those days, but we must admit that God has been rather silent these last few hundred years since we returned from the exile. Maybe He is starting to move again. These are strange times. Many, through violence, wish to restore the fortunes of Israel. Shall those of us who believe in another way, through ignorance and presumption emulate them and stone to death a young woman with child when God has put it into the heart of her husband to protect her? Let us watch and see what becomes of this child. Joseph has made his decision. Let him take his wife home. Why should we be offended if he is not?"

The crowd nodded in agreement at the wise words. Some were still unsure, but not clear what they were unsure about.

"I demand that we put it to the vote," protested the brother-in-law, desperate not to lose face. "Let the elders give their judgement."

The old man silenced him with his hand.

"This is not a court. It is the nighttime, and our law forbids a trial for grave offences at night." He turned to Joseph. "If you feel there is an issue to be investigated, the elders can hear your case in the day. Are you minded to return to continue tomorrow?"

Joseph drew himself up.

"When Mary went to visit her cousin, it was agreed that on her return she would become my wife. She has returned. I have come to take my wife home. I have no issue with my wife."

"Then go in peace. Love and care for your wife and bring up the child to love and serve God." He paused, looking at his feet. "In circumstances when there have been serious allegations, we make a charge that the husband may never divorce his wife as long as he lives. However, the details of this case are somewhat more complex and such a charge may not apply." He looked deeply into Joseph's eyes. "In this instance, I perceive that such a charge would be quite irrelevant."

Joseph squeezed Mary's shoulder as a signal to be ready, for they must now make a self-assured exit.

"Come!" he said firmly. As unhurriedly and confidently as possible, Mary and Salome stood and shouldered their bags, trying not to reveal how anxious they were to be gone. Joseph led the way out, his heart beating faster, for there were still scowls, and it would not be hard for the sensitised crowd to turn. But the way opened up; no one tried to stop them, and before they reached the back of the throng, it was already beginning to disperse.

Joseph turned up the road without speaking, walking fast, the girls keeping in step behind him. In a few minutes, they arrived at the door of the shop and the girls dropped their bundles.

"I will open the doors," he said, already moving the barricade to the narrow side entrance. Once inside, he took time to stoke up the fire, quickly sweeping up a handful of wood chips which soon caught, the bright flames from the pine wood lighting the courtyard. He fumbled through his workshop, knocking into some of his jobs in the darkness, but soon found the door and lifted the beam that locked it tight. The girls were sitting down now on their bundles, and in that short space, Salome, exhausted from the journey and the recent drama, had fallen asleep. In the way of children of large families used to sleeping in a bed with siblings, she was unrousable. Joseph, wanting to get the girls off the street and the door shut, hurriedly carried Mary's bag inside and dropped it behind the door before returning to pick up the sleeping

Salome. He glanced hurriedly up the street and, nodding towards the rest of their luggage, urged Mary on as he struggled through into the house with his load.

"Bring in your things and shut the door." Mary hurried to obey, dropping the remaining bags with the other as she tried to close the doors.

"Shut them both together and put the bar over," Joseph called over his shoulder. Salome was getting heavy and slipping from his arms, so he hurried with her into the back room and laid her on his bed. It was a big bed, and he humped her to the far side as she nestled in the pillows, turning instinctively away from the fire-light and pulling the cover over her head as Joseph laid it on her.

Joseph hurried back, collecting a lamp, which he lit from the fire, and entered the workshop where Mary stood hesitantly, unsure what to do next. She had put the door beam in as instructed, but upside down so it rested precariously on the supports. Joseph put the lamp on the bench and turned the beam round so it dropped neatly into place. Now safe and secure, away from any immediate danger, he felt suddenly confused about what to do next. He smiled sheepishly and spread his hands to gesture the workshop and house beyond, shrugged his shoulders and raised his eyebrows.

"Welcome!" he said, and after a pause, "Come through."

He carried the lamp and the sleeping girl's bag, dropping it at the foot of the bed, while Mary sat on the edge of the bed next to her, holding her bag close. It was really only a blanket tied around a bundle of clothes. Salome continued sleeping.

"You must be hungry. I will get some bread. Please… keep warm by the fire."

It had been the Sabbath, so the bakers had only just started baking at sundown: Sabbath loaves that needed no yeast. There was a baker a few doors further up the road and Joseph hurried there to buy some hot flatbread. In the brief respite from the embarrassment of the situation, Mary found a goat skin and knelt on it by the fire, stoking it up with some of the wood from a pile nearby. She made herself comfortable, curling her legs under her and leaning on her bag.

As Joseph returned, the smell of freshly baked bread made her realise how hungry she was. He put the bread on a platter and returned with a jug of watered-down wine, some olive oil and a few dates. Sitting on a low stool, he set the food between them so that they could both help themselves. They both looked into the fire, not knowing what to say, breaking off pieces of bread and dipping them in the oil. Soon the warmth of the fire on her face and the smoke made Mary's tired eyes burn and she closed them to give some relief, but then jerked awake as she nodded off. She tried again but again her eyes burned and this time she thought if she just lay her head against the bags…

She started as she felt an arm under her back and, realising Joseph intended to carry her as he had carried Salome, uncoiled her legs and put her arms around his neck to ease the load. Though she was not very heavy, Joseph knew he could not carry her for long but really had no wish to put her down immediately. He steadied his foot on a saw bench and supported her hip on his knee. She made no pretence of being asleep now and looked into his kind brown eyes, flicking from one to the other, searching for an answer, for reassurance. Speaking came more easily now. It would have been more complicated to remain silent.

"You knew about the baby?" she whispered. "Don't you mind?"

Joseph looked away briefly, considering his reply, then back into her eyes. He started to speak, looked away again and then more intently.

"I heard rumours. I was really confused." His gaze wandered away again as he tried to put the tumbling thoughts into words. "I had a dream… I was woken from it even as you were being accused and they called me. It was so vivid! So clear. Like a voice. I will never forget it: 'Do not be afraid to take Mary to be your wife, for the child that she is with is of God.' I just had to go and bring you home. Bring home my wife. It was so clear, there was no doubt what I had to say. To do."

Her eyes filled with tears and he smiled on her, his eyes brimming too.

"But what does it all mean, Joseph?" She began to cry softly, all the pent-up emotion now being released. She turned her face into his shirt and he watched, unsure how to deal with tears and ever more conscious that she was getting really heavy, and his arms, though strong, were becoming tired and he would have to put her down. She giggled nervously for fear of being dropped as he struggled clumsily to the bed.

Having no strength left in his arms to lower her, he had to bend and let her drop. In doing so, his face fell onto her shoulder as he sought to regain his balance. He tried to straighten up again, but she held him fast, whispering in his ear, "You are so good, so brave, so strong! I was so scared. We will keep this baby safe together. You will be his father. I will be a good wife Joseph, I promise."

She released his head slightly so that she could look into his eyes again. The faint smell of scent, her black curls and big dark eyes held him spellbound.

What would the future hold?

What was happening?

Her eyes closed and he kissed her cheek as her grip slackened. He gently removed her arms from around his neck, sitting on the edge of the bed for a long while, watching her as she slept.

Chapter 7

So Joseph took Mary into his house as his wife. The child was uppermost in both of their minds; while Mary made a home, Joseph became fiercely protective of both the mother and child.

The old man had called the next day. Sitting for a long time in the doorway of the shop where all who passed would not fail to notice, he reinforced his approval of the marriage. However, he had more practical concerns and after a long time of silence, while Joseph sat politely waiting on his guest, the old man turned towards him.

"Look after the girl and her child." Another long pause. "There may be those who wish them harm."

As he did not elaborate, Joseph presumed that he alluded to the brother-in-law who might be expected to carry a grudge.

It was not the custom of pregnant women to venture out of the home very much, which suited Joseph, and he made sure that their home was well stocked with supplies. He worked hard to get more money together to cover the extra expenses. He paid a widow to collect their water and either he or Salome shopped in the market. Joseph went to the synagogue less frequently now and few people called at the house. He had been disappointed that none of his friends had come to bless their new matrimonial home, as was the usual custom. Clearly people were not easy with the situation, though he was not sure how many were as hostile as the old man suggested.

What would be the reaction when the baby was born?

The conception and all that followed had been such an event. Now the baby was growing inside Mary's womb and one day... Both spent long hours thinking. They did not talk about it but were often silent together for long periods, each deep in thought. Pregnancy was a time when the woman would care for her body and prepare for childbirth and sexual relations were usually suspended. The whole situation was so overwhelming that Joseph treated Mary and the unborn baby with especial deference. To his way of thinking, his role was to provide for, and protect, the mother and child.

Not that there was an absence of affection between them, or no moments of intimacy. On cold nights she would lie with her back curled into the strong arch of his body with his arms protectively round her shoulders, his bearded face holding the covers tight against her neck with his chin nuzzling into her locks, his beard rough on her cheeks.

He had been confused the first time he found her bathing stripped to the waist, leaning over a bowl and running the water through her hair. Apologising profusely and trying to reverse out, he become entangled in the lengths of wood he was carrying and ended up in a heap on the floor of the courtyard. Mary was alarmed at first, quickly holding her towel up to her shoulders, thinking that they had company. As he stammered, wide-eyed and confused, that he was alone, she dropped the towel to go back to her bathing, scolding him, "For goodness sake, you're my husband!" Then quickly pulling the towel back, she looked up into his face, her dark eyes sparkling and irresistible. "Unless you've deceived me and we're not really married!"

From then on this was the joke between them, whenever she bathed or she towelled him down after his wash or she held his hand to her abdomen to feel the movement of the little life inside.

"Are you sure you are my husband?"

In fact, Mary was never certain when she had legally become Joseph's wife. The betrothal ceremony was, of course, of particular significance in those days and as binding as the final marriage. But they had never had a marriage ceremony apart from that evening with the elders, and certainly no celebration with friends and family. That they were man and wife was evident as both began to find that clothes that used to fit were becoming tight, as Mary's baby grew and Joseph benefited from Mary's culinary and housekeeping skills. Any doubt of the legality of the marriage was clarified when a census was called and Mary figured as Joseph's wife.

She would have to be registered with him at their hometown of Bethlehem.

Joseph could have registered them both himself, making the journey to and from Bethlehem in about seven days, but under the circumstances there was no question of Mary staying by herself. His concern for her security without his being there to care for her was compounded by his concern that the baby could be born while he was away.

By now, life had settled down and village concerns were directed elsewhere, but the birth of the baby could raise it all again – quite apart from the practical problem of sympathetic female relatives to help her during delivery.

It would be a tight schedule, as Mary had less than a month before she was due to give birth. It took them a few days to put things in order, shut down the house and leave it in the care of the widow. At least they had the old donkey, which Joseph used for bringing logs in from the countryside.

The journey was slow, taking five days even with the donkey, which was an uncomfortable ride for Mary in her condition. They knew Jerusalem would be busy, expensive and risky for the unwary, so they planned to stay a night in one of the villages to the north before crossing Jerusalem and making for Bethlehem the next day. But the crowded and confusing streets made their journey through the city painfully slow, and after wrong turnings and other holdups, it was well into the afternoon before they left the city limits. Evening was drawing in when, to their relief, they arrived at last in Bethlehem.

Joseph had not been there for many years, but he had cousins who would be expected to give them hospitality. They lived on a small farm, one of several in a cluster set into the hill around a cave system that over the years had been used to house the animals. Steps had been cut into the hillside, leading to the house above. Mary, who was quite worn out by the journey, was glad to sit at the foot of the steps while Joseph went up to greet the family. Mary heard the cries of welcome and feet running and fading as he was drawn into the house. The old donkey hung its head disconsolately and Mary sat on the bags, thankful that their journey was over, for she could travel no further. That day she had been feeling so tired and the baby felt heavy and uncomfortable. She gasped as a pain stirred her abdomen, taking deep breaths until it passed. She had been experiencing mild contractions over the past few days, but this was stronger and lasted for some time. Thank God that they were with family who would know what to do!

Joseph was gone for some time and she didn't hear him come down the steps in the gathering darkness. When he came, he was alone. He looked back down the road towards the main town, clearly worried, and started to untie the donkey. Mary was confused now.

"What is it? Joseph?"

He did not reply for some time.

"There's no room in the house. It's full." He looked at her dejectedly and smiled sadly, his eyes moist with tears. To be turned away by family in Jewish society was unheard of. Mary reached for his hand.

"What has happened, Joseph?" He did not answer. "It's me, isn't it? I'm so sorry."

She started to cry quietly, unable to contain it any longer with the tiredness and all the emotion of early labour. This rejection cut her deeply. She wanted to be secure. She wanted her mother. She wanted her little home in Nazareth. She wanted to be anywhere but here in a windswept street in a strange town.

"Joseph, I think the baby is coming." she gasped, sobbing and gripping his hand hard as another contraction started. "Why do people hate me?"

Joseph crouched down beside her and pulled her close against his chest, wrapping his cloak around her.

"Mary, it's not you. People don't hate you. They just don't understand about the baby. They are confused. I don't understand it either, but something big is happening and I know I have to care for you. Other people don't have that, Mary. We're going to be all right, I will look after you, I promise."

She had to push him away as another contraction started and she needed to have room to gasp. Joseph began to feel a growing desperation.

What could he do? Could he get her to mount the donkey?

She was in a lot of discomfort. She wouldn't be able to walk far, but she couldn't stay here. They had passed an inn in the village, but it was crowded, and while there might be room in the courtyard, it was hardly the place to give birth. Could he get her there anyway?

For all his brave words, he was totally at a loss. He had been given a job to do and it was rapidly turning into a disaster.

All the words of the angel and the old man in Nazareth were far away and useless. They were outside, in the cold, at the mercy of the vagabonds of the night not to mention the wild dogs that he knew would prowl the streets of the sleeping village. His imagination was racing now and he recalled a story of old of the girl from Bethlehem, gang-raped and killed because her husband got the travel plans wrong. He thought of Rachel, wife of the patriarch Israel, dying in childbirth on the road to Bethlehem, never making it to the relative safety of the town. Her memorial was just up the hill. And here he was, another man who had messed things up, and the wife was to pay the price.

In the distance, he saw a figure crossing the path. He called out urgently, but the figure just hurried on its way. There did not seem to be anyone else around. He called again for help, listening intently for any reply, but the houses remained silent. They were some way away and they might not hear.

He tried another shout, louder this time, trying to make his voice sound confident. Mary gasped again as another contraction gripped her and his cry ended in a choked sob of desperation: "God! God help us!"

Something touched him in the dark and he heard a strangled animal sound. He span round, the hairs on his neck tingling as he jumped back, almost falling over Mary. A lad stood in the shadows, gesticulating and making a crying sound. Joseph explained their plight rapidly and urgently, emphasising his need of help to get his wife to shelter, but the lad made no response. Joseph explained again in growing frustration. Then, in the gloom, Joseph saw him put his hands to his ears, shaking his head and waving his hands dismissively to indicate that he was deaf. It was getting darker by the minute and Joseph had to make exaggerated signs to explain their predicament. When the lad realised that Mary was in labour, he put one hand to his mouth to indicate horror and shook the other fiercely to give emphasis. He then became excited, pulling Joseph's arm as he pointed to the caves, and putting his hands together by the side of his head to indicate a head on a pillow.

Joseph could now see a faint glow in one cave as the light fast faded. The child seemed to be pointing, first at the cave, then at Mary and indicating a bed. Joseph knelt by Mary.

"There may be somewhere nearby we can get you under cover..." he began with growing hope. Then, a contraction started; Mary gripped his hand and pulled on his coat so that he had to sit back to prevent himself falling over as she rose up, then fell back as the contraction passed.

The lad could not hear her cries but was quite agitated by her obvious distress and waved his hand to Joseph to hurry. Joseph covered Mary with his cloak and hurried after. The ground around was soft, covered in straw and animal droppings, but the cave entrance was stone and swept clean. There were hurdles separating some animals from a fire, which glowed welcomingly. A crude lamp was fashioned out of a bit of broken pottery, obviously burning tallow by the smell. The lad grinned and snorted, pointing to the back of the cave. Squeezing past the hurdles, he led the way to the rear, clearly his quarters. Some meagre belongings lay around; a pitcher and a gourd cup, some clothes on a wooden bench and rags, which were obviously his bed. At least it was dry and sheltered. As he took in the surroundings, Joseph noticed hay piled onto a low wooden platform at the very back of the cave to keep it off the ground. He pointed at this and indicated a bed, which the boy quickly understood and hurried over to it, pulling the piles of hay down to make an even flatter area. He grinned, describing a pregnant abdomen with both hands and pointing back out towards Mary and back to the hay store, then cradling his arms to indicate a baby, which made himself clear.

Suddenly, there was hope. Joseph hurried out and tried to explain to Mary, but she was beyond caring. Hastily, he took one of their bundles into the cave, spread some of their clothes on top of the hay, then went back to Mary. He coaxed her to her feet and helped her walk to the cave. She leaned heavily on him as another contraction came, but soon they had Mary out of the cold and onto the makeshift bed on the hay. The contractions were coming every few minutes now, and though Mary was safe, Joseph had no idea what to do next.

Looking to the boy, he pointed to Mary, opened his legs, held onto an imaginary large object, spread his hands, then shrugged his shoulders and scratched his head. He pointed to the village, trying to think of how to describe a midwife, but the boy clearly understood. He cupped a hand each side under his chest to indicate a female then cradled a baby, pointed to himself and then to the village, and was gone. Between contractions, Joseph sorted out their baggage into a makeshift wall to protect Mary and give her some privacy.

A pipe carried water into a trough, indicating a tapped spring, so Joseph was able to collect some water in a calabash and give Mary a drink. He was doing this when he heard footsteps and the lad reappeared with an old woman. Though she was clearly unsure what to expect, she soon summed up the situation.

"When I saw him, I thought it must be one of his animals that needed help, not some poor wee girl. What do you two think you are doing with this motherless child? Shame on you! Now be gone out of it!" She banished them from any further part in the proceedings.

Joseph took stock of the situation. In the outer part of the cave were some sheep with young and some of the other caves were clearly occupied by other animals. This was where they kept the weaker animals and the orphan lambs. The lad was clearly employed to care for the animals at night. Joseph would not have been surprised if this was the only home he had, such was the prejudice in those days to any form of disability. The midwife had commandeered the lamp but by the firelight he could see how gaunt and sparsely clad the waif was. He was perhaps eight or nine. He would be exploited and teased and probably had a very hand-to-mouth existence. There certainly did not appear to be any food around the cave.

Food!

Joseph now realised how ravenously hungry he was. They had a bit of bread but maybe the lad could buy them some hot food. Joseph laid a hand on the boy's shoulders, rubbed his stomach, pointed at his mouth and rubbed his stomach again. He put a coin in his hand and held up three fingers, pointing at himself, Mary, then at the boy and again at his mouth. The youngster grinned and hunted around for a suitable receptacle to carry the food in. Joseph, seeing the rags and broken shards of pottery and cracked gourds, quickly went to his own bags and pulled out a large calabash and two of the cloth food bags Mary had made from old clothes. The lad would probably have bought the food just for them, but the thought of some for himself was good news indeed and he hurried off into the dark.

Joseph sat by the fire, periodically pacing the entrance to the cave and going inside, attentive when he heard a gasp or groan. He tried to work out what was happening without daring to approach too closely or ask, but he was reassured by the confident yet kind encouragements of the midwife.

The boy returned after some time with some bread, roasted grain and a lukewarm sauce made with beans and curds. Joseph separated some out for Mary before the two ate in silence out of one bowl, the child eating shyly and deferentially holding back, but soon Joseph could eat no more and waved the rest to the other, who took the calabash to the back of the cave where he noisily ate the rest, wiping up every trace with a piece of bread.

The night wore on, with Mary's gasps coming every few minutes and then more frequently and desperately, interspersed with loud panting. Joseph stood at the entrance to the cave, gripping the door post, eyes helplessly brimming with tears as he heard the long, strangled cries of pain and the midwife's authoritative commands: "Push! Now wait!"

The sounds pierced through the cold wind and dark night till one last scream was followed by a baby's cry. Joseph hurried to the back of the cave as a light glowed over the hills of Bethlehem, like the first glow of a new day. Mary lay back on the hay, pale and drawn but smiling and looking tenderly, as only a new mother knows, at the newborn baby suckling on her breast. The midwife was rummaging through their bundles and, finding a piece of cloth, deftly tore it into strips. Taking the baby, she wrapped him firmly according to the old way, though this was now quite out of fashion. Joseph stood transfixed, then stroked Mary's head. She looked up at him, smiling.

"Thank you! Thank you! Isn't he just beautiful?"

Chapter 8

The memories which tumbled through Mary's mind were not without pain, but things had worked out safely in the end. She was jerked back to reality by her companion Sarah, who was certainly not at peace with her own situation and became quite agitated.

"But did you have things to explain that people couldn't understand… or chose not to understand?"

"Well, yes. There were issues. But then I suppose I had Joseph to speak up for me."

"But I'm all alone… Who can I turn to? They will all be against me."

"Don't be so sure. There are some good men who will come to your aid and who you can rely on for help. Provided…" She looked up at Sarah, pausing. "Provided you tell the whole truth. You can't expect a good man to stand up for you only to find you have not been straight with him."

"But how do you find the good ones? They are all so pompous and opinionated."

"God's heart is for the fatherless and the widow. There are men after his own heart, but they are not so strident."

Sarah was quiet for a while. Thoughtful. While she could brazen it out with men who, like Abbas, were morally weak, she wasn't too keen on gauging herself against God's standards. She had never been devout or religious, although she had a niggling feeling, deep down, that she was just putting off the day of reckoning. She had been foolish and, if she was honest, rather rebellious. Did she count as a widow? Or her son as fatherless before God? Would God punish her? In any case, she was sure he would abandon her to her foolishness.

"I'm really scared," she admitted quietly. "It's all so confusing, and if I try and explain, it all sounds so bad. And if I bring God into it… Well, the religious ones are the worst!" She was quiet again, looking down the road towards Bethlehem.

Mary could see Sarah struggling and asked gently, "Would it help if you told me? Then you would know how it might sound when you came out with it later."

Slowly, shyly and with some lip biting to fight back the tears, she told her story to Mary, who listened carefully. When she had finished, both girls were silent. Mary was not sure what to say.

She too had been in a predicament, in danger of being misunderstood, but she had received so many affirmations. The angel in Nazareth; Elizabeth and Zechariah during her pregnancy. Then there were the shepherds who knew that she had given birth to a baby in a stable. And then in the temple, when they had gone to offer the sacrifice of dedication and purification, the old man Simeon, Zechariah's friend who had walked for miles to the temple, somehow knew they would be there. He had prophesied over the baby, his words confirmed by that sweet old lady, Anna, who had said such wonderful things.

Most of all she had depended on Joseph. How he had so selflessly cared for her! She looked up at him now, so strong and dependable. They had talked long into the night after the day of dedication in the temple until Joseph's eyes became heavy.

He had woken, startled, to a soft melody. The air was heavy with the sweet scent that had captivated him all that time ago, when he had found the scarf she had left in his carpenter's shop. The glow from the lamp silhouetted Mary's body against a thin full-length bridal veil, while her soft voice sang words from the Song of Songs:

Awake north wind
and blow south wind.

Let the air be full of fragrant spices.
My lover come into your garden
and eat your fill of choicest fruits.

And she had leaned over him, looking into his eyes through her veil. "What...? But I thought...? Mary... I mean..."

"Joseph, I have completed my purification. The baby is safe. That part is done. Maybe he needs some brothers and sisters. And I... 'I belong to my lover, let his desire be for me.'"

She sang on, parting the sheer silk veil and taking his face in her hands. The veil slipped from her head onto her shoulders as her song became an intimate whisper:

"Come. Come, my lover. Let us go..."

Strong arms wrapped around her. Brown, strong hands gently caressed the soft white skin of her back. The song faded and ended with the gentlest kiss, and the flickering lamp cast dancing shadows of lovers' secrets on the whitewashed walls.

She was now well into her second pregnancy.

Chapter 9

This poor girl has no man like Joseph and no one to champion her cause, thought Mary, returning to the situation of Sarah. The religious establishment may well judge her harshly, but that was not God's way.

"I said godly and good, not religious," she corrected, picking up the thread where they had left off.

"Look, there's a good man in Bethlehem, a shepherd. He's out on the hills, so he doesn't get to the synagogue a lot. He thinks things through while tending his sheep and has a real wisdom about him. Doesn't go on about it, but in the village when there's an issue affecting the shepherds and he speaks, everyone listens. He's had a tough life, lost his wife and baby 20 years ago in childbirth. I don't know the details; they were both young people. But he will do anything for a mother and child. You may know him – Daniel bar-David?"

"I don't know the name; Bethlehem is quite a big village. I don't know any shepherds and I never really went to the synagogue. But anyway, why should he help me?"

"He came to us the night that Yeshua was born. You see, Joseph's cousins wouldn't have us in the house because of how things were. When he saw that we were abandoned in a stable, he offered us a room in his house in the village. He doesn't spend much time there so we mostly had it to ourselves. Joseph was able to do some repairs to repay him, but he would have had us anyway. If you're up against it, look for him and mention our names. Mary and Joseph," she reminded her. "We became such good friends. If you see him, please tell him that you saw us and that we have got safely away. We had to leave in rather a hurry.

He had sensed that there was danger and had come back from the hills to help us. He's like that. He came the night the baby was born when… when he knew something had happened."

Sarah looked at the tell-tale curve of Mary's stomach.

"Not a good time to be in a hurry! What happened?"

Mary paused for a long time.

"I'm not really sure what was happening, but Joseph was also warned that we were in danger. He had a dream."

It sounded a bit thin in the light of day, but that night it had all been so real. Warnings, danger and deliverance had been so much part of their lives that they hadn't been surprised to have another. Joseph had been working in Jerusalem on the new temple. It was a long walk there and back in a day, but it was bringing them in a little income. In the last week there had been talk of a power crisis. The tyrant king Herod was clamping down on any dissent, locking up any possible opponents, so everyone was watching their step and their tongues.

It all started when a delegation from the Far East came to pay their respects to a newborn heir apparent. Herod was old and his son, Archelaeus, was already a grown man so it could hardly have been him. Though ruthless and scheming, the Herod dynasty was also extremely superstitious and there was a lot of speculation about what the omen could mean; Herod was obviously troubled by it. And when Herod was troubled, so was everyone else in the city! Joseph hadn't thought anything about it as he had little interest in politics or nationalism, but then he and Mary were completely taken aback by the arrival of the aristocrats from the East at their little home in Bethlehem just three days before! They were at first bemused when the visitors, with much pomp, said they were looking for a child who must now be 18 months to two years old and then, on seeing Yeshua, knelt reverentially before him, presenting gifts of precious perfumes and spices and a not inconsiderable quantity of gold in coins and jewellery. Such important persons did not arrive at a small town like Bethlehem without causing a stir, and the word soon spread. But in the morning, when the curious townsfolk went out to the small knoll where the visitors had camped, they found it deserted.

Two days later a patrol of Herod's soldiers came hurrying through, galloping off to the south-east into the desert in pursuit. They arrived back late in the afternoon and rumour had it that the visitors were already off Herod's territory before they could be apprehended.

Deeply troubled now, Joseph and his wise friend Daniel talked late into the night. Mary was woken from her sleep by Joseph in a state of agitation, calming her in her confusion, but urging her to get the child up and prepared to leave immediately. Daniel soon arrived with a donkey, so quickly bundling some clothes together and settling the sleeping Yeshua into a cloth sling, the family set off as quietly as possible, heading west and south on the old desert road towards Hebron.

A couple of hours later, Joseph had pulled over into a grove of trees, looking anxiously back down the road.

"There's someone following us," he whispered, while calming the donkey to avoid any sound. They waited anxiously, straining to hear anything above the sound of the insects chirruping in the night, looking back for any changes in the shadows in the path behind them. Suddenly, Daniel was there with them, their cries of alarm turning to joy and relief.

"I've brought you some food for the journey," he whispered.

"When you'd gone, I went out and bought some bread, flour and oil and some dried fruit as if they were for me in the hills. I went to the stable where the dumb lad cares for the sick animals and we milked a couple of ewes and have put the milk into this old skin for Yeshua. It will keep till morning. I came back round the top of the village, and crossing the Jerusalem road I passed a detachment of troops making for Bethlehem with lances and short swords as if they were expecting some resistance. Whatever is going on, it's best to be out of the way."

"But what about you? What if they catch you?" gasped Mary anxiously.

"I won't need to go back to Bethlehem for a few days and will take the sheep into the hills for pasture. Now hurry! I'll wait here for a while then double back and check the road. If you're being pursued, I'll make sure you're safe."

"Be careful, Daniel!" cautioned Joseph, but Daniel laughed softly.

"You forget that these are my hills and I know the sort of places where horses can't easily go and where the riders will have to walk. If they come this way, I'll make sure they follow my trail and not yours and they'll wish they hadn't!" With that, he hurried them on their way.

They made good progress and had now reached the edge of the territory under total Roman control and were moving into more wild country. They would need to move on swiftly in order to reach somewhere safe by nightfall.

Joseph came over and the girls looked up.

"I think we should press on, Mary." To Sarah, he asked, "Is there a village on this road?"

"About two miles on there's a tax post, but there were no soldiers when I went through."

"And the next?"

"Not for 10 miles or so."

"Any troops?"

Sarah laughed. "Looked more like Zealots to me."

Joseph smiled. It would be a long day, but it would be a good place to make for. He did not have much truck with the Zealots, but if he and the family were pursued by soldiers they would be on the same side and he could count on their help.

"If we can get past the next village, rest up during the heat of the day and then press on, we might even make it to Hebron before nightfall."

He would like to stop for a while in Hebron with Mary's cousin Elizabeth, giving Mary a rest while he made preparations for the long journey across the desert to Egypt, where they could merge into the large Jewish community already there.

Hebron was strongly Herodian, but Zechariah and Elizabeth lived in a village away from the city centre and they could probably be inconspicuous for a couple of days, then hopefully join a trade caravan making for Egypt. Even Herod had little influence beyond Hebron. Joseph sat thinking this through, then remembering Sarah was on a journey as well, looked up:

"And you, sister, are you going straight to Bethlehem?"

"It's her home, but she is not sure of the reception she will get..." Mary explained to Joseph.

"And I don't really have a choice," Sarah added grimly.

Joseph was thoughtful for a few moments.

"Look, I am not sure it's a good idea you showing up in Bethlehem just now. Strange things were in the air. Why don't you take your time?"

"I'll just have to take my luck. I don't really have the means to stop on the way."

Mary and Joseph looked at each other, each reading the other's thoughts. They were close in this way and could discern what the other was thinking. Mary glanced over to a leather satchel and back at Joseph, who untied the strap and opened it, taking out a small leather bag and going through its contents discreetly. He selected something and offered it to Sarah. It was a gold coin. She did not recognise it, but it was clearly valuable. She looked up, shocked.

"No, I couldn't!"

Mary said seriously, "The visitors who came gave gifts, including gold, to Yeshua. We are used to giving a tenth of our income to the synagogue and the needy. God has made our paths cross, so maybe it's for this."

When she still hesitated, Joseph said firmly, "Look, it may be important to us that we can get on without others knowing the road we have taken."

"But I wouldn't tell!" protested Sarah, a tinge of fear creeping into her voice.

"I realise that, but this is an easier way. This coin will help you delay for a few days."

"But Joseph, where can she change it? The inns on the way may not take it and it might put her at risk. Maybe we should give her some local money as well."

Ever resourceful and glad to enter into the subterfuge, Sarah broke in. "I'll take the road over the hill to Jerusalem. In the streets around the temple, they are used to changing foreign coins. Then I'll find somewhere to stay in Jerusalem for a few days. Also it will help me prepare to meet the elders… Oh! But where are the boys?"

In their earnest discussions, they hadn't noticed the children wander away. They all jumped to their feet, looking around anxiously. Although they were quite remote, the recent discussion sensitised them to possible danger. Joseph scrambled up a nearby hillock, then laughed.

"There they are, crouched down behind the bank, poking at a hole with a stick."

"Do go and check, Joseph!" called Mary, then turning to Sarah. "Yeshua spends hours looking under stones for beetles and investigating holes. One of these days he'll dig out a snake! He just loves it all, always asking questions. He so enjoys being with Daniel, who spends all his time outdoors."

Joseph arrived with the boys and deftly loaded the donkey, sitting Yeshua on top in a space between the bags while Mary collected up their last things. Sarah's load was so small she was soon ready and stood watching them wistfully.

Mary looked around to make sure all was ready, then purposefully went over to Sarah and embraced her longer and more firmly than polite convention might demand. Releasing her embrace but holding Sarah's shoulders, she looked into her eyes. Sarah looked away for a moment, then back at her with eyes full of tears. Mary sang softly and gently:

The Lord bless you and keep you.
The Lord make his face shine upon you
And give you peace.

"God be with you, my sister," she whispered as she finished.

"And also with you," Sarah responded hoarsely, quite choked up. She cleared her throat. "And if you come back to Bethlehem come and find me; you can stay with us. Ask for the widow, Joanna, she's my aunt. We're this side of Bethlehem – one of the last houses as the village thins out."

"We will see what the future holds, but thank you for your kind offer."

They set off in opposite directions and, after a few minutes, Sarah turned and watched the little family. She willed Mary to turn before the road dipped below the hill and at the last minute, she was rewarded with a backward look and a shouted Shalom. Joseph and Yeshua turned too, and all three waved as they passed behind the crest.

Sarah

Chapter 10

The sun grew hot and it became quite unpleasant to walk, especially carrying Issa and her bundle. Sarah pressed on for a while but in the end had to stop for a few hours at midday. She was glad to find a rivulet running out of the hills in a small wooded valley hidden from the path. The stream tumbled over a boulder into a small pool, in which she thankfully bathed her feet, wet her hair and allowed Issa to play and splash. She took the opportunity to wash his clothes, spreading them out to dry on the hot stones in the sun. It was so pleasant out of the heat and the journey ahead so full of foreboding that she delayed longer than she should, and though the day was now cooler, she would have to press on in order to reach Jerusalem before nightfall.

It was already well into the afternoon when they arrived at the fork where the road curved east to Bethlehem and north on the less familiar route to the city. For a moment she was sorely tempted to go straight home, but then she remembered the warning from Joseph. She could see the walls of Jerusalem clearly but it seemed an age till, with the sun low in the sky, they approached the gates. Issa was fretting, tired and hungry. There were merchants with their camels and goods lining the road, setting up camp for the night. Sarah enquired anxiously, fearing the gates were already closed.

"You'll be all right on foot," she was told by a stout lady with hair plaited and bangles worn in the way that had become familiar to her during her time on the edge of Arabia. "We have to wait here until the customs booths open in the morning."

Sarah hurried on and entered inconspicuously with others returning from the country, though few seemed to be distant travellers like herself. Though tired and dishevelled from the journey, she pressed on upwards towards the temple on the mount and into one of the small streets to one side, where she hoped to find a money-changer. The street was full of stalls selling wares and she was reassured to hear familiar accents and smell the local Judean street food.

Turning into an alley in the money-changing quarter, she chose a small shop at random. Entering, she dropped her bundle just inside the door, clutching the large gold coin and holding Issa on her hip. An old man sat on a stool behind a high desk in the shadows, his face just visible in the flickering lamp light. He raised an eyebrow, inviting her response.

"I have…" she started hoarsely, then cleared her throat. "I have some money to exchange." She nervously handed over the hot coin.

The old man looked at it and then went to a gold balance and weighed it carefully. He returned, inspecting it more closely.

"A royal gold coin… from the east!" he muttered slowly, glancing up and scrutinising Sarah's face, and then looking her up and down in a way that made her feel uncomfortable.

"There are lots of questions being asked about things that have recently come from the east," he said slowly, "but you, you are from here. I can tell. But maybe recently come on a journey?" he said enquiringly, looking at her bundle in the corner and her dusty clothes.

"From the east, maybe?" He smiled a little nastily.

Sarah's heart beat faster, searching for something to reply.

"If it's a problem, then I'll take it somewhere else," she responded timidly.

"Oh, but that is also a problem. You see, I should report anything from the east to the authorities. They want to talk to anyone who had trade with visitors from the east or who might pay with such coins as these." He held the coin up between finger and thumb.

"But you are a poor simple girl. I am sure we can come to some arrangement. Now, this coin would normally be worth…" He mentioned a sum which meant little to Sarah. "But of course, it does carry something of a risk. But…" He wagged his head as if weighing up the pros and cons. "I will take the risk from you. For a consideration, of course. But you, you can go on your way without having to explain to the authorities how a poor country girl – from Bethlehem, maybe – has such a valuable coin in her possession," he said with menace.

Sarah was by now quite frightened.

"How much?" she whispered.

He reached for a cloth bag and tipped out a handful of coins, placing a number on a small leather mat. It was still a lot of money to Sarah, although clearly this man had taken a cut. She guessed it was a sizeable cut, for 'his risk'.

She tried to count the money as she collected it together with trembling fingers and turned to go. It was too much to hold in her hand, so she quickly removed her headscarf, sweeping the coins into it and pushing it down the front of her dress. Tightening her belt for increased security, she hurried out into the twilight.

Sarah fled out of the alley, back into the main street and down some steps to one side. In a growing panic to get away from that quarter of the city, she continued to take any street heading downhill. She was so tired and Issa was a heavy weight for her to carry, so she took the easiest route. But where to go? Her visits to Jerusalem had been few and far between, and then only for the day. She had no relatives here. She dared not go to an inn. People hurried past in the gathering gloom. She really had no idea where she was, and soon she would be out by herself at night in the dark streets of a strange city.

Suddenly, the steps ended on a broad pavement with arches in front of her and she realised that she was by an open pool, into which a spring flowed from a tunnel cut into the rock of the hill. The water in the pool was grey and soapy. Obviously this was where the women came to wash clothes. There were few people about now, but she noticed two washerwomen piling bundles of clothes together, ready to return home. They, at least, would be humble working folk who maybe could help her, or tell her where she might go, where she might find a safe place for her to stay the night. As she hurried over, she saw that they were an older woman with a younger girl, presumably her daughter. They were busy sorting the clothes and didn't hear her approach.

"Excuse me," interrupted Sarah urgently.

The girl looked up and nudged her mother, who hadn't heard.

Sarah continued. "I'm looking for a room for the night. Do you know where…?" she looked around anxiously. "I can pay."

The woman straightened herself, looking inquiringly, clearly not having heard.

Sarah started to repeat the question, but by now the woman was more interested in Issa, who was crying softly.

"Look at the poor lamb – he's so tired."

Sarah started for a third time, but the girl had already understood and whispered something to her mother. She looked more closely at Sarah, her hair out of place, no headscarf, and her face dusty and sweat-streaked from the journey. She took in the small bundle on one shoulder and a young child in a sling.

"Are you running away?" Before Sarah could answer, she asked another question. "Where are you from?"

"Bethlehem," she replied timidly. It was true, and although she had been away nearly two years, it was easier to say that than trying to explain where she had just come from.

The girl gasped and clutched her mother's arm. The older woman looked quickly around them to see who else might have heard, and then whispered, "It's no wonder you're running away! You must be one of the few who escaped. Hannah, quickly get the clothes together." She turned to Sarah again. "Wash your face in the pool and wet your hair so you don't look so dusty. Then carry some of the clothes with your bundle so that we look as though we belong together."

Sarah was perplexed but too tired to argue. She was grateful to accept the protection of this woman and her daughter. Quickly and efficiently, they made three bundles while Sarah washed her face. The smaller bundle included Sarah's pack and the younger girl helped Sarah get it onto her back, passing the knitted wool strap, which held it all together, over her forehead. With her head bowed from her own load, she looked up at Sarah and smiled. The older woman swung her own bundle onto her back and the three of them set off back up the steps and along the streets down which Sarah had so recently fled. Thankfully, with their bundles, the women walked slowly and Sarah could keep up. In the dark, with a baby on her hip and a bundle of clothes, she looked the part, and tried to play the role convincingly.

But even with her lighter bundle, she found it hard going and had to stop and rest. The young girl whispered something to her mother, who turned to Sarah.

"Hannah will carry the baby for you."

Issa was rather nonplussed and looked as if he was about to cry, but when he saw that his mother would be just beside him, he accepted the situation. The girl asked something quietly, and though Sarah had not heard, correctly assumed it was to ask his name.

"Issa," puffed Sarah.

"Issa," repeated Hannah, smiling at the baby, and repeated his name until he looked at her in response. As they walked, Sarah could hear her talking quietly and laughing with Issa. She was clearly at home with younger children. Probably she had brothers and sisters of her own. They went back through the market streets where many of the stall-keepers were now closing for the night, bringing wares inside from the alleyway and pulling down curtains over them. Sarah guessed the stall owners would sleep with their wares for security.

They turned through a small archway and down a private but communal passageway with linked courtyards, into which numerous houses spilled. Old men and women sat on doorsteps; children appeared at windows and in doorways for as long as they dared while their mother's voices shrilly called them back inside, scolding their unseen household in general. The smell of cooking and charcoal braziers filled the air as evening meals were prepared, with the deeper cloying background odour of urine, soil and stagnant water that invariably hung over these poorer, densely populated city areas.

With a grunt of relief, the older woman swung her bundle off her back and, calling out a greeting, disappeared inside a doorway. The girl, Hannah, smiled at Sarah and indicated with an upward nod of her head that she should follow.

"You will be safe here," said the woman as she thankfully dropped her load onto the floor. "You can stay with Hannah in the roof chamber."

A boy of maybe ten and two younger children appeared. The youngsters pulled at their mother's skirts for her attention.

"Tsht! Tsht!" she scolded as she deftly swung the younger of about four onto her hip, simultaneously lifting the lid off a pot that simmered on the fire, inspecting the contents critically.

An old woman appeared with some bowls into which she slopped steaming red stew. She took it for granted that Sarah was to eat and proffered her a bowlful and a spoon made from half a gourd.

The mother said something sharply to the older boy, who cleared a space for Sarah. She sat down gratefully, and Issa reached out both arms to her, partly to be with his mother and partly because he was hungry and she had the food.

The lentil stew was simple but tasty and abundant, the few vegetables and spices available being expertly blended with generous quantities of the staple. The meal was both appetising and satisfied their hunger.

"The rest of the family have already eaten!" laughed the good lady, as she brushed aside Sarah's protests, tousling Issa's hair affectionately as she passed. "Your lad is hungry as I think you must be from so much carrying. But I must deliver some of the clothes that I have washed. Hannah...!" she called, turning to her daughter. "Hang the wet ones up on the roof." As Sarah rose to help, she shook her head. "No. You stay here with your lad. When I return, you can tell me what has been happening in Bethlehem and how you have escaped."

The old woman cleared up the remains of the supper, retiring into the back yard as Sarah settled down against the wall. It was now quite dark and the smoke from the fire stung her eyes. Issa, quite full of lentil stew, dropped off to sleep in her lap so she, too, closed her eyes, trying to think what she was going to say and wondering what could possibly have been happening in Bethlehem.

She woke with a start. Hannah was easing the sleeping Issa from her arms. Sarah looked around in confusion and then sank back, remembering where she was. She was so tired.

"Come with me to the room upstairs. I will take Issa."

Hannah led Sarah up some steep, mud brick steps between two houses, which gave each side onto the roof spaces over each of the two dwellings. The roof was covered in clothes hung out to dry, and in one corner was a small wooden lean-to room with a rush roof built against the wall of the next house further up the hill. The room was sparsely furnished but neat, with a small bed roll. Hannah pointed to this.

"You can sleep here with me. We will make a bed with some clothes in the space beside you for Issa."

Sarah was now a little more awake and opened her bundle, arranging the clothes on the ground. Hannah laid Issa on them, covering him with Sarah's rather thin blanket. When he was settled, Hannah pointed to a worn cloth curtain hanging from a stick making a small closet.

"For washing. There's a latrine across the alleyway outside, but in the night we use this," she explained, pulling the curtain to one side to reveal a shallow, crudely tiled area with a gutter that led to the roof edge and a chipped water pot that served as a slop bucket.

"Washing water runs off into the gutter, but we empty the slops outside in the morning," she continued, pointing clearly to make sure Sarah understood the domestic arrangements.

Chapter 11

Sarah woke with the pre-dawn light and the sounds of the city waking up. Someone was sweeping the next door roof, and the occasional greeting and laughter floated up from the alleyway below. She had slept well, appreciating the warmth of Hannah's back against hers as they lay together on the one bedroll under Hannah's thin blanket. Hannah and Issa slept on as Sarah crept out onto the roof, deciding to have a good wash before others were around. The bathing area was open to the sky and the curtain reached up to her shoulders. Anyone coming onto the roof would see that it was occupied. She scanned the houses on the hill above her but no one seemed to be around, and anyway, in the early morning light she would not be clearly visible. She was as concerned for the money she still had in her head scarf as for her modesty. She was pleased to be able to transfer it into a smaller piece of cloth, tying the top tightly. She kept some coins for ready use, and though she had no clean clothes to put on, the wash had refreshed her and she dressed quickly in the cool morning air and went downstairs. She found the latrine across the alleyway from the strong smell of urine and was just coming out and returning up the stairs when the mother appeared in the doorway of the house, her hands covered with flour.

"There you are. Come by the fire. We will have breakfast soon and you can tell me what has been happening."

The mother was expertly kneading a fat and flour mixture to make the flat loaves that were the basis of the common breakfast fare. Sarah felt she had been taken in under false pretences and needed to redeem herself.

"I must pay you for your kindness – the food and the night's shelter."

"Tsk tsk," chided the lady. "My door is always open to someone in need and we share what we have."

"Then please may I share what I have with you too," responded Sarah, quickly offering one of her coins, leaning forward and placing it on the bench beside the large wooden mixing trough. The woman kept kneading as if she hadn't noticed but called one of the boys and, pointing with her chin at the coin, sent him off to buy some milk and fruit.

"Take the jug… and there will be change," she called firmly after him. "So, young lady, tell me what's been happening in Bethlehem. We've heard some reports but no details."

Sarah was still confused herself.

"I need to be honest with you. Yes, I'm from Bethlehem, but I was returning there after having been away for two years and was warned on the road that things had been happening; that it may be dangerous to go there at present. So I came to Jerusalem, just in case." She shrugged.

"Hmm." There was a pause. The woman expertly flattened the rolls of dough into flat breads, turning them in her fingers and placing them on a flat stone which had been heating on the fire. "But what was it scared you just before we met you? You looked terrified," she asked, turning to look at her and raising her eyebrows.

Sarah looked at the ground for some time.

"I changed some money and the old moneychanger frightened me."

The woman still looked with raised eyebrows, wanting more.

"You see…"

Her explanation was cut short by a commotion in the alley outside and three soldiers forced their way into the house. The youngsters who had been playing by the fire ran to hide in their mother's skirts, while the older lad glowered sullenly.

"Well, well!" began one of the soldiers, recognising the woman, "The wife of Nathan the traitor." The woman's eyes narrowed and her lips pursed in barely suppressed hatred.

"Are you hiding any more traitors? We're looking for a woman and child from Bethlehem who changed a foreign coin from the East."

Sarah's heart raced and she felt sick, but the woman didn't look at her.

"There were no traitors here till you walked in the door. Why are you telling me this?"

"There's a reward for information. And," he added menacingly, "a penalty for harbouring them."

"Who would harbour such dangerous and desperate people as a mother and child? It is as well that there are three of you, or else they might overpower someone as feeble as you."

The soldier's eyes narrowed and he looked around the room. By now, the old lady had appeared with one of the boys.

"Be careful. We know all about you. A widow, one daughter, an old lady and two boys, two youngsters… but no man!" he laughed maliciously.

He counted them out deliberately, extending one finger at a time, finally drawing his hand across his throat and guffawing at his own crude humour. He was so absorbed in his joke that he did not notice Sarah's age or that the other boy had slipped in from the market breathlessly, though right on cue, quickly dropping his load behind a bench. "All present and correct unless there is someone hiding upstairs!"

The soldiers pushed roughly past the old woman and the boy to the back of the house and then up the stairs to the roof chamber.

"There is only clean washing on the roof so mind you don't get your filthy hands on it!"

Sarah wanted to scream and started as if to rush after them, but the woman held her back.

"Tsk! tsk!" she said quietly. "Just trust!" But her grip was trembling on Sarah's shoulder, betraying her anxiety.

To their relief, the soldiers reappeared quickly. There was little else to search and they found nothing. One of the soldiers picked up one of the small loaves as he passed and stuffed it into his mouth. Grinning, he drew his hand across his throat as his companion had done.

"I hope you choke!" the woman growled under her breath as they heard them burst into the house next door.

Sarah raced up the stairs onto the roof, fighting back the tears, trying not to cry out hysterically. Hannah and Issa were nowhere to be seen, but there was a pile of washing in the corner that had not been there the night before. It moved and Sarah realised that Hannah had been hidden with Issa and had escaped the soldiers cursory search! She knelt beside them, talking quietly, crying in relief, anxiously scanning the other roofs. There was no one out at this early hour so Sarah lifted the sheet and they quickly hurried downstairs.

Hannah was white and breathless. She had heard the soldiers enter and sensing the danger, had instinctively hidden with Issa, pulling a sheet from the line over them, praying that they were hidden and that Issa would not move or cry out, giving them away.

Sarah sat with Issa on her knee, now quite scared. The lads were posted in the alley ready to warn of any further searches, quite enjoying the adventure, while Hannah was sent back onto the roof to watch for anything happening behind the house.

"If you want us to help you, you had better explain everything," the woman said grimly, now that things were more settled.

So Sarah told her story for the second time in two days. Not so defensively as she had told Mary, but in a hurry to get it all out in case the soldiers returned. She guessed that the family the soldiers were after was Joseph, Mary and Yeshua, who she had met on the road, but she did not tell the woman any details about them – certainly not where they were heading. She just recounted that they had met on the road and rested together for a while. On reflection, she wondered if she may have helped their escape by diverting attention to Jerusalem. They might be safe now, but she was so frightened. At least she had no more incriminating foreign gold coins left and that the money she had changed was now safely tied in a cloth in the front of her dress.

The woman was quiet after Sarah had completed the story.

"So you haven't heard the rumours that Herod has killed lots of children in Bethlehem?"

Sarah pulled Issa even closer and shook her head, shocked at the news. No wonder Joseph and Mary had to flee! The woman stood up and went over to the fire.

"How I hate that evil man. Three years ago my husband was among some men taken and charged with treason. There was no evidence, but we could not save him. Herod has even killed his wife and several of his sons, so what hope is there for any poor person he chooses to kill? Some astrologers from the east came to Jerusalem and a rumour spread that they had seen in the stars a child had been born in Judea who would be king. Herod is extremely superstitious, but he is such an arrogant despot he really believes he can outsmart the runes. Some are now saying the astrologers went to Bethlehem, which is why he killed the babies there, but everyone with a small child is living in fear of what he might do next."

"I must go," said Sarah suddenly, getting to her feet and looking for her things. "I am a liability to you while I stay."

"But she'll be safest staying here, won't she, mother?" said Hannah, who had just come down from the roof and stood with her hand protectively on Issa.

"Yes, but what about your neighbours? Someone may have noticed me arrive yesterday or this morning when I went to the latrine."

The mother was silent, weighing things up.

"But where can you go? Who do you know? We're already in this with you. If you get caught, then it will only be a matter of time before they find out you stayed here." Sarah was quiet for some time. Then she remembered Daniel! Mary had told her he would help out and he had certainly helped them escape.

"There is a shepherd out on the hills around Bethlehem. He would help me, I'm sure. Maybe I could stay out on the hills until the coast is clear…"

"Nonsense," interrupted the woman. "How could you find him? You'll be in more danger wandering around alone in the hills. You shall stay here."

Sarah could see that she was worried.

One of the lads came back into the house and caught the last bit of the conversation.

"We could go and find Sarah's friend!" he said enthusiastically. The boys loved adventure, and the idea of roaming the Bethlehem hills, outwitting the soldiers, appealed to them. The woman looked doubtful, but, as she did not reject the idea out of hand, he continued. "No one would know what we were at. Lads are always in the hills searching for sheep."

"But what about bandits?"

"Oh, mother! The bandits are looking for rich people and merchants to rob, not poor lads out looking for a lost sheep in the desert! They keep to the Jericho road and other roads to the north." Not waiting for a reply, he rushed off to find his twin. They were soon back. The second lad glanced at Sarah and looked inquiringly at his mother.

"Who are we looking for?"

"Oh, I don't know. This is too dangerous for you. You're only children," snapped the woman crossly.

"We could ask Benjamin?" suggested Hannah. "He knows the Bethlehem hills as his mother's from those parts. I'm sure he would do it if I asked him," she added, colouring slightly.

The woman looked unsure. Worried. Thinking up more reasons to object.

"Yes, but the boys need to eat. A breakfast of bread alone is not enough for growing boys out on the hills all day," she protested lamely.

Grinning, one of the lads dramatically pulled out the bag of food he had been sent to buy before the soldiers came and set it down with a flourish.

"We could take some of this." Not only had he chosen food of his liking, but now he might get an even bigger share.

"That's Sarah's food…" began the woman, but Sarah waved this away. "They would be doing this for me. I am so sorry I have brought this trouble on you. I really should inconvenience you no further."

The woman gathered herself again, eyes flashing.

"You have brought us no trouble that was not already here. Evil pustule! You never know where he will burst its excrement next."

"Shall I get Benjamin, then?" asked Hannah timidly.

Her mother got up decisively.

"No, young lady. You stay here. Any arrangements will be between me and his mother. He will need to be out of the shop all day," she called over her shoulder as she went out.

"Benjamin's father was taken at the same time as ours," Hannah explained to Sarah. "His mother hates Herod as much as we do, and she will be discreet. But Benjamin will find Daniel. He is really clever and brave."

"And handsome?" laughed Sarah, and Hannah blushed as Sarah took her hand and squeezed it. "Clever, brave and handsome is good… but watch out for the charmers," she added quietly under her breath.

A few minutes later the woman was back and busied herself collecting clothes and checking the boys' sandals and headgear. Sarah guessed the trip was now on but felt it prudent to keep quiet.

After a short time, a sturdy young man of about 18 appeared. He looked around the room, politely greeting everyone, and was introduced to Sarah. The woman explained the plan quickly to Benjamin. The boys looked small and scrawny alongside him, but together they would look more like brothers than a band of Zealots or bandits. Sarah explained the little she knew about Daniel. Hannah sat demurely in the corner, watching Benjamin, averting her gaze whenever he glanced at her but just delaying enough for it to be clear that she had eyes only for him.

"All I know is that his name is Daniel Bar-David, but he is clearly well known in Bethlehem. The couple were called Joseph and Mary and they had a son called Yeshua. They used to stay in his house. They said Daniel would help me in a fix. Be sure to mention their names as he doesn't know me," Sarah added urgently.

"From what you have told me, young lady, everyone in Bethlehem will know all about you: You headstrong girls!" She glanced pointedly at Hannah, who looked from one to the other uncomprehendingly as she had not been party to the earlier discussion. "Quite apart from this present trouble, you will need friends in Bethlehem."

Benjamin was quiet for a while.

"I know one or two shepherds from Bethlehem," he said thoughtfully, "and may know Daniel by sight, but I don't recognise his name. It's soon after the rains so they won't have had to go far for pasture and most of the shepherds will take advantage of being closer to the town."

The three lads were about to leave when the woman instinctively looked down at her recently abandoned cooking.

"Which of you has my knife?"

There was a hesitation as the boys looked sullenly at each other.

"Oh, Mother! We might meet a lion or a bear!"

"Then kill them with your bare hands as David did!" she retorted. "The knife!"

Reluctantly they handed it over and Benjamin laughed.

"It's all right. I have a knife."

"Then mind you keep it on you, Benjamin. Those boys will cut off their fingers given half a chance!"

With that, they left. In the hills of Bethlehem they would indeed look the part of lads looking for a sheep, which in truth they were, for sheep would lead them to the shepherds, and hopefully, to Daniel.

It was a long day. Sarah tried to keep a low profile and certainly did not venture out with Issa, keeping inside the house except to visit the latrine. The woman and Hannah had customers wanting clothes washed and so Sarah had just the old lady for company, who said little, being quite deaf. She just pottered around the house or dozed on a mat by the fire, but would smile kindly at Sarah and clucked at Issa as she went about her chores.

Quite early in the afternoon, the women were back and were relieved to find everyone safe. The news of the massacre was everywhere, and with the soldiers searching, rumours spread like wildfire. Families were staying at home, especially keeping their young children out of view.

"There's no way you can go anywhere," the woman said anxiously, pulling back the curtain to look down the street. She was fearful for the safety of the family and especially of the boys. She felt guilty about it, but would be relieved when Sarah was safely on her way, although she wished her no ill.

The sky was red when the lads returned; tired but pleased with themselves.

As Benjamin had expected, the shepherds had been close to Bethlehem and after some enquiries they found Daniel. He had asked for news of the young family, but they could tell him no more than that Sarah had met them on the road.

Whilst very willing to help, Daniel had explained that he too needed to be cautious as the family that Herod was looking for had been living in his house. Apparently, everyone in Bethlehem knew of Sarah, as it had caused quite a scandal when she had left. If she returned to Bethlehem now there would be no suspicion, as she clearly had not been in the village for the last eighteen months. Paradoxically, it was probably the safest place for her to be. She would need to approach from the south and west as if she was returning from the Negev. This would fit her story, which would need no corroboration in the town.

"Yes, but how does the girl get out of Jerusalem?" the mother asked anxiously. Apparently Daniel had thought about that.

"He has to bring a small flock of sheep to the temple market some time, so he'll set off tomorrow at midday and pass through the Dung Gate late in the afternoon. He'll cause a distraction by getting his sheep to scatter as he comes through the gate."

"We are to help round up the sheep, but really make it worse!" put in one of the lads excitedly, pushing his twin and bleating like a frightened sheep.

"Boys! Behave!" scolded their mother, pulling them apart while looking to Benjamin to continue.

"This will leave enough time for Sarah to slip by in the confusion," added Benjamin seriously.

"But how will she even get to the gate? No one is out with a child and she would just arouse suspicion."

They all looked at each other, searching for ideas when Hannah suddenly brightened:

"I hid with Issa this morning under a sheet. We could do the same tomorrow with the barrow! I am the smallest, I could ride in the barrow with the baby under a pile of washing!"

"But what if he cried?" asked Sarah doubtfully.

Hannah thought for a moment.

"You could walk alongside, apparently steadying the load but actually holding Issa's hand. When the opportunity arose you could pick him up in a bundle of clothes and slip through."

The boys thought this was a great plan and elaborated enthusiastically. "We could make some 'deliveries' and 'collections' right near the gate so we arrive at the same time as the sheep and get well and truly muddled up with them!"

"And we could upset the barrow, then have to rescue the clothes and carry them through with the baby in the middle…!"

"Hang on, I'd be spilled on the road as well!" cried Hannah.

"Then Benjamin could rescue you and carry you safely through. You'd both like that!" said one of the boys mischievously.

Hannah blushed and the woman scolded. "Boys, this is not a game! If Herod was serious enough to kill little babies, he won't spare stupid boys like you."

They went on discussing and improving their plan late into the evening. To the boys it was pure adventure, but the woman was allowing her whole family to be put at risk for the sake of Sarah, who until the previous day had been a complete stranger. For Sarah herself, it was unreal and terrifying. She had been comparatively safe from the dangers of city life under Herod during her childhood in Bethlehem and had spent the last two years living in a remote village. The words of Mary's farewell song came into her mind:

'The Lord bless you and keep you.
The Lord make his face shine upon you
and give you peace.'

Someone, somewhere was shining their face on her and keeping her and her little boy safe.

Chapter 12

Early the next morning they embarked on their plan. It was simple and to an outsider would not seem suspicious. The boys left early to wait for Daniel on the Bethlehem road to explain the details and perfect the timing.

The woman and Hannah set off with a load of clean washing to another gate and passed through as if returning the clothes to a settlement outside the city limits. As expected, all the gates were manned. The guards checked their load briefly but there was nothing suspicious about a washerwoman leaving the city. Then after rearranging the clothes to look like a pile of dirty washing, they returned, but this time via the Dung Gate, through which Daniel would later come with his sheep. They made a point of talking to the guards manning the entrance, ostensibly to check on the time of closure of the gate as they 'had to return the load in the afternoon', bantering with them to ensure they would be remembered.

Later that afternoon they set off with the load again, this time with the clothes folded and Hannah underneath with Issa. By now he had quite taken to Hannah and enjoyed the game, though Sarah prayed he might fall asleep and not become fretful.

There were few people out on the streets and certainly none with young children. Within sight of the gate, they turned into a courtyard as if making a delivery and waited out of view. The two lads were hanging around in the way of youths whiling away the time, but keeping watch for Daniel, ready to signal for the women to emerge. Hannah was able to sit up a little and sang quietly to Issa who mercifully fell asleep in her arms. Suddenly the boys waved and nodded excitedly, and with racing hearts the women covered Hannah up again, though this time with Issa sleeping they could hide her quite thoroughly. They emerged into the street and made their way slowly with the other traffic towards the gate.

The boys moved into position as the soldiers halted the outgoing traffic to allow entrance to a load, which the women hoped would be Daniel with the sheep. The women pushed onwards towards the side arch, relieved when Daniel appeared ahead of his small flock.

A Bethlehem shepherd has total control over his sheep using gentle commands and whistles to keep them by his side or to scatter them should danger arise. Immediately under the archway, Daniel gave the scatter sign. The poor sheep looked around, bewildered and confused, bleating, pushing forward, trying to run in all directions. Then Daniel called them back and some, hearing this, returned, while others ran in panic, bleating noisily. The two boys ran into the melee and, under the guise of helping, caused more confusion, chasing the sheep towards the women and upsetting the barrow. The woman was able to slow its roll so the clothes tumbled gently into a heap on the ground and Sarah, heart racing, grabbed at the pile where she guessed Issa would be and felt him being pushed up into her arms by Hannah who appeared from under the clothes, unnoticed in the confusion, and loaded more clothes onto Sarah to cover Issa. He had awoken but his muffled cries merged with the cries of the sheep and the whoops of the boys trying to round them up.

Hannah quickly gathered the rest of the clothes, piling some back into the barrow and carrying the rest in her arms, while the woman shouted and scolded, upbraiding anyone who might come near her clean clothes, angrily ordering the girls through the small side gate, now abandoned by the guards, who were more concerned about the sheep milling around the main gate than about an angry washerwoman on her way back with the clothes they had seen pass that morning.

One of the lads gave the word to Daniel that the girls were through, so he quickly settled the sheep, rounding them up. The woman, shouting and scolding the world in general, pressed through the main arch with her barrow, declaiming as she went. One guard looked cursorily at the clothes left on the barrow, wincing from the curses this evoked, while the other guards grinned but kept their distance as she swept through.

No one spoke as they hurried along the road, Sarah's heart pounding, fearing a cry of alarm and the sound of pursuit, but they were safely away. Tired but relieved, they arrived at the house of a trusted relative in a nearby village where they were to await Daniel. The family welcomed them formally, but were clearly worried and a little unsure. They took Sarah to the small servant's room behind the main house where Hannah joined her a few minutes later.

"I'll stay here with you. Daniel's coming back at nightfall to take you into the hills under cover of dark. Mother's going on with the barrow back through the gate we came through this morning. Even if the guards from the two gates compare notes, it won't arouse suspicion."

"But how will you get home?" started Sarah.

"Benjamin and the boys will be here shortly. I don't know what plan Daniel has. He may want me to accompany you, but whatever happens, one of the boys may want me to stay with you."

Fortunately, it was not a long wait. The relatives' welcome to the refugee did not include any food, but Sarah had brought a little bread to keep Issa quiet. It was quite dark when they heard voices and the door was opened by the man of the house.

"Quickly!" he said. "Your guides are here." He hurried them across the courtyard and out through a small door into a narrow passageway.

"Now go! And God protect you," he added not unkindly, though clearly relieved they were leaving and, hurrying back, he barred his door. It was a moonless night, and a cold wind blew up the alley. For a few moments the girls thought they were alone and started tentatively in the direction of the main street, but a hiss from further up the passageway called them back and they found the three boys and Daniel. The twins whispered and laughed in nervous excitement till Daniel silenced them with short terse commands, leading them via narrow side streets to the hill at the back of the village where the track became a rough path along which they scrambled.

Sarah gripped Issa close to her, grateful that her bundle was being carried by the boys, but even so she found it difficult to keep her balance and fell a few times, scraping her knees and elbows in her efforts to protect the baby. Eventually, they reached the main path out of the village and into the hills. The pace did not slacken as they pressed on relentlessly, eventually stopping in the shelter of a scrubby stand of acacia bushes beside a stream.

"We can rest here for a while but then we need to get over that crest and down to the far Bethlehem road before daylight. That's the way you might have come if you hadn't diverted to Jerusalem. There's no path over the hills, so it will be rough going, but Benjamin and I will help you with the baby." Daniel spoke quietly, though there was no one to overhear. Sarah sat with Hannah, really tired but alert with the tension of the moment while the men moved away talking in low tones. Sarah could just make out Daniel pointing and curving his hands as he indicated the way they would go, finally sending the boys up a ridge to keep watch while he returned to the girls.

"So, my young sister, what's your story?" Sarah didn't answer immediately and after a few moments Daniel started again, but more gently. "Listen. You're in trouble. If I'm going to help, you'll need to tell me what's been happening. Your leaving caused a stir; no-one has heard from you for two years. Now you come back with a baby and no husband, Herod's soldiers are after you, and the village is still in shock from the slaughter of their infants."

"Then it's true... what they're saying in Jerusalem?" Sarah gasped, fear creeping into her voice.

"Yes, it's true. Nearly every boy under two has been killed on Herod's orders. Some have escaped, but not many, and the soldiers are hunting them down. Hence the trouble you are in."

"But won't I be in danger if I return?"

"If you are caught out here in the hills, certainly. In Bethlehem everyone will vouch for your story and though you may have problems with the elders, they won't give you over to Herod. But if I'm to help you with them, I need to know everything. Once you're back in Bethlehem, I'll speak up for you. But they mustn't discover that I helped you escape from Jerusalem."

Sarah sat for some moments. She was very conscious of Hannah's presence and wanted to spin the story carefully. In the end, she decided on a brief resume.

"I ran away with the young man and his family. He said he had married me, and we had a baby, but then I discovered he was marrying someone else. I don't know if he never really married me or if he was taking a second wife. They do that in Arabia."

"And you weren't content to be the second wife?"

Sarah considered this.

"No, it wasn't just that. The family never approved of me, so I thought I might be locked away or become a servant. I would have lost my baby."

"But they were content to take you away with them in the first place?"

"They didn't know I was with them. It was a big caravan. They didn't realise until it was too late. Also, they'd always indulged Abbas; that was my husband's name. When the new bride appeared on the scene, I knew that I needed to go."

"So you just walked out?"

She laughed bitterly. "'Just walked' is an understatement! I had to carry my son and couldn't take much with me." Tears came to her eyes as she thought of all she had suffered on the road, and how she'd had to beg and take menial chores just to keep body and soul together. "It was hard," she added, her voice breaking.

"And then you met the young family on the road… Tell me how they were."

Sarah was rather embarrassed to have so little to tell Daniel about them, especially as she realised that it would be because of this tenuous connection with them that Daniel had done so much to help her.

"They'd travelled right through the night. I met them in the early morning. They said they were heading towards Hebron, where they had relatives."

"Hebron? I understood they were heading for Egypt."

"They did say that was their eventual destination, so I guess they would cut across to the coast road below Hebron. It's the time of rains and the wadis will have water."

Although Sarah wasn't sure exactly where Egypt lay in relation to Hebron, she had learnt enough about the desert during the last two years to know that if the young family had to cross desert lands, they would be safer doing it now.

"Did you tell anyone you had met up with them? Is that why you got into difficulties?"

Sarah shook her head and told him of their generosity, and that it was the changing the gold coin from the East that had got her into problems in Jerusalem. Daniel was quiet, looking at the ground, putting it all together. Sarah broke the silence.

"Thank you for helping me. Why have you risked so much?"

He was thoughtful for a moment, looking up at the rocky outcrops and standing stones all around them.

"Look at the rocks. What do they look like? Have you ever seen an angel?" Hannah giggled nervously, but Sarah was taken aback and not a little alarmed at the turn of the conversation. She'd been aware of the shapes in the pale moonlight and now followed Daniel's gaze. Though not devout in her religious beliefs, like most people, she had a deep-seated fear of the spirit world which prowled through the night, and the hair on her neck tingled as she looked around quickly at the giant outcrops. Her recent terror at being pursued by the soldiers added to the menace of the rocky shapes.

Daniel sensed her agitation.

"Yes, they do look like giants and can appear forbidding, but you get used to them. But one night..." He paused, then went on quickly. "A shining light suddenly appeared... getting brighter and brighter until the sky was lighter than at full moon. We were all on our feet in a second looking at the light when suddenly, one of the rocks started walking up the brow of the hill, silhouetted against the sky!"

The hairs on Sarah's neck tingled again.

"We were frozen to the spot, most of us dropping to our knees; our legs were just like wet mud bricks." Daniel was in full stride now, reliving the moment. "This voice was all around us and seemed to fill our heads, deep and sonorous: 'Do not be afraid. Good news! Good news! A baby is born!'"

He dropped his voice. "It could only be the Messiah, the chosen one," he whispered. "The Promised One who will deliver us! The voice went on, commanding, insistent but full of joy: 'A baby is born. In a stable. In a manger. Go and see! Go and see! Go and see!'

"Then the air began to thrum and a sound seemed to well up all around us from the rocks and scrub. It filled our heads and rose to a crescendo coming from everywhere all at once so that our heads felt they would burst. We all stood transfixed as the sound swirled around us and though there were no apparent words, wave upon wave rolled over us and there was no doubt of the message: 'Glory to God in the highest heavens. Peace on earth to people of goodwill.'

"After what seemed like hours, though it was probably only minutes, the rushing noise died down and the sounds rose above us into a vortex, which seemed to be sucked into the bright light we had first seen. We know the stars well, but this was different from a star. It stood low over the hill like a beacon fire the Romans sometimes make to guide their troops to a rendezvous. It was setting in the north-west, so we climbed the ridge and it was there above Bethlehem. It seemed to light up the little town and as it dipped below the horizon, it looked as if it had dropped down into the village itself. One of the others said that he always felt that shooting stars brought messages from God, but this was something new. As we watched he became excited: 'Fix the spot! Where does it land? You always need to go to where a shooting star lands!'

"It was hard to see exactly, but from where we were it seemed to drop behind the ridge where the caves are, above the town, which fitted with what we had heard as the caves are used to house animals. We all set off at a run and it wasn't for some minutes that we realised that no one was left with the sheep. We stopped for just a moment, but somehow the sheep didn't seem important. So we pressed on, agreeing that we'd all help each other to round up the flocks and search for any sheep that might have strayed.

"It took us some time to get to Bethlehem. There was one cave with a light in it, the one where the dumb boy cares for sick animals from time to time. He was there standing watch at the entrance. He was so excited! He beckoned us in and we found the couple with the baby. Old Fatima was there. You may know her? She's a bit of a crone and lives by herself, but has a way with sick animals. The daft lad had called her to help with the birth, though I doubt if she'd helped a mother in labour for many years. She'd even wrapped the baby in bandages like she does for an injured lamb to stop it moving its limbs!

"The others with me split up, some rushing into the village to tell everyone about it and others to return to care for the sheep. I could see what was going to happen, so I offered the little family my house to stay in so they were away from the stable before the villagers came to investigate. I suppose I've come to feel like a bit of a protector. When the sages from the east showed up asking for the King of Judah, finally settling on the little family, it was confirmation that this baby would be someone special. And Herod's reaction was inevitable, but now they have escaped and the old tyrant's days are numbered."

"But why help me?" asked Sarah breathlessly.

"At last there is a light. The prophets spoke of a great light in the darkness. People are being touched by the light. I have seen the light – on the hills that night. The sages from the east saw a star in the sky and came to find the source of that light. Other people are talking of the light. Maybe you don't realise the significance, but the light has shone on your path too. The light of Israel will become a flame. It will light the whole world. There are dark forces who would try and put out the light but they will not overcome it. I do not know what part we may play but, little sister, we're in this together and when, one day, the family returns, we must be ready."

Chapter 13

It was three years later. Using a dried palm frond, Sarah was sweeping dead leaves from the front of the little guest house she had inherited from her aunt who had died a few months previously. She was largely ignored by the village folk, which quite suited her, and she busied herself with running the hostel and bringing up her son Issa. Daniel had been true to his word, championing her cause when she returned to Bethlehem. The plan to get back to the road she had been on and act as if she had just come from the south had worked well. No one questioned where she had come from.

There were two big hurdles she had needed to face to avoid being physically thrown out of the village: the legitimacy of her marriage and the fact that she was now the only mother in the village with a boy child aged under two. Daniel had made sure he was with the elders when they deliberated. However, with the pain and fury over the recent deaths of those other village infants fresh in their minds, they took little persuasion that they should protect at least one child of Bethlehem from the cruelty of Herod. The villagers themselves agreed with the decision. While they themselves might treat Sarah and Issa as social outcasts within the community, they could score off Herod by secreting at least one child from his evil designs.

Sarah's aunt was quite elderly. Though glad of Sarah's help, she regarded Issa as a bastard child – barely tolerating him, and for whose keep Sarah had to work twice as hard. Living on the outskirts of the village meant that she and Issa only crossed with the locals at the well or on other errands. Most of the women of the village fell silent when she approached, and though there were one or two old friends who might acknowledge her occasionally, even they kept their distance when in the company of others.

The guest house made little money, as there were larger and more elaborate inns nearer the central square. Sarah had to accept the custom of Gentile travellers who found it prudent to keep to the fringes of such an ancient and traditional Jewish village. This further alienated the locals, so when Sarah's aunt died and the local gossip deemed Sarah to be the cause of her demise, she was shunned still further. So, Issa was growing up with very little contact with other children and Sarah had nothing to lose in running a guest house without conforming to the strict segregation laws of the village. Her religious observance, though always quite rudimentary, slipped further away from the strict dietary and purification customs. She would have liked to return to Jerusalem to see Hannah and her family, but time had not erased the fear of those days and she was content to stay in the relatively safe backwater of Bethlehem.

Quite soon after returning to Bethlehem, while she was resting in the shade at the well before the long haul back up the hill with Issa and her full water pot, she had happened upon the deaf mute boy who Mary and Joseph had mentioned. He was being scolded by a group of women who wanted the shade he was resting in, slouching out of range of their cuffs and scowls like a beaten dog. Sarah instantly knew who he was and, feeling a kindred spirit with this outcast, gave him a kindly smile. He quickly looked behind him to see who she was smiling at but, seeing no one, eventually glanced furtively back. Sarah seized the opportunity to smile again, patting the wall beside her in invitation. He came, uncertainly, standing in the shade, too wary to sit and be close enough for a cuff. Sarah smiled again, reaching over to touch his arm. There had been a deaf girl in the compound in Arabia and she had learnt how to communicate simply with her. She pointed towards the hill where the caves were, curved her hand over her tummy to indicate a pregnancy, pointed back at the lad and made some excited faces. Then pointing at herself walked her fingers up her arm, looking behind herself, then pointed south over the hills.

The lad understood immediately, beamed and repeated the gestures, adding more in the same vein as he elaborated on the story. He pointed to his eyes, indicated tears and ran his fingers up his arm as Sarah had done. They sat for a while. The women who had shooed the lad away managed to show their disapproval without actually looking at them. Sarah, for her part, smiled at their averted faces in defiance of their rejection. Following that encounter, she had noticed the lad in the street from time to time, and they always exchanged smiles and waves. Unable to hear the gossip about her, he at least was a kindred spirit with unqualified friendship.

But today her mind was not on her sweeping. Her gaze kept being drawn to the road that led out into the hills to the west. She'd had a troubled night, with dreams about Mary and her husband and child. Her thoughts were crowded with the little family, Daniel and the deaf boy. She sensed that things were not right and she had relived some of the terror of her own brush with danger. True, the old tyrant, Herod the Great, was recently dead and everyone was glad to see the end of him. But his son, Archelaus, while not so cruel or unpredictable, certainly ruled with an iron fist. The words which Daniel had spoken that night kept coming back to her.

"We are all in this together. When the family return we must be ready."

Could this dream have been an omen? She felt restless, as if she should be doing something. As she looked once more up the road, there was a strangled cry from behind her, making her start. Turning sharply, she found the deaf boy grinning awkwardly. He seemed to want to tell her something. Though they had always greeted each other, he had never before been to her house, always keeping a respectful distance, but she was not surprised that he knew where she lived. He pointed excitedly up the road, gesticulating and shading his eyes, searching as if expecting someone to appear over the brow of the hill. He ran a few steps up the road, then came back, taking Sarah's hand, drawing her with him, urgent and insistent. This was all the encouragement Sarah needed. She ran back to the house to collect Issa, who was playing under the tree at the back of the house. He was reluctant to leave his game until he saw his deaf friend and then ran over excitedly. Without a second thought, the lad swung Issa onto his back. Sarah hurried into the house, barred the door and came out of the gate in the wall, securing it with a rope.

They toiled up the hill behind the town, turning back at the top for one last look to check the house, which was clear in the afternoon sun, then hurried down over the small stream in the ravine and up the other side. The lad was striding ahead of Sarah, even though he had Issa on his back, and waited for her at the top of the next rise. When she caught up with him he pulled her arm, pointing excitedly across the valley. In the distance there were some travellers, just appearing on the road. As they traversed a narrow part of the path on a steep part of the hill, they broke into single file and it became clear that there were two adults walking either side of a laden donkey. The lad gesticulated again and made to head off down the hill but Sarah stopped him, indicating that she would wait with Issa. He understood straight away and, gently putting Issa on his feet, scampered down the hillside as sure-footed as a mountain-goat, cutting across the zigzags of the path wherever possible, climbing the far side of the valley more slowly but nimbly, again taking short cuts wherever he could.

The group stopped to watch as he got closer, and from the enthusiastic waving it was clear that they recognised him. The warmth with which he was embraced was apparent even at this distance, and Sarah guessed that it must be Joseph and Mary, for she could not imagine that many other people had such affection for the poor boy. She could see him now pointing towards her and they waved too, their shouted greeting reaching her faintly as the wind carried it away over the hills.

Sarah waved back, her eyes filling with tears as she remembered the warmth with which Mary had spoken with her. Though it had only been for a couple of hours, it was a precious memory. How starved she had been of friendship over these last years. She would always be indebted to the family in Jerusalem who had risked themselves to save her, but the memory of those terrible days was too frightening for her to consider returning. In any case, as a single mother, she was always under suspicion and a trip to Jerusalem would certainly give rise to speculation. She would love it if Hannah or her mother came by, but their life too was hard. They would not have the resources to make the journey. She realised that at the back of her mind she had been hoping that Joseph and Mary might return to Bethlehem, but now they were here, she felt a deep anxiety mingling with the joy at seeing them again. She picked up Issa.

"Look," she said. "That little boy is called Yeshua, and his mummy is Mary and his daddy is Joseph. They helped us when you were very small. They are our very good friends. Yeshua, Mary and Joseph... And a new little one!" she added, a little choked, as she could now make out two children on the back of the donkey.

Issa looked into his mother's eyes, sensing her emotion, and smiled.

"Yeshua is my friend."

They took a lot longer to climb up the valley side than the lad had to descend, as they zig-zagged slowly up the path. Sarah could see the young Yeshua, now a big boy, holding another toddler who was sitting among the packs on the back of the donkey. At the steeper or rocky parts, Joseph would slow the donkey until Mary was able to steady the youngsters, keeping them safe as the donkey regained its footing on the flatter path. Eventually they were just below, and Sarah called out a happy "Shalom!" Mary looked up and gave a warm smile in return, too out of breath to speak.

Sarah held back as they arrived and Joseph settled the donkey, while Mary lifted Yeshua down and took the smaller child in her arms. Then, giving the child to Joseph, she held Sarah in a long embrace.

"Well, sister, how has it gone?"

"We are safe." Sarah could say no more. Her eyes were full and she was choked.

Mary looked thinner and a little more lined than she remembered her, but there was no mistaking the sincere warmth in her embrace.

"Joseph, we must rest here for a few minutes." She looked around, choosing the raised base of an acacia tree for a seat, then took the young child from Joseph as Yeshua shyly stood by her side taking in the newcomers. Issa watched, desperate to play.

"Yeshua, this is Issa," said his mother encouragingly. "Do you remember when we met on the road? You went looking for beetles together."

Yeshua looked from his mother to Issa and smiled, happy at the memory.

Sarah broke in. "And this is the little one you were expecting... another little boy!" Looking closely at Mary, she paused. "And are you...?"

"Yes, pregnant again! This little one is called Jude, and I hope this next one will be a girl."

"You poor thing! Travelling pregnant again." Sarah looked concerned.

"No, it's good," Mary laughed. "We always seem to travel when I'm like this. I've been so homesick in Egypt. When I found I was with child, I knew I was going home! But you! Why are you here? And with Moshe!" she asked, pointing towards the three boys who were all together, engrossed with something under the tree.

Sarah looked puzzled.

"Moshe? Is that his name? Everyone refers to him as…"

"Screamer, or the dumb boy," finished Mary. "Not very nice. No. We call him Moshe after Moses, who needed someone to speak for him. And he got us out of a predicament, so he is our deliverer. Has he attached himself to you? Yeshua adores him. There seems to be some deep understanding between them. Is he the same with Issa?"

"He doesn't come to our house, though we are friends. But he came today really excited and wanted me to come with him. He must have known you were coming. And I too have had dreams about you. And now here you are!"

Sarah watched the three boys who were now playing together, then turned back, her face anxious.

"I am worried about you. I wish I could say I am glad you have come back, but my dream came like a warning of trouble ahead."

"But we heard Herod was dead?"

"Yes, thank God, but things are still very tense, and his son is equally paranoid about possible usurpers."

The two women had not noticed Joseph, who was now standing behind them and heard the last exchange.

"I too have had dreams that have troubled me. I am sorry, Mary. I haven't wanted to alarm you." He sighed resignedly. "But it seems we may be in danger here. Maybe we should turn back."

Mary looked at the ground. It was clear that she had been hoping this would be the end of the journey. Sarah watched sadly, then had an idea.

"Look, why don't you come down to the village at dusk and stay with me? My aunt has died and it's just Issa and me. I am on the outskirts and the chances are that no one will know you are there. Then you can work out what to do."

Mary hesitated. "But we travel so slowly."

Joseph stepped in. "Mary, you could ride the donkey with Yeshua and Moshe could carry Jude. We could wait here till twilight and hide the large bags so we could travel at speed. I could then return under cover of night to retrieve them."

"How much further is it, sister?"

"Only about two miles, one valley down and up and then down the hill into the village. I will go on ahead and get things ready," she added enthusiastically, excited at the thought of them staying with her.

This sounded like a good plan and they explained to Moshe in signs that Sarah was going on ahead with Issa and he was to help Mary and Joseph later.

He understood fast, grinning, then gestured at Issa, mimed a piggyback and ran his fingers down his arm then back again, pointing to Mary and Joseph.

"He wants to carry Issa home then come back for you," said Sarah doubtfully, but Moshe already had Issa on his shoulders and was keen to get started. They waved from the first bend. Seeing the family making their way off the path into a tree shaded dip, Sarah pointed this out to Moshe, who grinned and nodded.

It was dark when Sarah heard them arrive. She had busied herself making a guest room presentable and preparing a meal. She did not have much food in the home, but had been able to make a big stew with some onions, pumpkins and lentils. She resolved to send Moshe to buy bread as well as fruit and milk for the children, although the poor lad had been running and carrying all day. She still had some of the money that Joseph had given her. She called it her 'danger money', after her escapade in Jerusalem, and only spent it in extreme circumstances, which she felt they were in now. She had a lamp lit, thankful that she had some oil left over from a previous guest, and she placed it at the back of the house near the room she had prepared for the family.

"What a lovely home," said Mary kindly but not untruthfully, as she was relieved to have such a welcome and somewhere to stay in contrast

98

to her experience four years before. Joseph too was pleased, as he could see that they were out of sight and on the edge of the village just as Sarah had said.

Sarah quickly dispatched Moshe to get the fruit and milk and hoped that her signing had been explanatory enough, having mimed milking a cow and drawn various fruits rather crudely in the dust. Her depiction of bread was rather nondescript but as it was such a staple, she thought he would understand.

They all ate hungrily and in silence as soon as Moshe returned with fresh bread. He took his own plate very carefully, retired to a dark corner to eat and then mopped up every last scrap from the corner of all of the plates with crusts of bread. Joseph sat pensively, picking the bits of his supper from between his teeth with a splinter.

"We should talk to Daniel," he said quietly but decisively. "Maybe I could try and find him when I go back for the baggage."

Mary looked doubtful. "But where will you start looking? Don't you think Moshe could find him more easily? No one would suspect anything, as it could easily be about the animals." She could not bear the thought of Joseph being away for what could be a long search with the added risk of being recognised and detained, while the women waited anxious and defenceless with the children.

It took a little while to identify Daniel to Moshe, but as soon as he understood, the night swallowed him up. Joseph too, left the house, heading back up the road to retrieve the cache. A few minutes later, the women were startled by the sounds of someone in the courtyard and, with a quick glance at each other, they drew the children in, moving silently into the shadows and watching the door with wide eyes and pounding hearts. There was a quiet and enquiring "Shalom!" from outside, followed by silence. Mary, holding tightly to Sarah's hand, squeezed it harder still and when a figure came bending through the low doorway she tried to stifle a scream, finally bursting out into a high-pitched "Daniel!" as she recognised their old friend in the lamp light.

Yeshua broke away and ran straight into Daniel's long cloak.

"What…? Why, Mary! Yeshua!" He took him in his strong arms, swinging him up high so they looked into each other's faces for a second or two, but quickly having to drop him to support him more comfortably on his hip.

"Haven't you grown, young man! Are you safe?" He turned to Mary, greeting her in low tones, his voice full of concern. Without waiting for a reply, he said to Sarah,

"Praise God, you have taken them in! I said we were all in this together."

Yeshua sat content in Daniel's arms while Issa watched them in puzzlement. Sarah squatted beside Issa, holding him reassuringly.

"Yeshua used to live in Daniel's house. He helped them like he helped us. When things are tough, it's good to have Daniel on your side. God bless you, Daniel Bar-David!" Sarah said warmly, bursting with pride that they were 'in this together'. Daniel smiled but quickly became businesslike again, looking round.

"But where is Joseph?"

"He's bringing some more of our baggage from the hill. We slipped in quietly in the twilight…"

"We met them on the road, and they came down the last two miles lightly loaded to get here fast and avoid being spotted – Joseph has gone back for the baggage," added Sarah.

"Were you spotted?" asked Daniel. "I have had no peace thinking of you these last few days and last night my dreams were so vivid that I had to come down from the hills. I thought of Sarah here and came to ask her to keep a look out for you, as I felt God was warning me that you were returning and might be in danger. You certainly would be if you showed up at my house."

Mary was now alarmed, though immensely grateful that they had the security of Daniel with them before being made aware of the danger.

"But why?"

"The people are still grieving over the children who were killed."

"Children who were killed?" said Mary, alarmed. "What children who were killed?"

"Didn't you know?" said Sarah incredulously. "Herod had all the children under two killed the night you escaped. All of them! There are no other boys of Yeshua's and Issa's age in the village."

Mary sat down heavily, clearly shocked. Yeshua, pushing away from Daniel, ran over to his mother and buried his face in her shoulder. Mary rocked him, stroking the back of his head.

"I knew we were in danger and had to escape, but we had no idea…"

"It's not your fault, Mary," said Sarah quietly, but Mary shook her head.

"It's not just that, it's… There's so much that is so painful… Oh, my little boy! My precious little boy!" She hugged him close and rocked back and forward. "Those poor, poor mothers."

Sarah and Daniel looked at each other helplessly and, when Sarah made to speak again, Daniel raised his hand to keep her silent. Instead, she put a gentle hand on Mary's shoulder who took it appreciatively, squeezing it hard.

They stayed like that for some time, when suddenly Mary opened her eyes.

"Moshe!" she exclaimed. "He didn't come back with you, Daniel!"

Daniel looked puzzled. "Moshe?"

"Yes, you know. The deaf boy. We sent him to look for you, isn't that why you came?"

"No, like I said, I came to get Sarah to look out for you. I never saw him."

"Oh, the poor boy will be all over the hills looking for you, and all the time you are here! He can't speak so he can't even ask anyone."

"Which maybe is just as well, in the circumstances."

"Oh, but we should look for him," said Mary, looking around concernedly, sniffing and wiping her eyes, diverting her recent grief into concern for Moshe. Daniel laughed kindly.

"That boy can look after himself and he seems to have a sixth sense. I'm sure he will work out where I am."

Just then Joseph arrived back and, finding Daniel, cried a joyous welcome, folding him in a warm embrace.

"You still smell of sheep and worse!"

But when there was no repartee from Daniel, Joseph looked around to see what was amiss and became aware of Mary's tear-stained cheeks and Yeshua's concern for his mother. He looked questioningly at Daniel and Sarah.

"She has just heard about how Herod killed all the baby boys the night you escaped," explained Sarah solemnly.

Joseph looked at the floor.

"Oh no! Not that! I knew he was ruthless, but I never knew it would have come to that. The poor families! How they must resent us."

Daniel nodded.

"I'm afraid your return will bring it all up again and who knows what the village authorities might do if it gets out of hand."

They were all silent. At last, Joseph spoke. "We must go. It will be for the best."

"I have been troubled these last nights, as if it were a warning," sighed Daniel.

"And I have had an omen, and so by all accounts has Moshe," put in Sarah.

Daniel put his hands on Joseph's shoulders, holding him at arm's length and looking into his eyes. "My good friend, we do not understand what is happening, but you must protect your family and God has put us in your path to play our part."

"You can't leave now," said Sarah, a little desperately. "It's late and you are so tired. We can lie low here at least until tomorrow evening."

It was sound advice, but Sarah had mixed motives for delaying their departure. She so yearned for friendship, and now this little family, who had shown her such kindness, were to be snatched away again. Could she not hold on to them for even a few hours? Joseph was thoughtful.

"We left in such a hurry last time. There are some things we could usefully take with us. But of course, they will slow us up, so maybe…"

"How about if you do the same as you have just done? Take some of your things early in the morning and leave them with a group of Essenes I know, about ten miles from here," interrupted Daniel. "Then we could return again over the hills and you could get away at twilight. Mary and the children could rest for the day and have the strength for the journey. I could borrow another donkey to make the journey faster still."

"That is wise advice," put in Sarah, delighted at the turn of events. She took Mary's hand. "And we can have a quiet day together."

So it was arranged. Joseph and Daniel set off before dawn and, much to Yeshua's disappointment, he was not taken along.

"He so loves doing things with his father," laughed Mary as she turned to her little boy. "Yeshua, you will get tired, and we need you strong for tonight. And besides, Issa will be pleased to play with you."

Sarah nodded, adding ruefully, "That would be so nice. He does not have any friends except Moshe."

Mary glanced up quickly then looked away, sadly shaking her head.

Moshe had appeared rather bleary-eyed but was dragged into the boys' game as soon as he had eaten. After spending most of the night diligently looking for Daniel, he had eventually camped outside his house, which is where he was when the two men arrived in the early morning to collect Joseph's kit. The boys were pleased to play together and Moshe, being older and stronger, happily took the brunt of the rough and tumble while Mary and Sarah sat together watching, with the little one playing around their feet.

Eventually, Sarah ventured, "Why do you really think Herod was trying to kill Yeshua?"

Mary sighed. "There are so many things I do not understand. I was told I would have the baby before I was married and I became pregnant without... without, you know," she said shyly.

Sarah was thoughtful for a while trying to take this in.

"Told?" she queried, as it was easier to focus on that rather than the other.

"Yes," she smiled to herself. "By an angel, actually."

Sarah smiled too. It was getting a bit surreal, but it was easier to play along rather than being incredulous.

"Daniel told me about angels he saw on the hills."

Mary laughed. "Yes, there have been angels and dreams and people popping up saying things about Yeshua, and then the sages from the East came along talking about stars appearing, then Herod getting threatened..."

"And then I have had dreams, and Moshe suddenly appears," put in Sarah, pleased again to feel she was part of this.

"I really don't know what is happening," continued Mary, sighing, "except that Yeshua is someone special and we have been asked to surround him with love and protection... and wait and see."

"See what?" prompted Sarah, after a long pause.

"I really don't know... I really don't know," she repeated quietly, and then her eyes filled with tears. "But sometimes I fear for my little boy." She instinctively pulled Jude into her arms, looking over to where the boys were playing.

"But surely he is safe with you. At least God, or someone, seems to be caring for him," protested Sarah.

Mary was quiet for a while.

"An old man called Simeon, a sort of prophet, I think, said that one day 'a sword would pierce my heart.'" She looked up at Sarah with brimming eyes and a choked voice. "And I look at my little boy, so lovely, so precious. What did he mean?"

Sarah took Mary's hand but said nothing. She remembered the terror of the soldiers in Jerusalem and her desperate escape. The terrible grief in Bethlehem was proof that the danger was real and not exaggerated.

Mary laughed again suddenly, sniffing and wiping her eyes and blowing her nose on her headscarf.

"When I get like this, Joseph gets me to sing one of the psalms. Do you sing, Sarah?"

"Not really…" Sarah shook her head. "I mean, I never learnt any of those psalm things," she answered clumsily and a little embarrassed.

Mary started to sing, quietly at first. Then, clearing her throat and sitting up straight, she started again, strongly and confidently:

"The Lord is my light, the one who saves me:
Who is there to fear?
The Lord is my safe strong tower;
who can frighten me now?
When evil men plot terror against me;
when enemies attack me
they will trip and fall."

She broke off, smiling at Sarah with moist eyes.

"That was lovely," Sarah whispered. She had never been very religious but the words stirred her, especially in Mary's haunting clear voice. "You are a good person, Mary. God will care for you. I wish…" She turned away. "I don't dare go to the synagogue. It's hard enough going for water. I tend to go when there won't be too many others at the well. I wish you could stay here and teach me to sing."

Mary turned to her, taking her hand.

"I am sure you have a good voice. Look, why don't you learn this one?"

Mary sang the first few words again and Sarah joined in the second time, albeit rather tunelessly. They sang it through several times, but stopped abruptly when the boys came tumbling into the room.

"Mama, are we going to eat?" demanded Issa, and the girls laughed. There had been a lot of stew left over from the abundant meal she had made the night before and it was simmering in the pot. Issa went to get three large gourd plates and handed one each to Yeshua and Moshe. Yeshua glanced at his mother and smiled. Normally they would have some ritual hand washing. Sarah suddenly realised and was embarrassed.

"Mary, I am so sorry, can… Issa, just wait… I'll fetch water. Oh dear, I am sorry."

Mary laughed.

"It will be fine. But shall we sing? When Joseph is with us, he says a solemn thanksgiving, but when it is just Yeshua and me we like to sing, don't we, Yeshua?" Jude ran over wanting to join in, climbing onto Mary's knee. Yeshua smiled as they looked at each other in mutual encouragement, Mary starting the song and Yeshua joining in quietly but confidently:

"How precious is your love, O God!
We are safe in the shadow of your wings.
We feast on the choicest of your food,
and drink cool water from your springs.
From you is the fountain that brings life;
in your light we delight."

"Thank you," whispered Sarah, not sure what they were expected to do next. She busied herself with the food and was soon chattering again brightly. "You must teach me that one too! What have you three been up to?" She turned to the boys.

"We found an ants nest and the flying ants came out. Moshe caught them and ate them. We had some too, but I didn't like them much," exclaimed Issa excitedly.

Sarah looked a little shocked, but Mary laughed.

"Moshe has a tough life and has learnt to eat whatever is going. The desert people consider them a delicacy. They won't hurt you."

"But aren't they all considered... how do you say... 'unclean'?"

"No, not at all! They are quite all right to eat if you like that sort of thing. The ants only come out to fly once a year, or so Yeshua tells me. It isn't exactly daily bread! Now locusts, that's a different thing. They are fat and juicy and the desert people roast them, which fries off their wings and legs and leaves the fat meaty bits."

Sarah shuddered. "I think I prefer the things I have grown in the garden."

They both laughed.

After they had eaten, the boys went out again, Sarah signing to Moshe the limits within which they could roam on the hill, away from the path and the village where no one would be likely to come. As soon as they had gone, Sarah pressed Mary to continue teaching her the psalm they had started to learn before the meal. The tune was simple and repetitive and it was well imprinted on Sarah's mind by the time they had got through all the words. Sarah was sure she would forget most of them, but having sung the first lines so many times as they practised, at least those would stay with her. Other lines had particularly caught her attention and she tried hard to memorise them:

One thing I would ask:
That I may have a place in the Lord's house for ever...
In days of danger he will keep me safe...
though my father and even my mother abandon me;

the Lord will care for me…

be strong and take heart and wait for the Lord.

Sarah got out some flour to make bread for the evening and added all the vegetables that remained, so as to stretch the leftover stew even further for Joseph and Daniel when they returned. She would have liked to have had some roast meat, but that was way beyond her danger fund. The couplet from the song Mary and Yeshua had sung stuck accusingly in her mind: "We feast on the choicest of your food."

As she glanced sadly at her pot of watery stew, an unspoken prayer flitting through her mind. Mary, without being asked, helped with the bread, taking the dough balls when Sarah had finished kneading, flattening them into thin loaves to cook over the hot embers. She was so like the sister Sarah had never had other than in her imagination. Sarah was an only and orphaned child and had been brought up by her strict widowed aunt. She could not even remember her parents. Another couplet stirred in her mind: "Though my father, even my mother abandon me, the Lord will care for me."

Could it be?

The sun was low on the horizon when Joseph returned. Mary was relieved to have him back with them safely. With a cry of 'Abba', Jude hugged his father's legs and Yeshua and the three boys ran in to greet them. Joseph swept Yeshua and Jude into his arms and spun them round.

Yeshua shouted with joy, crying, "And Issa too!"

Without any hesitation, Joseph put down his boys and lifted the delighted, fatherless boy into the air. Moshe grinned approvingly and put a hand on Joseph's shoulder.

"How was your journey?" asked Mary. Joseph became serious and put Issa down, wrapping his arms around the three boys.

"We found the Essenes. And also, your cousin Elizabeth with her boy, John."

"And Zechariah? Has he joined the Essenes?"

"It seems that after we visited, someone betrayed them to Herod and Zechariah was killed. Elizabeth fled with the John to the desert and found her way to the Essenes."

Mary was visibly shocked.

"But is she all right? The Essenes don't take kindly to women!"

"They have quite taken to John. Elizabeth makes ends meet by collecting firewood and doing other simple tasks for them, but she has only thanks to God for his provision and is so excited that we will be calling by. She says it is God's goodness to her."

"That is just like Elizabeth," Mary said wistfully, then turning to Sarah. "Elizabeth is my cousin. They are the ones we went to in Hebron on our way to Egypt. We wondered why they weren't there when we passed through on our way back. Oh, if only…"

She covered her face with her headscarf and sobbed. Sarah, sitting next to her, put an arm around her and Mary gratefully buried her face in her shoulder. The song so recently learned was still in Sarah's head and she started to sing it quietly in Mary's ear. Mary took her hand, squeezing it hard.

Sarah's singing faltered, but Mary pleaded urgently, "Please, please don't stop!"

So Sarah continued, self-consciously looking down to avoid everyone's eyes. A small hand rested on her shoulder. She glanced round to see Yeshua with one hand on her and one on his mother. Sarah's singing soon ended and as she looked up, Yeshua turned from his mother and smiled into her eyes. He held the smile for a few seconds, gently squeezing his eyes to show his appreciation. Everyone was silent for a while. Then, Joseph finally spoke.

"Daniel will be here presently. He had an errand to run in the village. Let's get ready so we can make a start as soon as it is dark and be clear of the village before the moon comes up, which will give us the advantage of the moonlight for the hills. Come and help me, Moshe and Yeshua." He beckoned to Moshe so he could understand.

He moved off, with Moshe following, the two smaller boys skipping after.

Mary and Sarah were left alone.

"I'm sorry…" Mary started, but broke down once more. She again turned her face into Sarah's gown. Sarah was moved and choked, but felt so privileged that Mary should find comfort in her, and she realised how starved she was of affection. After a few minutes Mary drew herself up, wiping her tears and forcing a smile.

"This won't do. I must get our things together."

"You do that, and I'll prepare food for you to eat before your journey. Joseph and Daniel must be famished."

Sarah was determined to make the farewell meal something to remember, even if it used all her funds. Maybe she could find some meat trimmings and a bone to add to the stew. Wrapping her headscarf round her face, she hurried out of the house.

"Please Lord! The choicest of food!"

A man was hurrying up the road in the twilight and Sarah made to merge into the shadows, but then she saw it was Daniel. Slung from a hook, he was carrying half a roasted lamb. He greeted Sarah formally but kindly, and with a smile.

"The baker roasted this for me in his oven while we were away. We can add this to the good food you have prepared. It will need a little more braising over the fire. We need to feed the family before the journey."

Sarah gasped, and whispered to herself, "The choicest of food!" before adding joyfully in a louder voice, "Thank you, Daniel Bar-David! You are so good to this poor family."

With the family's personal bags ready by the door, they were collecting up their last bits and pieces. Daniel helped Joseph arrange other bundles so that they could make a speedy exit. Mary smiled at Sarah as she came from her kitchen.

"Please. The food is nearly ready for you. You have to wait until it is dark before you leave so it won't hold you up. Please don't rush," pleaded Sarah anxiously.

"You are too kind," said Mary. "Let me help you."

"I will manage all right and you must rest. Daniel has brought some roast lamb so there is little to do except mix some herbs and oil and finish the lamb over the coals. But come and talk and teach me some more of that psalm thing we were singing."

The girls squeezed into the tiny kitchen as the boys sat on the bags, playing a simple game with some stones and a stick, which Jude did his best to spoil. Soon bored and tired, the toddler crept onto Mary's knee, pulling at her tunic, wanting to suckle as he obviously still did while falling asleep.

Joseph squatted beside Daniel, deep in conversation, and soon the smell of roasting lamb and the spicy stew wafted through the house.

They ate in their travelling clothes, and as the house was sparsely furnished, the men stood. Daniel used his sharp shepherd knife to slice off portions of meat expertly cutting up the bones.

As he sucked the meat off one of the ribs, Yeshua chuckled. "It's just like the real Passover: eating lamb ready for the journey to escape!"

Issa looked puzzled and Sarah struggled to remember the story. "Our people long ago escaped from a wicked king," she began hesitantly.

"And they had to mark the doors so that the angels would protect them, and they had to be all ready for the journey, just like we are. And we have come from Egypt!" Yeshua added brightly.

"And God protected them on that long journey just as he will do for us now, so come on, let's get on our way," added Joseph, turning to Sarah.

"May God bless you for your kindness to us today!"

Mary held Sarah in a long embrace.

"Goodbye, my sister," she choked through tears. Sarah was overcome and couldn't reply, so she knelt down to hug Yeshua, who gave her another of his warm smiles. At a signal from Joseph, who was checking the street, they all hurried out of the door. Moshe turned and grinned a farewell and they were gone.

Sarah found Issa in the kitchen eating some of the leftover food. She sat among the debris of the hastily eaten meal, tired after her cooking and sad at the farewells, not having the energy to clear up. As the lamp burned low, she took Issa in her arms till he fell asleep.

"I have you, my precious child. God at least has been that good to me." With a sigh, she lifted Issa off her lap and laid him on the rug, covering him with a blanket. She stroked his hair, looking at him tenderly as snatches of the song she had learnt so recently came back to her and she sang quietly while she watched him sleep:

"I hear a whisper 'seek my face'
My heart responds 'Your face I will seek my Lord'
So teach me your way.
 Lead me along a straight path."

The sound of scratching brought her back to the present. She clapped to shoo away the mice and started to clear away the remains of the food.

Chapter 14

Sarah would have been pleased to build on the stirrings she had felt with Mary, but life was hard, and it was easy to 'not have the time'. The truth was, she feared rejection at the synagogue. She was not sure that 'the Lord' in whom Mary and Joseph trusted was the same Lord that the hard-liners followed. So she contented herself with the warm memory of the time with Mary and would attempt to sing the psalm she had tried to learn. The first lines went along, more or less, but then there was a lot of 'la-la-ing' between the other snatches she could remember. The tune was simple enough and humming that alone gave her a lot of joy and reawakened the feelings of peace and security that she had felt when singing with Mary.

Now that Moshe had been to her house and found himself welcome, he turned up from time to time. Sarah would find him sitting on the wall of her yard, grinning and signing some bit of information, usually some small talk about the weather or a recent occurrence that Sarah did not always fully understand. But he also had a habit of showing up just when he was needed. Was he quietly keeping an eye on things, she wondered, appearing when he would be useful, especially when there were lodgers? Sarah was glad of the help and Issa was always pleased to have someone to entertain him for a while, although he would really have liked Moshe to himself.

Occasionally he would turn up late at night when she had a solitary visitor, as if he wanted to ensure her safety. Sarah held herself aloof from the travellers to avoid any misunderstandings, for she knew that some lodging houses were thinly disguised brothels where travellers could get more home comforts than food and a bed for the night. When a husband had displeased the authorities and disappeared, the women folk had to find a way to feed their household. Such women were shunned by the village people and largely ignored but were the convenient scapegoats for anyone who needed someone to blame. They suffered summary justice with rarely anyone to defend them. She supposed that there would be rumours about her around the village so she was cautious and sometimes she had no visitors for days on end. Moshe, though slight and barely into his teens, was sharp and quick-witted from bitter experience of being teased and pushed around. He could be relied upon to defuse a situation rather than confront it. He would often divert abuse onto himself by being excessively 'helpful' to a person insulting or obstructing Sarah at the well. But he was discreet in such a way that the villagers didn't notice his attachment to Sarah and Issa. It was their secret.

The years passed and Issa was now 11 and growing fast. He liked to wander on the hills behind Bethlehem and had no real friends beside Moshe. He would often be gone for several hours. Sarah was always a little anxious while he was away, but she knew he would be with a protector who would see him safely back to the road by the house. Then, with a grin and a wave, he would slip back into the village. Sometimes Sarah was quick enough to give him some bread or roasted grain, though often she did not have any such food in the house. She scraped out a small plot on the hillside, producing a few vegetables if the rains were favourable. At harvest time she went to glean in the fields but, having to be careful to anticipate visitors to her hostel, she was not always able to take advantage of the best fields.

Each autumn there was a big feast for the harvest, which was open to everyone: the poor the widow and the foreigner, who may not have anything to offer, were all welcomed. The first year after her aunt died she had gone, fearing rejection, but there were so many people and the feast so joyful that she was able to quietly eat her fill, enjoying the singing and dancing from under a tree, a little giddy from the wine and full of food.

A girl of Sarah's age and circumstances might have expected the attentions of some of the older widowed men looking for a young, hard-working wife to care for them into old age, but there was a 'bad omen' around her and Issa because he was the sole survivor of the massacre, so Sarah kept a low profile. In any case, she had no family who would normally do the negotiations. The festivals were the only time she saw Daniel, who would quietly seek her out, asking how she and Issa were keeping, before melting away. Though he never called by the house, from time to time a joint of lamb would come via Moshe. Sarah held him in awe and was comforted to know that there was at least one good man in the village who was concerned for her wellbeing.

Not all the festivals were quite as generous as the Autumn feast, but Sarah enjoyed them all the same. She was not really sure of their significance. Some were more solemn than others, but they all would have some singing and usually a little food was available to the poor. If she could, she would take a small contribution from her garden; a pumpkin or some beans, and quietly place it with the food destined for the common pot on the morning of the feast. Although this was never acknowledged, nor was she invited to help with the cooking, she didn't mind, being grateful she could express her thanksgiving. She would sing quietly the couplets that Mary and Yeshua had sung over the meal, those few years before and which had come alive to her when Daniel had arrived with the side of lamb:

'How precious is your love, O God!
We are safe in the shadow of your wings.
 We feast on the choicest of your food,
 and drink cool water from your springs.

From you is the fountain that brings life;
in your light we delight.'

There seemed to be any number of songs that the people sang, different words but often expressing the same thoughts of love, provision and protection. Sometimes everyone sang together and if there was a refrain, she would join in. One popular one started, 'Give thanks to the Lord for he is good, his love endures for ever!' and went through the history of Israel. A deep bass singer would sing the line, and 'His love endures for ever' was belted out with inebriated roars by the crowd.

At home, Sarah would invent her own lines telling her own story of her wayward adventure; the weary return and her chance encounter with Mary and Joseph and the deliverance from the evil Herod. She sort of knew the story of the deliverance of Israel in years long gone, but her own deliverance was so much more real to her and in the cool of the evenings she would sit at her door, humming her thoughts and singing the refrain, 'His love endures for ever!'

But one popular song troubled her. In each stanza, the couplets all started with the same sound, each one then speaking of God's law or his word. Sarah did not understand all that they said and certainly did not learn them all, as each time they were sung at the festivals, they started at a different verse. But always the same thoughts were expressed: 'Learn God's word… study his laws…' Yet she knew so little and could teach Issa nothing. She knew the synagogue school would be costly and anyway, there were no other boys of Issa's age. And she had no male relative who could take him on as an apprentice to teach him a good and upright trade.

It was at one such feast, when the villagers had sung their hearts out, merry on the abundant wine of that year, that one of the grandfathers called on his granddaughter to sing. She sang shyly and quietly, but it was lovely and the crowd roared its approval. Not to be outdone, other old men called on their talented young people to also come and sing, although most were reluctant. Sometimes the crowd joined in or sang the refrain while the old men and fathers noisily called for more. Cries of approval and encouragement and hilarious repartee interspersed the songs with a great cheer whenever another shy youngster stepped forward. Sarah recognised one of the girls from a house not far from hers. She was not as old as the other girls that sang, about the same age as Issa. While she had a lovely voice for one so young, it was her choice of song that made Sarah start. It was Mary's song! Her song! She had not heard it sung except by Mary. Her eyes filled with tears and she became quite choked. She recognised the words even though she couldn't have repeated them all, but it was the last couplet that arrested her:

"Wait for the Lord;
be strong and take heart.
Wait for the Lord."

The young girl sang them over several times as a coda to her song, ending in a deep whisper:

"Wait for the Lord!
Wait for the Lord!"

There was an appreciative pause for reflection as she finished, then a great cheer and applause. The girl smiled shyly; her grandfather roared with drunken approval while her elder brother pulled her back a little impatiently, almost disapprovingly, from the firelight into the family group. It was a fitting last song of the evening and after the rousing benediction, the crowd turned to go home in the dark. As they went their various ways, Sarah found herself amongst the singing girl's family. There was a lot of chattering and banter, but among it she could hear two or three of the children singing the song along with the girl, enjoying her moment of glory with her. They too liked the ending repeating it over and over, trying to get the haunting whisper right. Sarah found herself joining in quietly and as they turned into their home, she carried on singing quietly to herself:

"Wait for the Lord. Be strong and take heart. Wait for the Lord."

Issa was there when she got home and as the fire was made up, she guessed Moshe had brought him home, made up the fire and then slipped out when Sarah returned. They had all eaten well tonight. Moshe usually came to take Issa to feasts and she was happy to leave the boys to their own devices. Moshe knew how to work the system to get plenty of food and at least in this Issa was having good teaching. But now the words of the song stayed with Sarah and displaced the guilt feelings she so often felt about Issa's lack of education. In the end, she did not have so long to wait before her concerns were met.

Chapter 15

It was common practice for inn keepers to tout for custom in the village square to try and draw in travellers with extravagant claims of the superiority of their hostelry. Sarah was very cautious of this, as offers of accommodation by a woman on her own might well be misconstrued, but she did keep bedding airing outside her door, which was the usual indication of an inn, and kept an eye open on the road for likely customers, making sure everything spoke of a clean, well-cared for and respectable, albeit humble, hostel. She would be busy in full view if she saw a married couple or an obviously respectable citizen but often she kept out of sight until she'd had a good look and could decide whether to tout for custom, be cautious, or definitely not be at home. She was holding back in this way while she weighed up three young men, dusty from travelling, coming down from the hills. She had more or less decided to let them go past when they stopped outside her house, looking around and pointing. Something was familiar about them and her curiosity got the better of her so she stepped into the doorway, trying to look more suspicious than welcoming.

"Is this where Mistress Sarah stays?" asked the older of the three.

She was taken aback. Most people who knew her name did not treat her with respect, but she was still cautious.

"This is my house."

One of the younger lads nudged the other and grinned.

"Sarah! Don't you remember us? You stayed in our house with Issa and… and the sheep," he added in a quieter, conspiratorial voice.

"Hannah and Mother send you their peace."

Sarah's eyes filled with tears and she dropped to her knees.

"I thought I recognised…! You are welcome! You are most welcome, please… Please come in." In a louder voice, she called out, "Issa! Issa! come quickly!"

She took each of their hands as they passed. Benjamin, in taking both of hers, pulled her up, smiling.

"You are well, sister? And this must be Issa," he said as the boy self-consciously came out, standing close to his mother. The lads laughed and punched Issa playfully and Sarah noted that though older, they were still like a pair of puppies.

"Issa, these are the men who saved us! Who tipped you out of the barrow!"

The lads roared with approval and slapped each other's backs. Benjamin looked deeply into Issa's eyes with his hand on his shoulder. "And you have cared for your mother well since then… but who is this?" Moshe also appeared.

He smiled quickly but looked a little confused, overwhelmed by the sudden arrival of three men who seemed to know Sarah and Issa.

"This is Moshe. He is our protector!" She pointed to Benjamin and the lads and gesticulated towards the hills, cradling a baby and miming running away. Moshe smiled again quickly, but was obviously still confused. More explanations would have to wait, and Sarah turned back to the lads.

"But what are you doing here? It is late, and you must stay. I have no other guests. Issa, get water for them to wash, and I will prepare some food."

Issa wandered off in the general direction of the water pots, but it was the ever-observant Moshe who realised what Sarah had said and quickly fetched the water and a basin for the men to use, while Issa halfheartedly helped. Benjamin quickly realised that Moshe was the man about the house, and he gave him an encouraging smile.

It appeared that the lads had come to do some business in a village some way down in Judea, and as Bethlehem was not a great detour, they had been told to make contact with Sarah. After supper they exchanged news, though Sarah was cautious of mentioning Joseph and Mary. Benjamin was now married to Hannah and they had three children. The boys worked a market stall with Benjamin and were branching out into new commodities, hence the visit down to Judea, having heard of a cheaper supplier for their latest product.

Sarah did not dwell on her hand-to-mouth existence, though the lads could see that she was not well off, but she told them Moshe's story: how he was their guardian angel, always appearing when she had a need, and how he was such a blessing to Issa, who would have been totally isolated if it were not for Moshe. She became a little choked as she explained that she feared Issa would not get a chance to learn a trade, that he was ostracised as the only surviving boy of that age and having no father. She told them how they could go to festivals but she had not felt able to send Issa to synagogue school. The lads looked at their feet for they were not at all devout, never having attended synagogue school themselves.

One of the twins suddenly brightened, as he came up with an idea. "Why doesn't Issa come and stay with us during one of the big feasts in Jerusalem? There is so much religion in one week that it would last him a whole year!"

Sarah sighed. "But they are my busiest times; I rely on the travellers to and from the feasts for my income."

"We could take him! We usually buy some lambs before the Passover festival to sell on, so there's no reason why we shouldn't get them from Bethlehem and pick up Issa on the way through. We could try that shepherd who helped us the last time. Daniel, wasn't it?"

"But wouldn't Issa be in the way?"

"He could help around the stall. The market is always very colourful, and he will also be in the thick of it, for we hope to get a pitch in the outer courts of the temple this year."

"But how would he get back?"

"Business is usually slack after Passover, so one of us could bring him back."

"Or maybe I could go with Moshe!" suggested Sarah, warming a little to the idea, thinking of ways of getting something out of it herself as well as ensuring that she got Issa back without delay. "If you don't mind having him for a couple of days after the feast while the travellers go home. They usually disperse quickly after the feast."

Issa sat smiling, realising that an adventure was being planned. He always enjoyed feasts with Moshe, and the two younger lads, being so full of life, would probably make even more of any feast.

And so it was settled. Benjamin pulled some coins from his pocket. "We'd better leave a deposit, so he knows we are serious. It's not much, though."

Sarah remembered the spontaneous generosity of this family and realised how fortunate she had been to have fallen in with them all those years back. Here they were again at her time of need.

It was arranged that Sarah would get Moshe to locate Daniel and place the order for lambs. As there had been some rains, he could well be nearby. He might even come into Bethlehem. Moshe would bring word when he was around and Issa could go with him to explain in detail.

Though far too complicated to explain the proposed venture by signs, Moshe understood that Sarah needed to know when Daniel was nearby, so it wasn't long before he turned up indicating that Daniel was in the village. Sarah really would have liked to speak with him herself but he had never made any obvious direct contact with her and she respected his discretion. With Moshe carrying the money and Issa carefully schooled in what to say, the lads set off at midday. They were away for some time and it was a very excited Issa who returned well into the evening. They had found Daniel with the men doing the shearing who had just arrived from the distant hills with their flocks. Moshe was pulled in to help with rounding up the sheep and penning them for the next day's shearing. In great excitement, Issa explained about it all. It was all Sarah could do to get out of him that there was no problem with supplying the lambs. Daniel had apparently said that nearer the time he would make sure Moshe knew where he was to be found so that Benjamin and the lads could find him.

On the following morning, Issa was up unusually early.

"Mother, I'm going to see if I can help the shearers." Sensing her hesitation, he added quickly, "I'm sure Moshe will be there and he will look after me." Sarah put her hand on Issa's shoulder. She was most concerned that he might not be welcome and would be hurt by the rejection.

"Will Daniel be there?"

"Oh yes, Mother. I think he's in charge. Don't worry about me. The shearers are all from the hills and not from Bethlehem, so they don't say things like the people here." Sarah was a little taken aback that Issa was so aware of the hostility of the villagers. Little wonder that he had become a loner.

She looked lovingly at her son, rather gangly as he had grown so much recently and now was rapidly gaining her height. His father had been tall and handsome and she could see his fine features in the lad. A pang shot through her heart, her eyes brimming with tears. She turned away to busy herself and put away the painful memories, so Issa wouldn't see.

"You must have some food before you go and take some for later on," she insisted.

"Oh no, Mother!" The lad was anxious to be getting on. "All the shearers and helpers eat together. They gave me food yesterday," he went on, "and I'm sure they'll give me some today."

"That will do for later, but they will arrive well fed and you may have to wait some time. If you want to impress them with how well you work, then stock up first!"

There was not a lot of food in the house, just some bread and a few boiled vegetables left over from yesterday that Sarah was going to fill out with some roots from the garden, or maybe a marrow bone if she could afford it. Issa pulled at the rather stale bread and pushed the limp vegetables to one side. He spooned some olive oil onto the bread to make it softer, slopping it carelessly before Sarah could intervene. The oil was precious and she used it sparingly, never to moisten stale bread – they had water for that. But she let it go, not wanting to curb Issa's new-found enthusiasm.

"Well, just make sure you do what you're told and stick close to Moshe," she clucked as he washed the last of the bread down with some rather tepid water.

She watched him running off down the street, expertly skipping from side to side to find the dry mud patches, avoiding the sharp flints to spare his bare feet. When he had almost disappeared down the hill, she was relieved to see Moshe arrive. Ever the diligent minder, he had come to collect him and together the two boys raced off to the shearing pens.

As she went about her daily chores, thoughts of Abbas would not leave her mind. The pain of his betrayal was still there. Though not generally given to feeling sorry for herself, today bitterness was not far away. Issa was growing up, looking more and more like his father, and today she saw the first signs of independence. In a few weeks' time he would be going alone to Jerusalem. One day he would no longer need her. Sitting in the shadows at the back of her house, she let the tears flow; not tears from a broken lover's heart, though there were tender scars there, but rather from the foreboding that maybe, one day, her son would break her mother's heart.

The shearing lasted all week. Moshe called early each morning to collect Issa and together they would go off bounding down the hill. Issa would come home each evening quite exhausted but excitedly explaining the intricacies of herding and penning and throwing the sheep until sleep caught up with him.

On the final day he came back with a good piece of meat, which he proudly gave his mother as he explained that it was his pay. Moshe probably had been given a little cash and Sarah did not doubt that Issa, at eleven and a novice, was really playing, so she was pleased for him that he had been given any pay at all. She was a little taken aback when Issa added, matter of factly, that Daniel said he would be calling by to talk with his mother.

A few days later there was a hubbub in the lane leading up to the house and a flock of sheep appeared, led by Daniel. He said something as they arrived near the house, and the lead sheep wandered to the road side, the others following, spreading out and sniffing for grass to nibble. Daniel walked on till he was right outside Sarah's house, then leaned on his staff, watching his sheep browse. Apparently taking no notice of Sarah, he started speaking, slowly, carefully pausing and then adding another phrase as his gaze turned to her side of the road. Sarah stood discreetly in her doorway, holding her scarf over the lower part of her face, looking at the dusty road but attentive to everything he said.

"I received your friend's order for the lambs... They'll be ready before Passover, as requested."

Then a pause.

"Your lad has a fine way with sheep... He could make a fine shepherd boy."

"I will be up on the hills behind this end of town till the rains stop." He turned to look up the road and then back again. "You might send him out to me out for the day." Another pause.

"The dumb lad knows where I am. Maybe he will learn a thing or two."

By now, Sarah was staring wide-eyed. Aware of this, Daniel looked up and smiled kindly.

"Who knows where it might lead?"

Curling his lips over his teeth, he gave a sharp whistle. The lead sheep came to his side and he headed on up the road, the other sheep following. Anyone watching from a distance would have just seen the sheep pause, feed and pass on. No one would have guessed that Issa's future life had been planned.

Except one. Standing unnoticed, just behind his mother in the doorway, hearing all that had been said, was Issa. His eyes were bright and excited.

"Mother! I am going to be a shepherd boy!"

Issa

Chapter 16

The winter months had passed and spring was now here. The crops were ripening in the fields and the feasts of first fruits and Passover were soon to be celebrated. True to his word, Daniel had taken Issa on as a shepherd boy and the lad had taken to it as a duck to water. Though still slight, he was growing, becoming tough and wiry. His face had bronzed in the winter sun, but with hands soft and gentle from the oils in the sheep's wool. On mild nights he would often stay out all night, and Sarah was never certain when she would next see him. If it had not been for Moshe, she would have worried more, but the faithful friend would accompany him into the country and return to be around the house for a while, as if to reassure her that he had seen Issa to the flock, before going about his business. His extraordinary sensitivity to their needs meant he would turn up at just the right time to help Sarah out. If he called by in the evening and then quietly slipped away, she felt a surge of joy for she knew that he sensed that Issa would be coming back and had gone to meet him.

Benjamin and the boys had come as they had promised and Issa had very proudly appeared with a small flock of lambs, doing everything all very properly, tenderly picking up one then another of the smaller ones to give them a rest on the journey from the hills. In his arms, the lambs would nuzzle up to him, and it was obvious that he had a special way with them. They all recognised his smell and his voice. His mother watched proudly as he and Moshe quickly made an old, tumbledown outhouse with three standing walls into a sheep fold, lashing together some willow they had cut from a stream in the hills and fashioning a hurdle to close the fourth side. After they had eaten and Benjamin and the boys retired to sleep, Issa brought his bed roll from the house and stretched it out inside the hurdle. Making gestures as if he was a wild animal to explain the sleeping arrangements, Moshe turned to Sarah and winked. Though no wild beasts would come this near to the village, Issa was taking his role seriously and Moshe faithfully joined in, sitting on a stone by the hurdle, taking his turn to watch. Her heart bursting with pride in her growing son, Sarah quickly went inside, pulling her only blanket off the bed and giving it to Moshe. There were no spare blankets with Benjamin and the boys staying, but she could manage with a shawl and some extra clothes. She was in this, too!

They had all set off for Jerusalem early next morning. Moshe went a little way with them but was soon back. It was not long before the first pilgrims started arriving and Sarah was kept busy day and night. At first she had to ask for a little money to buy food to prepare, but, as the days went on, she was able to buy food in advance and have a pot on the go to tempt travellers to stop rather than pressing on for Jerusalem. It was now an advantage to be on the outskirts of the village. With so many hundreds of visitors pressing towards Jerusalem, no one knew how crowded the inns would be further on, so they were glad to take her spaces. With Issa not there, she could use his bed and she gave up hers to accommodate cooking for so many, sleeping in the kitchen area in front of the fire if it was cold. Moshe would keep the fire going, collecting wood and cutting it ready and carrying water from the well even though it was considered women's work. With so many visitors, there was often food left over and he was more than ready to scrape the pots clean, not wasting one morsel. There was a brief interlude at the height of the feast when she could regroup, clean and spruce up the house in preparation for the returning pilgrims. The return was never so lucrative though, as many wanted to get further than Bethlehem on the first day of travel. The main work was having food ready for those who stopped to rest and eat.

The returning pilgrims were now more spaced out, giving Sarah time to relax, sit in the shade and watch out for the return of Issa. Late in the afternoon she saw, in the distance, a lone figure hurrying up the road. A woman carrying a small child, clearly very agitated. There was something familiar about her. As she came nearer, to her joy, Sarah recognised it to be Mary! She ran down the road, calling out, "Mary! Mary!"

As the woman looked up, Sarah saw her red eyes and anguished face.

"Oh Sarah, Sarah it's you! Thank God! Please tell me he's here!" She caught hold of Sarah's sleeve, pulling desperately and crying almost hysterically.

"Mary, who? Who have you lost?"

"Yeshua," she wailed. "He was with Issa. Where's Issa? Is Yeshua with him?"

"Mary, Issa is still in Jerusalem," Sarah said quietly, deeply troubled now lest both boys might be in danger. Leading Mary into the house, she tried to calm her.

"Oh, Sarah! I so hoped he would be here, I have run all the way from Jerusalem! I thought he was with Issa!" She buried her face in Sarah's shoulders, sobbing, then slid to the ground in physical and emotional exhaustion.

Sarah knelt beside her, pulling her to herself. Mary didn't resist. Sarah's mind was in a whirl! What should she do? The child with Mary was now crying too, alarmed at her mother's distress as Sarah held her close, trying in vain to comfort her. Mary looked desperately into Sarah's face. Her hair was dishevelled; her face wet with tears. Sarah tried to think of what to say to console her.

"Mary, the Lord will look after him."

At this, Mary became quite hysterical.

"But God... gave him to us... to look after... and... and... and we've lost him!" she howled through sobs, burying her face in Sarah's tunic again.

Sarah was crying too now, both in sympathy and in growing concern for her Issa, searching wildly for inspiration.

A tune and snatches of words had been going through her mind all day. She wrapped her arms around Mary and the crying baby and sang tearfully and quietly the words she could remember, her face pressed against their heads so the song had a loving intimacy:

"I will sing of the Lord: He is my sanctuary my stronghold...
He will conceal you in his feathers; secure beneath his wings...
Neither the terror that lurks in the night nor the dangers of the day will you fear.
He will send his angels... to keep watch over you... to carry you in their arms...
call on me... I will answer."

Running out of the words she could remember, she sang snatches over again. Gradually the sobbing calmed. The baby pushed away, wanting to breathe, and they all leaned back into more comfortable positions.

Sarah went to get some water for Mary and she returned with some cushions and a blanket. Mary was slumped, looking into the glowing embers, exhausted from her crying, occasional sobs heaving her chest. The sun was now setting and Sarah wrapped the blankets tenderly round her friend's shoulders; Mary did not resist Sarah's taking the now sleeping baby and sitting with the child on a stool next to her. The baby was only a few months old and nestled against her, making suckling movements as she felt the softness of Sarah's breast through her light tunic. Mary continued looking into the fire.

"All generations will call me blessed... Huh! Dumb more likely!" Looking up, her eyes filled with tears. "Sarah, do you know what I've done? I've lost the Son of God!" she howled with a fresh wave of grief, but right then Moshe appeared, and Sarah had no time to think of what Mary could possibly have meant.

Though he could not hear what was said or the wailing of Mary, the smile of joy at finding Mary quickly turned to concern at seeing her red eyes and tear-streaked face. He looked from one girl to the other and then fixed on Sarah, eyebrows raised, looking for an explanation.

Sarah made signs indicating Yeshua, then spread her hands looking this way and that to indicate something lost. She pointed here and towards Jerusalem, shrugging and indicating growing panic. Moshe understood enough and took command.

He pointed to the east to indicate sunrise and to himself and ran two fingers up his arm. He looked with grave concern at both of the girls and turned to go, turning back at the door to incline his head while closing his eyes, so telling them to get some sleep.

The girls slept fitfully by the fire, both minds struggling with worry for their boys in the lonely early hours. With the first streaks of dawn, Sarah stoked the fire and roasted some barley and, going out of the house, she found Moshe waiting patiently. He proffered an earthenware pot, which was filled with ewe's milk and some fresh bread. He grinned sheepishly and Sarah wondered how he had come by it. Best not to ask. He lived by his wits and though she never doubted his honesty in her home, she knew he was sharp and would have cajoled the baker into giving him some bread. The milk was easy for a lad who lived among the animals and he often brought some to Sarah.

Quickly the girls prepared themselves. Though Mary had no appetite, Sarah made sure she had something to eat before travelling. Without prompting, Moshe shouldered the luggage and the three set off down the road to Jerusalem. It took only a little over two hours to do the journey and it was still early when they arrived, but the road was already busy with country folk bringing their wares to sell in the city.

Moshe seemed to know his way and Sarah guessed that he was a not infrequent visitor. Near the city gate Mary left them, heading round towards a village called Bethany where she had friends with whom she stayed. She was desperate to get news from Joseph. He had gone up to the fort 'Antonia' next to the temple. They had heard that some of boys had got into a scrape with the soldiers, and were fearful that Yeshua may have been caught up in it. It could take hours to get past the officious guards to make enquiries and Mary had left Joseph waiting with some other fathers while she hurried to Bethlehem.

With Sarah's scant knowledge of the city, they decided on a crumbling tower that was just inside the city wall as a meeting point.

"That's the tower of Siloam. Everyone knows it. Meet me there in an hour," Mary added, pointing to where the sun would be in an hour's time.

Sarah was really glad Moshe was with her. She shuddered as they passed through the Dung Gate, through which she had escaped. The old fears came back; her heart was pounding as she was sure someone would recognise her. She tried to remember the way to the house of her friends where Issa was now staying, but Moshe strode on and she realised that he knew the way. Of course! Moshe would have been keeping an eye on Issa and had probably tracked them to Jerusalem and checked out the house.

"He is such a protector!" she gasped gratefully, struggling to keep up with him as they climbed the steep streets into the city.

The houses and alleyways became familiar in style, and suddenly Moshe dropped the bags at a door propped open by a stool. She recognised the street door, but other things had changed. She looked up to the roof area where she had stayed and noticed that it was now covered in. Probably the home of Benjamin and Hannah, she thought. Moshe banged on the half open door and a small boy appeared, who looked at her quizzically, but he was pulled back quickly and a young woman appeared to investigate. Though she was quite a lot fuller than Sarah remembered, it was obviously Hannah with a small child in her arms. For a second the other did not recognise her, but then her face beamed.

"Sarah!" She turned to call inside. "Mother! It's Sarah, Issa's mama!" With that, she threw her spare arm around Sarah's neck in a warm embrace while the door was flung open and the portly figure of Hannah's mother appeared, rather stiff and breathless, but still just as much in charge.

"Now come in child, and wash. Hannah, what are you thinking of? Bring a bench and some water."

Sarah looked around, but there was no sign of Issa.

"Is Issa not here?" she asked, trying hard to fight off the panic.

"Oh, he's with the boys, closing down the stalls."

"But is he all right? He's not been in any trouble, has he?"

"Issa? No. I warned the boys not to get up to any mischief. No, he's had a fine time. He met an old friend and the two of them were off together, but he was a sensible sort of boy, not likely to get himself into trouble."

"Was he called Yeshua?"

"Was that boy called Yeshua, the one Issa was with?" she called out to Hannah, who was in the back yard collecting water. Hannah came into the room with a jug, which she poured into a basin for Sarah to wash in.

"I didn't get his name, but he came from Galilee by his accent. Issa said they had known each other when he was quite young."

"Yes! That was Yeshua. Do you know where he is? His mother and father are frantically looking for him. They haven't seen him for two nights now. His mother thought he might have been with Issa and came all the way to Bethlehem in the hope of finding him. She's in a real state. That's why I came back with her."

It was then she realised that Moshe was no longer with her. She looked around.

"But I came with a young man. Moshe." She quickly went to the door, but the street was empty.

"Has he gone too? These boys! I've got two and they're just the same, though they should have grown up by now. They will be the death of me," clucked the old lady. "Should be about their father's business, not causing anguish to us womenfolk. Hannah, go and fetch Issa and tell him his mother is here. And now, Sarah, tell me your news."

Sarah tried to be polite and fill her in on the last few years, but her thoughts were elsewhere. At least Issa was safe, but what of poor Yeshua? She struggled to remember what she was saying, as her thoughts wandered and she listened for Hannah's return so she could go to meet Mary. At last Hannah came with Issa, who was obviously resentful at his mother's presence. Sarah hugged her son, reluctant to let him go, then she held him by the shoulders and looked hard into his eyes.

"Issa, have you seen Yeshua?"

"Not for a couple of days. Not since the festival finished. I think he's gone home."

"But Issa, he's lost! His mother is frantic. They haven't seen him for three nights!"

"He won't be lost. Not Yeshua. He knows so much about Jerusalem. He took me all over and showed me all sorts of things. He knows all the back alleys and secret passages. He knows loads of stories about famous kings and about almost everything that goes on in the temple. You know…"

"Look," Sarah interrupted. "I'm sorry, but we must go and meet Yeshua's parents and see if we can help them. I said we would be by that tower. What's it called? Shiloh or something?"

"Siloam! A rough area around the Tower of Siloam," the old lady corrected. "All sorts of ne'er-do-wells hang out there gambling and drinking. And Issa, don't you go climbing on it. It is all crumbling and should have been pulled down ages ago. Not the best place to choose to meet."

"I suppose it was an easy landmark for me to find. I really don't know my way around." Sarah got up to go and Hannah gave the small child to her mother.

"I'll go with you, so you don't get lost. It's always better to be two women together round Siloam." It was sensible, of course, but underneath, Hannah was glad of an excuse to be in on the action.

"Well, you mind how you go. Sometimes you girls are as bad as the boys!" chided her mother.

So the three set off together. Sarah was pleased that Hannah was with them, for in the narrow streets she could not see the tower until they were quite close. Mary was not there when they arrived, but there was a very agitated Moshe. He motioned to them and pointed up through the old city to where the temple gleamed above them. He was grinning and waving, and in a state of high excitement, making more squeaks and growls than usual.

"Moshe! What is it?" Sarah asked by shaking her hands questioningly. After quickly explaining to Hannah that Moshe was deaf, she turned back to him and tried to calm him down so that they could better understand what he was trying to tell them. He waved and pointed, then suddenly broke off and ran across the street to where Joseph and Mary had arrived unnoticed. They too were perplexed as Moshe pulled on Joseph's sleeve, but when he bounded up the steep street towards the Temple Mount, beckoning them on, they followed as fast as they could. By now Issa had caught up with Moshe, and the two boys waited at each corner to keep in sight, before giving a wave and rushing on.

"He's going to the temple," Joseph called over his shoulder as the girls tried to keep up. "But I've been around the temple courts and he wasn't there. Anyway, Moshe should be careful going into the temple. If they find out he is deaf and dumb, he'll be in real trouble."

Breathless, they arrived at the large temple gates, but Moshe led them off round the side away from the public courts to the administrative and legal areas.

"That's where the lawyers and Sanhedrin meet. Whatever's going on? Is Yeshua in trouble?"

There was a knot of people around a terrace some 50 metres away across a small square, where some scholars were obviously engaged in discussion. Moshe stopped and grinned and pointed to the group. They followed his gaze uncomprehendingly, then saw, in the middle of the men, the slender figure of Yeshua, who seemed to be the focus of attention.

Mary quickly offloaded the baby onto Sarah and, hitching up her skirts, ran over the dusty cobbles towards the group, calling out Yeshua's name rather hysterically. The men turned in surprise and for the first time, Yeshua saw his mother. He ran to meet her, giving her a warm embrace and swinging her round in joy. Joseph was not far behind, but looking rather stern. Yeshua greeted him more formally, holding his hand as he turned and swept his arm towards the side wall of the temple. The others could not hear what was said as Yeshua pointed to the group of scholars and smiled at his mother while stroking her arm affectionately. He led Joseph and Mary over to the men and introduced them. From the way they shook hands warmly and gesticulated, it was obvious that Yeshua was far from in trouble but, rather, had made a deep impression on them. The discussion went on for some time between Joseph and the scholars while Yeshua talked excitedly to Mary, who did not appear to be in the least convinced. Then there were warm farewells; the scholars slapping Joseph on the back approvingly, putting affirming hands on Yeshua's shoulders and, with final wise counsel, discharging him to his father's care. With that, the three of them came over to where the others were waiting, talking earnestly among themselves.

Sarah looked questioningly at Mary as she handed her back the baby. Mary did not smile, whether from anger or relief Sarah could not tell.

"He has just had his Bar Mitzvah: he has come of age. He thinks he has a high calling. It seems we are going to have to get used to this."

"Boys!" Sarah sympathised. Mary looked quickly at her and then averted her tear-filled eyes while Yeshua, with a shining face, talked animatedly with Joseph. Hannah, a little perplexed, invited everyone to return to their house to eat, but Joseph and Mary were anxious to make up for lost time.

"We need to call in to Bethany, so we will eat something there then get on. The rest of the family are with the group from Nazareth and they will be wondering what has happened."

Mary looked round hurriedly to check Yeshua had not slipped away again, and saw him talking with Issa as they crossed the street to where Moshe was standing in the shadow of a tree. Yeshua gave the lad a warm embrace and clasped his hands in a number of ways in lieu of any words. Moshe grinned and looked self-conscious, glancing over to Sarah and Mary and slipping behind the tree. By the time the others had said their farewells he was nowhere to be seen, probably well on his way back to Bethlehem to keep an eye on the house until they returned.

Chapter 17

It was a happier evening with Hannah and her mother, who clucked and tutted as Sarah and Issa recounted their adventures. Issa and the boys had been packing up the market stall until well into the evening and came in tired and hungry. It was too late to return to Bethlehem after supper, so they planned to set out early the next morning. Sarah explained that she needed to be home to catch at least some of the later returning pilgrims.

On the way home, Issa talked nonstop about his time in Jerusalem. He had not realised the significance of the sheep from Bethlehem, that they were prized for their being purebred without blemish and were ideal for the Passover lambs. Benjamin and the boys were very pleased with their week's work and Issa was sure he would be able to return next year.

"And how did you meet with Yeshua?"

Issa was quiet for a while.

"The twins would shout their wares in the market, saying these were genuine Bethlehem lambs with a genuine Bethlehem shepherd boy to prove it. They made jokes about me killing giants and lions and bears, which is something to do with King David. I was really embarrassed, but I noticed this lad, a bit older than me, watching. He came over and said he had been born in Bethlehem and was pleased to meet me because there weren't many boys of our age left from Bethlehem."

Sarah did not reply, and Issa continued.

"Well, we got talking and discovered that you and his mother were friends. He could remember going through Bethlehem and staying

139

139

somewhere and leaving in the dark. I could only vaguely remember, but when we met his mother she was so excited and remembered lots about you. So we got to be friends and he told me lots of stuff. The other boys wanted to play being Zealots. Zealots are freedom fighters, see, and the boys wanted to hide in the trees and pretend to shoot Roman soldiers in the Antonia fortress. But Yeshua didn't like that sort of game, so we went round the old walls. He knows so much about the history of Jerusalem! He showed me a narrow cleft and he reckoned that was where King David's soldiers climbed up when they captured the city. We went down the cleft a little way, then waited till some people came by and then climbed up and burst out on them! You should have seen their faces! But they joined in the game too! All the visitors are so happy during the feast."

Sarah was a rather alarmed at the boys playing on cliffs and began to scold Issa.

"Oh, Mother! I do lots of rock climbing around Bethlehem. Moshe has shown me some great climbs. Anyway, when we're driving the sheep, Daniel sends me down the hillside to head them off so it's good to practise. Yeshua lives in Nazareth now, which is built on a cliff and he's so good at climbing rocks. He told me lots of other stories of kings and… you know, Mother, some were great heroes but others were really bad. The good kings wanted to defend Jerusalem. One, I can't remember his name, something …iah, even cut a tunnel to bring water into the city! Yeshua had explored the bottom of the walls before and found the spring and the tunnel, so we climbed down the cleft to the entrance. He showed me how to make a lantern out of dry sticks and leaves and we got an ember from someone's fire and we went through the tunnel. It was really smoky, but I wasn't scared – well, not much – but it was full of water and we walked for ages but he knew what he was doing. We kept slipping. Eventually we fell and the lantern went out, so we were in the dark but we held hands and went on through. At last we saw a light in the distance, so when we got close we slid down the last bit into this big pool where all these women were doing their washing. Some were a bit miserable, but others laughed and we splashed each other. We were right down in the bottom of the city, so we climbed back up through a valley on the outside of the city walls. Yeshua said it was a really sad valley called Hinnom where people did bad things. Bad things still happen there now, so we went carefully."

"I hope you didn't get into any trouble with anyone," put in Sarah.

Issa shuddered but, wanting to spare his mother, he said nothing about the crosses they had seen in the distance. Some things had troubled him.

"Another day we went to the Temple and Yeshua told me that we used to be slaves in Egypt and that God had rescued us from the Egyptians who were killing the baby boys, so we had to kill a lamb and put blood on the door so that the angel would pass over." He was quiet for a few moments. "Why do people want to kill babies? Yeshua said they used to do that in Hinnom valley, which is why it is so sad. Yeshua knows so much. We were in the temple and some religious men were having a discussion when suddenly Yeshua starts speaking sort of foreign to them. They were really surprised and talked for ages. Yeshua told me later it wasn't really foreign but Hebrew. It's what people used to speak years ago, but now it is only spoken in the temple. Anyway, Mother, that's why it's called Passover, and when you get to 12 it's called called Bar Mitzvah and you have to take a lamb and it gets killed for you. Then you become a Jewish man, sort of like a Passover or something. I get all confused. But it's something like that. Anyway, how old am I?"

Sarah wasn't sure. She was not good at counting; each year merged into the next.

Issa went on. "Yeshua's mother…"

"Mary," interposed Sarah.

"Yes. Mary said I was nearly a year younger than Yeshua so I will be 12 next year. So, I could have a Bar Mitzvah next year, couldn't I?"

Sarah was troubled.

"Oh Issa, that's all right for rich children, but we are poor. We don't have money to buy a lamb or any things you might need."

"But, don't you see, I could get a lamb from Daniel! I could work for it and then I could be a real Jewish man!"

Sarah was not convinced.

"But you probably need to know lots of things and learn things from the Scriptures."

"I could sing some of those songs and things we sing on feast days. I bet they come from the Scriptures."

"I don't think they're the only things you need to know. Look, Issa, it's a nice idea but not really for us. We're lucky that religion allows us to join in the festivals and collect leftovers from the fields, but going to the synagogue, let alone Bar Mitzvah, is only for rich people."

"But Yeshua isn't rich."

"Yes, but he has a father. Mothers don't count the same. Besides…" she trailed off, thinking bitterly that village prejudice meant that Issa, regarded as an illegitimate child, would under any circumstances be excluded from the synagogue.

But Issa did not notice. He was thoughtful. He would soon be back in the hills with Daniel and there was a lot to talk about.

Daniel had moved a little way away from Bethlehem and it was fortunate that Issa had Moshe with him or he may not have found him. Though Issa was bursting to tell Daniel all about his adventures, Daniel was rather dour, so Issa would have to wait till evening round the fire. After the busy-ness of the city, Issa was glad to be back in the wild. He and Yeshua had discovered they both shared a love of rugged hills, though, by all accounts, those around Nazareth were much more lush. From the higher points of Jerusalem they had sat, looking over the Judean hills as Yeshua recounted some of David's adventures as a young man hiding in the hills, escaping from King Saul and his army. Saul, who was jealous of David, was trying to kill him. But Yeshua also noticed the tiny things around; a small rock flower, or a beetle, or he would point out a particular bird, giving its name and explaining some characteristic of its flight or call that was the origin of its name. His face would shine; his touch, eyes and voice expressed awed tenderness that was a new experience to Issa who, like most small boys, pulled the wings off insects, trod indifferently on flowers and used birds as targets for practising slingshots. A flower caught his eye and he reached down, trying to emulate the way Yeshua would have so gently handled it. A thrill passed through his fingers and into his body as he paused to savour the moment, till a cry from Daniel brought him back to the present and he went scurrying after a straying lamb. Though no predator was apparently around, they would take no chances.

That evening around the fire, the shepherds' conversation moved round to the recent festival in Jerusalem. They weren't particularly religious, but the festivals in Jerusalem gave them an income and so they held them in respect. Issa sat on the outside of the circle, as befitted his status, but made sure he was just behind Daniel.

When the conversation lulled, he said quietly, "I was with Joseph and Mary. They send their greetings."

Daniel half-turned, eyebrows raised.

"And are they well? And what of that boy, Yeshua?"

"They are all fine. Yeshua isn't a boy anymore. He came of age; he had his Bar Mitzvah."

"What? Is he 12 already? Hardly seems yesterday they were here. Well, I'm glad they have kept him safe." Daniel spoke quietly, not wanting to engage the other shepherds.

"Was he in danger? Is he still in danger?"

"Potentially everyone is in danger. The Romans, Herod, the Zealot freedom fighters, bandits and outlaws – all have their fears and jealousies. It pays to keep in the shadows. They did well to move up to Nazareth."

"But we're safe here, aren't we?"

"Just you keep an eye out for fierce animals. David overcame a lion and a bear but had a lot more trouble with the wild two-legged variety, and on these very hills."

Issa was quiet for a while.

"I will be twelve this year. Am I allowed to have a Bar mitzvah?" After a long pause, he added, "My mother thinks we are too poor for that."

"It has nothing to do with being rich or poor, but sadly people have made up all sorts of rules and regulations which were not there long ago. It's true that it may be hard to get the approval of the law teachers, but what God wants is much more simple."

"I would need a lamb to sacrifice at least, wouldn't I?" Issa said hesitantly.

Daniel was quiet for some time.

"You know, God told the people that he was tired of their sacrifices. What he wanted was obedience. Live justly, love kindness and walk humbly with God. If you work at that, then you will get a lot of joy. And then if you do have a lamb to take to sacrifice, you will find peace even if you can't do all the other stuff they ask of you these days." Daniel stood up and stretched. "But if you're going to be man next year, we'd better get some practice in. You should be taking care of the some of the flock by yourself. We'll start this evening. The sheep are in the fold. You sit up there and keep watch while I sleep by the gate, then wake me when the moon is just over that rock. We'll talk again about Bar Mitzvah and a lamb."

True to his word, Daniel started putting more responsibility on Issa. It suited Daniel, now becoming less agile, to leave Issa to sort out the lambs and kids from the sheep and goats. When the animals needed to roam to find grazing, they would keep the suckling lambs and kids in the fold while the adults were taken into the hills for the day. One of the shepherds would stay with all the lambs together and the others would lead their flock to find pasture. Issa watched carefully all that Daniel did. There were commands and whistles which Issa tried to copy. The whistle was the most difficult to master. On his walks to and from Bethlehem, when he was by himself, he curled his tongue and lips around his front teeth blowing across them for hour after hour until, at last, he found the edge of a whistle. Then it was downhill all the way for, once he achieved the first sound, he could elaborate and copy the sounds he had heard Daniel make.

One day, sitting on a hillside but near enough for Daniel to notice, he sent up a call. To his delight, some of the sheep raised their heads and looked towards the sound. He tried to appear nonchalant, but his heart was full. Daniel, impressed, called over the valley.

"Boy! You've been practising! Keep it up, they'll soon get to know your calls!"

Chapter 18

As time went on, Daniel trusted Issa more and more. Now he would be sent out to round up some of the flock by himself, and by the time Benjamin and the two boys came back at the next Passover season, he was a confident shepherd boy.

Being on the hills so much more meant he was less at home. Daniel made sure he did go from time to time and would often send a gift of some meat with him. Though Sarah missed him, she was glad he was so happy in his new role and Moshe was always around when she needed him.

He also missed some of the festivals as, being low in the pecking order, he often had to stay with the flocks while the shepherds went to the feast. Though not particularly religious the rest of the year, they enjoyed the revelry fuelled with good food and flowing wine. Issa hadn't forgotten Daniel's words about justice, kindness and God and that, but wasn't really sure how to put it into practice. He thought it might be easier to do the God bit if he could go to the festivals and learn some of the songs. He tried to be kind, but easily got irritated with his mother. He often wasn't kind to Moshe, finding it all too easy, like the others in Bethlehem, to take advantage of Moshe's kind and generous spirit as well as his deafness. But Issa loved the animals in his care and was gentle with the most helpless of those, so maybe that counted as being kind. The justice bit puzzled him. It was hard being poor and he had learnt to keep a low profile. Moshe was much more up front doing whatever he saw needed doing, but was often being cuffed and chased away. That was so unfair. Issa wondered if a way of being just was to stick up for Moshe, but he wasn't brave in that sort of way. It would be easier if Moshe would learn to mind his own business anyway. The Romans were very strict and talked about justice, but that was all geared for their benefit. Whatever justice meant, it wasn't the concern of the poor. Maybe his mother was right. That was all for the rich people. Still, he would enjoy the festival even if he didn't have a Bar Mitzvah thing. Daniel had said he could go with Benjamin and the boys to get the lambs to Jerusalem, but not to stay on afterwards as he had done the year before.

Benjamin had ordered 30 lambs, which Daniel had separated out into a separate fold. Moshe arrived with Benjamin and the boys, who greeted Issa with whoops and hugs. Issa worried that all the noise and banter would scare the lambs, and fortunately Daniel came over and gruffly told them there wouldn't be any lambs left unless they calmed down. Issa had learned to count in the last year, for although he recognised the sheep by name, in the moonlight you needed to be able to count them quickly. He sidled up to Daniel.

"Daniel, there are more than 30 sheep here."

"Yes, there are 31."

Issa thought for a moment, not sure if he should say anything.

"But I thought…"

"30 for them, and one for your Bar Mitzvah, boy."

Issa turned to Daniel. "But…?"

"You won't always be a shepherd boy. You can stay to get the lamb sacrificed, then come back here. It's time to start to be a man." He turned back to Benjamin. "30 sheep for you and one for Issa for his Bar Mitzvah."

The twins roared with approval and Benjamin beamed. They weren't religious themselves, but they were pleased for Issa.

"Don't become a Pharisee yet. There's a lot of fun still to have. We'll have a party for you the evening before! We'll do it in style."

They called by Issa's house and stayed the night as the year before. Issa didn't tell his mother about the lamb for the sacrifice until they were alone later. She was pleased, though concerned.

"But do you know what to do?"

"Oh Mother, don't fuss," he grumbled, but underneath he was rather nervous.

He had watched last year, and everyone seemed to have their father with them. Maybe he could attach himself to another family and just follow on. There was something else the boys did with the teachers, but on Daniel's advice he would just offer the sacrifice and hope for the best.

They arrived in Jerusalem mid-morning and safely corralled the lambs behind Benjamin's market stall just outside the temple precinct. There were so many stalls that they spilled over from the outer courtyard of the temple. As relative latecomers to the market, Benjamin and the boys were still in the outer courts, but they might eventually get a stall in the more lucrative inner temple precinct.

Issa went off by himself to try and see how things worked, but there were no sacrifices today. The first day of the feast was the next day when the people from the North celebrated. He would join them – no one would know where he was from – then he would get off back to Bethlehem with the meat from the sacrifice. His mother would be pleased to get that and they would have a feast at home. But now, with the rest of the day to fill, he decided to go and look at the walls of Jerusalem he had been to with Yeshua.

Skirting one of the valleys to a point where he could see the walls from afar, he tried to spot some of the places they had climbed. At the time they had scrambled up the cliffs with little problem but looking from the other side of the valley, the climb seemed impressive. The walls certainly looked quite impregnable and he smiled as he remembered how they had found one way David's men may have broken through. He followed the valley round till it joined a second, Hinnom, which Yeshua had alluded to. This valley seemed more of a rubbish heap and the smell was getting overpowering, so he turned to retrace his steps.

Suddenly two Roman soldiers came into view, dragging something behind them. Like most of the Jewish people, Issa kept away from Romans, so he quietly slid into the shade of a clump of trees. To his horror, he realised that they were dragging a body of a man, naked and bloodied, covered in dust from the path! They stopped at a point where the path curved at a rocky outcrop and the steep side of the valley was a sheer rock face. As Issa watched, they held the lifeless broken form by the arms and legs, swinging him over the edge, letting him drop into space. He heard a crash as the body hit the bushes and black and menacing vultures soared up, wheeling round and round, before descending slowly back into the valley.

As the soldiers disappeared round the bend, Issa hurried to the spot, sick inside but unable to tear himself away. The stench was terrible and Issa could see the body lying 10 metres below, on a mass of other bloated and rotting corpses. He turned and fled the scene, scrabbling back to the path, trying not to vomit. He heard voices in front of him and, thinking they could be more Romans, scrambled up the valley side away from the path. Thorn bushes tore at his arms and legs, but he pressed on, desperate to get away from the Romans, the bodies, the vultures, the dreaded valley of Hinnom.

He was at the top of the rise now, where the hillside flattened. He stood up to run, but immediately sank again to the ground as he saw the Romans just 30 metres away and on a path just below him! He desperately hoped they would not look up as he crawled forward into some cover. He was on the edge of an old quarry dug into the hill. The grass, still green and lush from the rains, shielded him from view. Looking around quickly, he saw he was on the highest point for some distance so would not be overlooked from anywhere.

Carefully parting the grass, he peered into the quarry. There was a fire with a semi-circle of log benches around it with some of the soldiers' kit and jugs of wine scattered about. Some gnarled beams were lying to one side with bloodstained clothes thrown over them. This was obviously the Romans' camp and the two he had seen soon came into view down a path. They went to the fire and picked up the stone jug, talking and laughing in their foreign language. One of them picked up a staff with a large stone bound on the end to make a crude sledge hammer. The soldier ambled over across the quarry towards the cliff where Issa lay 15 metres above. Issa then became aware that immediately below him there were three wooden stakes: two with crossbeams and the third half collapsed, with the crossbeam detached. But on each of the two still standing hung a body with outstretched arms lashed to the cross beam! At first he thought they must be dead, but then one strained on the ropes and pulled himself up, groaning and coughing and crying out as the effort became too much and he sank back down gurgling. Then the other did the same. The soldier stood for a while in front of them, then took the sledge and swung it against the legs of the first man. There was a splintering crack and an earsplitting scream and he swung again towards the other leg. Issa waited no more but fled down the slope, slipping and sliding, not caring about the stones and thorn bushes as they grazed his hands and legs and tore at his clothes, making no attempt to hide in his desperation to get away from that awful place.

It was a very subdued Issa who arrived back at the family home. The lads were full of themselves, having had a good day selling the lambs. They joked about how they had made big profits from the gullible country folk who paid whatever they asked. Issa winced as he realised that he was one of those 'gullible country folk' and felt rather out of place among these sharp city boys.

The family had prepared a meal for his Bar Mitzvah and he tried to eat, but he still felt sick from what he had just witnessed. The boys toasted him and drank lots of wine and soon Issa felt very lonely. Going over to the old lady, he thanked her for the meal, excusing himself by saying he was tired and needed to prepare himself for the next day, though he had no real idea what he was supposed to prepare. He explained that he would bring them some of the meat from the sacrifice. That much he did know. Going up to the roof where he had his bed roll, he sat for a long while, unable to get the images out of his mind, listening to the hubbub of the city and celebrations around him. When the lads eventually came up quite drunk and noisy, he lay down pretending to be asleep, but when sleep finally came, it was fitful and full of fearful sounds and images and worries about the next day.

He eventually awoke with a start in the early morning, still not sure what he was supposed to do. The family, being rather irreligious, could not offer any help.

The lads were also up early in spite of the previous night's revelry, though they obviously had sore heads. Together they went to the market stall where Benjamin had stayed overnight, keeping watch over their merchandise. Collecting his lamb for the sacrifice, Issa made his way nervously to the Temple courts. The lamb nestled against him, feeling secure in his arms as Issa had a familiar smell and recognisable voice. There were lots of other boys of his age with lambs, but all seemed to be with their fathers.

Watching from some distance away for a while, he saw that on arrival they would go to have the lamb inspected, for only lambs without blemish were acceptable. Daniel had prided himself on only selling perfect lambs for sacrifice. The inspection seemed to be cursory, but he did notice that from time to time there was a discussion, some money changed hands, and only then was the lamb declared fit for sacrifice.

Joining a queue at random, he waited his turn. The inspector took the lamb and asked briskly, "Where is your father, boy?"

"He's not here... He... he can't come," he mumbled.

The man looked slyly at his colleague and they took the lamb away.

"No good," they pronounced as they returned. "Look!" They pointed to a black streak on the lamb's belly under a foreleg.

"But... that wasn't there before, mister!" protested Issa.

The inspector passed the lamb over to his colleague while handing some strange coins to Issa.

"Here boy, you can have that for the lamb."

"But I want my lamb!"

"Sorry boy, once you have presented a lamb you can't take it back. But to help you, we've given you some money for the meat. Can't be fairer than that!"

Issa was bewildered and close to tears. He tried to protest, but was pushed to one side as the next group presented their lamb.

"But, mister!"

"Clear off, boy, or I'll call the temple guard!"

Issa slunk off, colouring and fighting back tears. The other boys in the queue looked on, wondering what was happening, but no one came to help. So his mother had been right all along. This was not for him. Wandering aimlessly around the temple, miserable and rejected, he came upon some stalls selling meat and decided to buy some with the money he was given. At least he would have something to take to the family and back to his mother, but he received a very modest amount of meat in exchange, considering it represented the payment he had received for a whole lamb. Hardly enough to share, but it would have to do.

Pushing his way against the crowd to find the way out of the temple area, he passed near one of the many slaughter stations. A man was presenting a lamb for sacrifice and Issa saw with indignation that it was his lamb!

"Hey! Hey! That lamb is mine!" he protested, running over. Everyone turned in surprise. "He's mine. The inspector said it was blemished and took it away." The lamb, hearing Issa's voice, bleated plaintively. "See! He knows me. He's mine!"

The man presenting the lamb was indignant.

"Now see here, I just bought this lamb!"

"But they stole it from me. He's mine!"

Just then, a voice called out from the crowd.

"Don't trust that boy. We know him. He is a bastard child and his mother is a prostitute."

Issa turned and recognised one of the Bethlehem villagers, but carried on protesting, pulling at the man holding the lamb.

The crowd, which until now had been bemused, turned against Issa. He was jostled and cuffed and pushed to the back, each adding another blow for good measure till he fell to the pavement, bruised and crying, clutching his meat, which by now was covered in dirt and stones from the ground.

As he struggled to escape the growingly violent crowd, another boy crouched beside him with an arm around his shoulder, protecting him from any further blows. Issa looked up. It was Yeshua, his eyes full of concern, but with an angry determination to withstand the crowd.

"They stole my lamb, and all I got was some scraggy meat," Issa wailed, as Yeshua led him protectively through the back of the muttering and disapproving crowd.

They found a trough and washed Issa's cuts and bruises and cleaned the dirt off the meat. Issa's sobs subsided, but he was left sullen and angry. He just wanted to get away from the temple, away from that city full of cheating traders and hostile crowds, away from the memory of slaughtered innocent sheep and of smashed bodies rotting in the Hinnom valley. He yearned to get back to the Bethlehem hills and his beloved sheep. He was not very gracious about the help he had received from Yeshua, who walked with him till he was well away from the crowds. Issa made to hurry on, but checked himself and turned.

"Thank you, Yeshua." Yeshua's kind smile was in stark contrast to the hostile cries and blows of the crowd. It drew Issa back and the boys embraced. Issa said again, more quietly still, "Thank you … Yeshua."

He walked away bruised but somewhat comforted, and turned at the temple gates. Yeshua was watching him and waved.

"When you need me, call out to me," he heard above the din from the crowds around them.

Had he really said that? Was that what the look in his eyes, in his smile, his warm embrace, his protective intervention wordlessly conveyed?

But how could he be there when he most needed him?

One day he would know for real.

Chapter 19

Issa returned to the house and collected his things.

"But are you not staying for the evening meal? One of the boys will go home with you tomorrow," the old lady chided.

"No, I must get back. Something has happened and I need to get back to Bethlehem."

Half-truths would have to do. Hurrying out, ignoring the old lady's protests and running to the city gates to avoid meeting the twins who would be upset that he had gone without saying goodbye, he left Jerusalem, he hoped, forever.

When Issa arrived home safely, much to Sarah's relief, she wanted him to tell her all about his time in Jerusalem but he just clammed up. The crucifixion experience had severely traumatised him and he could not rid his mind of it, and he was raw from the humiliation of his experience in the temple. His mother would be dreadfully hurt to have been labelled a prostitute. That night he had bad dreams and he must have called out, for he woke to find his mother sitting by his bed. Her face was full of concern as he held out his arms to her and she cradled his head against her breast.

"Do you want to tell me now?"

So Issa told her everything about the temple debacle, though he avoided the words 'bastard' and 'prostitute'. Nor could he bring himself to tell her about the men hanging on the crosses in the dreaded Valley of Hinnom.

Sarah did not say anything. In the dark Issa could not see the tears, but he would soon realise if she spoke. Eventually, she composed herself.

"Mary taught me a song she had made up. Things weren't easy for her when Yeshua was born. I am sure Yeshua understood that too. I can't remember it all, but one bit says: 'The mighty are fallen, the humble are raised. The hungry are fed; the rich sent away empty.'" She smiled at her son. "Let's have that meat you brought home tomorrow!"

True to her word, Sarah prepared a special meal for Issa, buying a few choice ingredients from her meagre profits from the pilgrims. Of course, Moshe smelt out the food, so although things had not worked out in Jerusalem, they had their own party and the next night they went to bed full.

Issa was in two minds about meeting with Daniel. He longed for the hills and the sheep but was embarrassed to tell Daniel about what had happened. Although he rose early, his mother was already up, sweeping the dust at the front of the house. She smiled at Issa.

"Have some bread before you go. You'll feel better when you're back with Daniel." She still ached inside with pain for her son but was determined not to show it. Once he was gone, she would be free to let the tears flow again.

Moshe was waiting just over the brow of the hill and they set off together. He pointed to a crest in the distance and swept his hand down and up again, indicating that Daniel was a few miles away. After an hour of walking, they came upon some sheep and one of the shepherds called out a greeting.

"Hey Issa, you're a man now!"

Issa coloured, thankful that Moshe did not understand, and hurried on.

Daniel was as gruff as ever and set the boys to work, separating the lambs from their mothers in the corral and sending the sheep off to graze. They would not roam far from the lambs and the whole flock would stay together. The lambs and kids having been separated out, Moshe headed back to Bethlehem and Issa found a hillock where he could watch for wanderers. Glad to be alone with his thoughts, he vented his anger and frustration with the slingshot, sending stone after stone crashing across the valley.

That evening, he sat in silence by the fire.

"You're very quiet, lad," Daniel said to Issa. "How was Jerusalem?"

"All right."

"And your Bar Mitzvah?"

Issa threw a stone into the darkness.

"I don't want to talk about it," he muttered, slipping away to his bed roll for the night.

The next day, he sorted the lambs without being asked and hurried to the distant hillock, where he resumed his watch.

"I brought you some water."

Issa started. Daniel had come up the hillock without Issa noticing. Seeing him jump, Daniel laughed.

"Good job I wasn't a lion or a bear!"

Daniel sat down next to Issa and for a long time did not speak. Eventually, he broached the topic. "Jerusalem can be tough. Do you want to tell me about it?"

Issa was silent for a while. He felt choked and his eyes brimmed. He looked down, trying to blink the tears away so he would not have to wipe them away with his hand, digging savagely in the stony soil with the end of his shepherd's stick. The sniffs blinks and coughs told their own story and Daniel laid a hand on his shoulder.

"Take your time, boy," he said kindly.

Eventually it all came out, as Issa told Daniel all about being tricked out of the lamb and the crowd turning against him.

"They would probably have killed me," he exaggerated, "but suddenly Yeshua was there and he rescued me. He's not very big, but no one dared mess with him. I reckon he would have taken the whole lot on and they knew it and all backed off. I should have listened to my mother. She said that religion wasn't for poor people like us. We should be content with the gleanings and a bit of food at the festivals."

Daniel was quiet for a while.

"Listen, boy. You took the lamb for sacrifice, and even though they stole him from you, he was sacrificed. The Lord knows where your heart is and he isn't fooled. It was not the normal celebration, but you are now a 'Son of the Law'. That's what Bar Mitzvah means. For most religious people, the law is something they learn but don't do. They will carefully tithe their herbs, but things that really matter like caring for the poor, the widow, the orphan and the foreigner are left to someone else.

"But, for people at the bottom end of society, their experience of the law is usually through suffering injustice. You know the reality of the law from the raw side. You know what is right and wrong by suffering the wrong of others. So there are three ways ahead for you to choose from. One is to collaborate with the system and get rich while others suffer. Some of our people become tax collectors for the Romans, and some just cooperate and get the perks, like the Sadducees. The second way is violent rebellion, which may seem better but sadly the end result may be more oppression. There were freedom fighters, the 'Maccabees', who stood up against the evil regime of the Seleucids and fought for the oppressed Jewish Nation. They were great heroes. But after they won and got power, they too became corrupt and from that dynasty came all the evil of our present 'king'."

Daniel spoke quietly, even though there was no one around to hear. Such talk was dangerous, and he was careful not to mention Herod's name, though he was obviously referring to him.

"The third way we have spoken about already. Remember the words of the prophet: 'Do justice, love mercy and walk humbly with your God.' Let this be the law that guides your life."

Issa thought this through.

"But what about King David? He was a great warrior and conquered his enemies. Yeshua told me about him. We climbed the walls of Jerusalem like he did when he beat the Egypticites who were living there."

Daniel smiled at the conflation of Egyptians and Jebusites. "Yes, you're right. He was the greatest King we have ever had. His words and advice were sure and reliable."

Daniel started to sing, and Issa recognised the tune from the festivals, though he had never paid attention to the words before.

"How can the young keep on the upright way…?

By reading and acting on your word.

With all my heart I search for God, do not let me drift from your high call.

Your word is deep within my heart that I might not fall short of your ways."

He continued humming the tune for a while, looking into the distance, obviously not sure of the rest of the words. They sat in silence for a while, then Daniel started again.

"But you know, even David slipped at the times when he chose power rather than justice. The scriptures are clear. Stand up for the just way; always be ready to show mercy, kindness, gentleness, and don't think of yourself too highly. Walk humbly with God."

Issa was quiet for a while.

"I can sort of understand the justice and mercy bit, but what's the walking humbly with God about?"

"It's thinking about God and praying to him. For instance, at present the devout ones will be counting the Omer." Daniel laughed when saw Issa's puzzled expression. "Between the Passover festival and the feast of weeks are 50 days. You're supposed to stop and think on each day and prepare yourself. It's called 'counting the Omer'. You remember the Feast of Weeks? It's called that because it is seven weeks from Passover. I'm sure you have been to it with the dumb boy."

Issa remembered the festival well. It was not as great a feast as the Feast of Booths but provided a good spread of food all the same.

"That's the one where they tell the story of Ruth, isn't it? I think they sing that song you just sang."

"Good lad," encouraged Daniel.

"They remember the giving of the law and that psalm is all about God's laws. But for you, the story of Ruth is really important. Ruth was a foreigner from a despised race. She was a poor young widow caring for her destitute widowed mother-in-law and she came to live right here in Bethlehem. But though a misfit, she became the great grandmother of King David. You know that King David was a poor shepherd boy and had a problem with his brothers. He also got on the wrong side of King Saul and became an outlaw in these very hills. He wrote lots of the songs we sing at the festivals like that one I just sang. Many were written during his time in the hills as an outlaw."

"Do you count the… what was it you said… the Omer?"

"I used to, but for years now I have been away in the hills and all that sort of thing tends to slip. I like to sing some of the psalms I can remember."

"Does Yeshua's family do it?"

"They're sure to. Joseph is very devout, honest and upright and he will teach Yeshua well."

Issa was quiet now, as he thought how good it must be to have the stability of a father like Joseph. He looked into the distance over the desert hills. Somewhere out there, he had a father.

Sensing what was going through Issa's mind, Daniel continued. "I could teach you some of the songs and things. Don't worry if you don't do it like the others. God looks on the heart. And you'll be learning about walking with God like David did on these very hills!"

Issa was still not convinced, but he was pleased to hear Daniel's positive angle and he liked the thought that David had been a poor shepherd boy too. Yeshua had told him some of the stories, and as he thought about roaming the hills and climbing the walls of Jerusalem as King David had done, he felt a warm kinship. The grandees in Jerusalem could do what they liked! He had done what he could and was proud to be a man; a man King David would be proud of. He wasn't sure how to do the counting bit, but he would try and stop each day and think of justice, mercy and walking humbly with God. And Daniel would teach him some songs, and then maybe one day...

Issa did try. Some days were really busy and he would forget, but when he was sitting in the hills he would think of David, justice, mercy and walking with God and true to his word, Daniel told him more of the old stories of the people of Israel or sang some snatches he could remember from the songs that David had written.

Apparently, there were over six hundred laws, but only the really religious could remember them all. David had summarised them in ten and similarly the prophets in six. Daniel hummed a few lines from a psalm he was struggling to remember:

"Who may go to your Holy hill - your sanctuary?
The one who is blameless and righteous
with a truthful heart which does not slander or slur...
keeps his promises... lends to the poor
and accepts no bribe..."

"Was that ten? I forget now. Well anyway, you just remember the three we talked about."

Chapter 20

Issa wondered how he would know when the festival was approaching. Although trying to 'count the omens', as he called them, he had got in a muddle with the number of days. But he need not have worried. On cue, Moshe appeared, grinning and pointing back towards Bethlehem and signing a festival, then rubbing his stomach to indicate a good feed. No one knew how Moshe worked out where the shepherds were. In spite of the lack of hearing and speech, his other senses were sharpened.

Daniel would not be going to this festival; he was staying with the sheep. It was some distance to Bethlehem and Daniel was becoming a bit stiff and really did not want to be bothered with walking back and worrying about the sheep on the hills. The boys set off, and a few hours later came over the hill to Issa's home.

Sarah was so pleased to have Issa back after so long. She clucked and fussed over him but was immensely proud of her bronzed young man. Moshe had always been near at hand and she had sent him off to the hills to fetch Issa back for the festival, which she knew followed on from Passover. The feast was the next day and Sarah had some pumpkins and some lentils to share, but she had enough spare to make a tasty stew. Issa excitedly told Sarah of all the adventures of the last few weeks and explained how he had been learning songs and sort of counting the Omens, which Sarah had heard something of and she was pleased that Daniel seemed to be teaching Issa something. At the festival the boys who had come of age were presented by their father, or sometimes by a brother or cousin who had also recently become of age. They would recite bits from the law. Sarah had hoped that Daniel might be there and that he might present Issa, for there was no one else who could or would do it. She sighed sadly, thinking of what might have been, but still immensely proud of how Issa had learnt things from Daniel.

The next day the boys set off in great excitement, looking forward to the food. The feast started rather sombrely with the law being read. At the point where all the boys who had come of age that year should step forward, there was a long pause. Issa was acutely aware that he was the only boy of that age. He certainly wasn't going to push himself forward after all that had happened in Jerusalem, so he slunk into the shadows and watched from a distance with Moshe, wondering if anyone might call him forward but never really expecting it. Someone pushed up next to him and took his arm, and for a second he thought someone had come to present him, but looking up he saw, to his dismay, that it was the man who had turned the crowd against him in Jerusalem! Issa tried to pull away, but the man gripped his arm more fiercely.

"Don't even think about making a fuss here. You're not just a bastard-child but you're a scheming scoundrel, now clear off!" He released Issa's arm, raising his hand to give him a clout to send him on his way, but Issa ducked and the blow missed.

He pulled his arm away and sidestepped as the man made a grab for him. Issa shot his elbow out, catching the man in the midriff. With a grunt and a cry, the man fell heavily to the ground. Issa, looking over his shoulder, saw Moshe helping the man to his feet and dusting him down. The man was cursing Moshe and the crowd gathered round started to chide and cuff Moshe, who slunk off in his normal fashion.

Issa waited no more but hurried home bitter and angry. Daniel was right. He was learning about justice from the bottom up. He got his things together and waited at the back of the house for his mother to return. It was no good. He would return to the hills and not bother about the festivals anymore. God was obviously not bothered about him and would be quite indifferent about how religious he was.

Still busy with his bitter thoughts, he did not notice the return of Moshe with a loaded cloth over his shoulder. He grinned at a puzzled Issa. So much food, but the feast had not really started. He looked questioningly at Moshe, who grinned again. He held Issa by the arm as the man had done, swinging his fist, ducking then pointing to himself and sticking out his leg, stumbling forwards, rolling his hands as the man tumbled in a heap, exaggeratedly helping the man up, dusting him down and finally shielding his head from cuffs of ingratitude. He crept away, grinning, and both boys rolled with laughter after the performance.

Continuing to sign, Moshe described a man he did not know with a beard who had pressed a coin into his hand, obviously pleased at seeing the other fall in the mud. Moshe had gone to some of the traders on the road and bought provisions, though Issa couldn't believe anyone would have given enough money for so much food. Moshe knew how to bend the rules just enough in order to survive, or maybe God was just looking after him. Just as well, for he was obviously not looking after Issa, so he would have to benefit from Moshe's good fortune. The food was ready-cooked festival food and the boys soon dispatched it all, lying replete and dozing under a tree.

It was late when Sarah returned home, surprised to find the boys already there.

"I didn't see you at the festival. I hoped you would be there for the blessing of the boys who came of age. Where did you go?"

Issa had got over his initial anger at the incident, but he was still feeling surly.

"It would have been bad enough if there were other boys coming of age, but I would have been the only one. Anyway, I wouldn't have been allowed. It's only for the rich and privileged. That's why we came away. The festivals aren't for us, Mother."

"But everyone goes, rich and poor, and no one is turned away!"

"It may be all right for you, but I don't fit in. I stick out because I'm the only one of my age." He certainly was not going to repeat the hateful accusations against his mother. "It's better for me to be in the hills with the sheep. That's where I belong. The religious stuff is not for me."

"But you can join in on the fringes like I do. I know that we wouldn't be welcome in the synagogue, but the festivals are different."

In truth, Sarah was worried that if he did not come to the festivals then she would see him even less, but she did not say anything. There was an ache in her heart. He was so young, and she was losing him.

Issa sensed her thoughts and softened.

"Don't worry, Mother. I'll come to the festivals for the food. There are a lot of people who stay on the outside, foreigners and others like Moshe. I'll just keep out of the religious bits then everyone will be happy and there will be no more trouble."

Sarah looked at him quickly, a little alarmed.

"Were you involved with that incident at the coming-of-age ceremony? Some people said that some boys had caused a disturbance. Is that what the problem is?"

"We didn't cause the disturbance, but we were there, and a man fell over Moshe and got cross," he told her, bending the truth. "So I came home. I didn't want any trouble."

"And where did the food come from?" she asked sharply.

"Where do you think…? Moshe, of course. Best not to ask!"

This was true and Sarah had often benefitted from Moshe's quick wits, but she was concerned. She knew that she belonged on the fringes with the poor, the widow, the orphan and the foreigner, but she had hoped for something else for Issa. She sighed, but she felt she had done all she could. Maybe God would accept them even if the religious leaders would not.

Chapter 21

So, life developed a pattern. Issa would go to the hills and return for the festivals at least three times a year. This suited Daniel, who would come back to the village from time to time, usually when they were in a group with other shepherds. At festival times, when many of them would want to go back for the feast, he was content to stay and watch over all the flocks.

Issa was still a slight lad, but growing stronger with the healthy lifestyle of the shepherd. He was acquiring a lot of desert skills, too: not just calls and whistles and accuracy with the sling shot, but reading the signs, developing a heightened sensitivity to his surroundings, and recognising bird alarm calls giving warning of predators. He learnt to watch the sky to recognise signs of an impending weather change, how to find water and which desert plants and roots were edible. Daniel would try from time to time to teach him some of the psalms. Although he listened politely, he did not really try to understand what they were saying, for they were not for such as him.

But he was aware of the greatness of the night sky and sometimes would feel so puny, so insignificant, while a whisper, swelling into a clarion call when he paid it attention, declared something, someone all-powerful was out there beyond the stars. Although it awoke a deep longing in him, it was all so confusing.

Benjamin and the twins would come each year for the lambs and they would enjoy the evening together, but he steadfastly refused to go back to Jerusalem. The whole festival, either the commercial side the boys represented or the religious side, was an anathema to him. God was out there somewhere, and if he tried to love justice and mercy, and live simply and humbly under that ineffability he experienced in the desert night, maybe, one day, God would deal kindly with him.

In the dry season, the shepherds with large flocks would roam further afield looking for grazing, way over towards the Dead Sea, which they knew as the Arabah. The land nearer the settlements had more pressure from the locals. Few people lived in this area but there were some religious groups who wanted to live separate lives away from commercial and political life, but they were not apparent. Issa didn't know what they got up to, but he understood their love of the wilderness. He, though, would miss the trips to the village to enjoy the good food and fun on the feast days in the unlikely event that he became part of such a group.

One day they found themselves on the edge of the escarpment way above the Arabah. Daniel pointed out a green strand in the distance and explained that this was the Jordan, which flowed down from Mount Hermon, way up in the North. That was one of the ways the people would travel to Galilee, and was the way preferred by Yeshua's family. Though it was not the most direct route, there were settlements all the way up the river. Also, it avoided crossing the Samaritans' land; a people the Jews did not like associating with.

For some time Daniel kept the flock in that area near a well he knew of, and Issa liked to perch on a high rock looking out over the valley beneath him, where he could both watch the sheep and also enjoy the dizzy views across the arid rift valley with the blue Arabah below him and the hills of the Arabian desert in the distance. Daniel had explained that the Arabah was quite dead; the only life being in the valleys where streams and springs fed into the sea.

One day, to Issa's surprise, an old lady appeared seemingly out of nowhere, gathering sticks from the bushes that had dried up in the fierce summer heat and working her way along the ridge till she was just below Issa. The area was so remote it would be churlish not to make contact, so he called a greeting, making it as warm as a shout could be. She looked up at his cry and waved as Issa scampered down the slope, jumping from rock to rock.

"Shalom, young brother," she greeted him, smiling. "I didn't see you there, but I have seen the sheep for some days now so I knew you would not be far away."

Issa was puzzled.

"Do you live near here? I have seen no dwellings."

She laughed.

"I live near the Essenes. You won't see their homes; they live in the caves in the steep slopes under the crest of the valley. Even if you knew where they were, you wouldn't be able to find your way to them. They are quite hidden."

"Who are they scared of? Are they fugitives from the Romans?"

Daniel had told Issa of the outlaws who sometimes came through these parts. Some were freedom fighters, the Zealots, and some were just bandits. Daniel surmised that most were a mixture of the two, supposedly fighting for freedom but also terrorising the locals. They generally left the shepherds alone, as their sheep represented a regular supply of meat to which they would help themselves to from time to time.

"The Essenes are scared of everyone, or rather, they try and keep away from everyone in case they get contaminated – especially by women!" She laughed again. "But they put up with me as I am too old to tempt them, and I do chores for them and run errands for the things they don't have, although they would never admit that they needed anything from the outside world, or for me to do their chores. My son is about your age, or a bit older, and they're teaching him a lot and would like him to join them, but I don't think he'll stay now he's come of age. He loves the desert too much. He says he feels closer to God in the desert. He doesn't really like the formal religious stuff."

Issa was more interested now.

"That's a bit like me," he put in ruefully. "I once tried religion in Jerusalem, but it went badly wrong, and the village was not much better. So I just try to do justice, love mercy and walk humbly and maybe sing a few of the songs I have learned from Daniel."

The old lady started. "Daniel? Is that the shepherd from Bethlehem that I met once?"

"Must be. There's only one that I know of. I'm his shepherd boy, though he treats me loads better than most shepherds treat their boys. He's always talking about God and that, but he doesn't go to the religious festivals much these days."

"I remember him well. He helped my cousin and her husband when they had their first baby," said the old lady. "They live up in Galilee now, but he was born in Bethlehem and things got pretty hot for them."

"Do you mean Mary and Joseph and Yeshua?" asked Issa excitedly. "I know them! My mother met them when Yeshua and I were both small boys, and I met them again in Jerusalem. I had a great time exploring the walls and valleys with Yeshua. He told me loads of stuff about history and King David and that. He was loads more religious than me. But I could cope with the way he did stuff."

"So you know my cousin Mary and Yeshua? How are they? Have you seen them recently?"

Disappointed that he had to tell her he had not seen the family for five years, he added again that Yeshua was the one highlight of his adventure into religion. Maybe one day they would meet again.

The lady was pensive.

"My husband and his good friend Simeon would talk for hours about Yeshua and our boy. But they are both dead now and we wonder what it

170

was all about. There were prophecies and angels and royal visitors. Then Herod started killing people… small children even." She looked away and when she looked back, her eyes were full of tears. "He killed my husband, my boy's father, too. He would have killed Yeshua and maybe our boy as well if he'd had the chance, but they were spared. And then it all went quiet. We had hoped that God would liberate his people, but now we're not sure what's happening. Yeshua and his family are up in Galilee and we're here in the desert."

Issa was not sure about all this. He had heard some things from his mother and knew only too well that the other boys in the village had all been killed.

"Are the Essenes liberators like the Zealots then?" he asked.

The old lady quickly corrected him. "Not at all. They really despise each other. The Zealots want to start an uprising and take the land by force, while the Essenes just want to read their holy books. We believed God was going to do something new and maybe my boy John and Yeshua were going to be part of that. But now we're not so sure."

They would have talked some more, but Issa noticed a commotion among some birds which might indicate a predator after his sheep, so with a hurried explanation to the old lady he made his farewell.

"Maybe you'll meet my son if you are here for a while," she called after him. "He gets a bit fed up with the Essenes and goes into the desert whenever he can."

That evening Issa told Daniel of his meeting with the old lady.

"Yes, I remember meeting her myself a number of years ago. Joseph and his family had to make a hurried escape from Bethlehem and stayed in Hebron with Mary's cousin. Herod got wind of it and took in the old man, but the mother and the boy escaped to the desert and were taken in by the Essenes. The old man died in prison, probably tortured and killed. Mary was distraught to hear about it. She felt it was all her fault for going there, but the truth is that no-one was safe from Herod's whims." Daniel shook his head sadly.

"She said something about her son and Yeshua being liberators, and that there were prophecies and angels and royal visitors which was why Herod killed all the small boys," explained Issa.

"I don't know about her boy, but there have been some amazing things around Yeshua." Daniel told Issa about his encounter with the angel as he had recounted it to Sarah all those years ago. "I don't know what it all means, but there is something special about Yeshua. Joseph and Mary have the responsibility of bringing him up to grow into that. It was a privilege to have been able to help them."

Issa was quiet, thinking back over the time he had spent with Yeshua in Jerusalem. That was an amazing experience, and if his cousin John was of the same sort, he would really like to meet him. He decided that if he was able to, he would try and lead the flock to where he had met the old lady.

The next day he set off in the same direction and was pleased to find some grazing a little way off the crest but still quite visible to anyone who was around. This was going to be a hot day and Issa sat in the mottled shade of an acacia tree, keeping watch. The animals noticed first that someone or something was approaching, and Issa was instantly alert in case it was a wild animal. Seeing a fleeting glimpse of a figure, who immediately disappeared below a ridge, he scanned the area when there was a cry from behind him. Spinning round, he saw a youth a couple of years older than him laughing and holding out a hand in welcome.

"I'm John. I think it was you who met my mother yesterday." They clasped hands, an immediate bond forming between them.

"Yes, that was me. But you crept up on me! Just as well you weren't a lion or a bear..."

"Or a Zealot," put in John. "But they aren't as subtle, using brawn rather than brains."

"Are they around these parts?"

"Not at this moment apparently, but they do move fast and will appear without warning."

"Are they a problem?"

"Pretty grim if you're a Roman or a collaborator and you meet up with them in these hills," answered John, drawing a finger across this throat. "But mostly they just want a bit of protection pay."

"Protection pay?" enquired Issa, puzzled.

"We look after you, so you need to pay us."

"Do they look after us?"

John looked furtively around.

"'Nice flock of sheep you got here; it would be a shame if anything happened to them… which it just might, if you don't pay up.'" He spoke in a conspiratorial tone with a heavy accent. "It's an old trick. David used to use it to feed his warriors when he was a fugitive in these hills."

"What! David the King? I thought he wrote songs about God and religious things and justice and that? I didn't think he did bad stuff!"

"He was a fighting man and times were tough. He knew what was right and would sing about it. But 'knowing' what's right isn't the problem, 'doing it' is what is tough. He would live by his wits, bend the rules and even take advantage of his power."

"So do the Zealots think they're following King David when they ask for protection pay?"

John was quiet for a while.

"David often sang about asking for and receiving forgiveness. That's the difference. He knew there was a right way and would hold up his hands when he was caught out or realised his mistakes. Many of the songs he wrote are admissions of failure, confessions of sin or asking for forgiveness. It's easy to see the mistakes in others and either kill them as the Zealots do, or shun them and separate from them as the pious do. David railed against injustice in the world and longed for the day when God would put things right, but when he spoke of individual sins, he more often than not was talking about his own."

"Blessed is the one who is forgiven,
whose sins are covered.
When I kept silent, my bones wasted away.
Then I confessed my sins to you
and you forgave the guilt of my sin.
You are my hiding place. You will surround me with songs of deliverance."

He sang softly, looking into the distance. Both lads sat quietly when he finished.

"Is that one of David's songs?"

"Yes. One of many."

"Did David write the bit about doing justice, mercy and walking humbly? Daniel taught me that. But it wasn't in a song."

"That was one of the prophets, but David said a similar thing in one of his songs:

Sacrifice and offerings you did not desire.
My sacrifice is a broken spirit:
A humble and repentant heart you will not despise.

People were doing all sorts of religious stuff, but the prophet said that what God wants is justice mercy and humble walking with him. But when God's kingdom comes, it will be different from what either the Zealots or the pious expect. That's why I love it out here in the desert. So natural, so far from any human influence. You can sense the presence of God here," John said wistfully.

They were quiet again, looking out over the rolling hills on the far side of the Arabah.

"My mother tells me you have been with my cousin, Yeshua. I haven't met him since we were very young and I can't remember much. Will you tell me about him?" asked John, breaking the silence.

Issa recounted some of the story of his childhood: how they met on the road when they were infants, and later when Yeshua's family had passed through on their way home from Egypt. He explained that they were only distant memories and mostly things his mother had told him. But when he got to the adventures in Jerusalem, he became more animated.

"I learned loads of things from him about King David and the history of Jerusalem. We climbed the walls and went through a tunnel made by a king, but I don't remember who that was. He explained about the coming-of-age ceremony, of how a lamb had to be killed when the people first escaped from Egypt and about other sacrifices and things. The funny thing was that after all that, he got lost and his mother got really stressed like mothers do, but he was safe in the temple and we found him in the end," he went on, laughing before growing more serious. "It was such a good time I decided to go back the next year, but that went all wrong."

John raised his eyebrows. "What happened?"

Issa was silent for a while, then went on more quietly.

"I didn't meet up with Yeshua at first, but then I shouldn't have expected to. There were so many pilgrims in Jerusalem. I had this lamb for the sacrifice; Daniel had given it to me as pay. I was so excited."

"Then what happened?"

Issa picked up a handful of stones and threw them vehemently one by one towards a spike of rock.

"The inspectors turned it down. Then they sold it to someone else to sacrifice… but when I complained, the crowds turned nasty and I got roughed up." He paused. "Suddenly Yeshua was there and stuck up for me. I don't think he actually hit anyone, but the crowd didn't wait to see. I never thought he could get so angry. He's not that big, but no one messed with him."

"So you gave up on religion?" enquired John with a sidelong glance.

Issa was quiet for a while.

"I went back to the hills and Daniel tried to make it good. He said I had taken a lamb and it had been sacrificed, so that counted before God, and he said I should count the omens..."

"The Omer," corrected John, smiling.

"Yes, that's it. The Omer thing. I didn't always remember to do it, but then I went to the festival in my village and they chased me away from there too. My mother had warned me that religion wasn't for the poor like us, so now I just go to the festivals for the food with my friend Moshe and spend my time in the hills with the sheep. I like to think of King David in the hills and sometimes Daniel sings some of his songs, but I like it best when I find out new things about living in the desert. I would like to meet Yeshua again, though."

"You're lucky. He's my cousin and I hardly know him. Not like you. Maybe one day when we are men, we'll have the chance," added John hopefully.

"But I thought that becoming a man is what the lamb was killed for?"

"That's when you come under the law. That's what Bar Mitzvah means: 'son of the law'. Then you start to learn, and you are still learning till you are 30 years old. That's when you are ready to take on your father's trade."

"I haven't got a father," murmured Issa.

"Nor have I," said John, slapping Issa on the back. "So we'd better make the best of what we have." He waved his hand expansively towards the desert hills. "God is our father and there's a lot to learn in these hills." He sent a stone spinning towards the spike.

They sat together, watching the sheep while John told Issa some of the local secrets of the desert where they were: hidden caves and valleys, how to forage for good things, showing him some roots he could dig up – some even Daniel hadn't shown him – and explaining about the bees that made wild honey from the acacia blossom.

The sun was dropping towards the horizon when they eventually separated, and it was getting dark by the time Issa got back to Daniel, who chided him for being out so late but listened as Issa explained that he had been with one of the Essene boys.

"Do you ever meet the Zealots?" asked Issa when he had finished.

Daniel shrugged. "We try to keep out of their way. They're pretty violent and desperate anyway, but it would be worse for you if you were to be seen with them and Romans appeared. In any case, it's time we started heading back to Bethlehem, where they never venture. The rains will soon be starting and there will be plenty of pasture."

Chapter 22

The rains were good that year, so the people were blessed with an abundant harvest, though the wet winter was not comfortable for the shepherds out on the hills. Once again, before the hot dry summer began, Daniel moved closer to some of the wells he knew. The festival of Tabernacles was approaching again and promised to be a great feast. As usual, Moshe had come to the flock to meet him, and although Issa was quite mature enough to travel back by himself, he was happy with the custom as it served as a reminder to Daniel that Issa would want to go to the feast. Sarah was delighted to see her boy again, fussing over him, taking his clothes to wash and proudly presenting him with a new waistcoat. She made him take off his shepherd's head scarf to wash and exclaimed at his long matted hair.

"I rather suspected you wouldn't have washed in weeks so I've filled the pitchers," she said, pointing to the large stone jars that, in some more pious bygone time, would have been used for ritual washing. She took Issa's clothes and shooed him to the back of the house, turning on the grinning Moshe, who she scolded, and gestured for his clothes also. He gave her his tattered shirt, but she snapped her fingers for more, till, grinning sheepishly, he too was stripped naked and joined Issa by the pitchers.

In the late afternoon sunshine the boys threw water over each other, whooping and laughing like small children. Sarah, washing their clothes, looked on indulgently. Though Moshe was almost 10 years older, Issa was now as tall as he was. Their faces had a striking resemblance too, as did their bronzed bodies, so they could easily have been taken for brothers. Sarah did not know who Moshe's parents had been. He was probably the illegitimate child of some poor girl who may have died when he was young, so he had been abandoned to fend for himself. In a small community they could well have been blood relations, but Sarah was excluded from the circles of gossiping women who might have enlightened her. But better that she did not know: he was now part of her family and she loved him dearly. She was the only one in Bethlehem who claimed him for her own.

The boys were in high spirits when they got to the festivities and joined the watching fringe of misfits – those with physical or mental difficulties, and others ostracised on account of their lineage, or lack of it. There were none among them of Issa's age and only one or two as young as Moshe. The rest were decrepit old men.

As ever, Moshe melted in and out of the crowd, collecting food. His recent ablutions and washed clothes made him less obvious in the crush, but the food and drink were abundant that year and soon everyone was merry and in good humour. By late afternoon, the singing and dancing started. The richer villagers having eaten the choicer fare, it was time for the old men from the fringe, together with the widows and orphans, to be welcomed to the table, eating their fill of the spread and secreting extra food in their headscarves and shawls for later on.

Once again this year, between dances, proud fathers brought on their daughters to sing. The humour was often coarse, fathers extolling the eligibility of their daughters and roaring with appreciation as each girl sang. While women were excluded from formal worship, they could sing at social events, weddings especially, and their songs, although from the scriptures, were usually romantic in theme.

Moshe and Issa were sitting on a bough, high up in a tree, full of food and a little lightheaded from the wine they were not used to drinking. The girls' singing awoke an interest in Issa that he had not experienced before. The lamps cast shadows, emphasising each girl's fine features;

179

the occasion, the passionate words and the effect of the wine gave each a particular beauty.

One of the girls passed just under the tree with her mother as she went to sing. She was a little older than most of the singing girls, making her voice stronger and more mature, but it was also crystal clear and perfect, even when hitting the high notes that few of the others had attempted. She sang a romantic song from the Song of Songs:

"My lover! See him come,
leaping down the mountain side
springing over the crags.
My lover is a sleek gazelle –
Look there he stands beside the wall;
waiting, watching,
now through the windows,
now through the trellis.
'Come away my darling. Come away with me.'"

The verses became more erotic, each one finishing with the refrain,

"Come away my darling.
Come away with me."

She finished, taking a breath before holding the highest of high notes on the final refrain.

There was a ribald and appreciative cheer at the end of the song, the humour coarse and drunken, and Issa was indignant that such pure singing could be so trivialised.

While she had sung with confidence and conviction, as soon as she finished the girl struck a modest pose, quickly following her mother back through the crowd, keeping her eyes lowered demurely.

Issa was captivated. He watched her closely as she approached, hoping she would pass under his tree again on her return. There was a lamp attached to the tree and, as if sensing his gaze, she glanced up discreetly into the branches, hardly moving her head, searching out the boys and smiling a fleeting smile as her eyes met Issa's. Heart thumping as he watched her go, he deftly swung down out of the tree, keeping her in view and following until he found where her family group was. He recognised some of their faces and realised they were near neighbours, though he had never had cause to speak to any of them. They were of another class, quite well to do and very religious. This must be the singing girl his mother had spoken of over the years.

As the night drew in, the folk songs were used up and the crowd turned to the well-known songs of David, their most famous son.

There was a rousing chorus of 'His love endures for ever' as they started on the ancient round of songs that the pilgrims would sing as they approached Jerusalem. Issa stayed near the family group, joining in with the singing as well as he could, waiting for them to head home so he could steal another smile. But the opportunity did not arise.

Moshe and Sarah were at home before Issa, Sarah sitting happily by the fire as the autumn evening was clear and chill.

"That was a really special feast," commented Sarah. "I do love it when the girls sing. That girl who lives in the big compound just below us sings so beautifully. The mother's a real harridan, though. I remember how strict she was from when I was younger. All the other sisters and brothers are older and married with their own children of almost her age."

Issa tried not to appear interested and wished his mother would carry on, but there was no more to tell. Tomorrow he would have to return to the hills, but he would look for any excuse now to visit Bethlehem and try and find a way, any way, to see that smile again. The next feast was some months away, but the winter was approaching and the rains would mean they would probably be on the hills nearby.

Chapter 23

Moshe went back to the flock with Issa and as usual stayed for the day. He too enjoyed being on the hills. Daniel was always a little gruff when they returned from the feast, as he had to do all the menial work that Issa usually relieved him of, but after a couple of days Issa was able to ask Daniel about the song the girl had sung. He couldn't remember much except about the lover bounding over the hills and gazing though the branches. He had so entered into the song that he had imagined the lover being hidden in a tree as he had been, rather than behind the walls of the house. Daniel recognised the passage immediately and explained that it was a long love song, supposedly written by King Solomon. Solomon had hundreds of wives and concubines, but some suggested that his true love was a girl he had met in the hills behind Jerusalem, which he loved to escape to as a young man.

"So, what happened to the girl?" asked Issa, a little hoarsely.

"Who knows…" They sat in silence for a while, then Daniel continued. "Some disagree and say it tells of God's love, which is not concerned whether a person is rich or poor, but is pure, passionate, faithful and overwhelming. Take it either way. Or both."

"Do you know any more of it?"

"It's a lover's song. Quite beautiful. But I buried the love of my life and her baby many years ago. My songs are sadder now."

Issa was quiet.

"Are there sad songs in the scriptures for you to sing?" he enquired at last.

Daniel laughed. "Many of our songs are sad, angry even. Calling out to God, asking, 'Why?'

"My God, my God, why have you forsaken me?
I cry out all day long but do not hear you answer me;
at night I call and call, but find no peace, no rest."

He sang to a mournful tune.

"Life can be tough, both because of bad people or ourselves doing wrong things. A lot of David's songs are because people were trying to kill him, and then in the prophets there are sad songs from people suffering under the punishment for what they have done wrong. Some of David's songs are confessions of wrong as well."

"We don't sing those songs at the feasts, do we?"

"No. You need to go to the synagogue each week, that's all they sing! They feel the oppression of the Romans and they long for the Messiah to come and deliver them. But the feasts are all times of celebration. The main three each year are a celebration of God's goodness, so the festal songs are all praise and thanksgiving."

"Isn't it a bit strange that they sing angry songs most of the year, but then happy ones at the feasts? Can you be angry and sad and happy all at once?"

"There is one book which is all lament. Jerusalem had fallen because Israel had forsaken God and got into all sorts of bad ways. The people who had not been killed were taken into exile and were desperate. The prophet wrote this lament summing up how they all felt. In this song each couplet continues the lament, getting more and more desperate as the song goes on. But here's the thing: Right in the middle of the most desperate part, in the middle of the chant, the prophet suddenly alters his tone from grief to hope:

"Yet this always comes to mind and brings me hope:
Because His love is greater, we are not destroyed
for His mercies never end;
 refreshed every new morning;
so great your faithfulness."

Daniel paused, searching for the words. He was quite animated now. "I can't remember it all, but there are other bits that have helped me...

"How good it is for man to learn endurance while still young...
for the Lord is not angry for ever...
Let us look at our hearts and test our ways,
turn back to the Lord and feely confess:
We have fallen short and turned away from you."

"My father taught me loads of stuff, but I have forgotten so much. But I remember that even in the darkest times there is hope. You know that song I tried to teach you, the shepherds' one?"

"The Lord is my Shepherd one?"

"Yes, that's it:

"Even though I walk through a dark valley, even in the shadow of death, I will not fear the power of evil, for you are always with me."

Issa was quiet for a while.

"But... are there any other songs... you know, other love songs?" asked Issa innocently.

Daniel roared with laughter. "Have you fallen in love, boy?"

Issa coloured and flung a stone from him.

"I'm going to check the lambs." He scampered off, Daniel's good-natured laughter following him.

Chapter 24

Issa was in love.

Being close to Bethlehem, the shepherds would take turns to have a break away from the cold and rain of the hills. Daniel would go back to his house for a few days at a time, but Issa had visits home too. On his way home he would make a detour to go round by the house where the girl lived, but she was never anywhere to be seen.

He decided to change his strategy. Making the excuse to Daniel that his mother needed him for a couple of days, he set off as usual, but this time he found a sheltered spot where he could watch the main gate to the girl's home from a distance.

He was rewarded when, an hour or so later, a girl left the house carrying a water pot and made her way down the main path into the village. Issa hoped it was the right girl, for the full-length gowns of the women made them rather indistinguishable. Hurrying after her as she turned towards the main path, he was almost certain she was the right one. He moved on quickly, taking a parallel track that ran behind the houses so that he could cut her off and be heading back up the road when she passed. The plan worked well for, as he rejoined the main path, she appeared round a bend a few houses further up. He sauntered up the road slowly, watching, waiting to catch her eye. She was just a few feet away when she looked up, brushing a lock of hair from over her face. Their eyes met and he smiled, his heart racing and, though she looked away modestly, he thought he saw a smile forming as they passed. Issa turned and watched her go on down the street. Had that been a smile for him? After years of being ostracised, he was ever ready to assume it was a smile of condescension or disdain, but as she came to the next bend in the path, she swung her water pot off her shoulder to change sides, and in the same movement, looked back up the road to where Issa stood. His heart felt it would burst! He quickly looked around to see if anyone was watching, but the street was deserted.

There was only one path to the well. She would have to come back the same way. There was still no one else in street and all the houses were quiet. A clump of large trees formed a small copse at a crossroads nearby where people would rest out of the sun, so it was quite natural for a lad like Issa to be sitting idly in the shade, though until now he would never have had the confidence to do so.

Sure enough, half an hour later, the girl returned, but to his disappointment she was with two other girls of the same age. She made no sign of recognising him as they approached, but to his delight they all swung their water pots off and sat under the trees on the other side of the road to chat. Frustratingly, she was in the middle of the three, and though she occasionally leaned forward, she never looked over. Issa tried to appear uninterested and occasionally one of the other girls looked over in his direction without seeming to notice he was there. He tried to listen in on their conversation but could only hear occasional words when their voices were raised in laughter.

After a good few minutes, the other girls stood and swung their pots onto their shoulders saying farewell and heading off on a side path between two houses.

"Come and sing outside our house one morning. It would be good to get the old man out of his bed!"

"I have enough trouble with my own household," she laughed. "That's why I sing to the hills in the back yard at daybreak before I start my chores." The two girls laughed too as they set off, while the other took time rearranging her headscarf and generally delaying until the girls were well on their way. This time she turned to face Issa, and there was no doubt of the smile and that it was intended for him. Issa grinned foolishly but made no move as she passed by.

The next morning he was up at the crack of dawn, creeping out, careful not to disturb his mother. He bounded over the low mounds which marked the far boundary of the village, so approaching her house from the hill behind. No one knew why the mounds were there, but they served as a barrier for further development of the village in that direction and meant Issa could almost approach the house without being noticed. There was a high wall with a ditch in front, which added to the height of the walls and thus increasing security. Stones would have come from the ditch for the wall's construction, but now it served as a place for a hopeful lover to hide!

Issa had arrived as early as he could and had to wait a while before at last he heard her singing. Most were religious songs, but at the end she sang the love song that had captivated him at the feast. She seemed to sing this more quietly, more intimately, than the other songs. He was mesmerised! The next day he had to return to the hills, but whenever he was able to go to Bethlehem, he would creep out early each morning to be in time for the serenade.

Yet he didn't even know her name! Convention held that a girl should not be seen speaking to a man unless she was a near relative, and in any case, he was struck dumb. He longed to know more of the family, so he eventually he plucked up the courage to ask Daniel about them. He tried to make it sound as if he was just curious about his near neighbours, but Daniel was not fooled.

"They're very religious and very strict. The eldest daughter was always strong-willed and a free spirit and disappeared a number of years ago. Rumour had it that she'd eloped. A few years later a child appeared, who the family like to call an orphaned relative, but the truth is it was the eldest daughter's child."

Though the resemblance to Sarah and Issa's situation was glaring, it passed without comment.

"I think the child's name may have been Miryam. Is that the girl you've fallen in love with?"

Issa coloured, but it was so dark that Daniel did not notice. However, judging from the delayed and hesitant response, it clearly was.

"Do you know if she's promised in marriage? Girls who are wouldn't sing in public, would they?"

Daniel laughed silently in the darkness.

"Not usually." Musing, he went on. "I don't know why she isn't betrothed; She must be nearly your age. Possibly men are wary that she may be as headstrong as her mother and not seen as a good catch." He paused. "Possibly her grandparents want to keep her to look after them in their old age. It's a common situation. Take in an orphan, often a relative, who then is expected to forgo any independence or marriage and in gratitude, to look after you as you get old and infirm."

Issa reflected that the girl certainly seemed to have lots of character. But that was enough for the moment. At least he knew her name.

But soon other things were to preoccupy him.

Chapter 25

Sarah was worried. Recently the Romans had appointed a revenue man in their area. He was Jewish, from Galilee, and therefore regarded as a traitor to Israel. That he was corrupt went with the job. Everything to do with Rome and the occupation was corrupt and it was taken for granted that the tax collectors charged much more than the Romans demanded. How else could they get Jewish people to do the job?

At first he would walk to Bethlehem, setting up a stall in the market and collecting from the people as they passed. Being Jewish himself, and so knowing their language and ways, it was hard for traders to pull the wool over his eyes. After concentrating on the market where the richest pickings were, he turned his attention to the home-run businesses, including inns and lodging houses. Sarah's guest house was very modest compared to the larger inns in the village, so she had hoped she would escape notice, but before long he found her out and called round. She was quite anxious about what to expect and certainly had no money to pay any taxes. When Issa came back one day, he found his mother agitated. The tax man had been asking probing questions about her business, making demands she could not possibly meet. He was due back that day, so she was relieved that Issa was there to offer some protection.

Issa, for his part, was quite intimidated by it all, but tried to look tough when, later that afternoon, a rather portly man with a large leather satchel came up the road. Wearing his rough tunic and headscarf, firmly holding his shepherd's staff in his hand and with his sling and bag of stones by his side, Issa tried to look bigger and older than his 17 years. Sarah was at the back of the house and so did not see the taxman approach.

"Ah, a lodger. Can you call your hostess?" he began, stroking his chin.

"I am Mistress Sarah's son," Issa replied coldly. "What do you want with my mother?"

"Just a matter of back tax. Your mother has not paid her taxes for many years." He looked Issa up and down. "Ah, but you are a shepherd I see. We'll need to talk to you about your taxes too."

"You'll have to talk to my master about that."

"And is your master in the house too? With your mother maybe?" he said with a leer.

"He's in the hills," hissed Issa, reddening.

"Maybe I'll pay him a visit. Where can I find him?"

"Just beyond the lion's lair. You'll need to watch out for the bear traps," added Issa sarcastically, watching the man closely while waving towards the hills.

"Very amusing," replied the other coldly. "Call your mother. I have a proposition for her."

Narrowing his eyes, Issa turned slowly, calling his mother who had heard their voices and been hiding just inside the door. She came out, holding her scarf nervously over her face.

"Ah, Mistress Sarah! Has your son brought you enough to pay the taxes you owe?"

Sarah did not move or say anything. Issa stayed still.

"I see not. Well, I have a proposition," he said, spreading his hands. "You see, the people hear that I am on my way, so the market is already emptying when I arrive. I need to be a little more, let's say, immediate? Now, it seems to me that this is a good lodging house and conveniently placed. Both in the village, yet expediently on its edge, away from any possible interference. I am willing to consider waiving your taxes in return for accommodation."

Issa started angrily, but the man waved him down.

"Of course, I am quite within my rights as a tax collector to requisition accommodation for no payment at all. So it's your choice."

"But if you stay here, then my mother will not be able to have any other lodgers! It's her only income," protested Issa.

"Ah, but I would only stay a few days each month, so for the rest of the time she would be free to take in lodgers as usual. If the fare is good I might recommend her to others, and she could get more trade. Anyway, think about it. I will be here tomorrow for either the back tax or a bed for the night. I will bring some food from the market for you to cook. The traders do tend to give me their choicest produce. They are very generous," he added unpleasantly as he departed.

Issa was furious! He did not trust the man and feared for his mother's safety while he was away in the hills. Sarah was more circumspect.

"I've been here all these years with some pretty scary lodgers and God has looked after me. Anyway, we can arrange for Moshe to be here when he comes to stay. He will make sure I am safe."

Not convinced, Issa went and found Moshe in the cave with the lame animals. There was no formality between them so greetings, while silent, were always warm and prolonged, but today Issa quickly dropped Moshe's hands, obviously troubled. After years of being together, they had developed signs and gestures so could quickly communicate. Issa signed Romans and money, their house, a sleeping man and for Moshe to be on guard. Moshe grimaced, pointed to his eyes while drawing his finger over his throat indicating what would happen if he saw any nonsense. Later, at the house, they were able to discuss a detailed plan, Moshe nodding and looking around, all the while flapping his hands as he did when planning and preparing. He was soon off back to his cave to get the animals secured for the night. There were not many at the moment, and those he had would soon be returning to the flocks.

The next day Moshe returned with his cloak, a stout staff and his small home-fashioned shepherd's knife. He was sitting on a boulder sharpening this when the taxman arrived with a bag as well as his satchel.

"I'm glad you saw sense," he said when he heard they had agreed. Opening his satchel, he pulled out a cut of meat wrapped in plantain leaves, a pumpkin and some beans and handed them to Sarah.

"Please show me the guest room and prepare the food. You boy! Bring me water to wash," he demanded, turning to Issa. Then he started on seeing Moshe sharpening his knife. "Are you another son?" he asked a little nervously.

"He is my brother. He can't hear or speak, but don't let that fool you. He sees everything, even in the dark. And even in the darkest mind. You may not always see him, but he will not be far away. He will look after my mother, the house… and you… as long as you stay within the agreed boundaries."

"Is he safe? Can I trust him?"

"He is as straight as they come, but he's had a tough life and knows how to look after himself and those who look after him."

Moshe grinned, running his thumb over the edge of the blade before turning back to the stone to continue sharpening it.

The first night was tense and the boys stayed awake all through, but the taxman snored and slept till morning, having drunk a lot of wine with his meal. He was not difficult, and the boys appreciated being able to share the food he brought, though Issa felt fleetingly guilty that this was part of ill-gotten gains. The next day, the taxman went to the market and Moshe returned to his animals, but Issa knew that with his extraordinary insight he would be back as soon as the taxman arrived, and being so fiercely loyal, he would protect Sarah from any danger.

The spring lambs were being born and so Issa was seldom able to return to Bethlehem. When he did, if he found the taxman there, he wasn't happy leaving Sarah alone while he went to hear Miryam sing. When he heard about the unwelcome guest, Daniel had only nodded grimly, which Issa knew, from experience, meant that he was worried. Before Passover, the boys from Jerusalem came for the lambs as usual, but having been warned by Issa, they stayed in another lodging. To Sarah's disappointment, at Passover, which should have been her busiest time, the taxman stayed on, not only taxing the pilgrims, but also provoking the people of the village who muttered darkly about Sarah. Whenever she could, she would try and explain that she had no choice, but it made no difference. She was still ostracised and few people gave her any credence or attention and her protests fell on deaf ears.

Chapter 26

The Feast of First Fruits was imminent, bringing the boys, full of anticipation and excitement, down from the hills for the celebrations. As they prepared to go to the village square, Issa found his mother still in her house clothes sitting sadly by the fire.

"Come on, Mother! Aren't you going to wear your good dress? You'll be late!" he chided. Sarah looked up, her eyes full of tears. "I won't be going to the feast."

"But why not? You love the feasts! Are you unwell?" he questioned anxiously.

She poked the fire with a stick before replying quietly, "I'm not welcome. People say I get enough of their food from the taxman, and they don't want me. But I don't eat his food! I would rather choke!" she protested, her voice rising, breaking.

"But mother! What do you eat then?" He noticed for the first time that his mother looked gaunt and thin. "Why didn't you tell me?"

"I manage."

Dropping to his knees before her, he took her hands and looked into her eyes, his own filling with tears to see his mother so broken.

"Mother, I'm so sorry. You must come! You'll miss the singing. You do so love the singing. Couldn't you come to the fringes, in the shadows? We will be nearby to defend you. No one would notice."

"Thank you, my boy, but I'm so tired. I can't fight any more." She wiped her eyes and blew her nose on the corner of her headscarf. Issa stood, angry but helpless, clenching and unclenching his fists.

"Well, you'll eat tonight! We'll bring you some food." He thought for a while. "But is that parasite here? He is the cause of all this! He certainly can't go to the feast. If you don't go, then I'll stay with you. I'll not leave you alone with him."

Sarah protested tearfully but the boys insisted, and in the end it was agreed that they would take turns. Issa stayed first, while Moshe soon returned with choice pickings of the food in his usual way. Sarah was in no mood to eat. She picked at her plate listlessly, but Issa knew that some of the food would keep and she would be stocked up for a while at least. By the time Issa arrived at the feast, he knew that most of the best food would be gone, but he had come for the singing, or rather to see Miryam and hear her sing. He was not in the mood for singing himself. The villagers were people of habit and he suspected that each family would gather in the same place in the village square at every feast. Sure enough, he found Miryam's family in the same spot, but could not see the girl. The community singing had already started and there were speeches, but as the evening wore on, it seemed that tonight the girls were not to be called on to perform. Disappointed, he made a quick visit to the now nearly empty tables, together with the other outcasts from the margins of the crowd, who always saw to it that none of the food was wasted. Quickly choosing more of the food that he thought might keep for a few days, he followed the crowd back up the hill in the moonlight. The path narrowed as it passed through a grove of trees and in the darkness, the revellers bunched together, hemming Issa in and slowing the pace.

"Miryam! Miryam! Where is that girl?" a voice shouted crossly from up ahead. A shadowy figure called out in response.

"It's all right, I'm here, grandmother! I'm just coming."

She made to squeeze past Issa. In the dark and confusion on the narrow path, his heart in his mouth, Issa reached out to steady her, and in response she held his cloak, stumbling and swaying against him. He put a supporting arm around her, holding her up more firmly than really necessary, feeling her slender shoulder through her tunic. She glanced up and giggled.

"Sorry, I slipped. You're so kind to help me."

And she was gone. His heart leapt again! How long had she been there? Had she planned it? He had broken every convention by holding her, but even if anyone had been able to see, it would have seemed an innocent accident. It was anything but innocent! And she was the chief conspirator.

Issa had to return immediately to the hills, for now it was into the summer, the flock would have soon to travel further in their search for pasture and Daniel was impatient to start. There would not be so many opportunities to return home the further they travelled. Issa was now really concerned for his mother, but could he ask for leave to return to check she was all right? Moshe was on hand for Sarah, and Daniel knew the arrangement, so he might not be sympathetic. Issa would have to choose his moment. That evening by the fire, Daniel was in a good mood.

"How was the feast, boy? Did your girl sing more love songs for you?" He roared with laughter.

Issa grinned shyly in the darkness.

"The girls didn't sing this time." He did not elaborate and certainly was not going to tell Daniel that he had held her, albeit briefly, in his arms. They still tingled with the memory. "I couldn't go to the feast till later anyway. There are still problems at home with the taxman. I stayed to look after mother till Moshe came back with some food. The people won't let her go to the feasts now. I am worried that things are getting worse and she may have serious problems. I would really like to know she is safe before we go further away," he added tentatively.

Daniel was quiet for a long time. "Yes. You're right. We do need to make sure she's safe. But maybe it's time for me to go and see what's to be done. There must be a way of getting the wretched man to leave."

Deep down, Issa was torn. He wanted to go himself to try to see Miryam, but he knew he could do little to help with moving the taxman on. Daniel had much more influence, but by the way the taxman pushed everyone around, he could not see how even Daniel could help. They sat in silence. Issa had broached the subject. It was for Daniel to respond. After a long time, the shepherd started somewhat hesitantly.

"Boy, tell me about your father."

Issa was taken aback at the turn of conversation.

"I don't remember him. Mother doesn't talk about him. Well, not much. Except sometimes when she's angry with me and tells me I'm arrogant like my father."

Daniel stoked the fire before continuing. "Did he divorce her?"

Issa dug at the ground with a stick, as he did when nervous. This was getting a bit difficult.

"I'm not sure he ever married her," he said quietly. "The villagers say I'm a bastard-child, so they must assume he didn't. She gets tearful when she knows they're saying that, but I think it's because she knows it's true. I think he had a bit of a reputation. I know she thought they would get married, but he abandoned her for another woman. She said once that men could have more than one wife in Arabia. But I don't know. They were Jewish. Maybe he did marry her. Maybe he divorced her. I don't really care. But one thing I do know – he's never been anything of a father to me."

He paused. "Not like you," he added under his breath.

They were silent again. Eventually, Daniel stretched and yawned.

"Leave it there, boy. We'll see in the morning. I need to think."

Issa rose before sunrise, but Daniel was up before him. He had his cloak on and was packing a small bundle.

"Get the flock ready for travel when I get back. Check on any lame animals. Look at that ewe that got caught in the briers. See if she's fit.

197

Some of the lambs may need to stay. I'll come back with the dumb boy to collect those that can't make it." He paused, seemingly deep in thought. "Don't worry about your mother. I have a plan."

He looked back at Issa and smiled, then turned away again, nodding, as if weighing things up in his mind.

"I have a plan," he repeated quietly, as if to convince himself.

Though sorry not to be going, Issa had the consolation of having the flock to himself so he could practise his calls to get the sheep to do manoeuvres without Daniel being around to criticise if it went wrong. While the other shepherds had not yet travelled far into the hills, they had all separated as pasture was getting scarce, meaning Issa was all alone, not only with the sheep, but also with his dreams. That evening, with the sheep safely corralled, as he sat alone by the fire, it was his thoughts of Miryam that wandered far and wide; one moment passionate fantasies and the next heart-aching doubts. The truth was, he had no idea what to do next. She seemed to be aware of him, to seek him out even, but was there any hope? Did she know he was considered a bastard-child, as last night's conversation had forcibly reminded him? Would he ever be allowed to marry her? Could a bastard get married at all? He knew she too had a doubtful parentage. Maybe that was why she had noticed him. Could they even elope together as their mothers had done? He imagined them living as outlaws in the Judean hills.

But that was too complicated, so he changed tack and pictured her at home with his mother. The house was big enough for them all, and this was a common enough domestic arrangement. Sarah would be a devoted mother-in-law. This worked much better, so he imagined doing some heroic deed that endeared him to her family, such as saving one of the children from a mad dog and winning Miryam's hand in gratitude! Even better, he imagined being seriously injured thwarting a robber raiding their home in the night, and lying unconscious in the street, being mistakenly accused of the crime. Unseen, Miryam steals into his lockup and secretly nurses him back to life, learning from his semi-conscious ravings the true identity of the culprit, and revealing the whole story. Vindicated, the hero of the hour, he marries her and, sweeping her into his arms, he carries her slender form to his home! The fantasies always ended with him taking her in his arms. He tried to remember exactly how her slim shoulder felt to his touch; how she had leant against him as he felt her breath on his face; her giggled apologies.

A shrill howl in the distance cut through the night air, quickly bringing him back to reality. Grabbing a burning ember in each hand, he patrolled around the flock, waving the brands above his head. The sheep huddled nervously together, shifting restlessly, watching him, aware of a wild animal nearby. From experience, he knew the light of the flames would deter the predator, but he would have to be alert and repeat the exercise regularly.

He thought of Moshe keeping silent vigil at their home, protecting his mother from the threatening menace snoring in the guest bed rather than howling on the hills. Reassured by Daniel's promise to speak with the village elders, his usual nighttime anxiety about his mother was eased. He looked back over the hills towards Bethlehem and wondered what Daniel's plan could possibly be.

When the first rays of dawn streaked over the eastern sky, he busied himself sorting the animals before the heat of the day. The sun was just rising over the hills when an excited Moshe arrived, gesticulating and clapping his hands. After their warm embrace, Moshe tried to calm himself and explain – the taxman had gone! For good! So Daniel's plan had worked! For a second he feared that Daniel had slit his throat, but he would not be as crude as that. Moshe did not know the circumstances, so they would have to wait for Daniel to explain on his return.

Turning their attention back to the sheep, Moshe expertly inspected the animals Issa had separated out for possible return to Bethlehem. He pronounced the injured ewe as fit to travel – the wounds would be completely healed in a few days. Clicking his fingers over two of the lambs in concern for their state, he indicated that he would have to carry them back to Bethlehem, while a further three could walk slowly with rests. From experience Issa knew he would set off in the cool of the evening, walking at the pace of the weakest, taking frequent rests, travelling through the night to arrive before the heat of the next day. Moshe had saved many animals who would otherwise have perished, yet, though appreciated for his skill, he was still regarded by the shepherds as a simpleton and relegated to the fringes of shepherding.

Later in the afternoon Daniel appeared over the crest and Issa bounded up the hillside to meet him.

"Thank you, thank you, sir!" he shouted excitedly, as soon as he was within earshot. "I understand from Moshe that the taxman's gone! Is it true he's gone for good? Your plan worked! Thank you so much! I've been so worried for my mother. Now maybe she'll be safe," he finished tearfully, falling on his knees and taking his master's hands in gratitude.

"It was not me, boy. He was going anyway. I spent some time discussing it with the village elders and they confirmed that he has moved away to Galilee."

"Thank you! Thank you!" Issa repeated over and over. He was so relieved; he wasn't interested in the details. As far as he was concerned, Daniel had saved the day.

"Well, that's that," said Daniel businesslike, closing the subject. "Let's get on, boy, and get the flock in order."

Issa scampered down the hill, whooping as he went, to join a grinning Moshe who, even at a distance, understood what was said.

Daniel watched them go without smiling. It wasn't modesty, but a deep loneliness that had come over him. His journey had not been an unqualified success. He had been taken aback by the vehement attitude of the village elders towards Sarah. That she had proved herself to be an honest hard worker, deferential to the villagers and a good mother, counted for nothing. They still regarded her as little more than a whore and a collaborator, and Issa as a ne'er-do-well bastard-child, making no secret of their disdain towards Daniel for having taken him on as a shepherd boy. He was stung. After Daniel's years of being alone with no son and heir, this poor, fatherless, shepherd boy had come into his life and aroused fatherly love. But the village hostility forced him to be cautious. Could he cope with being marginalised further himself? Shepherds, generally, were looked down on; he was a privileged exception. He knew his status was as precarious as it was precious to him. He watched grimly as the two lads enthusiastically worked the sheep. He would do his best for Issa. He would continue to try and treat him a bit more as a fostered son. But any other ideas were obviously a step too far. He sighed and turned away sadly, putting any further thoughts of taking Sarah as his wife far from his mind.

Chapter 27

The barley would be ripening in the fields around Bethlehem and Issa was happy in the thought that his mother would soon be benefitting from the gleanings of the harvest. While Issa had long since stopped counting the Omer, Daniel would allude to it sometimes, so he was aware of the progression of the countdown to the Feast of Weeks when he would surely see Miryam again. Bethlehem was still a long walk away, but the joy in his heart would give him wings. Impatient for the time to pass, he would sit on a perch in the hills, thinking about her, dreaming of ways to make possible an encounter for long enough for them to be able to express what was on their hearts.

It was, therefore, a surprise when Moshe appeared two weeks early, agitated, gesticulating and pointing as he hurried over to Issa. He signed Sarah and indicated injuries, cowering as if avoiding blows. Moshe was too distressed to elaborate further, but it was enough for Issa to understand that his mother was in trouble and he urgently needed to go to Bethlehem. The sheep he was with were grazing some way from the main herds, scattered over a large area. Desperately the two boys started rounding up the flock, a task made more difficult by their urgency and impatience, and also because it was still the middle of the day rather than evening when the sheep were accustomed to return. At last they arrived back at the makeshift shelter by the desert well at the hottest time of the afternoon. Daniel awoke from his afternoon sleep in the shade, not a little irritated, but also wary, in case bandits or Romans were around.

"What gives, boy?" he shouted gruffly, looking cautiously in each direction. "Why so early?"

"It's my mother!" Issa called out wildly as he approached. "Moshe says she is hurt. Beaten by someone." His eyes were full of tears and he looked desperate.

Daniel thought fast, cursing himself for not anticipating such an eventuality. He had been given due warning. He felt the urge to go too, but he would need to settle the animals. There were other shepherds nearby, as they were all heading back towards Bethlehem in time for the autumn rains, so he may be able to leave the flock in their care.

"Boy, of course you must go to your mother. But first help me get the animals sorted so that they won't wander. When you see how your mother is, send me word by the dumb boy... if I can understand him," he added under his breath.

It was late afternoon before the sheep were safely corralled and the sun had quite set when they eventually arrived at Bethlehem, breathless from their run over the hills. Fortunately there was a bright half-moon and they could find their way with ease. The house was in darkness and the fire out when they arrived. Issa called out for his mother, but there was no reply. She was not in her bed, nor in the yard. The boys searched the house, but there was no sign of Sarah. The ashes were cool so she must have been gone some time. Flapping his hands in agitation and looking around with grave concern, Moshe gave a cry and pointed to the door. As Issa did not understand, Moshe ran to the door, gesticulating to make Issa realise that her staff was missing. She only took it when going into the local hills. The boys looked at each other and up into the hills. The people had been so hostile that she would surely not have gone into the village. Pointing to the fire, Moshe indicated that if she came back while they were out it would be good for her to find it lit, so she would know they had returned. In the meantime, they would search.

Expertly they got the fire into a blaze and set off for the hills, Issa calling as he went. The search took them back and forth across the hill,

Moshe returning from time to time to the silent house in case she had returned, while Issa continued calling. They searched all night and eventually found her in a ravine about a mile from the house. The moon had just come out from behind a cloud, making her light headscarf glow against the dark rocks as she lay on her back, immobile.

"Mother!" cried Issa desperately, scrambling down the ravine, fearing the worst, closely followed by Moshe. "Mother!" he said again, gently shaking her.

She opened her eyes, smiling weakly.

"Issa, my boy. I knew you would come. I'm so sorry."

"Mother, are you hurt? Where is the pain? Can you move?"

"My head hurts so much," she answered in a whisper, "and I can't move my legs. I can't feel them."

"They must be broken," Issa said quietly, lifting his mother's skirts and gently moving her legs. She made no sound. The moon came from behind another cloud and Issa could see a wound on her head and dried blood and cuts to her face. One of her lips was purple and swollen. She eased herself and a spasm came over her. She called out in pain, then started to cry softly. That's enough talking for now, thought Issa grimly.

"Mother, we need to get you out of here. Just hang on while we make a hurdle."

The boys, being shepherds, were expert at making hurdles, but here on the hill there was not much to use. They looked around hurriedly. The nearest willow clump was probably at the entrance to the village, so Issa decided they should cut their losses and fetch one ready-made from the house. He indicated as much to Moshe who, understanding straight away, bounded off down the hillside. Issa slid back down to his mother.

"Mother, can you tell me what happened? Gently. Take your time."

She spoke slowly with frequent pauses.

"I went to glean and the women attacked me… They beat me with their sticks... When I tried to get away, they threw rocks at me... I fell, I think."

"Didn't anyone try to help?" gasped Issa, incredulous. He knew that the fields would have been full of workers.

"The reapers just watched and did nothing... I think the women might have killed me if Moshe had not arrived."

Issa made no comment on the good fortune of Moshe turning up. He was always there when there was a need.

"He was so angry and rushed screaming at the women." Sarah managed a little laugh. "You know how scary he is when he screams. He scared them, and they all ran away... then he came and picked me up and carried me home. He was so upset, he was crying too... Poor boy, he was so worried. He laid me on the bed and washed my wounds... He was torn between staying with me or going for you, but I needed you so much... Once I had settled, I told him to fetch you... I am so glad you came." She pulled his hand to her chest, crying again.

After she had calmed a little, Issa pressed her some more. "But Mother, why are you here?"

"I got so scared... I thought the women might come to the house, so I decided to go up into the hills a little way to hide and watch for you to return... It was so hot. I thought of these trees where I could hide and be in the shade, but it was a lot further than I thought... I was so tired and thirsty when I got here. I climbed down the bank and up this side to the trees but suddenly felt dizzy... and that's all I remember. I must have slipped and fallen... Issa, I'm cold, so cold."

It was not a cold night and Issa had little extra clothing that he could use to wrap his mother in. Her clothes were matted with dried blood and there was quite a pool of fresher clots on the ground by her head, which Issa supposed had come from the fall rather than the attack.

Holding her hand, he spoke tenderly to his mother again. "Hush now, we'll soon have you out of here and home."

Moshe was back in half an hour and the boys discussed how to get Sarah out of the ravine. It turned out to be a lot more difficult than they had thought. The sides were too steep to carry her up so they had to take her further down the stream to where the ravine came out onto the hillside. A number of clumps of small thorn bushes obstructed their path and it took over an hour to get her out, leaving the boys' arms scratched and their clothes torn. Sarah said little, except for an occasional groan when jolted, which made Issa realise, to his dismay, that she was probably losing consciousness.

Once on the hillside, the boys could take an end each and travel much faster, but it was still slow work over the rough ground in the near darkness, for by now the moon was low in the western sky. Eventually they reached the house and were able to slide Sarah off the hurdle onto a blanket and then lift her onto the bed. Although it had made moving her a bit easier, Issa was shocked and dismayed at how light his mother was.

But what should they do now? Being poor they normally slept and rose with the sun, maybe sitting late by the firelight, but lamps were a luxury. Sarah did have some rudimentary clay lights but rarely lit them, unless there were guests who provided the means to buy the oil, so Issa doubted that there was any left in the house. There was certainly none in the lamps which were gathering dust on a shelf.

It was the darkest time of night and still a few hours till daybreak, but he urgently needed to look at his mother more closely, to see how bad the wounds were and get her blood-soaked clothes off. No store that sold oil would be open now, and anyway, he had no money. His only hope was to wake his neighbours, Miryam's family, and ask them. He felt as though he knew them well, since he had taken a keen interest in all the family members because of Miryam, but the truth was he had never spoken to anyone. They were comparatively well off, so probably did not glean, and they would not have been involved in the incident though they may well have heard about it. Perhaps they would feel some sympathy for Sarah.

"Please God let them help me," he prayed as he went to their doorway.

He banged on the courtyard door, clapped and called out. Immediately the dogs inside came to life with loud barking, but there was no reply or movement from the house. Gradually the dogs settled, and their barks became intermittent threatening growls.

Issa tried again, more persistently this time. Once again, the dogs started baying. This time there was an angry voice from within the house. Issa called out between bouts of barking.

"Please help! My mother's had an accident and I have no oil for the lamp to see to clean her wounds."

There was a murmur of voices and the sound of a bolt being drawn. A voice came from the window, though it was too dark to see a face.

"Who is it…? It's the middle of the night!! What do you want?"

"I've come from next door. Please help me. My mother has had a bad accident. She has fallen and hurt her legs. She can't move. I need oil for the lamp so I can see to clean her wounds. Please! Please help me!"

A woman's voice from further inside the house called, "Who is it?"

"It's the bastard son from next door. He says the prostitute has had an accident and is hurt. He wants some oil."

"What about the taxman? Get him to give you some oil. He takes enough from the shopkeepers."

Issa persisted. "He has been long gone and he never paid my mother anything anyway. Please, please have pity on us. Only a little oil. I will repay you."

"The shops will be open at daybreak. It's dark and the family are asleep."

Issa noticed that they had a lamp burning deeper in the house.

"Could you lend me a lamp for a few minutes? I only want to look at her wounds."

"It might get broken and then what would we do?"

"Please!" begged Issa, but the window was shut, and he was left with the growling dogs.

Issa returned home angry and tearful, smarting at the rejection and the words they had used. Moshe was by his mother's bed and turned to look enquiringly. Issa shrugged. It was too dark to sign and explain what had happened. Issa wiped his face and nose with his arm, the tiredness and anxiety for his mother taking their toll.

They tried to make a taper out of wood from the fire, but it just smoked with no flame to see by. Sarah always kept the yard cleanly swept so there were no twigs to make a torch with. They were scrambling around in the dark, trying to find something with which to improvise, when there was movement in the courtyard and a shadow appeared in the doorway.

"Who's there?" Issa called out hoarsely. Moshe leapt up to confront the visitor. A girl's voice answered.

"I'm Miryam from next door. I heard about your poor mother. I'm sorry my family are so hard. I have brought you a small lamp which is half full. I couldn't get any more oil, but this one will last a little while. I had to creep out of the house, and this is all I could bring."

"Oh, thank you, sister! You shouldn't have put yourself at risk!" said Issa as he gratefully took the lamp to the fire and tried to light it.

"Let me," said the girl. "I know how to get it going." Soon she returned with the lighted lamp, gasping when in its glow she saw the state of Sarah.

"Oh, your poor mother! Can I help her? Please let me. Get water. Can you warm some so I can try and get the dried blood off?" She leaned tenderly over Sarah and looked closely at her wounds.

"Sarah, isn't it?" She leaned close to her ear without waiting for a reply. "Mistress Sarah. I'm going to clean you up. I'll try to be gentle. Please let me know if I hurt you."

Sarah opened her eyes and tried to focus.

"Is that Mary? My old friend Mary? Thank God you have come!"

"No, I'm Miryam. I'm from next door. I'm so sorry you've been hurt. The boys are here. We'll try to help you."

She sat up, turning to the boys, who peered at Sarah in the lamplight, "I don't know very much about this, but I know we must get the wounds clean, especially the deep ones. This one on her head looks very bad."

There were whitish-yellow fragments, which she thought might be bone, but she had never seen such injuries before. She kept this concern to herself.

Issa began to calm down as he watched Miryam clean the wounds with her delicate fingers. Issa and Moshe's strong shepherd's hands were so rough in comparison, but they took the rags they'd found and washed them as they became filled with blood before bringing them back to Miryam.

"Do you have any clean cloth for bandages?" the girl asked, when she had done the best she could to clean Sarah.

Issa had to admit that there were few garments they could use for making bandages. His mother wore old and patched clothes. The bedding generally was rough and not suitable.

"I will see if I can find some for you. Are you coming to my wall tomorrow?"

Issa was taken aback!

"To your wall?"

"Yes, when I'm practising. You come when you're home from the hills," she replied matter- of-factly.

"How do you know when I'm home?" he asked in a somewhat defensive tone.

"Oh, I notice. I see the dumb boy come by then go up into the hills. It tells me you will be coming later that day. Sometimes I go on the hill behind the house and watch you coming," she giggled. "You're like the boy in the song leaping over the rock and crags. I imagine you when I am singing it and it gives me inspiration."

Issa was quiet for some time. They were talking in whispers, pausing, all the while attentive to Sarah, so long pauses weren't unduly significant. It was his turn to reply and the truth was he was dumbfounded and didn't know what to say. He had never noticed her on the hill, and the front of the house was always barred. On the times he had seen her go to the well, the gate was opened and closed by a man he took to be her elder brother. He assumed he was the one he'd spoken to just now.

"So how do you get out? How did you get out now?"

"There's a hole at the base of the wall under a thorn bush, near where I sing. It was probably made by some wild animal. I found it a little while ago and scraped it out so that I can squeeze though. It can get muddy, but I found an old goat skin which I lay over the earth. The hairy side is easy to slide on. It also covers the entrance and I put stones on it. Being grey it doesn't show through."

Sarah stirred and the conversation stopped. She woke and look around, disoriented and confused, and tried to sit up. Issa took her hand again and spoke in her ear.

"It's all right Mother, I'm here. You've had an accident and need to be still."

She sank back onto the bed and started to cry.

"They were throwing stones at me. They said bad things. Why is everyone so against us? I am so sorry, Issa. I am so sorry."

"Mother, it's not your fault! But we do have friends. Look, Moshe is here, and Miryam from next door has come too."

"Mary, my dear friend Mary. Is she here? She's so kind. Do ask her to sing."

"Mother, Mary isn't here...' started Issa, but stopped when Miryam pulled at his sleeve.

"I could sing for her. I know a psalm that might help. I can't remember all the words, but I'll sing what I can for her."

She cleared her throat gently and took Sarah's hand, singing a soft gentle melody:

"She who hides in the shelter of the Lord Most High
will rest under the care of El Shaddai.

I will sing of him; my hiding place, my strong tower,
my God, in Him I trust.
He will save you from the trap of the wicked,
from deadly disease,
covering you with his gentle feathers,
for under His wings you will be safe;
you will be freed from the nighttime terrors
and the abuse and rocks thrown by day.
She will call on me;
I will answer.
I will be with her,
I will deliver and honour her."

Sarah was quiet and they thought she had fallen asleep, but when Miryam stopped she stirred.

"Sing 'Wait for the Lord'. I do love 'Wait for the Lord,'" she murmured without opening her eyes.

Miryam thought for a while, looking up at the rough beams of the ceiling as she mouthed words, trying to remember the lines of the song. Then she gathered herself and leaned forward, singing softly:

"The Lord is my light, the one who saves me.
Who is there to fear?
The Lord is my safe strong tower –
who can frighten me now?
When evil men plot terror against me,
when enemies attack me,
they will trip and fall.
One thing I would ask...
that I may have a place in the Lord's house for ever...
In days of danger, he will keep me safe...

though my father and even my mother leave me the Lord will care for me…

Be strong and take heart and wait for the Lord."

When the song ended, Sarah lay peacefully, the faintest smile on her face. There was now a glow in the east, and Miryam, seeing it through the small window, gave a sudden start.

"I must go now before the house wakes! If the dumb boy…"

"His name is Moshe."

"Sorry," apologised Miryam. "If Moshe sits with your mother, I will show you the hole in the wall and fetch some cloth for bandages."

They left by the back of the house. Miryam signalled Issa to be quiet as they neared the house, whispering, "Wait here till you see me safe into the ditch, then follow me. I will show you the hole."

She moved deftly and silently along the hillside, keeping low down so that she would not easily be seen from the house. When she reached the ditch, he saw her wave, and Issa hurried over to her, bending low to stay hidden. They waited a few moments in silence. Then Miryam pointed to a dark opening at the base of the wall. Reaching in, she pulled what Issa assumed was the goat skin towards her.

"The cloths will be here. I will get them to you either before or after singing. But now I must go." She smiled warmly and, crouching down, squeezed through the hole on her stomach.

"Just as well she's slight," he thought, noting her slender calves and small bare feet as she wriggled through. She was gone, but he stayed for a few moments, rather dazed by the evening's developments. His heart ached for his mother, but now he had an ally to help. Moshe was a loyal brother but the two boys were clumsy. Miryam would be able to give some feminine help to his mother. He thought of how he had dreamt of being so close to her, able to talk to her. But why did it have to be in such cruel circumstances?

Chapter 28

Issa crept back along the hill and soon reached his house. Sarah was still asleep and Moshe indicated that she had not moved.

Now that the initial drama was over, Issa realised how hungry he was. He indicated this to Moshe, who nodded, touched Issa on the shoulder and, pointing to the village, was gone.

He was soon back with some bread and a melon. The ancient law for the poor stated that someone like Moshe could eat fruit in the field in which it was grown; he was not supposed to carry it out. But Moshe bent the rules. He had taken a large slice out of the melon, eaten it before he left the field and thrown the rest over the wall, retrieving it later rather than letting it rot in the ditch.

He had these elaborate rules for getting round the system, which over time he had explained to Issa. Issa never tried them himself; Moshe was an expert and got away with it, probably by not ever being caught but ready to play the dumb imbecile. He certainly was no imbecile, but it was often convenient that the villagers regarded him as such.

Getting bread would have been more difficult, for Issa had long realised that Moshe never stole. He limited acquiring bread to the most pressing situations, probably playing on a previous favour or making the promise of help. Issa never asked. As ever the melon was large and well-chosen and the boys ate every scrap. It was not a lot for active boys but at least it filled a hole and gave them some energy to face the day.

Sarah had not improved overnight; if anything, she was less aware. The boys tried to get her to drink but she could not sit up to use a gourd cup. Moshe produced a cleanish handful of wool and by soaking it they could squeeze water onto her lips. Much of it ran away, but she swallowed the small amount entering her mouth. With practice the boys got better at it and tried to give her water regularly.

When the sun was just rising behind the hills, Issa went back to Miryam's wall. She was already singing by the time he arrived. They were the songs from the night before – Issa appreciated the gesture. He scrabbled down the bank of the ditch to the hole and found the cloths. He was struck by how clean and new they appeared. He wondered if these really were 'old cloths' as Miryam had said and hoped they would not be missed. He was amazed at how small the hole was and wondered how she could possibly have fitted through. He lay down and pushed his head in. He had to turn it to one side to fit and probably would not be able to get his shoulders through. But then, it needed to be as small as possible to avoid detection.

Back at the house he and Moshe tried to bandage Sarah's wounds, but it proved more difficult than they imagined. When they had first found her, she would stir and cry when moved, but she now showed little response.

They sat with her all day, taking turns to sleep and for Moshe to go and forage for food. As the evening drew on, Issa wondered if Miryam might come back, but he tried to put the thought from his mind. He kept nodding off and waking with a jerk as his head lolled over, so he rested his head on the bed next to his mother.

He woke with a start, instantly alert. His heart gave a jump when he heard a rustle from the door behind him. It was now quite dark, and the moon was again high in the sky.

"I have come," came a whisper, and the shadowy figure of Miryam passed behind the lamp.

"How is she?"

Issa shrugged. "Much the same. Worse, probably. She hasn't really spoken all day."

Miriam pulled out a cloth from under her cloak.

"I have brought some more oil and some food for you. I'm sorry I couldn't get more." There was a roast pumpkin, some lentil cake and four small flat loaves. "There was some stew left after supper, but I couldn't get a pot small enough to fit through the hole. The bread got a bit muddy too, I'm afraid, as the bundle unravelled on its way through."

Issa was so grateful. He and Moshe started on the food, dusting the mud off on their clothes. Miriam, quite at home, went to the other side of the bed and sat with Sarah, gently stroking her hair.

"Sarah, I have come. Hush, hush." She gently stroked her arm, then turned to Issa. "Do go and rest; I am happy to sit with your mother. Shall I dress the wounds again?" She had apparently noticed the clumsily applied bandages and started to remove them without waiting for a reply.

Though exhausted, the last thing Issa wanted was to miss any time with this angel of a girl. She couldn't have been more than sixteen, a little younger than he was, yet she was so in command of the situation.

"No. I'll stay with her as well. You must not overstay and be missed. You take a big risk coming."

The girl laughed quietly. "I like taking risks! The family are asleep. I could hear the old man and my uncle snoring. I sleep at the back of the house with one sister. She's my aunt really, though she is quite a few years younger than me. She's used to me coming in late and going out early. I have many chores to do while the family are asleep. That's how I earn my keep."

Issa was puzzled. That she should have chores was expected; that she should need to earn her keep was odd.

"Earn your keep?"

"My mother is dead. At least, I suppose she is. I am a granddaughter.

My mother ran away when she was young. Someone brought me back when I was a small child. I was wrapped in my mother's shawl, which they recognised. They say she has brought disgrace on the family, and though they took me in as I am their daughter's child, I have to earn my keep for being my father's child."

"Your father?"

"No one says who he was, or even if they know. They refer to my mother as if she was a prostitute. I think she was with a man who abandoned her. She would have had a hard life. Maybe she had to work the streets out of desperation."

"Or maybe because she was abandoned people assume she must be a prostitute like they do with my mother," said Issa grimly.

"Yes… exactly."

They were both quiet.

Miryam wiped Sarah's face tenderly. "I wonder if my mother was like yours. Your mother looks so lovely."

"She is," Issa said, choking a little. "She is so good to me… but I am not always kind to her. It wasn't her fault she was abandoned, but I often feel angry and resentful about it, especially that I have no father."

"I understand. At least I have a family to protect me, even if I am treated as the servant girl. Everyone seems to be against you. I heard about your fight with Bar-Simon. He's a friend of my uncle. They are so religious, so pious and self-righteous. I laughed when I heard how he had fallen in the mud. The family were scandalised and went on and on about how terrible you were. That made me want to find out more.

"Then I found the hole in the wall. I had found a way to escape onto the hill behind the house, even if it was just for a few minutes. I love the hills; I'd love to be able to roam in them like you do. Sometimes we go into the hills to collect wild plants for herbs with my grandmother. But it's best when I'm by myself in the early morning before the sun is up. My family don't know I go. My grandfather's a kind old man and he might turn a blind eye. He knows I am a bit rebellious and free-spirited. I think he loved my mother very dearly and he sees her in me. My uncle and my grandmother are really religious and strict. They would beat me and lock me up if they ever caught me! So I only stay out for a short time and only when they are still asleep. They're so pious that they pray at all sorts of silly hours and then sleep long into the morning! I used to sit on the hill behind both our houses and watch till your mother got up to attend to the fire. That's when I first saw you bounding up the hill with, um...?"

"Moshe," he reminded her.

"Yes. Moshe."

"I would have been going back to the sheep. I'm a shepherd." He tried to sound important.

"I guessed you were. I tried to find out about you and your mother but there was such disapproval. My grandfather would just say 'another wayward girl' rather wistfully. Then one day, I saw you at the feast. You were in the tree. I was going to sing something else but all I could think of was the song about the lover bounding over the hills like you did." Issa was taken aback by her frankness. He so wanted to hear more of the same. They were silent again, watching Sarah breathe laboriously.

"I loved your singing. I so felt like the lover in the song looking through the lattice."

She looked up cautiously, sensing where this was leading.

"I must be going," she said suddenly. "The night is far gone. I will sing for your mother before I go."

"I don't know if she will hear you."

"She may... but I'll sing for you too. There is a lovely one about God being like a shepherd in the hills." She leaned forward and stroked Sarah's cheek tenderly once more.

The song had a gentle melody, flexible enough to allow the words to be adapted. Issa instantly recognised it as one of the songs Daniel had sung. He had really liked it but had not been able to learn the words properly.

> "The Lord is my shepherd. What else do I need?
> He leads me to green pastures and cool still waters;
> he restores my soul.
> Even though I am in the dark valley of death, I will not fear evil
> For you are with me. You staff protects me; it doesn't beat me.
> There is a table before me laden with food that my enemies can see.
> My cup is full to overflowing with wine as at the feast.
> You anoint my wounded head with oil.
> Goodness, love and mercy will be with me all my days,
> for whatever happens I know I will dwell in God's house for ever."

They were quiet for a while. Miriam looked up at Issa. He was watching her out of the corner of his eye so he could look up at the same time. Their eyes met. Both were full of tears.

"Issa, I fear for your mother."

He wanted to accompany her back to the wall as he had on the previous night, but she was insistent that she should go alone to avoid problems. If for any reason her absence had been discovered, it would be essential that she was alone.

Issa was worried now. He had noticed his mother's breathing changing, becoming more laboured and rasping. She was not swallowing water anymore. All that morning they sat with her and through the hot afternoon. Her lips were encrusted and her eyes half open, but there was no response.

As the sun set behind the western hills, she stopped breathing. Issa shook his mother and called in her ear. He ran and woke Moshe, who came in bleary-eyed and a little disoriented. The boys had never been with a person who had died, but were used to animals succumbing, and they knew that Sarah had gone. Issa buried his head in his mother's breast and sobbed. Moshe, crying too with a high keening sound, put his strong arms around Issa and Sarah and held them both close. What was Issa to do? His mother had been such a constant in his life and now she was gone. He loved his life in the hills, but he loved coming home and being spoiled by his mother. A lonely, unknown future stretched before him.

Chapter 29

The next 24 hours were a blur in Issa's mind.

He needed to tell Miryam.

He went with Moshe to the neighbour's house and banged on the gate. The elder son, Miryam's uncle, came out.

"My mother has died!" he cried, sobbing.

The man was clearly shocked but not sure how to respond.

"Don't you understand? My mother is dead. The people have killed her!" Issa shouted again, even louder.

The man became defensive. "No one from this house was involved! I am sorry for you, but we can't be accused of murder. Be careful what you say."

Suddenly, there was an older man in the doorway. Issa recognised him from the feasts and guessed he must be Miryam's grandfather. He looked frailer now that he was sober, but still commanded respect.

"What's happening? What is it, boy?" he asked, seeing the distressed Issa at the gate.

"He is accusing us of killing his mother…"

"Be quiet, Judah! Let the boy speak."

"My mother has just died." Issa spoke quietly now, his voice heavy with sorrow, tears coursing down his cheeks. "Please help us! We don't know what to do."

By now the whole house had gathered in the courtyard. The elder son was protesting to his mother, who clicked her tongue, looking on disapprovingly. The old man turned on them.

"Can't you see that the boy's suffering because his mother has just died? If you can't be more helpful, woman, then go inside! Judah, bring me my stick."

The old woman turned, grumbling, into the house; the son returned, handing the old man his stick rather ungraciously.

"Be careful, Father, these sort of people can be dangerous when angry," he warned, before releasing the cane to the old man's grasp.

"Then you stay away and don't provoke them!" he growled.

The old man accompanied the boys; Miryam stealing along behind. They came to where Sarah's body lay. Miryam's lamp was burning on the table, but the old man didn't recognise it, his eyesight failing.

"My boy, I am so sorry. Your mother has been badly treated. Whatever anyone's opinion, she is still someone's mother... someone's daughter," he added quietly. Miryam, by his side, looked up at his face, searching for a deeper meaning. "I'm sorry you have had no help, boy. I never realised how badly hurt she was."

"Grandfather, we can help now. Issa is so upset. They are just lads; they won't know what to do," put in Miryam carefully, not ready yet to confess that she had been helping them over the last two nights.

He turned to looked at her again, clearly wondering how she was familiar with the boy's name. Miryam coloured at the mistake, but it didn't show in the twilight.

"Ay, ay, ay. So sad. Boys, you will need to dig a grave." Issa looked at his feet, then around the house. The old man understood. "Do you have a spade? I thought not," he added, not waiting for a reply.

The boys only had their knives and the stout sticks they used to dig shallow holes to bury excrement. There were some wooden hoes somewhere that Sarah used on her vegetable patch, but no other tools. Out on the hills, when they needed to be rid of an animal carcass, it was thrown in a gully and left for the vultures and wild animals. They had never had cause to dig a grave.

Turning to Miryam, he ordered, "Go and tell your uncle to get the mattock and the spade. Then go and prepare some food for the boys... Something they can take to eat on the hill where they will need to dig the grave." The last part was shouted after her as she hurried to obey.

He watched her go, then turned and eyed Issa closely.

"So, how does she know your name, boy?"

Issa blinked, puzzled by the question, but had the presence of mind to cover up for Miryam's mistake.

"My mother loved her singing. My mother goes... used to go... to the well. Maybe they talked." He shrugged. He was past caring what the old man thought.

The old man let it pass.

"Look, boy, get a straight stick and measure how long and wide your mother is. You will need to dig a hole for her to fit into. Dig it as deep as she is tall. At the bottom, dig sideways along the whole length far enough so that there's a small chamber to slide her into. You can then put rocks into the hole beside her without damaging her body. When you have filled in the hole with soil, if a wild animal should dig down through the soft earth it won't be able to get past the rocks." He was business like and practical, obviously having buried several family members during his long life. "It's already sundown now, so you have until tomorrow evening to complete it. Do you have any male relatives to help you with the burial?"

"We have no-one. My mother has no family... and no real friends. They say she is, was, a prostitute because her husband left her. But she was a good kind woman! She was my mother and a mother to Moshe!" he blurted out angrily and with a sob. The old man was silent. He had no answer to the accusation. Issa made an effort to control himself. "I do have a master: Daniel Bar David. I am apprenticed as his shepherd boy. He has always been good to us."

The old man thought for a few moments. "Yes, I know of him. He is a known to be a good man. Is he far away?"

"About three hours walk, less if you run."

"Would the dumb boy be able to find him?"

"Moshe," corrected Issa. "His name is Moshe." He said it again, this time loudly enough for Miryam to hear as she returned with the spade and mattock. After the blunder with his name, he wanted to avoid a repetition.

Her grandfather took the mattock and turned to Moshe to give him practical instructions, so Miryam had the chance to take a long look at Issa. Her eyes filled with tears as she mouthed,

"I am so sorry," turning away quickly before her grandfather could notice, hurrying back to the house to prepare the food.

The boys chose a spot on the hill in a dip close behind the house but out of sight of the road and any other dwellings. They did not know how the villagers would react, so they wanted to avoid any contact. The moon was now three-quarters full and high in the sky so they started straight away. They had a willow branch marked with notches for the length and width, and they had already cut through the hard compacted surface marking out the shape of the finished grave when Miryam arrived with another girl, carrying some food for them.

They stopped for a break, eating half-heartedly but gratefully. They needed the energy for the digging and had hardly eaten for the last two days. The girls sat on a nearby boulder while the boys dug. Miryam sang quietly, a sad melody, a lament probably, but Issa could not catch the words. Although nothing passed between them, Issa was grateful for her presence. After some time the old grandfather appeared and gruffly sent the girls back to the house. They obediently did so, stopping to for a long look back before disappearing behind the crest.

It took several hours of digging in the stony soil before the grave was finished. At last, the boys could get some sleep. In the morning the old man inspected it, pronouncing it adequate. The boys had collected larger stones ready to fill in the base. The old man eased himself heavily onto the pile of earth.

He turned to Moshe. "Away now and fetch Daniel," he ordered, forgetting that the lad couldn't hear a word.

Issa quickly signed and Moshe set off, first to the house to have a drink of water and collect his staff before beginning his mission. In spite of having had little sleep for three nights and having worked hard on the grave and now having to walk three hours into the hills, he showed no resentment. He was tough and would probably run all the way.

Once he had gone, the old man motioned for Issa to sit beside him. They were quiet for some time.

"Boy, I had a daughter who went away, but unlike your mother she never came back and I never saw her again. It broke my heart. Then someone brought a child to us. She was wearing a headscarf as a shawl, which we recognised as one my wife had woven for our daughter. My wife has never forgiven our daughter for running away and is still bitter. Miryam, who was here just now, she is my daughter's child. My wife is rather hard on her. She thinks our daughter became a prostitute and Miryam is a child of sin. But I think she ran away for love, to be with a man. We never found out what happened except that she died, leaving the child an orphan. Foolish. Tragic. But not wicked."

He was quiet for a long time. Then he continued still more softly, looking into the distance as if to where his daughter may have been.

"My daughter would have been about your mother's age... I did not bury my daughter, nor was I allowed to grieve for her." He stopped, a little choked. "Boy, would you let me... do me the honour of letting me... be with you when you bury your mother?"

"Sir, it would help me to have you with us. We won't know what to do," replied Issa, touched by the old man's openness. He thought for a long moment before asking tentatively, "I know that it is usual for men to sing at the graveside, but would you let your granddaughter sing for my mother? She did so love her singing."

The old man was quiet for some time. "We all love her singing. Have you heard her sing?"

Issa decided to trust the old man.

"I have heard her at the feasts. I sometimes hear her singing in your compound."

"Do you come to specially to hear her sing? I have seen you on the hill behind the house in the early morning and wondered what you were doing." The old man smiled and stood to go. "I am so sorry for you boy. I hope your master will be here soon. Tell me when you are ready." He turned, looking kindly at Issa, and held out his hand.

Issa took his hand shyly.

It was the first time any man in the village had ever taken his hand in friendship.

Chapter 30

Daniel arrived late in the afternoon and without a word followed Issa into the house to where Sarah lay. Miryam and her sister had done their best in preparation of Sarah's body, though as Issa was poor and could not afford any spices, this did not amount to much more than washing her body and covering it with wild aromatic leaves they had collected from bushes around the village. They had wrapped her carefully in one of her better cloaks, tying it round with strips of cloth to make it secure. Daniel stood for a long time with his head bowed and when he turned back his eyes were full and his face streaked with tears. Sarah would have to be buried before evening as the law required and it was now only a couple of hours to sundown. Miryam's grandfather was now present and, holding each corner of her blanket, the four men carried Sarah's emaciated body gently to the graveside.

Daniel composed himself as best he could, quoting words from the scriptures with long pauses, his voice breaking. Miryam, accompanied by her sister, sang a lament as requested; her grandfather stood on the other side of the grave with the boys. Normally interments were men-only affairs, but norms did not apply here. The old man joined in singing a dirge, which was effectively a duet with Daniel, as no one else knew it, having never been to a funeral before.

Placing Sarah's body into the grave was a struggle. Eventually Moshe squeezed into the grave beside her body, tenderly tucking her into the slot at the base. He emerged covered in soil, tears making muddy streaks down his dusty face. They piled the large stones into the grave alongside her to seal her in, shovelling the loose soil on top. The girls stood some distance away as the grave was filled in, Miryam quietly singing.

When it was all done, Issa wandered listlessly back to the house followed by the girls and the old men. Issa stoked up the fire as the evening was drawing in and sat wearily on a stool, looking into the flames. Moshe sat on his heel opposite him. The girls continued on with the two old men, who walked together to the neighbour's house in deep discussion. Some time later, Daniel returned, drew up another stool and sat with the boys. They sat quietly for some time. Daniel spoke first.

"I am so sorry, Issa. This is a badly done. I will speak with the village elders in the morning." He remembered bitterly his recent discussions with them. "They will need to investigate. I understand there are no witnesses, and we need at least two who agree. But we can at least try to get some justice."

"It won't bring my mother back," countered Issa with a cough and a sob.

"No," agreed Daniel sadly, "but the village needs to take this seriously."

"It's nothing new. They have always been against us. They call me a bastard and my mother a prostitute. Then they wouldn't let Mother attend the feasts. Now they have killed her. There is no one to care for the house. I don't know what will come of it."

"One day at a time, boy. We all need to rest now. I will come back in the morning."

True to his word, Daniel came in the morning and they went to the village square where the elders had gathered. Miryam's grandfather was there as well. The elders heard the report formally, but as there were no witnesses who came forward there was no one to accuse. Daniel protested in vain, and though one or two looked uncomfortable, the meeting broke up with no redress.

Issa took little interest in the proceedings in any case. He was still numb and walked sadly home with Moshe. He had become used to injustice. He collected his few things from the house and walked back into the village to Daniel's small house near the caves.

"I'm going back to the sheep," he told him dully.

"There's no rush, boy. I've arranged for the others to care for them. I'll go back tomorrow. We could go together."

"I want to go now. Why would I stay in the village? I need to be in the hills away from this evil place. I need to be alone," he retorted bitterly.

Daniel was troubled and looked at the distraught young man. He had the face of a little boy who so needed his mother.

"Is the dumb boy going with you?"

"Don't know," he replied sullenly, although he knew full well that Moshe would be at his side.

Chapter 31

A deep sadness settled over Issa in those early weeks and he completed his daily chores mechanically. Moshe had returned to Bethlehem, indicating that he would watch the house. Issa did not really care one way or the other. The dry summer was on its way and Daniel moved the flock further into the hills to the well where he knew there would be some pasture. He had suffered bereavement himself, but life was tough in the hills and there were practical everyday realities which must be faced.

The sadness gradually congealed to a lump deep inside Issa's chest, which from time to time would rise to choke him and he would go off by himself to weep. Daniel was sensitive to these times and made allowances, arranging for him to have time alone but not be far away in case he was needed.

A few months later, when they were sitting round the fire, Issa seemed in a better place.

"Are you hoping to go back to Bethlehem for the feast?"

Issa did not answer immediately.

"There is nothing for me in Bethlehem. I'm not sure I can face the feasts anymore."

"There was a girl."

"Huh!"

"Was she the one who sang by the grave?"

Issa threw a stone angrily.

"She was kind to me. She sings nicely. But what's the point?"

"I think there might be a lot of point. Her grandfather seemed kindly disposed to you."

Issa had been thinking a lot about Miryam; fantasising, but not able to make the dreams into any plan that might work.

"What can I offer a girl? I am a shepherd boy. I have no money."

"You still have your mother's property."

"I have a house, but I don't have a home. If my mother had been alive… but now…" he trailed off, throwing another stone viciously into the darkness.

"Does the girl feel the same way about you?"

He thought of how she had looked out for him coming home, how she said she sang songs inspired by his leaping from crag to crag, how she had stumbled into his arms in the darkness and risked her reputation to help him with his mother. Was she just a kind person? He thought of the looks and smiles. Might this be love? But he knew nothing of how a girl's mind worked.

"Look, boy, when you're feeling better, go back to Bethlehem and try and talk to the old man. I'm getting older and soon will need you to take on the flock. It may be that you have to wait a little while, but if he knows your mind and is in agreement, she may yet be your wife."

Issa listened carefully. Could it be? He said nothing. Eventually he got to his feet.

"I'll go and check the lambs. Then I'll sleep."

Daniel smiled in the darkness.

"Don't forget my words."

There was no chance of that!

Issa really did not want to go to the feasts, even though it might mean he could see Miryam. He would wait until the autumn rains, then he could slip into Bethlehem from time to time when they were nearby on the hills and the days were shorter. Maybe he could meet her on the hills if she was still using the hole in the wall.

But it was to be many years before he returned to Bethlehem.

Chapter 32

They were now in the far desert overlooking the Arabah. The other shepherds had travelled to their favourite places in the Negev where there were other wells. Issa kept looking out for John or his mother, but as yet there had been no sign of them. From the crest of a ridge, he watched lazily as the sheep scoured the ground for the few plants there were for grazing. Suddenly he froze! His sharp eyes had noticed a shadow flit past a boulder. He watched the spot closely and then slid behind the crest. He scurried fifty yards along the ridge, removed his headdress and carefully crawled on his front to look back over the edge. There was a man creeping out from behind the shoulder of the hill opposite. He couldn't see him clearly, but knew it was neither John nor one of the Essenes, who would have had no reason to hide. He was obviously not a Roman, so he could be a bandit or a Zealot – or a mixture of the two. Fortunately the sheep were all on the hill away from the stranger and towards Daniel's encampment. Issa whistled once, short and sharp to call them together. Thankfully they all responded and he led them quickly down into a gully where they would be more hidden, then along and back round towards Daniel and the corralled kids and lambs. He waved urgently placing his hand over his mouth as he approached, in a warning to Daniel that all was not well. Issa told what he had seen and Daniel sighed.

"Maybe he didn't see you. We'll just try and keep a low profile. There is no way we can outrun anyone with a flock to manage."

They came in the evening as the sun was setting.

They had obviously been watching them, for the men arrived from several directions at once and soon they were surrounded by a group of bearded tough-looking warriors.

"Zealots," said Daniel under his breath.

Issa wondered how he knew. It was only later that he learned that Zealots kept the old laws regarding trimming of beards and hair, which made them distinctive from the lawless bandits.

There was a bit of relief in Daniel's voice as he called a friendly greeting, though Issa sensed he was quite tense. He had explained to Issa that the Zealots might steal from them, but rarely did them any physical harm.

There were five men and they all carried long knives. Four squatted in a circle surrounding them while the fifth came and stood by the fire.

"We've seen you here for a few days and have made sure you were safe. We have done the same for the last couple of years, though you may not have seen us, so we wondered if you could return the compliment with some sheep."

Daniel paused before answering. "That might be possible. How many do you need?"

"We expect friends, so need about twenty animals."

"Twenty is a lot of beasts. That will be almost a quarter of my flock."

"You have so many? Maybe you cold spare us thirty animals then."

"And if I don't have thirty to spare?"

"We'll take what we need anyway, but of course we can't really guarantee that the others won't be taken by a wild animal, or worse, over the next little while."

The message was clear. There was no point arguing. Daniel turned to Issa.

"Boy, separate out the sheep as the man says." He turned back to the Zealot. "I presume they are for slaughter, so we will give you all male animals."

"Sure. That way we can ensure a good supply if we need them next year!"

Daniel kept his cool and Issa hurried to do his bidding. The sheep were all together in a depression in the hill and it was now dark, so it took Issa some time to separate out the male animals, having to feel the rear ends of some, but others he knew well. He tried to choose the smaller and less good breeding stock and it was some time before he had them sorted. He had counted out 28, reckoning that with the sheep milling around in the dark it would be difficult for the Zealots to check. He stood with the animals, expertly keeping them together while milling around him so they would be difficult to count.

"Thirty?"

"Yes mister, but I'm not very good at counting always," Issa lied. He knew very well exactly how many he had.

The sheep began to wander away, so Issa whistled and using his staff soon had them back as a group.

"Impressive, young man," remarked the leader, genuinely impressed. "I think it might be good if you came along as well, to help us with the sheep. We are better at rounding up legionaries!" He turned to Daniel "We'll take the boy with us. He'll be back late tomorrow. We're just down by the springs."

Daniel presumed that they were at En Gedi and was a little alarmed. It was too obvious a place to hide, and the Romans must have checked it out regularly. It was why he had stopped going down to the springs himself many years before.

"Mind you care for the boy. He's a good lad."

"We've cared for him up till now, though you may not have realised it."

You weren't around when I needed you a few months ago, thought Issa bitterly. He wondered if the 'justice' the Zealots fought for would have extended to his mother's situation or were they just as bad as the villagers.

Daniel came and embraced Issa.

"God be with you, my boy," he whispered. "Watch for Romans. If you can, run! I will start for Bethlehem immediately. You can outrun the Zealots, and the Romans unless they have horses, and you will easily catch up with me."

"What are you telling the boy?"

"It's a psalm we say together.

'I will look to the hills?
Where does my help come from?
My help comes from the Lord.'

"Amen," said the leader. "I think it goes on, 'He who watches over you will not slumber or sleep.' That's us!"

Daniel grunted and squeezed Issa's arm. Issa was encouraged by his confidence, but inside they both felt fear and foreboding.

The group travelled through the night. As the sky brightened behind the eastern hills of Arabia, they began the descent into the hot and humid rift valley of the Arabah. The sea was clear and shining in the dawn light and they went on cautiously now, alert. As they came over a crest, they saw the silhouette of someone on a ridge a hundred metres away.

"That looks like Eli. He was on sentry duty last night."

The figure did not move and presumably had not seen them. They carried on down the slope as one of them ran on and up the hill to where the sentry was posted. His head was bowed and he did not move. The leader spat.

"He has fallen asleep at his post. We'll have to deal with that later."

The Zealot approached the sentry, stopping 20 metres away before turning and rushing wildly back the way he had come, shouting and waving.

"Run! Run! Romans! It's a trap!" He fell forward as an arrow pierced his back and Roman soldiers appeared over the ridge.

"Run for your lives! Regroup at Elgodgi!" shouted the leader.

Issa needed no second command. He didn't know where Elgodgi was and didn't care. He must get back to Daniel. With second nature he wasted a few precious seconds looking round for the sheep, then realising the stupidity of this, left them to their own ends and scampered up the hillside. There were Romans appearing all around and Issa desperately looked for a way through. Wherever he headed, he found he was cut off. He saw one of the Zealots lying motionless on the ground and another cut down as he tried to make a break, and realising that it was hopeless, stopped, fell on his knees and put up his hands in surrender. A legionary came up to him, giving him a blow to the head with the butt of his sword. Issa fell to the ground feeling sick and terrified. The soldier quickly removed his knife and slingshot then tied his hands behind his back with a leather thong, dragging him to his feet and pushing him towards the other soldiers who had the leader on the ground and were tying him too. The other Zealots lay still. The soldiers rolled them over with their feet, laughing and kicking their dead bodies.

"Leave them for the vultures."

Using their spears, they drove Issa and the leader, who had gash on his neck bleeding freely, ahead of them. As they crossed the ridge by the sentry, they realised why he had not seen them. He was long dead, with his throat cut, his body propped up by stones. They went down a valley and soon came to the upper pools of Engedi. There had obviously been a skirmish here; they stepped over the dead body of a Zealot on the path and another was floating in the pool. Further down there were more bodies and, though cold comfort to the leader, he saw there were some dead Romans also. At least they had been able to put up something of a fight. As they got to the end of the valley where it opened up to the sea Issa saw, to his dismay, bodies hanging from crosses. He felt sick and terrified. There were some other prisoners sitting on the ground while Romans cut and fashioned crude crosses out of the trees of the valley.

"Here are two more. Hope you won't be hanging around too long!" He laughed unpleasantly.

Terrified now, Issa was pushed to the ground with the Zealot. A cross was soon ready and they dragged the Zealot leader over, ripping off his clothes and spreading his arms, lashing them to the cross-beam. Issa's mouth was dry. He knew he was next! He could see his cross being fastened together.

A centurion came over to supervise the execution.

"So, you had gone for sheep. Well you won't be needing those where you are going."

The Zealot leader strained to look at the terrified and white-faced Issa.

"Look. This is just a shepherd boy. We forced him to bring his flock with us. He is not one of us. Have mercy on him."

"He'll become a bandit like you, given the chance. But thanks for bringing the sheep. It's a while since we had some meat. We'll need to be here for a few days, seeing off you criminals."

The Zealot tried again. He had seen a few sheep being brought down from the hills and realised that most of them were scattered in the desert.

"How many sheep did you get, three, four? The sheep know the boy. He'll round up them up for you."

The centurion watched as the cross was thrown heavily on the ground next to Issa. Two soldiers held him while the third removed his bonds. They stretched him out on the cross. He could feel the rough wood and splinters cut into his back. They were about to rip off his clothes when the centurion ordered them to stop.

"On second thoughts, it may be worthwhile having some more sheep. If you really are a shepherd boy and can retrieve the sheep, we'll see if we can spare you."

He barked an order and two of the soldiers pulled Issa to his feet, tying a rope to his ankle. "Don't even think about trying to escape."

Issa knew that his life depended on him finding enough sheep to satisfy the centurion.

The soldiers, grumbling in the heat, went back up the valley and were soon at the spot where the bodies of the three Zealots lay. The vultures were already overhead. Issa pointed to a hillock, gesturing. The soldiers understood and led him there. From the height, he could see for a distance. He whistled. And prayed! Presently, a sheep's head appeared, then another from behind a thorn bush, alert, looking around. Issa recalled the shepherd song Miryam had sung, and tried to remember the words. 'The Lord is my shepherd. He finds my sheep by the waters and pastures,' or something. There was a bit about 'the valley of death' and he felt he was in it. 'Goodness and mercy' came into it somewhere too, and he prayed for both. He whistled again and this time the sheep looked in his direction, starting to trot towards him, followed by four more. They stopped, looking suspiciously at the group. One of the Romans spoke some Aramaic, so Issa was able to explain that he would need space in order to round them up. The soldiers deliberated, eventually agreeing, but first taking the precaution of tying his legs together, leaving him room to walk but making it impossible to run away. He brought the five sheep to the Romans, then found six together a little further on. The soldiers sat under some shade, watching while Issa worked until, by midday, he had found seventeen in total. He had considered making a run for it and trying to cut the leg tie, but decided that escape was futile, and it would be best to cooperate.

The centurion was impressed when they returned and the soldiers seemed to give a good report. Issa was taken off to find pasture for the flock, thankful that he did not have to watch the death throes of the dozen or so Zealots hanging on the crosses, though it was impossible not to hear their agonised screams and cries, which went on all through the night. As each hour passed, Issa felt more confident that he would be spared crucifixion – but what then? They might just cut his throat. He felt growing hatred for the Romans, but from years of being ostracised in Bethlehem he knew not to antagonise. To maintain a low profile would be the best way to keep out of trouble.

After three days, when the last of the Zealots had been taken down from the crosses, the soldiers gathered their equipment, ready to leave. Being a small detachment, they had stayed together, fearing a counter-attack by Zealots. Now that there was a flock of sheep in tow, the centurion decided to take Issa with them to care for them.

"But don't get the wrong idea. You are still a condemned man. Behave yourself and you may become a slave rather being executed. What is your name, boy?"

"Issa."

"This is the army, lad, we don't use first names. What is your family name?"

"I don't have one... don't use one."

"Do you have a father?"

"Yes. But I don't know him. He lives in Arabia."

"An Arab stallion, I see."

Issa ignored the jibe. "No, he was Jewish. He came to Bethlehem for the census. He married my mother and took her to Arabia but abandoned her."

"So, you don't know his name?"

"His name was Abbas. I heard my mother talk of him."

"Abbas... Abbas. Hmm." He called one of the soldiers over. "Make out a certificate of imprisonment for this man."

"What name shall I put on it, sir?"

"His father was Abbas. Put him down as... Barabbas."

The soldier guarding Issa pulled him roughly to his feet.

"Come on, Barabbas!" he mocked, pushing Issa towards the squad of legionaries. "Get your sheep into formation!"

As the column marched away, with Issa in the middle with his little flock, a figure broke from behind a distant clump of trees and watched them go.

It was Moshe.

Barabbas

Chapter 33

It was twelve years later. Two travellers appeared over the hills behind Bethlehem in the late afternoon of a winter day. They were wrapped against a cold wind and drizzle which would have kept most people at home. Rather than hurrying into the village to look for lodging, the two stopped for some time on a hillside above it, examining the ground and moving aside the scrub. Just below them were the ruins of a dwelling; some of the mud walls still stood, but most of the timbers had been scavenged. After a while the two figures reached the dwelling, spending some time poking around the ruins. Eventually they moved on down the road, pausing briefly at a larger but rather ramshackle house next to the ruined one, before heading into the village.

Passing the inns in the village centre, they made for a small house in a sorry state of disrepair just below a steep hill. By way of a door, sacking hung over the entrance and the mud bricks of the walls were worn away by the rain running unimpeded off the roof. At the entrance, one of them called out while the other held back. Eventually the sacking was pulled back by an elderly man who peered at the two strangers outside.

"What do you want?" he asked gruffly.

"Daniel?" enquired the visitor. "Daniel! Don't you recognise me?"

"I don't see a lot these days, but the voice… I may know the voice!"

"Daniel, it's me; Issa. Your shepherd boy."

"Issa? Issa?" He reached for the door frame for support.

"But Issa is dead. What is this about Issa?" he barked hoarsely.

"No Daniel. I am Issa, and this is Moshe. You remember. You used to call him 'the dumb lad.'"

"Come in; come in; I need to sit down." The old man beckoned with a trembling hand and he led them into the one-room house, sitting heavily on a large chair padded with some old clothes. He motioned to a bench and the two travellers sat down, putting their blanket rolls at their feet.

"Now tell me what's this you are saying. How can you be Issa? Issa is dead. He was crucified at En Gedi."

"How do you know, Daniel? Did you find his body?"

"No. I didn't. But we found some of the sheep in the desert and some of the shepherds bravely went down to Engedi where they found the remains of the crosses and the bodies. They were badly decomposed, half eaten by wild beasts. They buried them hurriedly in shallow graves, fearful in case the Romans returned."

"Daniel. I am Issa. They didn't crucify me in the end. I was kept alive to manage the sheep, then taken as a slave."

Daniel looked hard and closely through his dim eyes at Issa, still unconvinced.

"Look, why would I lie? I have nothing to gain. Who would want to pretend to be me anyway? My mother was poor and regarded as a prostitute. She had died shortly before I disappeared. She had an accident. You remember? You helped me bury her."

Daniel was quiet.

Issa went over to him and said softly, "'I lift my eyes to the hills, Where does my help come from? My help comes from the Lord…' That was the last thing I heard you say."

Daniel reached out his hand for Issa's and gripped it desperately.

"My boy! My boy! Is it really you? Have you really come back? Oh my boy, my boy!" he cried, his voice breaking. He composed himself and went on. "But things are not the same. My sheep are all gone. I found I couldn't manage without you. Gradually I lost more and more sheep, and now look at me!" He let Issa's hand go, throwing up his own. He laughed ruefully. "I couldn't see the sheep now anyway."

Issa looked around at the sparsely furnished room. A small fire burned in one corner, the smoke escaping through a hole in the roof. Daniel's shepherd's staff still hung over the door.

"How do you manage, Daniel?"

"I have some family in Bethlehem. My cousin's children, and some of my wife's family. They're kind to me but they are poor also. I can't do a lot, so I don't need much to eat. At least they bring me firewood and water. But you boy! You aren't a boy any longer, you're a full-grown man now. And is this the dumb boy?" he asked, taking Moshe's hand, who grinned self-consciously.

"When he disappeared too, we reckoned he'd somehow got involved and was crucified as well."

Issa thought bitterly that no one would have cared much about either of them, so no one would have taken the trouble to find out if it were their bodies among the Zealots found by the Arabah.

"I felt so guilty that I had put you in danger. I don't know how I could ever have told your mother. It would have broken her heart." Daniel went quiet. He stared at the ground in front of him, reflecting quietly. "I couldn't understand why God had allowed your mother to die and leave you alone, but maybe he spared her the heartbreak of losing you… I have never been by your old home. Too painful. Too sad."

They were both quiet for some time. Then Issa sighed. "We went by the house. It's all a ruin now. We looked for mother's grave but there is nothing there."

There was a long silence, then Daniel put his hand on Issa's knee.

"So, they didn't kill you. But tell me, boy, what happened to you? You've been a prisoner. Are you a runaway?" he asked anxiously.

"No. I have served my sentence. I am free now, thanks to Moshe. He always turns up when we most need him."

Issa told him everything: from the first encounter with the Romans, the crucifixions, how the Zealot chief had managed to save him and how he had been made a prisoner.

In the journey up the Jordan Valley, the Romans had demanded food and provisions from the poor villagers, plundering and leaving many homes destitute. They had carefully kept within their 'code' by provoking the people until they reacted and then 'justifiably' suffered retribution for their protests. The soldiers joked about the small flock under Issa's care, taking every opportunity to steal another sheep or goat to add to it, expecting him to keep the disparate group together. If an animal strayed, they would curse and cuff him. He lived in a mixture of pain from his shackles on the long marches, fear of the retribution from the legionaries and misery for the plight of the villagers and his part in herding their animals, for which he felt treacherous.

The soldiers became more circumspect in their behaviour as they passed through more populous Galilee, but the pace was relentless until, with some relief, Issa was confined in a garrison prison while he waited for his case to come up before the magistrate who would decide his fate. The centurion wanted to formalise things and keep Issa as his personal slave, which filled him with dread. The other inmates of the lock-up, mostly petty criminals, listened to his story with respect. The exploits of the Zealots were legendary, though they seldom ventured into this busy part of Palestine. They discussed what fate awaited Issa and he soon realised, from the way they looked away, that a death sentence would not be unexpected. He spent sleepless nights under the terror of an agonising execution, or possibly a hard life as a slave of the centurion whose harsh treatment of the legionaries under his command made that a bleak prospect too.

Eventually, in chains and between two guards, he was taken before the magistrate. The case was conducted in Latin and though Issa could not understand what was said, it was clear the centurion was not getting his way and was angry. Finally, the magistrate pointed at Issa, gravely uttering his sentence, at which the centurion stormed out of the courtroom. With a dry mouth and pounding heart Issa stumbled back to the jail, presuming that, as the centurion had been denied, he had received the death sentence. The jailer, who spoke some Aramaic, unlocked the gate, looking inquiringly with raised eyebrows at the guards, who detailed briefly the sentence Issa had received. Issa pulled at his chains to detain the guards, desperately clutching at the jailer's cloak.

"Please! Please! What did they say? I didn't understand. Am I to die?" he cried in terror, his voice breaking, eyes wild with fear.

The jailer shook him off, closing the heavy gate.

"No, boy. The magistrate has a share in a quicksilver mine in Asia," he called over his shoulder. "He sends any prisoner he can to work there. You have been sentenced to 10 years labour in that mine."

As the guards dragged him away and the gate crashed shut, the jailer muttered in a mocking echo, "10 years… if you live that long. You may end up wishing they had killed you."

Issa was transferred to a ship and chained below decks in the cramped, foetid hold, amidst the cargo. There was little room to move and the heat was stifling. Eventually they set sail, and though there was some relief from the breeze that blew through the hold, on many days the sea was rough, adding seasickness to the sufferings of the prisoners, making their grim conditions even more unbearable. Sometimes they stopped at a port where they were disembarked to help unload or load the cargo. At least that meant they got some fresh air and could wash their vomit-sodden clothes and exercise their stiffened limbs.

After a few weeks trading along the coast, they arrived at a wharf where all the prisoners were taken ashore. This was quite unlike any of the other ports. Emaciated men were working beyond the jetty, carrying loaded baskets of deep red ore, or breaking them ready to be loaded into a smelter which belched out acrid smelling fumes. As they toiled to and fro, they watched the new arrivals listlessly. So these were the mines where he could expect to spend the next 10 years. Cutting deep into the cliff which overhung it, the mine's shafts and tunnels followed the seams still further into the hillside. Crude, lean-to shelters were built against the quarry edge; the stone building in the centre was obviously the guard room or administration block. The cliffs above towered sheer and high, and as Issa strained his stiff neck trying to visualise the top, a whip cracked, stinging his back. He hurried after the other prisoners to get out of range. Further visual exploration would have to wait. They were ordered to strip, then sluiced down with sea water before being examined like cattle in a market. Finally, with their legs hobbled with light chains, mercifully in leather anklets rather than shackles, they were assigned to their work detail.

Being young and strong, Issa was given the job of raising the loaded baskets from the mineshaft and carrying them to the smelter, a task which probably saved his life. The smelter was sited downwind of the prevailing breeze, as it had long since been realised that the fumes were toxic. Knowing this, if the wind changed, Issa took the trouble to make a detour to keep out of the fumes, even though it meant a longer journey with the heavy basket, but few others had the freedom of movement to do this. Many of the older men worked in cramped conditions, digging and filling small baskets with the ore. The dust irritated their lungs and Issa would hear them coughing all night. But a more deadly sign was the onset of the shakes. Over time, the workers developed a tremor which became more pronounced, together with increasing disorientation and confusion. If these did not result in a fatal accident, the sufferer's decline was inexorable and eventually the affected prisoner, unable to get up from their bedroll, would be dragged away and pitched over the cliff into the sea below.

There were frequent beatings for minor infractions, but after initial mistakes, Issa learnt the ropes and generally kept out of trouble. The food was inadequate and living conditions harsh. Whilst most of the men slept on straw in one of the shelters, Issa, accustomed to the vast Judean desert, sought out an open space on a ledge where he could at least sleep under the stars. Although escape seemed impossible, Issa knew it was his only hope of survival. But it would be make or break. The guards paid for any escape attempt with their own lives, so were ruthless in their control of the prisoners. As the only path out of the mine was closely guarded, any escape would have to be up the imposing cliffs, which Issa carefully reconnoitred. The lower slopes he examined covertly at night, scanning the upper crags from the seashore, where he made a point of going before each meal to 'perform ceremonial washing'. It was accepted that Jews had elaborate purification rites, so these habits did not arouse suspicion. Eventually he identified a route that might just be possible along some ledges and cracked seams. But would he ever have the opportunity to try? Could he do it in leg chains, anyway?

As his second winter in captivity began, the anxiety and mood swings that Issa was increasingly suffering made him suspect that the evil red rock was beginning to affect his mind.

Late one night, he awoke from a vivid dream. He was back in the hold of the ship on the storm-tossed sea. Waking with a cry, he found not the ocean, but the land heaving to and fro! There were thunderous roars, rocks crashing down, narrowly missing him as he scrambled desperately for shelter by a large boulder. After what seemed an age the earthquake stopped and he got unsteadily to his feet, gasping at the scene before him. The whole cliff above the mine had collapsed over the entrance burying the smelter, the guardhouse and the miners. Nothing and no one could have escaped.

In an instant, he saw his opportunity! Running and scrambling across fallen rocks, he made for the start of the climb, but among the new landslips and boulders, had he found the right spot? The hobbling chain impeded him, but with care he manage to scale the rock face, finding, to his relief, the first ledge of his planned route. The cracked seam from there was narrow but sufficient for hand holds. He felt with his toes carefully, aware that the shocks may have dislodged the crumbling rock face. As he reached the second narrow ledge, he rested his cramped muscles and took stock, desperately trying to recall the details of the route he had gone over and over in his mind as he planned his escape.

Suddenly, he froze: he could hear shouting! Two guards with drawn swords were hurrying down the path just twenty metres below him! He knew his fate should he be caught – in the bright moonlight, he would be clearly visible. His heart in his mouth, he crept along the ledge in a futile attempt to find some cover. A rock fell as he scrabbled against the cliff face, and there was a cry from below – he had been spotted! He swarmed along the fault, starting to climb frantically, all thoughts of the planned route lost from his mind. As he did so, a strong after-shock dislodged stones around him and he felt himself slipping. He grabbed frantically for a hand hold, crying out in panic. Mercifully his hand closed over a small bush and he held on desperately praying it would hold as his feet kicked and found a foothold and he pulled himself onto a narrow ledge. From here he looked back to the two guards, but they had lost interest in him and were struggling for their own lives. The path beneath their feet was giving way following the aftershock and with a great crash, a section of the cliff slipped into the sea, taking the two men with it. Even above the roar of the rockfall he could hear their screams. Then there was silence, while more stones and dirt poured down on top of them.

Lying for some time and panting from the effort, wide-eyed from his narrow escape and the terrifying thought of another landslip carrying him with it in the same way, Issa froze, trying to take stock whilst not daring to move lest he should dislodge more rocks. Were there more guards further up the path who might have heard the alarm raised by the other two? He could not see beyond the landslip, so he was probably out of sight for the moment. Forcing himself on, he found the courage to proceed, till after what seemed like an age, his hands and feet cut and bleeding, he reached the top of the cliff and sank into the grass. The hill above him was still steep, but he pressed on urgently. He was all in when eventually he found himself on the summit high above the sea. But where to now?

Instinctively he headed inland, keeping the moon behind him as it dropped into the western horizon. The strain of the climb and the hunger were making him dizzy as he stumbled on over the rough ground, looking over his shoulder, fearing pursuit. His heart failed as he saw a figure silhouetted against the moon. It must be another guard! Trying to keep down low, he scrambled on over the rocky mounds and round bushes as fast as the hobbling chain would allow him, desperate to get away, gasping for air. His foot caught in a hole and the chain pulled tight, tripping him so he fell heavily on a rock, smashing his knee and winding himself. He was spent. He awaited his fate, sobbing in pain and frustration. The figure was upon him now and Issa put his arms over his head as protection against the blow that must surely follow. But no blow came, just a hand laid gently on his shoulder. Eventually he turned to face his captor. It was not a guard.

It was Moshe.

"My boy, the Lord was with you! What an escape! But how did Moshe find you?"

Issa shrugged. "That's Moshe. Who knows how he finds us?"

"But boy, you said you were not a fugitive – but you escaped. Aren't they searching for you?"

"No one knew I had escaped so there was no pursuit, and now my sentence is over."

"So what happened, then?"

"I can't really remember what happened that night, except Moshe urging me on. The next thing I knew, I awoke in a rough shelter. I was so weak I could hardly move and I lay there for some weeks before I could move at all. It was one of those encampments you find on the fringes of towns where the misfits and outcasts live. Many people had been badly hurt and made homeless in the earthquake, so our arrival passed without comment. The people had so little and were in a desperate situation, but somehow Moshe managed to find food for us. He even had enough to be able to share some around.

"Then one day he came to me very agitated, indicating that the authorities were clearing the area. I was scared in case I was recognised and sent back to the mine, so although I was still weak, we set off deeper into the city. I could not believe the destruction! Hardly a building undamaged, with few left standing. Moshe seemed to know where he was going through the chaos, and we arrived at a tottering wall with a gate, where we waited. Presently, an older man came out and Moshe excitedly told me to greet him. I realised that he was Jewish from his dress so I ventured a, 'Shalom, Master,' which delighted him. He was a wealthy Jewish merchant called Solomon. Moshe had been helping him rebuild in return for a little food, and Solomon had always wondered if he was of Jewish stock.

"From the start he treated me kindly, but the old man was no fool and sensed from my agitation that I was more than a refugee, that I had something else to hide. I had to trust him. I explained about the destruction at the mine; that I was the only one who had survived, unbeknown to the authorities. Fortunately he was a well-connected merchant and so took my case to a friend of his who was a magistrate. The mine had been destroyed; all the prisoners registered as dead. The magistrate made me over as a slave to Solomon and money changed hands. The old man was canny. He explained that, as a devout Jew, our laws forbade him to enslave any of his own people, so we agreed that in return, we would both become bond servants for seven years. Bond servants are supposed to be released in the seventh year, which would have been the length of my sentence anyway. He was a good master and we worked hard for him rebuilding and restoring, and true to his word, he released us after seven years."

"But did he give you a manumission?" queried Daniel with some concern.

"He gave me a paper which says I was freed." Issa took a piece of parchment from a leather purse, which was hanging round his neck.

"Is that a manu… what was it you said?"

"A manumission, yes. Thank God," said Daniel, sinking back in his chair in relief.

"So, I have served my time, and now I am free."

Chapter 34

After Issa had finished his story, they sat in silence for some time. He had one burning question in his mind but did not dare to ask.

"Do you know what became of Miryam?" He eventually asked, almost casually. "The girl who sang at my mother's graveside?" It had been a long time, but he had never forgotten her.

Daniel sighed and shook his head.

"It's a sad story. Her grandfather died soon after you were lost, and her uncle became head of the family. The girl Miryam was to be married off to a rich old man who needed a young woman to care for him. Then just before the wedding, she disappeared. No one knew what had really happened, but it was assumed that she had run away to avoid being married to the old man. Her own mother had also run away from home many years before and the gossip said, 'like mother, like daughter'. It was assumed that she too would have ended up as a prostitute. But no one knows for sure what became of her, and if the family did find out, they are not saying. I am sorry, my boy. I know you were interested in her."

Issa was quiet. In his heart, he had always had the faintest hope that Miryam was still in Bethlehem waiting for him. He had steeled himself to expect that she was married with a family, but this? This was mixed news. What had happened to her?

"What of the family? Do they still live there?"

"There was a scandal, of course, and many recriminations when the girl ran away. The family of the old man wanted the bride price returned, but the village elders couldn't decide for a long time who should bear the cost. The uncle, Judah, was quite influential in the synagogue. In the end, the village found against him and ordered the money returned. He withdrew from the synagogue in anger. A short time later the grandmother died and then after a while the uncle left the village. He had never married and some say he had joined a strict group of Pharisees in Jerusalem. There are so many religious factions these days. The only ones left in the house are some poor brothers and sisters who keep themselves to themselves. Sadly, in a village, people don't forget and they still live with the shameful stigma of two wayward women."

Issa resented this. Miryam was a strong character who broke free from a life of virtual enslavement. In this he felt a kinship. But where had she gone?

"So what will you do now, boy?" Issa returned to the present and looked up at Daniel, who continued, "I may be able to persuade some of the shepherds to help you start again?"

Issa shook his head grimly.

"I could never live in Bethlehem after all that's happened! I only came to see you… and find out what had happened to Miryam." He muttered under his breath.

Daniel nodded understandingly.

"I'm all right, boy. Life is hard, but I manage." He stared pensively into the fire. After a long silence he looked up. "So what will you do now?"

"I have some scores to settle," came the determined reply, but when Daniel looked up in alarm, he quickly sought to reassure the old man.

"Don't worry, not here in Bethlehem. I'll spare the village for your sake. You have been good to me and I wouldn't want the village to hold anything against you for having been my master. I know that all the boys of my age were killed by the soldiers and I was spared. I don't want to be the agent of more suffering even after all these years. No, there are others. First, I plan to kill Romans to avenge the Zealots. They saved my life and I will avenge theirs. If the same soldiers are around, I will seek them out and kill them. I haven't forgotten their faces, especially the centurion. That might even redeem me in the eyes of the villagers! Then there's the tax collector who destroyed my mother's reputation. And I have some business with the traders in the temple market. And I'll look for Miryam. If I don't find her or if she has died, then I may find her uncle and make him suffer for the evil he has done her."

Daniel shook his head, looking at Issa with concern.

"Boy, don't destroy yourself in seeking revenge. There's another way. There's something new happening. People are talking about news of a new kingdom coming. There's a preacher by the Jordan. Many are going to see for themselves. I would go myself if I could get there. They say he's saying that what he calls 'the Kingdom of Heaven' is coming and he's baptising people as a sort of initiation. He's calling the people to turn from their old selfish ways because..." He leaned over to speak in a hushed whisper: "The Messiah is coming soon!"

He sat back looking at Issa, who was nonplussed. He saw Issa didn't understand.

"The scriptures talk about the Messiah. It means the promised one, a liberator, coming from David's line who will start a new kingdom. Do you remember Yeshua? I know you do; how could you forget that boy? And do you remember his cousin, John?"

Issa looked puzzled, trying to think who Daniel was referring to.

"You may remember the young man you met over by the Arabah?"

Issa recalled it well. John had made a deep impression on him. They had much in common in their love of the desert. He had been disappointed that their friendship had not been able to develop.

"Well, I think that's who the preacher is," went on Daniel excitedly. "When you were a small boy, I helped your mother escape from Jerusalem."

"Yes, I remember, or rather, my mother would often talk about what happened."

"I remember her asking me why I had done it and I explained that it was because she had been with Mary and Joseph and the boy Yeshua. You see, something was happening and I thought you may have been part of it. I have not been that good in my religion, but I am waiting for the Messiah and there were words... a promise from God over the boy Yeshua. That's why I took you on as a shepherd boy and tried to teach you some things. Now this John has started to preach..." He thumped his knee for emphasis. "I am certain it's the same John! And I'm sure Yeshua is part of that, too. And now you have come back from the dead! Something is moving and we are part of it. Boy, do this thing for me! Go and see who the Baptiser is, what he is saying and come back and give me word. I need to know."

He leaned over and took Issa's arm, gripping it firmly and searching his face with his misty eyes.

"Promise me you will go and hear him before you embark on a vendetta that lands you in trouble. I know there is another way."

Issa was moved by the old man's words. He was bitter and angry; he had his heart full of hatred for the Romans and those who had rejected him and his mother. But for all his brave words, he did not yet have a plan of how to put into practice. Killing Romans was not that easy. Maybe John was raising an insurrection that he could join. He thought it through. He wanted to find out what had happened to Miryam. Maybe she lived in Jerusalem, though that would probably have been too close to Bethlehem for safety. But she would almost certainly have had to go through the city. He would start by going to Miryam's old home, though he doubted they would know anything. Then he would go through Jerusalem and on to Jericho and the Jordan and hear the Baptiser. Maybe he was the promised one? If it was the John he had met, then he would be pleased to be in his army.

"All right," he said at last. "I'll go and hear what he has to say. If it's the same John, then I will be pleased to meet him again."

Issa got up to leave and Moshe followed suit. He was used to sitting quietly, knowing that Issa would explain what had passed between him and Daniel in their now quite elaborate sign language.

Issa decided to go to Jerusalem to stay that night, even though it was now late afternoon. Maybe they could stay with Benjamin and Hannah if he could find them. He had got over his fear of Jerusalem and the crooked traders of the market. They had more to fear now for what was in store for them.

Daniel embraced Issa warmly. Moshe held back and Daniel turned to resume his seat and then, noticing Moshe, looked at him kindly. "You have been such a faithful friend to the boy!"

Moshe could not understand the words but read Daniel's face and body language. Tentatively at first, but feeling the warmth of Daniel's embrace, he relaxed and held the frail old man long and firmly in his strong arms.

The old man returned to his chair, tearful at the reunion with Issa, but also at the thought of how he had regarded Moshe as a dumb imbecile, while, in the end, he was the one who had shown himself to be the most faithful friend to his old shepherd boy.

"Goodbye, boy. Come back soon," he called after them. "But you are not a boy any longer. I must learn to call you by your name: Issa."

"I have not been known by that name for many years," Issa turned and answered sombrely. "I am now called Barabbas."

Chapter 35

As he suspected, Miryam's family were no help. They had reacted with fear at Issa's appearance and insisted they knew nothing of Miryam. Nothing more had been heard since she left all those years before. They readily told Issa that their brother Judah was living in Jerusalem, grateful that they could give him some definite information and obviously anxious that he should leave them alone and seek out Judah.

Jerusalem had been a disappointment. They arrived so late that they had to sleep under the arches of one of the pools. The next day the streets were crowded and squalid, and Issa realised the futility of looking for Judah or Miryam. The tottering tower of Siloam had fallen down, killing a number of people, and the city authorities had taken the opportunity to renew that part of the city, pulling down many of the poorer houses in the area, changing the streets so that Issa couldn't locate Benjamin's house, even assuming it was still there.

They had found the quarter where the street women plied their trade; a squalid narrow street near the Hinnom valley. The women assumed that the two men had come in search of sex and, as competition for trade was fierce, they were not interested in helping a prospective customer find one particular prostitute who might be or have been known as Miryam. It was a hopeless quest, and the men escaped from the sordid scene as quickly as they could to head for the city gates. Issa was angry and disappointed. His opinion of Jerusalem had not changed with time and he was keen to get out of the city bounds. They found a small inn at the top of the Jericho road to stay the night. The road down to the Jordan was notorious and it was inadvisable to let night catch up with you on the way, so most travellers started in the morning, travelling in groups for mutual protection.

The next day, they fell in with some merchants and a family, and set off on the twisty road that dropped down the 1200 metres into the Jordan valley. Moshe soon made friends with the small children and they took turns being carried on his back. Issa was not as generous and his thoughts were more on possible plans for the future. It was mid-afternoon by the time they saw the palms of Jericho in the distance, and the evening was drawing in as they passed through the city gates. There was not a lot of talk about the baptiser among the travellers at the inn where they stayed, but the next morning, as they set out on the road towards the Jordan, they saw other groups obviously heading out to hear the preacher.

Arriving at the Jordan, they found him in full flow. Issa watched for some time and decided from his height and build that it may well have been the same John he had met. His clothes were of coarse cloth tied with a rawhide belt and his hair, though of the same colour, was long and windblown. His voice was clear and resonant. As the people went into the water to be baptised, he would speak some words quietly to each one, sometimes raising his voice again to address the crowds.

"Make a way in the desert for the coming Kingdom" was the gist of the message. Issa worked his way round to the beach, where the people came out of the river. They were all talking together excitedly, exchanging experiences.

"What did he say to you?"

"He said I should share if I had two shirts or cloaks."

"He told me to share my food!" said a stout woman who probably worked a busy kitchen.

Issa listened in, then noticed in disgust that a taxman was being baptised. As he came out of the water he asked, a little sarcastically, "So what did he say to you?"

"Don't collect more than you are required to."

Issa thought that was a little simplistic. He would have liked a bit more irony. But when a group of soldiers waded into the river, John divided them among his followers to be baptised, but addressed them as a group in a louder voice:

"Don't extort money! Don't blackmail! Be content with your pay."

This was more like it, so Issa settled down to listen to the preaching, which became quite subversive at times. The preacher spun round on some religious types standing on a rocky outcrop, who were watching the proceedings disdainfully.

"Snakes slithering down in the sun! Have you come, thinking to hedge your bets? Don't say to yourselves: 'At least we are descendants of Abraham.' God can make children of Abraham from these stones! All this is coming to an end! The axe is already at the root of the tree."

Issa was warming to the preaching now. He remembered how he had suffered in Jerusalem. He remembered telling John about it all those years ago above the Arabah, and if this was the same John, it resonated with their discussion. When he got on to the subject of Herod, the crowd were stunned!

"And that Herod! Adulterer! Stealing his brother's wife! Thinking that by power he can do whatever he wants!"

Issa loved it. He hated the Romans and had no time for the puppet Hasmonean dynasty, even if they were somehow related to the heroic Maccabees.

A murmuring started in the crowd as they realised the import of what was being said and the preacher stopped talking for a while to let the noise settle. He turned to survey the crowds and, as he looked in their direction, fixed his gaze on the two friends. Issa looked around, thinking maybe there was someone significant behind him, but no – it was he and Moshe John was looking at. Issa could now see quite clearly that this was the John he had known all those years ago as the Baptiser took a step forward, still silent but with a penetrating look, clearly inviting them to come and be baptised.

To Issa's astonishment, Moshe flung off his cloak and waded into the water. Issa was on the point of calling out that his friend was a deaf mute when he saw John gesture and sign, understanding somehow how things were for Moshe without being told. Moshe looked up intently into John's face then bowed his head and sank beneath the water. John held his shoulders as he came up, looking long and warmly into his eyes before Moshe turned to come out of the river and back to Issa, smiling broadly. To his chagrin, Issa realised that John was holding out his hand to invite him into the water also.

"The time has come at last, my friend! The time we were waiting for in the Judean hills." So he had recognised him! "Time to make a highway of righteousness in the desert. Turn from the hatred and wait for the coming one. It won't be long! He has come!"

Issa was perplexed. How could John have remembered him from a chance encounter all those years ago? A powerful desire to go into the water, to be reunited with his old acquaintance and become part of this new movement, welled up in him, but he hesitated. John beckoned to one of his disciples to take his place in the water and waded over to Issa.

"My good friend, we thought you were dead! There was so much talk of the skirmish with the Zealots and that a shepherd boy had been caught up in it. I realised it must be you, but here you are!" He wrapped Issa in a warm, though rather wet, embrace. The smell of smoky unkempt hair and the sweat of the hard-working poor was all too familiar to Issa, and he felt a kinship with this rugged man, just as he had all those years ago as desert-loving young men.

"Are you raising an army?" Issa asked quietly, looking around cautiously. "If so, I will join you. I have a lot of scores to settle."

John held him by his shoulders at arm's length, squeezing firmly and looking hard into his eyes.

"Issa, there is a new kingdom coming. It is the Kingdom of Heaven."

"And you will lead it?"

"No! No!" John dropped his hands and looked down. When he looked up, his eyes were bright and excited. "Yeshua. You remember Yeshua? You met him before I did. I only met him the other day, but straightaway I knew that he was the Messiah, the Anointed One!"

"The Lion," said Issa, surprised at himself for pulling that out of his subconscious, presumably from something Daniel had taught him years ago.

"The Lamb of God," said John quietly but emphatically, "who takes away the sins of the world."

Issa thought of all the wrongs he had suffered that and was getting excited too. Maybe vengeance would come through Yeshua!

"I baptise with water," John continued, "but he will baptise with the Spirit and with Fire!"

"Yes!" exclaimed Issa.

"So will you come and be baptised and repent of your sins?"

Issa was puzzled.

"Mine? My sins? John, I've had a hard life! I was abandoned by my father, rejected by my village, called a bastard and my mother a prostitute, robbed by a taxman and then saw my mother murdered! I've just spent years as a slave in a colony, seeing fathers and husbands getting sick and dying in the mines. The Romans are killing innocent people! I had to watch them crucify the Zealots! They and the others are the ones who need to repent!"

John persisted.

"My friend, look into your heart. If you were one of the privileged ones, would you not have been the same? We need to be straight and honest about how we are inside. We need to be on the straight pathway ourselves if we are to welcome the kingdom in."

Issa thought for some time. If this was what John was teaching, he realised he couldn't go through with baptism and still harbour the anger and hatred in his heart. He might be baptised one day, but first he must avenge his mother and the Zealots, get even with the tax collectors and pay back those crooks in Jerusalem.

"Maybe later... One day... Maybe. I have things I need to do first," he called out wildly and pushed John away. Moshe at his side pulled his sleeve, encouraging him to go into the river, but he shook him off angrily too and hurried off. He turned at the top of the bank.

"I'll be back when I have finished the business," he called, his voice breaking. John stood watching, a look of deep sadness growing on his face.

Issa walked briskly away without looking back. Only when well clear of the crowds did he slow down, and it was then he realised that Moshe was no longer with him. Somewhat irritated, he looked back and eventually saw him coming, hurrying through the crowds. He had obviously stopped for some reason, but Issa didn't want to know. Having made sure Moshe had seen him, he carried on towards the road that lead back to Jericho.

Chapter 36

Spring had arrived and though the rains had ended, the land was still quite green and the wadis would still have water. Issa had the idea of cutting over the hills to Bethlehem and he gestured this plan to Moshe, who considered it for some time before signing a general direction. Issa knew that if anyone could find their way Moshe would, but he had no desire to go near the Arabah. He anxiously spread his arms to indicate crucifixion, wagging fingers of both hands for emphasis. Moshe blew out hard through pursed lips, shaking his head vigorously. That place had bad vibes for him too. They would not go back there.

They enjoyed being back in the desert, hunting birds on the way with their slings, grubbing up edible roots of the plants that survived the harsh desert climate and roasting them and the fowl they had caught over a fire in the evening. Issa thought a lot about John during this time, both about what he had said and about the time they had spent together, especially whenever they found a root or plant that John had taught him about. After two days they arrived back in Bethlehem and went, as promised, to see Daniel to tell him about John. Issa felt a little ashamed that he had left John so abruptly and didn't have much to say to Daniel. He recounted how Moshe had been baptised, signing at the same time so Moshe would understand what he was telling Daniel. At this Moshe became quite animated, signing unintelligibly to Daniel, who looked on bemused, before turning back to Issa.

"So, you were not baptised?"

"No," he said simply, then pausing for thought. "There was a lot about repenting. He went on about the religious people and Herod and that.

They are the ones that need to repent, I agree. It would be good to see that they are sorry. Then maybe there would be some justice. But why should I repent? I don't think Moshe understood what it was about. What has he got to repent about?"

Daniel was quiet for some time.

"Do you remember the chats we used to have? The psalms we shared? David was our hero. A Bethlehem shepherd like you. He was badly treated and called for justice. But he also knew he needed to repent."

Issa looked away. He made an effort to control his anger as he spoke.

"Do you remember, Daniel, how you taught me, 'Do justice, love mercy, and walk humbly with God?' I tried doing all three at once like you said, but it didn't work. So I have decided I will first do the justice. When I have seen justice done on the worst offenders, maybe I'll try some mercy on the rest and then, when I am old like you, I will do the humbly walking with God bit."

Daniel looked at him sadly.

"Are you so sure you'll get to be old like me? If you really want to do them one at a time, why not start with walking with God?"

"That's precisely the point. The religious people think they are all right because they do all that 'humbly walking' stuff with their noses in the air. I aim to show them what justice really feels like and rub their noses in the dirt!" He thumped his fist into his hand.

They left Daniel later that day and headed on the road towards the coast. They had no definite plan in mind but, having travelled for many weeks, a few more as drifters while Issa formulated a strategy would not hurt. There was always work where ships unloaded, and they would not be out of place among the moving population of the seaports.

So they worked their way up the coast in this fashion, eating well and moving on from town to town. Issa had two resolves: one for vengeance, and the other to find out what had happened to Miryam. He suspected she was either with a man, eking out a life on the streets, or maybe dead. In all these years, she had apparently not gone back to Bethlehem. In each town he would be on the lookout for her and always set aside time to scout around the poorer parts, especially where the street women plied their trade. He knew that many were forced into the trade by similar circumstances to his mother's, which is why the villagers so readily assumed that of her.

It was in Caesarea that things changed. Thus far, they had just drifted while Issa mulled over ideas in his head. They were in the port area when they came upon a group of wretched prisoners being led in chains to a ship to be transported to a penal colony, maybe even the same mine. Memories of that voyage years ago welled up, he even felt seasick as the familiar smell wafted from the open hold. His heart pounding, hatred for the Romans searing his soul, he decided then and there that he must join the Zealots and fight with them for freedom from Rome. Burning with anger, he gathered up his bundle and, beckoning Moshe, left the port area out of the city gates and headed east for the interior.

The coast was not a good place for Zealots, with its busy ports and the danger of having your back to the sea in a confrontation. They always needed hills for escape. Issa knew there were wild ranges east of the Lake of Galilee where he might find the Zealots, so they travelled across the coastal hills and into the plain of Jezreel. When he heard another traveller mention that the town they could see from some distance away was Nazareth, he pricked up his ears. He thought he remembered his mother mention that it was here where Yeshua lived with his parents, so he decided to make a visit. Daniel had told him that Joseph had been a builder and carpenter so he asked around the village, soon establishing that Joseph had died a while back and that his wife Mary and family had moved to Capernaum on the lake. An older lady, overhearing them asking after the family, enquired if they were looking for the miracle worker. Issa looked puzzled.

"Who?"

"The miracle worker. The son, Yeshua. Bit jumped up now, they say. He lived here as a boy. Nice lad, but nothing startling. His father died a few years back and he took on the business. The people hoped he would carry on with it, as he was a good worker and honest. Been taught well by his father. But then he went off, ooh let's see, must have been a year ago. Just like that! Next thing we know, there are all these stories of him doing miracles. I mean good things. For poor people. Not magic tricks like those travelling charlatans. Healings mostly, things never heard of before, like blind people seeing. But other things as well. Some said he could even change water into wine! That's what caught some of the people's attention here, especially the old soaks!" she cackled. "But I don't really know the truth of it. When he came back here one day a while back, he wouldn't do anything. Or couldn't. The religious lot tried getting him to the synagogue to explain his-self, but he just upset them by what he said. So all the village turned against him and decided to teach him a lesson. The common lot turned on him because he wouldn't perform for them; they thought he could have provided a big meal for his old village, or at least heal some of the sick, and the pious, religious lot, because he offended their niceties. They took him to the top of the hill to throw him down the cliff!"

"And did they?"

The woman laughed. "Got the better of them somehow. Just disappeared. He always was agile, mind you. Used to see him bounding up into the hills whenever he could. Knew those cliffs like the back of his hand."

Issa remembered their adventures on the steep slopes around Jerusalem and nodded, smiling at the thought of Yeshua dropping down one gully and appearing up another. Just like him!

The woman shrugged. "Anyway, next thing we hear the whole family are down in Capernaum."

"Where's that?"

"Down by the lake. Never go there myself. Can't stand the smell of fish and that's all they do: catch fish, dry them, eat them. Their clothes, hair, everything. Fish!" She wrinkled up her nose. "If he was going to move, I don't know why he didn't go south to Bethlehem. That's where they came from originally. Sounds like that's where you're from too?"

"Yes, I am," he nodded, before adding bitterly under his breath, "I hope I'll always will be *from* that place, never again in it." Trying to sound casual, he then asked, "Anyone else here from Bethlehem? There was a girl from there called Miryam. I heard she may have come to these parts."

"Miryam? Can't say I've heard of a Miryam. Most girls with that name use Maryam or Mary in these parts. How old would she be?"

"Late twenties."

"Nah, no one brought a wife with that name to these parts," she replied, assuming that a girl would only move for marriage. "What was her husband called?"

"Judah, I think," he lied, choosing a southern name. If she did have a husband, it wouldn't make any difference what he was called.

"No one of that name here... Your brother's quiet," she remarked, looking at Moshe, who just grinned.

"He's deaf," Issa explained.

"Best way of keeping out of trouble. Though, if you do meet the miracle worker, he could change that."

Issa wondered how Moshe would manage if he could hear. He wasn't sure it was a good idea, anyway. It really suited Issa to be the one in the know and to filter the information. That way, he could keep Moshe dependent.

The friends got up to leave.

"You off, then?"

"We may stay around a couple of days then probably head off for Cap… where did you say?"

"Capernaum."

"Capernaum, Capernaum," Issa repeated to himself to fix the name in his mind.

"Hope you like fish!"

They laughed and made their farewells.

Chapter 37

In each of the villages and towns they passed through, Issa continued to look in the poorer areas. They were easily sniffed out, often literally, such was the depraved condition of the poor women living there. He did not know what he would do if he found Miryam working the streets. It might be better if he never found her at all.

At last they arrived in Capernaum, their funds running low. They would need to find work soon. As the woman in Nazareth had said, it was all fish. The houses were mainly along the lake shore, boats pulled up the beach in front of them, wet nets hanging from poles in the sun and fish drying on raised rush matting platforms to keep them from the dogs. A group of boats had not long landed and a knot of fishermen were gathered together. Hoping for some casual work, the friends approached them but found, to their dismay, a tax collector demanding his quota. He emptied out each string bag counting the catch and exacting a tariff. When he at last stood up, Issa gasped as he recognised the stout figure. It was none other than the man who had terrorised the people of Bethlehem! Issa remembered his Galilean accent. So he obviously had taken a posting nearer home and now here he was, still terrorising the hard-working poor! Burning with hatred, Issa watched as the fishermen gesticulated before turning away in frustration, indignant at the taxes they were being forced to pay. Moshe pulled a face at Issa, for he had recognised the taxman too. Disgusted, the pair turned away, heading back to the main street of the village. Clearly there was not going to be any spare money to pay a couple of casual workers.

Issa had hoped at least to find out about the miracle worker and discover if indeed he was the same Yeshua from his childhood, but was disappointed to be told that he had gone off across the lake with some friends in a boat.

Deciding to cut their losses, they headed back up to the plain to look for a farm where they could find work, realising that they had few skills which might be useful to the fishing community. As it was not yet harvest, it took time to find any labour at all, so it was some time before they were able to return to Capernaum. Issa now had a little money ready for immediate expenses, but had a daring plan for getting more funds forming in his mind. It was audacious. He would rob the taxman, slit his throat if necessary, and then escape into the hills to find the Zealots. He would then have avenged his mother, become richer in the process, and endeared himself to the Zealots with his escapade. He broadly explained the plan to Moshe, who looked alarmed. Issa sauntered down to the booth by the lake with a view to staking it out, but the taxman was not there today. Moshe had hung back, clearly not happy with the idea, and he was obviously relieved that their target was away. They found some cheap lodgings in the village, returning the next day to the booth, but there was still no sign of the taxman. It was going to be a problem if they didn't act soon. Two strangers hanging around town would arouse suspicion, especially when they disappeared, leaving a taxman with his throat cut and his taxes gone. Issa had hoped to make a quick job of it and get away without anyone linking him to the crime. Maybe they would have to abandon the idea. As a last resort, he tried enquiring casually about the taxman.

"Why do you ask? You in a hurry to pay your taxes?"

"No. I was looking for a rebate," he quipped.

"Well, you're too late. Given up, they say. Gone off with that miracle chap, Yeshua."

"Yeshua?"

"That's what they say. The taxman used to stay in a big house he requisitioned on the hill behind the village. Don't know if he is still there, or off with the miracle worker. Good riddance whatever!"

They headed up the hill and easily found the house. There was a noisy party going on inside with a disreputable group of people crowding around the doors and windows.

"Taxman throwing a party for Yeshua and his friends," said a passerby, as Issa and Moshe looked on.

"Yeshua? At a party?"

The passerby shrugged and spat in disgust.

"Never know what he'll do next. But the poor love him. Goes for the outcast whether leper, taxman or prostitute," he moved on, shaking his head.

Issa was perplexed. Surely Yeshua must know what taxmen did? He could cope with the poor. Not too sure about lepers and prostitutes. But taxmen! There was no way Issa was going to mix with taxmen! Though it would have been easy to join the crowd at the windows, they retraced their steps to their lodgings.

The next day, Issa set out to find Yeshua in the town, but was told he had again left early in a boat. To his disgust, he learned that the taxman had gone with him. Issa pondered what to do next.

On reflection, he realised that it would have been hard on the villagers of Capernaum if he got his revenge in their town, as the Romans would surely take reprisals on the locals if one of their revenue men was murdered. It was probably just as well his plan had failed. But Yeshua too had gone down in Issa's estimation. They were now on different paths. One to befriend tax men, the other to kill them. Issa now came up with a better idea: he would go to a Samaritan village and do the deed there. That way, the Romans would take reprisals on the Samaritans, who were enemies of the Jews anyway. He would leave Galilee to Yeshua.

"Let's see who achieves the most," he growled to himself.

The two friends set off, pleased to find the loose-living town of Tiberias full of thriving businesses on account of Herod having a palace there. There was plenty of casual work here, portering and labouring, and they were able to earn some good money. With plans for revenge and murder filling his mind, Issa had stopped thinking so much of Miryam. He did make a cursory visit to the poorer parts, as was his habit, but he didn't enquire after her by name.

It was only later that he would discover how close he could have been to finding her trail in Tiberias.

Chapter 38

Now with reasonable funds, the pair set off into Samaria, but it was not going to be as easy as Issa thought. The Samaritans were generally poor and none of the villages they passed through had rich enough pickings for a taxman. Issa didn't confide in his friend what he had in mind, but Moshe was suspicious, his caution growing as Issa's reckless plan took hold of him. Reaching a more sizeable town, they stopped at a tavern just off the main street for some refreshment, sitting on some fixed benches under a shady tree out of the midday sun. It was obviously a regular stopping place and presently a group of four rough-looking Jewish men came by and occupied the other benches, noisily calling for food and wine. Issa and Moshe exchanged somewhat anxious glances. They were obviously not Zealots by their hairstyles, more likely vagabonds or low-level bandits. They were quite self-confident and the two friends could see that the landlord was cautious and deferential in spite of the cultural hostility between them. As the men were loud and brash, Issa could listen in on their conversation, which soon turned to talk of the miracle worker.

"What do you reckon? Are they really miracles?"

"He's mostly in Galilee, so I haven't actually seen anything myself."

"The people seem to think it's true. They're always running around the lake to follow him wherever he is. He's taken to travelling by boat, probably so he can get a bit of peace. A number of his followers are fishermen, so there are plenty of boats at his disposal, though you wouldn't catch me in one of those tubs. It's dangerous, that lake."

"I was in Capernaum a while back. It was evening and crowds were still going to see him. People said that many were healed, so I thought I'd go and take a look myself the next day, but by the morning he'd gone."

"Nah, I'm not convinced. People often get better anyway. Too easy to say you've been healed. There was this rich man from my town whose son was sick. He went to see this Yeshua. Didn't take his son, though. When he came back, the son was well. He said he got well exactly the time he was with Yeshua, so the whole family believed. Don't believe it myself. Probably a coincidence."

"Yea, but what about Silas, an old man from my town? Silly old soak went and fell down a well when he was drunk and broke his back. That was a few years ago. Couldn't move his legs. He was in a right mess, but luckily for him, his drinking friends didn't abandon him and somehow kept him going. When they heard Yeshua was around and healing people, they carried him on a hurdle all the way to Capernaum. Must have fortified themselves at the inns on the road, as it was a long way to carry even skinny old Silas. I reckon they were probably pretty drunk when they got there, cos when they found they couldn't get into the house for the crowd, they only went and made a hole right there in the roof! Truth! Mud and wattle dropping on everyone inside! Then they dropped the old cripple through. Wonder they didn't break his neck! People were pretty angry getting covered in dirt, but Yeshua didn't bat an eyelid. He said the word and the old man got up and carried his bed roll!"

"What, back through the roof?"

"No, stupid! The people were impressed, cheering and laughing, slapping him on the back as he walked through the crowd. But the religious lot were pretty angry about it."

"Why? Because Yeshua made a cripple walk again?"

"No. It was because he said he had been forgiven his wayward years.

The religious lot say only God can forgive sins, but really what they mean is that they are the ones who decide who God can forgive."

"Yeah, they don't like Yeshua because he associates with the poor and fallen women and…"

"Scoundrels like us!" There was a roar of drunken laughter.

"Yeah, but also tax collectors. I don't approve of that." The speaker spat into the dust.

Issa shared the sentiment. He was impressed with the stories of healing, but Yeshua should be discerning. If he was the liberator, then he needed the right people on his side.

The conversation had moved on…

"Well, you see, James was pretty fed up that he'd lost the girl to Benjamin. She'd made a good choice, though, cause James has a vile temper. The two rivals had been good friends once, but now they were enemies and James was real mad and swore revenge. The wedding was in Cana by the lake. Benjamin isn't that rich, but he'd done his best. Got a lot of cheap wine and with the promise of a good drinking session, the local people had rallied round with food and that. Well, the night before the wedding feast, someone, and everyone assumes it was James, slit over half of the wine skins – the inside ones, so it wouldn't be too obvious, and they didn't notice till half way through the wedding!

"James was seen walking by, grinning, probably waiting for the rumpus. The villagers had provided the food and wouldn't take kindly to the wine running out. Benjamin's a good man and had invited the whole village, the poor and everyone. Yeshua hadn't long been in the area and even he and his family were invited. James kept waiting and waiting, but the wine kept flowing and flowing, and everyone was shouting to Benjamin that this was the best wine they'd ever had! No one realised the truth, but I heard directly from one of the servers. Said it was down to Yeshua. Somehow he had got gallons and gallons of wine into the water jars used for washing! No one knew how. This servant said that he knows they were full of water for he'd filled the jars with water himself. Most of the water had been used up by the guests as they arrived, but Yeshua told him to refill them, which is how he knew. Anyway that feast went on for days. Wine just never ran out! What do you make of that?"

There was a lot of banter about free wine and suggestions about kidnapping Yeshua to have it on tap. They roared with laughter, draining their cups in unison, calling for more wine.

Issa decided to join in.

"But what about the talk of the kingdom?"

They turned, noticing him for the first time.

One of the men looked around before replying, leaning forward and answering quietly, "You need to be careful talking about 'Kingdom' if there are Romans are around." He gestured to Issa to come and join them. "Best keep such opinions to yourself. John the baptiser is in prison for not watching what he said. Yeshua will be in trouble if he's not careful, and so will you. So don't drag us into it."

"Oh, it's all religious teaching anyway," said another.

"Maybe, but the religious lot don't like him either. Don't do religion myself, but if he gets up the nose of those pious hypocrites, then good luck to him."

A large jug of wine arrived and they filled their cups, offering one to Issa, which he sipped cautiously. He had never been good with wine.

One of the group, who until that point had been quiet, spoke up. He was obviously something of a leader, better groomed with an aloof manner, and certainly commanding respect. They listened without interruption.

"Talking of getting at the religious lot, here's a good one! A month or so ago I was mooching around Jerusalem. I was just minding my own business, or rather watching other people go about their business, on the lookout for any opportunity to mind mine to advantage of course." There was a rumble of approving laughter. "Then a couple of religious no goods sidled up. 'We wondered if you would like to earn a bit of money,' they says. 'Depends,' I says. They looked this way and that, obviously a little embarrassed. 'We'd like you to be with a woman.'"

"Yeah!" came the drunken reply, encouraging him on.

"Well, it took a long time for them to explain, but in the end, it seems they wanted to catch this woman in bed with me. 'Is she a prostitute?' I says. I'm careful which women I go with, see. They said that she wasn't a real prostitute, but she desperately needed money to feed her child and wouldn't need much persuasion. They were so convinced of this I reckon they'd maybe had a go themselves. They gave me some money for 'ongoing expenses' and said I would have more when the job was done. They took me to a well and waited a bit and then this girl, only a kid really, comes along with a baby on her back and they say, 'That's her.' Well, I saunter over and ask for a drink and we get talking. I have a way with women, see," he bragged.

"So I got chatting and found out that her man had been taken by Herod some while ago and she was living alone with her baby. She had fallen on hard times. I said maybe I could help her, I was a traveller and needed somewhere to stay, but more than that I needed… well you know," he leered.

"She thought about it for a while, then told me to follow her and we went to her place. She put the baby in its bed but was then unsure and started to cry, so I got firm with her and told her to stop messing me around and she gave in with a little pressure. I was just finishing and hadn't even paid her, when the same religious lot burst in, grabbed the girl and dragged her out. They gave me some more money and told me to leave quickly, but I followed them to see what they would do. They hauled the poor frightened girl to the temple precincts. She was desperately trying to cover herself up, but they had her arms and her clothes were half off her. They took her to Yeshua. He didn't look at the girl, just wrote in the sand. They started shouting at him that she was an adulteress, that they had caught her in the very act, that the law said she should be stoned. What did he think? They were all leering at her as well, waiting for an answer. He waited till they were silent then spoke. Quietly, but firmly.

'Let the one who is without sin cast the first stone.' Clear as day."

"That shut them up! Like I said! You know! Yeshua didn't look up at the girl once. They let the girl go and she quickly pulled her clothes on. Then one by one they left, till she was left alone with Yeshua. I decided it was time for me to go too, somehow couldn't stay longer, but as I left I saw Yeshua look at her, so kindly. Told her he had nothing against her but to go and live another way."

The others were silent, a little shocked in spite of their coarseness. The speaker, wanting to gain their attention again, went on boastfully, "So I got my pay, saw the religious types paid off, and I got the girl for free..."

Issa leapt to his feet and threw the contents of his almost full cup of wine in the man's face! He stood facing him, crimson with rage at the mistreatment of the girl! A girl like Miryam, or her mother, and from somewhere deep inside, all the suppressed anger of years of accusation and mistreatment of his mother welled up inside him.

"You're no better than a tax man!" he yelled. "You and those religious people are the worst scum on earth! Curses on you! Curses! Curses!"

The man reeled from the sudden unexpected onslaught, smarting as the wine stung his eyes. Recovering, he wiped his face, eyes narrowing. Quick as a flash, he drew out a knife with a long, curved blade. Issa stepped back as the other three men drew out similar knives, facing him menacingly.

"You are going to pay for this with blood on your face before I slit your throat," he said with his knife held straight before him, towards Issa's face. Issa stepped back, slowly looking for some weapon, any weapon, while the four men advanced. His small shepherd's knife wasn't readily accessible and, with such a short blade, was no match anyway. Even if he went for it, the other would be on him in an instant. Suddenly, there was a whizzing sound! The knife flew from the man's hand! Then another, and the stone jar of wine exploded on the table in front of the men, making them recoil from the shock. The man searched for his knife on the ground as another stone lodged in his headdress...

Issa turning to run as Moshe's sling blurred and another stone flew towards the group of men, whose hands were instinctively covering their faces. One took a hit on the knee. He yelled as he doubled up in pain. A further shot caught the elbow of another. Issa knew that Moshe was good with a sling but had never before seen him in such blistering action. Years of practice had obviously made him a formidable enemy. Issa knew that the men would soon regroup and then not even Moshe's accuracy would be enough to keep them at bay.

"Run!" he yelled, even though the sound was lost on Moshe, who stood his ground till Issa was past, letting off two more stones in quick succession before he raced after him through the archway of the inn and into the main street.

They had no idea which way to go, but instinct made them head upwards on paths leading them in the direction of the hills, where Issa knew they had a chance to outrun the others who looked unfit and were loaded with wine.

They took the first side alley almost opposite the inn. It curved sharply, so they were immediately out of sight, but to their dismay, they found that it was a dead end! Though safe from view for the moment, they could hear the men running by, and it was only a matter of time before they explored this alley.

Suddenly a door opened, and a woman beckoned them in. Quickly, but quietly, she closed the door.

"Under the bed! Move, or we're all dead!" she ordered, in a strong Samaritan accent.

Without further encouragement they scrambled under the bed, which fortunately was large. The woman pulled a braided cover over and lay on the bed, propping herself on the pillows. They could smell a strong scent, even under the bed. They held their breath as with a crash the door burst open.

"Excuse me, handsome!" said the woman in a drawling voice. "My, you are desperate! Need me so badly! I haven't even got up yet, I've had such a busy night." She yawned.

The man cursed and withdrew, slamming the door behind him. They could hear him going up the street, throwing open doors or banging on the locked ones.

Then silence. The woman warned them to stay quiet and not move. Sure enough, the man was back.

"Have you seen two men go past here?"

"I've seen lots of men, though most don't go past. They usually call in for a while. Do you want to stay?"

Again, the man cursed and went on his way. They heard the woman go out and return some time later, but they stayed quietly under the bed until it was getting dark. Only then did the woman lift the covers and beckon them out.

"I went to the main street and couldn't see anyone, but we must be careful. They may be waiting."

"We are indebted to you, Mistress," said Issa thankfully. She waved away their gratitude, indicating that they should be quiet.

There was some food on the table and she invited them to eat; they did gratefully, using their own knives, which they had to hand in readiness. When they had finished, Issa could not contain his questions any longer.

"Why did you put yourself in danger?" he asked with a whisper.

She smiled. "I was cleaning in the inn and heard what that man said and saw what you did. We knew there'd be trouble, so we all ran and

281

hid. I came out of the door onto the main street and across to my house and had just got safely in when I saw you coming. I couldn't let you be trapped in the dead end. Those ruffians are notorious around these parts; we're always glad when they leave. They'd have carved you up."

"But why put yourself in danger?"

The woman was quiet for some time.

"I've seen the tough side of life for abandoned women. They're regarded as easy prey. Some just have to fend for themselves on the streets. For my part, I was passed from man to man after the man to whom I was betrothed cast me off. Sometimes there was the sham of a marriage for religion's sake, just to keep it respectable, but they would use me for a while and then pass me on. I soon discovered how to seduce men. I knew what they wanted and how to dangle them along. I got to hate them, but nearly always managed to have one around, providing for me. I never had to solicit on the streets. But I know the form." She shuddered. "Thank God that's all over now!"

They carried on eating, but she noticed that Issa kept looking up at her, trying to work out the rest of the story, so she continued.

"I had a reputation in the town. The women would shun me. They assumed I was after their men, which of course I might be, if the current one had dumped me. So I avoided the women, going to the well during the day when they wouldn't be there. There's one in the village and another a lot further away, up on the hill. The water in that outside well is a lot sweeter. They say it goes back to the time of Jacob. But the women usually only go there in the evening when it's cooler. If they need water during the day, they go to the village well, which is a bit salty but less of a trek.

"Well, a little while ago, when I arrived at the far well at midday, there was a man there, sitting in the shade. He was Jewish, so I was a bit wary but not overly troubled. I know how to manage men of all types! I thought I would string him along a bit, but it was he who really tied me up. He seemed to know all about me. But, you know, I was relieved. I've been with lots of men, but this was the first man I had met who made me feel safe. Like I could be me. As he talked, it was as if I was being washed through. Living water, he called it. You know how it is when the rains come and the water washes through the wadis and all the dead leaves that have accumulated there get washed away and then the spring flowers start?"

Issa smiled. He knew it well. There were fewer trees to shed leaves in the wadis of the Judean hills, but the contrast between the barren hills of the winter and the spring flowers after the first rains was striking, and always filled him with hope.

"He seemed to know all about the men who'd had me, and though I felt ashamed, I also felt cleaned and renewed. My life changed from then on. It's a bit hand to mouth now, but I manage, getting a bit of work here and there. I was cleaning in the inn when you came along. When I heard you sticking up for that poor girl, I knew you were an ally. Are you one of his followers too?"

"Follower of who?"

"Yeshua, of course! That's who I was talking to by the well. You're a Jew. You must know of Yeshua!" She leaned forward secretively, though there was no one else to hear. "They say he's the Messiah, the Promised one!"

"But you are a Samaritan. You don't follow our God, do you?"

"We do really. Used to be all the same years ago. I don't understand what happened. It's all an ages old feud. Some say we still have the some of the same scriptures. The difference is you Jews worship in Jerusalem; we have a Holy Mountain. But Yeshua says that the days are coming when both will be no more, and worship will be in 'spirit and truth.'"

Issa reflected that he had never been allowed to worship in Jerusalem and certainly wasn't going to try again.

"What did he mean by 'spirit and truth'?"

The woman wagged her head from side to side, trying to work out what to say. "Don't really know, but sometimes when I'm out on the hills I feel the nearness of God. And I just tell him what I feel. I mean really feel. Do you know what I mean? I think that might be spirit and truth."

Issa nodded. "I used to feel some of that on the Judean hills when I was a shepherd boy."

The woman chuckled. "I thought you and your brother were shepherd stock by the way he used his sling."

She looked at Moshe, who grinned warmly. "Doesn't say a lot, though."

"Doesn't say anything. He's deaf."

"Makes up for it with his sling."

"Makes up for it with loads of stuff. Apart from not hearing or speaking, he is sharper than most people realise. To their cost!" he added, laughing quietly.

"But haven't you heard Yeshua's teaching? You could easily because you are Jews. It's so difficult for me as a Samaritan and a woman. He doesn't come this way much, or at least if he does, he doesn't stay. Most of our villages are hostile to him. If you do find him, come and tell me. You will always be welcome here."

By now it was quite dark, and the lads were restless and wanting to get away. The woman led them to her back yard and indicated a route. After crossing her elderly neighbour's property, they could clamber over a crumbling wall and would see the steep track to the hills ahead. They'd find plenty of cover up there.

She placed a ladder up against the wall and the two dropped over into the old man's yard, effusive in their thanks to the woman who had saved their lives, risking her own.

"And don't forget! Find Yeshua, and if you are back this way bring me word!"

Chapter 39

The friends crept up the hill, keeping as low as possible to avoid being exposed against the moonlit sky. As soon as they felt a safe distance from the village, they broke into a quicker pace. By morning they were well away through Samaria and nearing the Lake, so they found a group of trees where could shade from the sun and sleep through the day. Issa had been struck by the account of Yeshua's meeting with the woman and reckoned that if even the group of outlaws were impressed, though cynical, then he needed to find out more. He had failed to locate a taxman in Samaria and they also needed to get away from the gang they had so perilously encountered.

After a few hours' sleep, they headed off to the lake, skirting its western shore. They had no idea where to find Yeshua; he seemed to move from place to place with no apparent plan, certainly not subject to the whim of the people. The western side was more populated and more likely to offer protection than the wilder east if they encountered the outlaws again.

It was a good choice, for later in the afternoon, they came upon a large crowd on the lakeside. As they drew closer, they could see that they were gathered around a group of men and women, standing in attendance on a rabbi who was teaching. He was sitting in a fishing boat a couple of metres from the shore where he was more easily visible, especially as the beach was steep, so making a natural amphitheatre. The boys joined the fringe of the group; Issa listened in while Moshe looked at the crowd and took in the scene. Issa enquired of the man beside him if this indeed was Yeshua. He glanced at Issa, nodded quickly, returning to listen, while others turned and hushed him, irritated at the interruption. There was no wind and the water helped carry Yeshua's voice, but because of the size of the crowd, from time to time Yeshua would pause while his disciples standing near him went into the crowd to repeat and clarify what he had just said. Yeshua obviously preached the same message in different parts, for they had little difficulty concisely repeating his words.

The message spoke of another Kingdom: the Kingdom of heaven, a kingdom not like those of this world, which espoused different principles, be it military might or the religious legalism. Yeshua said that there were many people who were waiting to hear the message.

"The harvest is white and ready, but the labourers are few," he proclaimed.

It seemed he wanted the message to spread and was inviting his followers to take it to those who had not yet heard. Twelve had already gone. Now he wanted to send out many times that number. He invited others to become his followers so that he could teach them and they in turn could take the good news of the kingdom far and wide.

When he added that they would do greater things than he had done, there was a buzz of excitement and people turned to each other in discussion. Food and wine were high on the agenda.

Soon people were going forward to Yeshua. Issa watched as they he spoke to them in small groups. A few knelt before him, but many more listened to what he had to say and turned away.

Yeshua raised his voice and said clearly, "If you want to follow me, you must take up your cross. Foxes have holes, and birds of the air have nests. But the Son of Man has no house or home to lay his head."

People were returning sadly.

"It's all very well, but he doesn't understand. My father expects me to be in the business. But when he dies, I'll be free to choose."

"It's all right if you've been brought up to it, but I've got lots of friends to explain it to. They will get the wrong idea and cut me off."

Issa would have liked to remake his acquaintance with Yeshua, but he had certain scores to settle first. It was clear that Yeshua did not accept anyone with an agenda of their own. All or nothing, it seemed. And there was nothing he had heard that even remotely suggested killing Romans and Jewish traitors.

He turned to Moshe, who looked questioningly, waiting for Issa to explain what the preacher was saying. He clearly hadn't realised that this was the same Yeshua from his childhood or he would have been right up there at the front. Issa knew he needed to get Moshe away or he would lose him. The events of the last few days had shown that he would be vulnerable without Moshe, who, though clearly not happy about what he understood of Issa's plans so far, would hopefully fall into line.

Disappointed and looking back, clearly drawn to Yeshua, the ever loyal Moshe reluctantly followed his friend. They hurried back the way they had come and rounded the southern end of the lake, crossed the river as it flowed out into the Jordan Valley and climbed the hills on the eastern shore of the lake. With fewer people there, Yeshua would not be so likely to visit. Issa didn't want to hear that message again. Too compelling. Also, he had an idea that they'd be more likely to meet up with some Zealots in these rugged heights than on the more fertile Western slopes. They would have to take their chance with the outlaws.

Little did he realise that they would be not long in meeting both, and it would change the course of their lives.

Chapter 40

That evening, Moshe begged Issa to explain what had been said by the teacher. He had been very taken with John and clearly wanted to know about this preacher. Issa fobbed him off with some general information, then, irritated, indicated that he was tired and lay down. Moshe looked rather crestfallen and sat up for some time while Issa feigned sleep, though his mind was in turmoil from what he had heard. In the morning, after a disturbed night, Issa wasted no time in getting off on the road. With no plan in particular except to get away from thoughts that were troubling him, he set a frantic pace and, on impulse, struck up over the hills into the heights.

The lake shimmered in the heat below them and the spring flowers were in abundance. Stopping to get their breath, they took in the view. Moshe swept his hand in an arc, tracing the far shore, his face lighting up in appreciation. There were a number of small boats on the lake, and the villages on the distant shore were quite distinct, with the larger Tiberias and its whitewashed villas sparkling in the sun, which rose in the sky behind them. A stream gurgled over some rocks nearby, the water clear and cool. It must have been what Yeshua had in mind when talking to the Samaritan woman. Vivid memories of his adventures with Yeshua as young people flooded back: climbing the walls, gently touching flowers and admiring their beauty, and grubbing around for insects. Yeshua seemed to love beetles! Issa sat down on a stone by the stream, lost in thought, poking at a hole with a stick. All at once, Moshe grabbed his arm and squealed as he did when alarmed, pointing out four men who were running towards them over a nearby hill. Putting his hand over his mouth in alarm and with eyes wide, Moshe tugged at Issa's sleeve as he made off. Issa could not tell if these were the four outlaws they had encountered in Samaria, but they weren't waiting around to find out.

Carefully slipping into the stream bed and moving fast along the gully, they peered over the bank in time to see two of the men running in their direction, but still some way off. The other two were not evident. There was no time to lose. Their best plan seemed to be to carry on down the gully, which would eventually lead to the lakeside where they were more likely to find refuge in a farm or even a village. As they raced on, there was a cry behind them and one of the outlaws appeared on the hill above. Although they had a head start, the boys had made the wrong choice: the valley narrowed into a gorge and trees blocked their path, slowing their progress. When at last, to their relief, the lake came into view and they thought they were safe, to their dismay, the stream became a waterfall, dropping away over a sheer rock face to the lakeside meadows twenty metres below them.

By now the outlaws had caught up with them, covering each side of the gorge while one scrambled down the hillside to cut off any chance of escape down the precipice. A rock crashed down, then another, making the friends crouch for cover. Now they had their slingshots out. Smooth stones from the river bed provided ammunition. Moshe found cover behind an outcrop and was able to wing one of the outlaws as he looked over the edge. There was a cry of pain and a curse. But their situation was hopeless. It was only a matter of time before a rock would find its mark. Issa crept over to Moshe, signing a plan. He would climb the side with just one outlaw while Moshe covered him with his sling. The plan started quite well. The outlaw above Issa had to lean over to get a view of him, giving Moshe time to get a shot in. His shots were so accurate the outlaw could only throw rocks at random, and in the pauses Moshe concentrated on the other outlaws, who now had to throw stones across the valley in a futile attempt to dislodge Issa, swarming expertly up the rocks with his knife held ready between his teeth. He was rapidly traversing the rock face while out of view to try to get some element of surprise, when there were shouts and a scream and the outlaws all disappeared. Moshe, hearing nothing, stood with his sling in readiness while Issa scrambled on, cautiously pausing below the summit, knife at the ready, alert, expecting a trap. A head appeared above him but quickly ducked from view as a shot from Moshe pinged off a rock, inches from him. And then, as if to order, two lines of armed men appeared and stood silently on the cliff edge on each side of the gorge. There would be no escape now. Issa prayed they were not hostile, but from their dress he thought they must be Zealots. As the two friends climbed out of the valley the men surrounded them, at the ready, cautiously keeping their distance, knives in hand. Issa dropped his small shepherds' knife, held his hands out palm upwards, and Moshe quickly followed suit.

"Shalom. God sent you just in time. I think we owe you our lives." Issa tried to sound calm, but his heart was thumping.

The men weighed them up silently. Their leader nodded imperceptibly and two men stepped smartly forward, holding each in an arm lock, expertly searching for hidden weapons, then roughly pushed them towards the leader, who held out his long blade menacingly and asked curtly.

"Are there others in your group?" he demanded, flicking his knife in their faces, indicating that he would not tolerate any lies.

"We are just two," replied Issa hoarsely.

"From?"

"Bethlehem... Once we were from Bethlehem... A long time ago."

"Two brothers from Bethlehem. And what are you doing in these hills? So far from home?"

Issa desperately searched for an answer that would let him stall but found none. He dared not lie. But were these really Zealots? When he did not immediately reply, the leader went on. "And what part had you with these four outlaws? How had you offended them?"

"We had a disagreement with them in Samaria. We escaped but did not expect to meet them in the hills."

"So, you used to be part of their gang?"

Issa was horrified! "No! No! We had never met them before! I... threw a jar of wine in the leader's face when he insulted the memory of my mother." Issa shrugged.

There was a ripple of approval from the others. The leader was also clearly impressed.

"Huh. I'm glad someone at last has had the courage to stand up to these vagabonds. We've been after this gang for some time. Thanks to you, they were distracted and didn't hear us approach. They've been terrorising the neighbourhood, robbing farms and villages. People started accusing us, so we had to deal with them. But go on. You were about to tell me what you were doing in the hills."

Issa took a deep breath. "We were looking for the Zealots..."

The leader turned his back, then quick as a flash, spun round and held Issa in a head lock, the point of his knife against his throat.

"So you could betray us and get a reward?" he snarled.

"No! No! I was at En Gedi a decade ago. I was a shepherd boy then. I saw the Romans crucify the Zealots. I was sent as a slave to the mines. Moshe rescued me. I vowed to avenge the Zealots who I saw murdered," he gasped, as he struggled to breathe.

The leader let him go and looked hard into his eyes. "You were at En Gedi? But no one escaped from En Gedi!"

"Yes, they did. I did. The Zealots had... had commandeered some sheep from my master. When we arrived at En Gedi, there was a trap. I was to be crucified too, but the Zealot leader spoke up for me. He persuaded the centurion to take me with them to care for the sheep and I was spared."

"And why should we believe you?"

"The leader had a scar on his face. He was a good man…" Before they could discuss more, the other group of Zealots arrived, dragging the leader of the outlaws with them. He had been beaten and his face was bloodied.

"The others?" queried the Zealot leader, slapping the helpless man about the head. His hands were tied behind his back so he couldn't defend himself.

"Dead. This one tried to escape, but Thaddeus soon caught him."

The leader looked disdainfully at the outlaw. "String him up and leave him hanging as a warning to others," he barked.

They found a tree and slung a rope over a branch, dragging the outlaw over to it. By now all the brashness had gone and he looked terrified. They cut a forked stick and stood it on the ground with another across it in the fork. With the rope around his neck, they made him balance on the stick, ready to kick away the upright to leave him hanging. Issa watched the cold efficiency of the summary justice. Then, an impulse seized him.

"Wait!" he called out. "I have a score to settle. Let me do it!" He wanted vengeance. And he wanted to prove himself to the Zealot leader.

The man stood on the rocking structure, desperately trying to maintain his balance, eking out the last seconds of his life. He looked imploringly at Issa.

"Mercy! Mercy!" he pleaded.

Issa looked at him for a few seconds, enjoying the moment of revenge.

"Mercy is for later. Now is the time for justice!"

He kicked away the stick, the scream of the terrified man becoming a gurgle as his body contorted, desperately struggling against the tightening rope around his neck.

Issa had imagined he would see images of his mother and the poor girl in Jerusalem whom he had avenged, but imprinted on his mind were the desperate eyes of the outlaw as he implored him for mercy.

The leader of the Zealots was suitably impressed.

"We'll make a Zealot of you. These men are trash. You'll get more pleasure out of killing Romans."

This was what Issa had wanted, but right now, he just felt sick. He turned to face the other Zealots, who held up their hands in salute.

"I'll join you," he said hoarsely, looking at the ground, trying to erase the image from his mind.

"What about your brother? He impressed us with his skill with the sling."

They turned to where Moshe had been watching some distance away. But Moshe had quite disappeared.

Chapter 41

Issa slunk into Jerusalem with the pilgrims arriving for Passover. He now wore the conventional shepherd's headdress he always used to wear, having shorn off the distinctive haircut of the Zealots. Carrying an appropriate bundle, he attached himself to a group of pilgrims coming from the north so as not to attract attention to himself as a lone traveller. He had been with the Zealots for over two years now and, after an induction into their philosophy and fighting methods, had become a feared member of the insurgency. At first his daring and zeal had been appreciated, as he was always the first to volunteer to slit a throat or carry out a summary execution. But then things started to go wrong. His killing had become indiscriminate and the Zealots were having difficulty keeping him in check. Just a few weeks earlier, he had come into Jerusalem on an unauthorised mission to rob some rich merchants regarded as collaborators. But the plan had gone wrong and ended in a riot, during which a number of innocent people had been killed in the Zealots' desperate escape attempt. Most of Issa's companions on that day were either killed or imprisoned; he had been lucky to escape. The Zealot leadership was not impressed with either the loss of innocent life or the depletion of their ranks, and Issa realised it was time to slip away before they took action to curb him. He would head south into the desert where he could disappear. But there was one last score to settle, and he had a daring plan.

As the pilgrim band entered the narrow streets of the city, he slipped away into a small alley, looking for somewhere safe to wait till the evening when he would move into action. The streets and lodging houses were busy, but he found a tavern in an alley with a courtyard where he could be hidden from the street, yet keep a close eye on those who came and went. It was not perfect, but it would do.

He ordered wine, bread and oil from the girl who came to serve him, leaning his head on his hand as if weary after his journey, but in reality to partially cover his face. She returned with his food and drink. He thanked her gruffly without looking up, pulling his headscarf down low on his forehead. Covertly, he kept an eye on the other customers as the girl moved around serving them. He'd not seen her face, but her movements were familiar. He watched her slim figure as she moved among the customers. A man appeared in the doorway, wiping his hands on a cloth.

"Miryam, we need water. Please go to the well."

She looked up, smiled and followed him inside. Issa's heart jumped. Could this be...?

All doubt was gone when she returned with the pot on her shoulder. The years rolled back to a dusty street in Bethlehem...

This was Miryam. His Miryam.

He tossed some coins on the table and quietly left the inn. He had been schooled well and no one, if questioned, would have remembered him departing, or even being there.

He followed Miryam down the street, keeping her in sight. He knew that he wouldn't be able to talk to her at the well – that was a woman's world – but on her way back up the steep path with a heavy pot she would have to rest somewhere.

He followed at a distance until he saw her arrive at a well, swing her pot off her shoulder and await her turn. Issa turned in to a baker's shop, where a knot of customers were waiting for a batch of bread to come out of the beehive oven. The baker, seeing him join the queue, nodded in his direction.

"A few minutes yet. So many people, I can't make the bread fast enough!" he said apologetically. A few minutes was perfect.

The bread was ready and Issa served just as Miryam started back up the street. Issa stood against the wall, carefully wrapping the bread in a cloth to put in his roll, taking his time as she laboured up the street with the heavy water pot. As she drew level, he clumsily dropped his roll, spilling the bread onto the path in front of her. As he had expected, she swung her water pot off her shoulder to good-naturedly help him gather it up.

"Miryam? It's Issa," he whispered as their heads came close.

She turned to stare at him eyes wide, unbelieving.

"Issa?"

"Shh. Not here, not in the street. Where can we talk?"

Times were hard, and it was no surprise when people were covert. She looked quickly around, but no-one was taking any notice. Without further sign of recognition, she whispered, "This way," tossing her head to indicate that he should follow her.

She walked on up the street without looking back, while Issa repacked his roll. He waited until she was well ahead before following on, increasing his pace so that he would be close behind when she entered the alley leading to the inn. She walked past the main entrance and opened a gate in the wall a few metres beyond, presumably the side entrance to the rear of the property. The gate was still open when he arrived and she was at the far end of a passage. She beckoned him urgently and he slipped in, closing the gate behind him. She held a finger to her lips as they passed an open door, going on into the back courtyard. A wide stairway led up to a second storey, then narrowed as it continued up to the roof. She stood blocking the doorway of the upstairs room, indicating the roof, waving her hand urgently. Issa bounded silently up the stairs and out of view. The roof had no balustrade and was obviously used as a store area and probably for drying produce. Issa expertly assessed it for safety. He could sit against the wall of the next door house and be hidden from view but still keep an eye on the stairs. The flat roof of the single storey house next door led to an alleyway which would serve as an escape route. Not perfect, but adequate.

Presently Miryam appeared with wide shining eyes, her face flushed with anticipation. Issa smiled.

"Issa, is it really you?"

"You thought I was dead?"

"For years, yes. Then I heard about someone who had escaped crucifixion and I prayed and hoped it might be you. And at last, here you are. But are you safe? And why the secrecy?"

"I joined the Zealots." He saw a shadow fall over her face. "But I'll not be with them for much longer. I'll explain in good time. But where have you been? I went to Bethlehem and Daniel told me you'd run away. I came though Jerusalem and have been all over looking for you ever since but couldn't find you. What happened?"

This wasn't exactly true. He had given up searching for her since joining the Zealots.

"Is the innkeeper your husband?"

Miryam held up her hand, silencing him. The sun was now high in the sky and time for the afternoon rest. They sat side by side in the shade of the wall.

"Calm yourself. We can talk for a while. The inn is closed for the afternoon and the others are resting. But tonight is the Passover meal and we'll be busy again soon. So, quickly: the innkeeper is a follower of Yeshua, as I am. As we all are here. He is not my husband. I have no husband. I have… I have lived with no man, as a husband," she said hesitantly.

Issa sunk back against the wall, closing his eyes in relief.

Thankful he did not probe further, Miryam continued, "It's been a tough few years. I was devastated when news came that you had been

297

killed by the Romans. No one else cared much, but I wept and wept for you and for dear Moshe." She stopped, turning rapidly on Issa. "But what happened to Moshe? Did he die on a cross?"

"No. Moshe is safe. He followed me somehow and rescued me from the colony where I was imprisoned. But he didn't want to join the Zealots," Issa added somewhat sadly.

"Thank you, Lord God," she said with relief. "But where is he now?"

Issa shrugged. "I don't know. Probably best that he went away. He'd have struggled with the Zealot cause… would have been a burden." He was pensive for a few moments, thinking of his old friend, but he needed to put him from his mind, so he pressed Miryam further. "More importantly, where have *you* been hiding?"

Miryam hugged her legs, putting her chin on her knees and thinking back over the years.

"My grandfather found me crying and I told him everything. About the hole in the wall, and helping you with your mother. He was proud of me, and so sad that you had died. From then on he was quite different. When my uncle suggested marrying me off to some old man, he was furious. But then my grandfather died, and soon afterwards my uncle went ahead with the arrangements. I had no choice in the matter. When I eventually met the old man, he was awful. I could smell his rancid breath from metres away. I couldn't face life with him, so I ran away. Like my mother did."

"But how did you manage? They said in the village that you must have become a prostitute."

Miryam laughed bitterly. "That's what they're like. They think my mother was a prostitute, but there are other ways for a runaway girl to manage… just about. I could sing, so I would sometimes perform at drinking places. You can get a few coins that way and it was enough to get by. I had heard that my mother may have gone to Galilee, so decided to see if I could find any trace of her. But I found nothing. I got to Tiberias and when I was singing at a tavern, a man noticed me and asked if I could dance as well as sing. I said yes, though I couldn't really. My grandmother had never let me join the dancing girls at the feasts, though I would have loved to. I really envied the girls who did those group dances."

She hesitated, looking down sadly.

"And?" encouraged Issa.

"It wasn't that sort of dancing. It was the sort that drunk men like."

Issa knew what she meant. It was becoming increasingly popular among the Romans. The girls would perform erotic dances with veils, wearing little else, arousing the drunken men. It was dangerous work, so the girls often worked in troupes with a male escort.

"So did the men use you?"

"No. No, not like that. Sometimes men would try and force themselves on you. It was disgusting. Some of the girls were raped, but the Romans had slave girls for that. Young girls enslaved by the Romans from rebel towns that fell. What I did was worse, really. I aroused the men and they took it out on those poor slave girls. We were very unpopular among the Jewish community in Tiberias and around the lake, especially girls like me who were obviously Jewish. And fallen. Beyond hope."

"But you don't do it now?"

"No, not now. Not since I met Yeshua. In Tiberias we would often go to Herod's palace. If Herod was there, we sometimes danced for him. We must have impressed him, for we were taken to his fort at Masada to dance for his birthday. It was a lavish affair. His stepdaughter Salome fancied herself as a performer and we were to be part of her act. We went there some time before, waiting for the guests to arrive. There was a preacher man in prison there. John the Baptiser, they called him."

"I know John," put in Issa, cautiously.

"Knew," corrected Miryam quietly. "He had railed against Herod for stealing his brother's wife, Herodias. She hated John for it and wanted him dead, but Herod was fearful of killing a Holy man. By having him in prison, it silenced John, placated Herodias and suited Herod. Herod thinks he's Jewish, or at least tries to endear himself to the Jews, and is pretty superstitious. He was actually scared of John.

"Anyway, I got to visit John in prison. There wasn't a lot else to do. His followers used to be around and they were kind to me. Made a change in that hellhole. John heard that I used to sing psalms and that, and he persuaded me to sing for him. It brought back loads of memories. I used to listen to him teaching his followers through the dungeon gratings. He said the Messiah was coming, was here. He said the blind could see, the deaf hear, the lame walk, the good news was being preached. It was all to do with Yeshua. I had heard of Yeshua, but I had not paid much attention. But now I wanted to know more. So, I used to steal down to the dungeon and hear John's teaching whenever I could. Then…"

Her voice broke and her eyes filled with tears.

"Then it was Herod's birthday and we danced with his stepdaughter, Salome. Herod is a lecherous old man. He would drool over Salome while she played up to him, and we made him and his guests wild with passion with our dancing. He made all sorts of rash promises: 'Anything you want – up to half my kingdom!' Stupid, evil, sex-craved man! His wife Herodias, Salome's mother, cunning witch, had probably planned it all. She didn't care that her husband was lusting after her daughter. She just wanted John dead and got Salome to ask for John's head. On a silver meat dish." The tears streamed down her face as she turned to Issa. "They killed him because of our… my dancing. I was so sick."

She composed herself. "I have never danced again since that day. After that, the party broke up. Herod was in a bad way. We all got paid off. More money than we expected. Blood money, I suppose. I split from the troupe; walked back to Tiberias, in turmoil. I gave all the money I had earned at Herod's palace to a beggar. I couldn't bear to have it.

"Then I heard that Yeshua was in the next town, and in desperation, I went to hear him. He must have heard that John was dead, and I was so ashamed of my part in it. But he said he had come to call sinners to repent. That was what John had said, too. I knew that sacrifices were offered for sins, but I thought it was only for little ones, like getting tithing wrong, or working on the Sabbath. People like me went straight to hell. But what he taught was different. There were all sorts of people following Yeshua. He made you feel that God loved you, was not angry with you, wanted you back however far you had fallen.

"It really offended the religious people. People said the Pharisees and the others were planning to kill Yeshua. And I knew from being with Herod that what he was teaching would certainly not endear him to the Romans. I had just seen John killed and the religious people hadn't liked John either. I reckoned Yeshua would go the same way. I was so ashamed of what I'd been doing! Like some of the other girls, I had used my earnings to buy expensive perfume oils as a way of saving. It wasn't as obvious and so less likely to be stolen. I wanted to give it all to Yeshua. Crazy, wasn't it? What was he going to do with perfume? But I walked round the lake till I found him. He was having a meal at a Pharisee's house and I was so scared for him. What if they had tricked him into an ambush? I wanted to warn him, wanted to protect him, wanted to let him know.

"So I pushed my way in and saw where he was reclining at the table. I crept to where he was before they could stop me. Everyone was shocked when I appeared. Even though I'd tried to dress modestly, they could tell where I belonged, but he just looked so kindly at me. I didn't know what to do then, so I just knelt down and started to cry, right there by Yeshua's feet. I just cried and cried. My tears were wetting his feet. Funny what you notice, but his feet were so dusty and my tears were making them streaky so I wiped them with my hair." She giggled, embarrassed at the memory.

"Then they got all sort of muddy so I did the really dumbest thing: I poured all the perfume over his feet! Well, I didn't have anything else to wash them with and I just wanted to clean them up and care for him. So what that it was perfume? He is worth it! Obviously no one had washed his feet, as normally happens to guests before meals, and I wanted to care for him. I felt this real love flow over me and well, after that I just started kissing his feet. Until then, everyone was just shocked! Embarrassed, I suppose. Women like me aren't supposed to go crawling round the feet of guests! But then a hubbub started. I didn't know what do next, but Yeshua sat up and put his hand on my shoulder. I have never felt so loved in my life. There was a bit of an argument going on about me. Yeshua just kept his hand on my shoulder, reassuring me. Eventually I left. I was so embarrassed, but Yeshua was so kind. I reckon anyone who hears about it will reckon I am the dumbest woman on earth. But I would do it again tomorrow!" she exclaimed defiantly. "The men disciples weren't sure how they were meant to react, but then I saw a familiar face. It was Joanna, the wife of one of Herod's stewards, Chuza."

Issa remembered the name. He had long been a target of the Zealots, but Tiberias was too well guarded.

"She just opened her arms, and I buried my face in her cloak and we both cried and cried. She had recognised me as one of the erotic dancers yet didn't reject me at all. We became good friends. She uses her money to support Yeshua but can't be with him all the time as she needs to be at court. Because I know how the palace works and the guards recognise me, I can come and go easily. I have a little house in Tiberias, so I stay there when necessary and take provisions from her to Yeshua. Whenever I can, I travel with the women who help Yeshua. That's why I'm here now. The religious Jews are scandalised that Yeshua has women disciples. But that's part of his teaching. It's so different. You know, some of the men even go and collect water! That's how radical he is!"

She paused, weighing up carefully before sharing any more. Yeshua was expected to arrive that evening to use the room below. They had kept the location secret. She wasn't sure she could trust Issa, so she decided to say nothing more. Yeshua had so many enemies. She didn't know what the Zealots thought of him. She needed to change the subject.

"But you? Are you really a Zealot?"

She asked this almost sadly. Quite apart from the danger Issa faced, the Zealots did not have a good reputation. Many innocent people had suffered in reprisals and most people, though hating the Romans, wanted a quiet life. Also, the Zealots expected the locals to support them, and often forced them to give food and money they could ill afford to 'the cause'.

Miryam went on. "I heard from some of John's disciples who are now with Yeshua of a shepherd boy he had known, who he thought had been killed by the Romans but had somehow escaped and maybe joined the Zealots. They had no more details, only that they'd met up at the Jordan when he was baptising, and John was really sad that he'd chosen that road rather than that of the Kingdom. By then John was dead, so I couldn't ask him any more, but I wondered, hoped and prayed it was you! Tell me what happened?"

Issa recounted briefly how he had been spared at the last minute and sent to a penal colony, about the earthquake and his escape, and how Moshe had found him and nursed him back to strength. He spoke of how he had been fortuitously redeemed by the Jewish merchant, then worked as his bond servant for the allotted seven years before being released. He went on with details of meeting John by the river and hearing some of Yeshua's teaching, but had become a Zealot, believing that was the way forward.

"Do you see Moshe at all now?"

Issa's face clouded.

"No. Not since I joined the Zealots. He was quite taken in by John, but he couldn't have understood what it was about. A bit of an innocent, poor guy," he added condescendingly, then wistfully, "but I do miss him."

"But what are you doing in Jerusalem? It must be dangerous for you here. Do the authorities know you, I mean would they recognise you?"

Issa smiled.

"They know me by my name, but not my face. Maybe you have heard of… Barabbas?" he said his name very quietly.

Miryam opened her mouth wide in astonishment and gasped. She looked around and put her hand on his arm.

"You are Barabbas? The Barabbas?"

"The same," he said rather proudly. "But don't believe everything they say about me. A lot of the stories are exaggerated."

"But Issa, even if some of the stories are true, you are in great danger, and…" Her face clouded. "Were you really involved in that terrible attack recently? So many people killed! People say it was Barabbas. Was that really you?" she queried anxiously, her eyes filling with tears. She withdrew her hand.

"Sometimes innocent people get hurt," he answered lamely. The eyes of some of the terrified people were impressed on his mind. He had thought that getting his revenge would ease his thoughts, but these days he was more troubled than ever, and now he covered his eyes to block out the images.

Miryam put a hand on his shoulder, sensing his confusion, speaking quietly and intimately. "Issa, I know that is not the way. So much suffering! So many dead! And where is it leading? Issa, there's another way! One of Yeshua's group, Simon, used to be a Zealot. We all have a past. He says he doesn't come for the righteous but for sinners. I know he will accept you. Oh, Issa! Now we've found each other again, could you not give up all this and follow Yeshua?"

Such was the amazing coincidence of their meeting again; she had no doubt God was in it. The situation being so desperate, she wasn't going to stand on ceremony and wait for him to take the lead.

Issa wavered, then spoke in a determined voice, more to convince himself than Miryam. "There is one more thing I need to do, then my vengeance will be complete. I have a plan that will make me rich, and after that I'll take you away somewhere outside the borders of the empire and we can live together in peace."

"No! Issa, please! Don't do any more!" she implored. "God has spared us both and brought us together now. Don't do it! I don't even want to know what it is. I don't care if we have no money." Her voice, though a whisper, was becoming hysterical and Issa put his hand on her arm to calm her.

Something nagged again in his mind. This was the third time he had felt a powerful pull towards this unknown Kingdom. He hesitated.

"I don't know." He turned, wrestling with indecision, to face Miryam, and saw the tear-stained face he had last seen at the grave of his mother. The hurt, hatred and thirst for revenge welled up inside him.

"It's all right, I have a good plan. It will work," he added grimly, his teeth clenched, then looking up defiantly. "And everyone down the ages will remember the name of Barabbas."

Chapter 42

Miryam had returned sadly to her work preparing for Passover. Issa seemed determined to go through with his plan, whatever it was, and she rather reluctantly agreed to him staying on the roof. She brought him a little food and water. He was trained to endure long hours of discomfort and so it was no hardship for him, even when the sun moved round and there was no shade.

As evening approached, he heard a group go up the stairs and into the room below. Others came and went, bringing food from the inn kitchen below; he could smell the roast lamb and herbs and was grateful that he at least had some bread to chew on. When it was quite dark, he crept down the steps. He was almost at the next level when the door of the upstairs room burst open and someone came hurrying out. Issa froze, pressing himself against the wall in a futile attempt to hide, but whoever it was seemed to be in too much of a hurry and soon disappeared into the darkened alley. Issa held his breath until his footsteps died away, then let it out in relief, waiting a few seconds more before slipping down the stairs to the alley before anyone else appeared. The street was deserted, but he could just make out the silhouette of the stranger who he had seen on the inn stairway passing the lighted windows of houses where people were celebrating Passover.

Issa rehearsed his plan. It was simple.

He had always held a grudge against the temple market traders who had robbed and humiliated him all those years ago. He well knew that Passover was as commercial as it was religious and there would be a lot of money in the temple courts. The temple money changers recycled the same temple coinage, accumulating large amounts of real currency. These were the last days of the market and he planned to relieve the temple of some of it's ill-gotten gains. On previous secret missions to Jerusalem, he had spent time carefully memorising the temple layout, watching the guards and timing the intervals between their patrols Surely this plan wouldn't fail! At least this time it was night – no innocents around to be hurt.

Turning into the large square in front of the temple, in the moonlight he could see not only the figure from the inn still ahead of him, but an unexpected detachment of temple guards.

He stood uncertainly in an archway, taking stock. Should he abort his plan? But this was his last chance to get rich! How else could he give Miryam the life she deserved? Casting caution to the wind he set off, but from the start nothing went to plan. It wasn't easy slipping past the guard; once inside, he wasted precious minutes hiding in the shadows to avoid detection before he was able to even access the courtyard where the money changers had their safe store.

At long last the coast was clear, and he reckoned he would have a few minutes before the next patrol passed through. He was working on the lock, which was proving more stubborn than he had anticipated, when there was a cry. He span round, knife in hand, and quickly overpowered a guard, pinning him to the ground and holding his knife to his throat.

"Benjamin!" a voice called out from the distance, obviously in response to hearing the scuffle. "Are you all right?" Two other figures appeared, running.

Issa looked closely at the man. It was Benjamin! The man who had rescued his mother and the one who had been so kind to him! This must be the twins coming. Hannah's face flashed through his mind. Gentle Hannah, who had loved him as a baby. He could not cut Benjamin's throat, betraying Hannah and his mother and the generous family! Miryam's plea, "Issa! There is another way," echoed in his mind, and with a curse he leapt to his feet. What a fool he had been! He must escape! He fled back the way he had come and into the square. By now the alarm had been raised and there seemed to be soldiers whichever way he turned! Escape was hopeless. He was soon cornered and clubbed down. He hadn't even been able to use his knife.

"This must be one of that Yeshua mob. We knew they'd be back after he'd run riot in the temple. Just as well we're here in force tonight. We'll soon have the whole lot of them."

They dragged Issa over to a lamp pulling off his headdress. There was a gasp from the crowd as one of them exclaimed, "It's Barabbas!"

The news that Barabbas had been captured spread around the temple courts. He was hustled before the temple authorities who, for some reason, were still in the precinct. They weren't sure what to do. Barabbas did have a following among some of the devoted patriots, though many of the people would have liked to see the back of him. The temple authorities couldn't be seen to be doing Rome's work for them. In the end, it was decided to hand him over to the Roman governor, Pilate, as the civil authority. That way, they could both demonstrate their willingness to be subject to Rome and at the same time rid themselves of a trouble maker. The people wouldn't need to know too many details.

Issa was led under guard to the Roman fort and handed over to the soldiers, who beat him thoroughly about the head, and would probably have killed him there and then had not an officer taken charge. They led him in chains down the streets to Pilate's court, his face cut and swollen from the many blows the guards had landed on him. Dazed and bloodied, Issa struggled to keep his balance and the soldiers beat him all the more, prodding with their staves to keep him moving. He tripped on a step and fell forward. Suddenly, strong arms were around him, lifting him to his feet. He felt his arm being put around the other's neck, taking his weight and supporting his dazed and staggering body.

"Here you!" yelled a soldier. "What do you think you're doing?"

They tried to pull the man away, beating him as well, but he hung on determinedly.

"You watch out or we'll take you in as well!"

"Hang on! Look at him! It must be his brother! Let's have him too!"

It was Moshe.

As Moshe wouldn't leave Issa's side, they allowed him to support him, having spent their ire, leaving them alone till they got to the governor's residence. The attending officer at the gate added a few more blows to Issa and ordered him thrown into the cells below the praetorian.

"I will be glad to see him spread-eagled on a cross!" he added as Issa was led away. "The governor will deal with him in the morning... and this man, too." He turned to look at Moshe.

"Interfered while we were arresting Barabbas. Looks like his brother. No violence, but he interfered in the apprehension of a criminal. What's your name, knave?"

Moshe looked blank and the officer struck him for his insolence, again demanding his name. Moshe put his hands to his ears and shook his head, making a keening sound.

"Deaf and dumb idiot, it seems. Anyone who wants to help Barabbas is a fool, even if he is his brother. Probably as bad as him. Lock him up. We'll get the governor to see him in the morning. Probably get a flogging at least. But if the governor is in one of his moods... that will be a lesson to them all," he added under his breath.

Moshe was roughly led away and flung into the cells with Issa and another prisoner. Issa was dazed and bloodied, totally confused at the presence of Moshe, who became businesslike and, by the light of the moon coming through a grilled window high up on the wall, used his headdress to bathe Issa's wounds, damping it in the half-broken earthenware jug that was the prisoner's only water supply.

Issa thought hard and fast. By now he was little interested in why Moshe was there or how he had found him, but more concerned with the immediate problem of how they could possibly get away. Their predicament seemed hopeless. As he had been led away he had heard the officer say that Moshe may just get a beating and escape with his life. But he knew the Romans well, and on a whim they might nail him up too.

Issa sat against a wall on the straw. From time to time he would look at Moshe, who was always watching him, ready to give his old friend a kindly smile.

Early in the morning, through the grating high in the wall, they heard the commotion of a large crowd gathering outside. Something was going on! Issa hoped it had nothing to do with him.

Chapter 43

On the early morning streets of Jerusalem, Miryam hurried towards the governor's residence. News had been garbled and confused. One by one the disciples had returned to the upstairs room. Yeshua had been taken by the temple authorities! He had been betrayed by Judas! They were numb. They could not believe one of them had betrayed Yeshua! Although, they recalled that Yeshua had always warned them that this would happen.

Peter and John had followed on and the others were all waiting for news from them, to know what they should do. The innkeeper was very anxious about the disappearance of his son Mark. The lad was devoted to Yeshua, though considered by his father too young to join the close band of followers. He had stolen out during the night but had not returned. Now there were worrying reports that a young man had been seen being chased by the temple guard.

Then news came that Yeshua was being taken to the governor's residence. Most of the others, being from Galilee, were wary of Jerusalem at the best of times and didn't want to go anywhere near the Romans. They would wait until Peter and John reported back. Miryam could see they were all very frightened, but being a woman and also used to the ways of Herod's court, she had more confidence and decided to go for news. She hurried down by the city walls taking a short cut she knew, when a voice called from behind a low wall.

"Miryam! Miryam!"

She turned, a little alarmed.

"Miryam! It's me, Mark. No! Don't look! I haven't got anything on. Give me your cloak or something. I'm freezing."

Gladly, Miriam tossed her cape towards the dark alley where the voice had come from.

"What are you doing, foolish boy? Your parents are so worried about you!"

"I sneaked out last night. My father was a bit suspicious, so he took all my clothes away. They do that sometimes to keep me in, but I went out with my blanket. I followed Yeshua after they had arrested him but they saw me and chased me. Almost caught me, but they only got the blanket."

He looked a bit odd in a woman's cloak, but with the hood up and his young face could have passed for a girl. Mark might sometimes be an impetuous young man, but he was brave.

He only knew what Miryam already was aware of, so the two of them hurried to the governor's residence, where a crowd was gathering and people were all discussing what was happening.

"What's this about then?"

"Something to do with that miracle worker Yeshua."

"Not to do with Barabbas? I hear he was taken in by the Romans last night!"

Miryam's heart missed a beat.

"No, this is about Yeshua."

"What? Yeshua? The one some people say is the Messiah?"

"Yeah, he came to the feast with the pilgrims from the north singing, 'Hosanna!' 'Save now!' Then he went and smashed up the temple market!"

Miryam sidled up to the man who had mentioned Barabbas.

"Did you say Barabbas had been taken in?"

"So they say. Governor probably going to have him crucified. Good riddance, I say."

Others standing by looked on and nodded. Barabbas was not popular after the recent riot.

Miryam felt sick. Yeshua and Barabbas both taken in. Her world, which just yesterday, though precarious, was full of promise, was now crashing round her ears.

There was a cry from those at the front and the crowd surged to the railings around the governor's court. Some Jewish officials were there and presently Yeshua was brought in. Pale and unsteady, he stumbled as he entered, his tunic torn and bloodstained from the beatings he had suffered. He stood, head bowed, his hair matted with blood. Those gathered before the dais bowed in reverence as the governor, Pontius Pilate, entered, taking his seat on the chair of office. He gestured towards Yeshua and a guard pushed him forward with the shaft of his spear, causing him to slip and fall to one knee. He rose painfully before standing erect and looked steadily at Pilate, who, turning away, questioned the Jewish authorities.

It was impossible to hear what was being said but Pilate's gestures became increasingly animated. From time to time the governor looked over at Yeshua, but quickly averted his eyes, unable to hold Yeshua's gaze. Pilate tried to question him, but he didn't move and didn't appear to answer. The governor became agitated, leaving his chair and pacing to and fro in front of Yeshua, pointing and and waving his finger. When Yeshua did speak, it was clearly not what Pilate was expecting. Pilate slumped back in his chair, clearly troubled. Yeshua was on trial, but it was obvious who was in command. The governor mopped his brow and turned to the Jewish authorities, waving them to silence. He shrugged and spread his hands.

Miryam saw that as a sign that he was unconvinced by their argument and felt a flicker of encouragement. Then the authorities all started talking at once, gesticulating and pointing at Yeshua, waving their arms around the court and pointing to the Imperial Eagle above them.

Pilate was obviously wavering. Then, standing again, he went to consult with some of his advisors. He returned as one of the Roman officials stood to make an announcement and everyone strained to hear it.

It was the governor's custom to release a prisoner on Jewish festival days. They had recently arrested Barabbas, who was a bandit wanted for murder, riot and theft and even an attempted robbery of their Holy Temple.

Miryam felt sick. So that was what Issa had planned. Why? Why? Why? Oh, if only he had heeded her warning, he might be safe now!

"Choose between Yeshua, the king of the Jews, or Barabbas," the announcement continued.

Miryam felt as if she was in a nightmare. She didn't want to be there. The two men she had loved more than anything in the world were being put up against each other. Some of the religious people scattered in the crowd around her were stirring up the people.

"Choose Barabbas! ... Choose Barabbas!"

A few voices shouted "Barabbas!" Next to her, she could hear Mark shouting, "Yeshua! Yeshua!" but he was alone, and soon his voice was drowned out until everyone seemed to be shouting, "Barabbas! Barabbas!"

Miryam stood rooted to the spot. She hadn't said anything. She looked at the lonely figure of Yeshua, almost totally rejected by the crowd, but she didn't shout his name.

The governor was trying to say something else. The crowd quietened.

"What shall I do with Yeshua?"

The question was barely audible above the rumble of the audience.

"Crucify him! Crucify him!" came the cry from the religious leaders, swelling louder and louder, becoming ever more frenzied as it swept round the crowd. "Crucify him! Crucify him!"

Miryam turned away, ashamed that she had made a choice even by her silence.

"Oh, Yeshua! Yeshua! Yeshua!" she wept bitterly.

Chapter 44

In the dungeons below the governor's court, the prisoners sat waiting while the noise of the crowd increased above them. Moshe was not able to hear anything but could tell from the others' faces that something was amiss.

Issa started. Above the general commotion he could hear his name being shouted, now louder and louder! What was going on? Then his mouth went dry as another cry went up.

"Crucify him! Crucify him!"

Issa looked around, desperate now. There was no hope. What a fool he was! He had just found Miryam and now he would lose her forever. The crowd were calling for his death. Then he saw Moshe by the door looking through the small grating. Of course! Moshe! Moshe always stood up for him; always took the knocks. If he could understand, he would go in his place. But there was no time to lose.

He went over to Moshe, pointing to his headdress and cloak. He quickly removed his clothes, indicating to Moshe to do the same. Then Issa gave him his to put on, urging him on. Soon Moshe, a little bewildered, was wearing Issa's clothes and Issa was putting on Moshe's. Once dressed as Issa, Moshe turned round again to look through the grating. Issa nudged him, holding his shoulder. As Moshe turned round, Issa hit him with all his might, full in the face. Moshe looked unbelievingly at his friend as he staggered backwards; Issa hit him again, trying to cause wounds in the same places as the ones he could feel on his face.

In the end, Moshe crumpled to a heap on the floor. Issa kicked his head again to complete the job and went to the back of the cell, adjusting

Moshe's headscarf to cover his own face as much as possible.

Moshe lay still for a few minutes and was just staggering to his feet when there was the sound of the bolts being drawn and the door of the dungeon burst open.

"Barabbas!" they yelled, but there was no reply. As their eyes became accustomed to the dark, they saw Moshe standing dazed against the wall.

"There he is. He's still pretty dazed but I remember that headdress. Come on, you."

And they grabbed Moshe by the arms and pulled him roughly out of the dungeon.

Issa sat against the wall, feeling sick at what he had just done, trying to reassure himself that it was what Moshe would have wanted. In any case, Moshe had run away scared when he had joined the Zealots. He didn't fit in this tough world. When he and Miryam went off together, what would he do? It was kindest this way.

There was a great roar and more cries of 'crucify him'. He hoped no one would notice the switch, but they were so often mistaken for brothers, he trusted that with the clothes and the bloodied face the subterfuge would pass. Moshe wouldn't be able to tell them and, anyway, would not understand what was happening.

Soon there was another gasp from the crowd at the sound of a flogging. There was no mistaking it. The Zealots used the same scourge on their Roman captives and on traitors to make them talk. He could imagine the cruel lead barbs and broken bones tearing into Moshe's flesh. He covered his ears, now crying for his friend who had been so loyal and whom he now had betrayed. It would be all over soon for Moshe, but no, he must concentrate on playing the part of Moshe and endure a flogging without speaking. Moshe's interference should only receive a flogging with rods rather than a scourge.

The other prisoner had heard the shouting and, finding Issa still there and not Moshe, realised what Issa had done.

"That was a dirty trick. But hey! He was a dumb imbecile and the world won't miss him. Let's hope the governor is kindly disposed to us and we get away with our lives."

The scourging seemed to last forever. Issa slumped deeper and deeper against the wall, trying to shut out the results of what he had done. At last, it finished. But then the door of the prison burst open and two guards came in and ordered them out.

"Bad luck for you two. The governor's in a bad mood after this morning's business and has ordered everyone in the cells to be crucified. Come on, on your feet." They prodded them with the ends of their spears.

Issa was terrified! All that for nothing! Now he too would be crucified! What a fool not to heed the pleas of Miryam. They dragged the two felons out of the dungeon into the courtyard. Moshe was already there, his back torn to shreds from the scourge, kneeling under the weight of the crossbeam. Two more crossbeams were each loaded onto Issa and his fellow prisoner. The sad procession made its way through the streets, the onlookers jeering, spitting and throwing dirt in the way crowds have treated condemned men down the ages. After a short way, Moshe was unable to carry his crossbeam any further and fell to the ground. They pulled the crossbeam off him, pressing a bystander to carry it and dragging him back onto his feet. As they did so, Issa saw that it was not Moshe.

It was Yeshua!

Where was Moshe? Issa tried to look around, receiving a blow from the shaft of a spear. There only seemed to be three of them. They climbed up the narrow streets out of Jerusalem. Now away from the governor's residence, the crowd was more sympathetic to the condemned men, women crying and wailing for Yeshua. What was going on? Suddenly, someone appeared at his side.

It was Moshe! His face was cut and swollen from the beating Issa had given him. He was crying and wanting to help Issa carry his cross, but the soldiers pushed him roughly away. Issa was totally bewildered. What was happening? How was Moshe free? Why? He had no more time to think, as they arrived at the place of execution and now the men were stripped of their clothes and thrown to the ground. Rough hemp ropes lashed his arms to the crossbeam, which had been inserted into an upright. He remembered with terror the last time this had happened to him and knew what was in store.

"No! No! No! Not this!" he screamed desperately. The soldiers only laughed.

As he cried out for mercy, into his mind came the image of the eyes of the outlaw with the rope around his neck, pleading for mercy, as he kicked away the stick; an image that had haunted him ever since.

He felt now the futile hope the man would have felt: a last desperate, hopeless plea but knowing all hope was gone. Terrible pain. A lingering end. Then the blackness of death awaited him.

As he lay spreadeagled on the cross, he tried to move into an easier position. A sharp spike of wood on the upright dug into his back, gouging a wound as they pulled the gibbet into the air and he took the whole of his body weight on his arms. They lashed his feet to the upright beam, allowing him to use his legs and so prolonging his agonising death. Now he could hear them cruelly nailing Yeshua to the cross. He knew from stories the Zealots told that this was another way of fixing someone to the gibbet. It was excruciating, but death often supervened more quickly.

Issa hung from his arms for some time, crying out curses on the Romans, but gradually he found it harder and harder to breathe without pulling himself up to relieve the strain on his chest. Being strong he was able to do this at first, but the sheer effort, the pain and fatigue in his arms and legs and the chafing from the rough ropes quickly became severe. Then the cramps started as the blood supply to his arms was cut off. He tried arching his back, but those muscles became cramped too.

He tried to allow himself to suffocate to hasten his end but the urge to breathe was too strong and his body contorted in every way possible. As fluid accumulated in his throat he couldn't cough, now entering a cycle of desperate body contortions, crying out in pain as he gasped and gurgled; his screams became muffled as he foamed at the mouth, trying to fill his lungs with air.

The cycle of choking contortions and unbearable pain was endless. As the hours passed, what was going on around him became a confusion. Was that a woman's voice calling his name? He strained to look, and thought he saw Moshe and Miryam, but every effort was on breathing. There were others round the cross next to him on which Yeshua was hanging, with the other condemned man agonising beyond.

He was hallucinating now. As waves of pain and the desperate struggle to breathe came over him, the image of the outlaw's eyes were always before him. In the distance was his mother imploring, beckoning, but there was an abyss between them. He heard Daniel's voice calling from far away.

"Do Justice. Love mercy. Walk Humbly with God." But his voice was fading away...

It was too late.

Snatches of songs that he had heard at the feasts came back to him. He saw Miryam singing at his mother's bedside. Then he saw her standing between the two crosses.

He strained to look for Moshe – he must make amends to his loyal friend Moshe – but sweat rolled off his forehead, stinging his eyes, and flies buzzed around the dried blood of his wounded face and his mind wandered again.

Then those eyes were back! The terrified eyes facing death filled his mind and he felt himself sinking into unconsciousness.

"God...!" he cried out loud in desperation, and the scene around him merged into his hallucinations.

He was a boy again, one lone friend standing with him while a hostile crowd bayed for his blood.

He saw eyes again, but these were the eyes of his friend Yeshua. The vivid memory of the last time they had been close together at the temple market years ago. As the images whirled around his head, he heard again Yeshua's parting words to him.

"Whenever you need me, just call."

The scene faded and he was back in agony on his cross, the blackness of death growing and growing even as the daylight seemed to be fading. He could hear jeering and baying directed at Yeshua.

But what had Yeshua done?

Why was he there?

It was he, Issa, who had rejected, betrayed and let down his mother, Daniel, and all his friends from childhood, especially Yeshua.

Again, the image of the outlaw's eyes grew large in his mind. Then other eyes of the Romans he had killed; the traitors he had tortured; the innocent people he had robbed and killed to fund his campaign to do so-called 'justice'. An orgy of vengeance and hatred.

There had been no mercy. No humility. No walk with God.

Why should there be mercy now? Why should God hear him?

Then there came a voice: gentle, calm, unhurried, but rising in intensity, insistent, persistent. "His Kingdom is not of this world! His Kingdom is not of this world! His Kingdom is not of this world!"

What hope was there for the Kingdom? John had been executed, and now Yeshua hung on a cross next to him. Where was this Kingdom now?

The other criminal joined in the mocking of Yeshua.

"If you... are the Messiah... save yourself... and us!"

The cries and jeers welled up, but the voice in his head was stronger still.

"My kingdom is not of this world. My kingdom is not of this world."

As the mocking increased, Issa was transported once more to the angry crowd at the temple market, where he had felt the arms of his friend Yeshua around him, protecting him, and his kind and gentle voice saying, "When you need me…"

It was his only hope! But would he still know him?

He turned and called.

"Yeshua… Yeshua! Remember me?"

Why should he remember him after all these years? He'd been invited to join the Kingdom and had rejected it three times. Gone his own way. So why should Yeshua care?

"Yeshua… in your Kingdom… Remember me!"

He desperately pulled himself up with all his strength to have one last desperate look at Yeshua. Their eyes met for a second, but there was no mistaking that same look he had seen all those years ago, a look that he had all but forgotten, but had been burnt into the mind of the hurt, lost, lonely and humiliated boy in the temple market and which welled up in his mind now.

"Today… with me… in paradise," came the gasping reply.

The image of the eyes of the outlaw faded to be replaced by the loving eyes of Yeshua as Issa slipped in and out of consciousness and agonised, close to death, his tortured muscles still not allowing him to give up.

Then he saw a Roman approach with a sledgehammer, and he knew what was about to happen.

"No!" he screamed as the stone head smashed against his shins, smashing first one leg then the other. Pain exploded again and again as the broken ends of the shattered bones grated together as he tried in vain to lift his broken body and breathe.

His arms were pulled from their sockets and could no longer support him. He felt his lungs full of fluid and tried to cough. He was choking, fluid welling up into his throat. He was suffocating. Darkness started to come over his eyes and he pitched forward into the black tunnel of death.

Then he saw a glow at the end of the tunnel, a light growing brighter and brighter. As it did so, the pain of his body was fading and he found his arms were no longer bound to the cross! He saw the three bodies on gibbets below as he rushed towards the light, arms flung wide and free as a young Yeshua appeared before him, looking as he had done on the crest of the cliffs of the Kidron valley! His eyes full of love, fun and friendship, arms outstretched to pull him over the summit ridge and embrace him in welcome.

Miryam

Chapter 45

As the hammer had smashed Issa's legs, so Miryam's own legs gave way and she crumpled to the ground, burying her face in her cloak, covering her ears to his strangled dying screams. Then, silence.

All had gone quiet, and she looked up. The callous guards hadn't broken Yeshua's legs as he was already dead, but in a final act of brutality, they slashed open his side with their spears, the blood collecting in a pool at the foot of the cross. The other women now stood together some distance away, weeping together.

Miriam felt a hand on her shoulder. It was Mary.

Someone had told her that this was Yeshua's mother Mary, though she'd not met her personally before. She'd understood that Yeshua's family hadn't really approved of what he was doing, hadn't supported him. But she was still his mother, and clearly had always loved her son and would have been heartbroken at seeing him on the cross.

Mary spoke, quietly. "Miryam?"

Miryam looked up into the tearstained face of Mary, nodding blankly.

"Miryam, the others tell me you sing beautifully. Will you sing a lament with me for Yeshua when they take him to the grave?" She looked up at the body of Issa and back at Miryam. "Did you know him, too?"

Miryam nodded. "I once thought we would marry." She shrugged and buried her face in her cloak, sobbing again.

"Then we will sing for both."

Miryam was quiet for a while, then looked up. Staring into the distance, she said quietly, "I cannot sing for Yeshua. It would be false. I could have called out for him in the crowd. I could have called out,

'Let Yeshua live!' but I didn't. It may not have made any difference, but at least he may have known someone loved him! You see, my love was divided." She looked at Yeshua and then at Issa.

The two women were silent for a while, then Mary said quietly, "None of us are worthy, Miryam. I haven't supported Yeshua as I ought. My love was divided too. I wanted to keep Yeshua as my boy. I was his mother; he was my son. I wanted him at home with me. But God was... is his father, he was... is the son of God. He had to do what God, his.... our Father had called him to do. I should have learnt this years ago. He told me when he was still a young boy, 'I must be doing my father's work.' And he meant God, his heavenly father, not Joseph, his earthly father."

The two women waited patiently at the horrific scene, wanting to at least see the broken bodies of the men they loved so dearly laid to rest. Would the Roman authorities allow them to recover the bodies or would they be thrown into the Hinnom valley? They knew that as condemned criminals, even their bodies had no rights, but sometimes the Romans would turn a blind eye and allow the families to take bodies away, so avoiding the hard work of dragging them the not inconsiderable distance to the edge of the Hinnom valley. But if they were not on hand when the bodies were taken from the crosses they would lose the opportunity, and so they must stand and wait till the Romans did their gruesome work.

The first waves of grief having passed, they were now in that surreal time when the reality of the dreadful truth seems suspended. There would be all too much time for mourning in the days ahead.

"Tell me about your man?" asked Mary tenderly.

Miryam looked up at Mary and smiled through her tears. She recounted all she knew, which in reality was scant. She told her his name was Issa, but when she mentioned that they were from Bethlehem, she felt Mary start.

"Did you say Issa? Was his mother's name Sarah?"

"Yes, that's right," she replied, puzzled by how Mary might know.

"Then I know Issa," she said sadly. "We met years ago when we were escaping from Bethlehem… when the baby boys were slaughtered by Herod. We met them on the road. Sarah was returning to Bethlehem, that is why Issa wasn't killed then. Sarah was so kind to us. She will be heartbroken at losing her son!"

"Sarah died some years ago," continued Miryam quietly. "That's when I met Issa, when I really met him. We had always liked each other before. But I was able to help as she died. We fell in love… but he was taken by the Romans to a colony, and I thought he was dead." She choked and a sob broke out as Mary laid a tender hand on her shoulder.

Though they'd never declared their love for each other, Miryam had always assumed that Issa had loved her as dearly as she had loved him.

"I never saw him again till yesterday. He'd joined the Zealots and was in Jerusalem on an assignment. We met by chance. I begged him to leave and come with me and follow Yeshua. Some Zealots have followed Yeshua, you know," she added defiantly. "But he was captured. I thought he was being released instead of Yeshua. We had to choose and I couldn't choose!"

She looked up at Mary and wailed. "I failed, Mary. I failed both of them! Then they released Moshe instead of Issa. He looks so like Issa that the guards wouldn't have known. You see, in the end Issa did the right thing. He let his friend be saved!"

"Moshe?" questioned Mary. "Deaf Moshe?"

"Yes, he was here." Miriam looked around. "But he didn't stay. I think he couldn't bear to see his friend die. He is so good."

"Issa would have known that he deserved to live and done everything to save him. Did you hear what Yeshua said to Issa? See, Yeshua knew the truth! He knew what was really in Issa's heart."

Mary looked on at the young girl wrestling with the pain of loss, her stricken conscience and the mixed memories of the man she had loved.

"Yeshua seemed to know exactly what was in people's hearts," she agreed, nodding knowingly. "I think he would have known exactly how things really were."

The Romans seemed in no hurry to take the bodies down from the crosses, so the women continued to wait.

Mary had been quiet for some time.

"Please sing with me, Miryam. None of us are worthy to sing for Yeshua our Lord, but I think he would want us to all the same. He loved to hear me singing for him when he was a boy... But you lead. I have heard about you at the Pharisee's house. You have loved Yeshua as your Lord for longer than I. I will follow. I need to learn from you, Miryam." After a pause, she continued, "And I will sing, both for myself and also for Sarah; a mother's lament for our sons. Sarah did so love him. And you follow me and sing your lover's lament. Sarah would have been pleased to see the two of you together. She would have gladly given him up for you."

The women looked up. There was movement around the crosses. The Romans were starting to take them down.

First the other condemned man's cross was toppled, smashing to the ground, the body twisting as the crossbeam bounced and came free of the upright. Then Issa came crashing down. There was more of a wait with Yeshua. Two Jewish men, obviously rich from their attire, and probably religious leaders, were talking with the centurion.

"What do they want? Haven't they done enough? Haven't they had their fill?" gasped Mary. But the men were insisting the soldiers treated the body of Yeshua more gently than they had the other two, and made them lower the cross slowly to the ground.

One of the Roman soldiers approached with the heavy sledgehammer, ready to knock out the nails, but the rich man restrained him, looking around for help. It became clear that the rich men were not there to cause trouble, but rather to treat the body of Yeshua with dignity and respect. They also had servants with them who carried cloths and spices for burial.

This gave the onlookers confidence, so Mary, Miryam and the others standing apart approached. One of the rich men tugged at the nails, looking around for help, and a figure pushed forward.

It was Moshe, face bruised and bloodied, his clothes, Issa's clothes, dishevelled and covered in dirt and dust. He held a granite stone to use as a hammer and, not waiting for permission, knelt beside the cross, loosening the nails, banging them carefully to and fro until he could pull them from the wood.

Rigor mortis was setting in, so the women, who had been waiting for this moment, wasted no time in straightening the limbs and wrapping the body in a makeshift shroud they had brought, together with some of the grave clothes brought by the rich men.

Moshe gesticulated to the two other bodies. Understanding, the rich man turned to the Romans, who shrugged. If he wanted all three, it was fine with them.

As the women worked, Mary and Miryam sang their laments, first for Yeshua their Lord and then for the lost sons; Mary singing also for the unknown and unloved man who had no one with him as he agonised. Some mother's son who would have been loved once as she had loved Yeshua and Sarah had loved Issa.

Moshe begged some cloths from the supply brought for Yeshua to wrap around his friend, and he also took the trouble to cover the naked body of the other felon.

The women stood back after the initial preparations had ended and everyone, including the centurion, stood reverently while Mary and Miryam finished their laments.

The laments ended; the servants moved to carry the body of Yeshua, but Moshe pushed forward. He lifted the broken body, tears streaking the dust on his face, while the two servants supported Yeshua's head and legs, and the two rich men led the procession down the hill that Yeshua had so recently climbed, turning off the path into a new garden under

329

construction. It wasn't far away, and though Miryam couldn't see the actual tomb, she could see some of the crowd gathered round it.

She waited by the two other bodies, now feeling alone and afraid, aware of the soldiers' suspicious looks. She was relieved that the garden was so close by. Soon Moshe returned, humping the body of the other man and hurrying up the slope and over the hill. He soon reappeared and did the same with Issa, the feet dangling alarmingly from the ends of the shattered limbs such that Miryam feared they might come away.

Thus he carried the bodies, always keeping one in sight while he carried the other, until after a short but arduous journey, they arrived at a freshly dug grave on the lonely hillside, outside the city limits. Now Miriam realised that Moshe had been here all day, digging the grave in preparation.

The grave was like Sarah's, but with two slots, one on each side for the two bodies. So Moshe had even planned beforehand for the other friendless condemned man! He then had to unceremoniously drop the bodies into the grave, struggling to accommodate the broken and stiff limbs. Eventually it was done, large stones blocking the base and the grave filled in.

Tired and exhausted, Moshe dropped to his knees. Miryam, ignoring the dirt, dust and blood and cultural inhibitions, knelt beside him, and he drew her close, wrapping his strong arms around her as they wept together.

As the sun was setting, they walked together back over the hill and to the new garden where Yeshua had been taken. The tomb was obvious. For some reason there was an armed guard and ropes and a seal over the large stone door. Everyone else had gone; it was the day of preparation. Moshe had never understood religious rites, and Miryam no longer cared. He walked with her back to the inn where she was staying, but as ever, when she turned to say farewell and to thank him, he had gone. She suspected that he would sit in vigil between the grave of Issa and the tomb of Yeshua.

Chapter 46

Miryam sat in the inn with some of the women. There was not room for everyone to stay in one place, so followers of Yeshua were scattered all over the city and in some of the villages around.

The sabbath was long and sad. Everyone was numb. In shock. Someone asked Miryam to sing the lament she had sung with Mary at the tomb. She wasn't sure she would manage but struggled on through and everyone appreciated it. The night drew in and though some retired with the setting sun, no one slept much.

Miryam crept out in the middle of the night to sit on the flat roof. She could hear the murmur of voices in the room below where Yeshua had celebrated Passover just two days before, but it seemed like an age ago. She sat where she had sat with Issa, thinking of what might have been. She realised that he had changed from the shy and awkward young man she had known. Was it all a fantasy? Could he have left his life of vengeance and killing?

But now what was to become of her? All her dreams shattered. What would become of the followers of Yeshua? Would they all drift apart?

Although she still had the little house in Tiberias, she knew she could never go back to her former life as a dancer. She would somehow have to find a new life in Galilee.

And what about the other women? Several of them, like her, had sordid pasts.

Would the men know what to do with them, even if the disciples stuck together? Yeshua had as many women around him as men, even though the inner twelve were all male. She wasn't sure that the men really approved of the women being so much part of things, though content enough to eat the food they'd prepared and 'allow' them do the washing!

The sky was just lightening in the east when she noticed a movement on the stairs. She thought it must be one of the disciples coming in from an outlying village, but saw to her surprise that it was Moshe. He was highly excited, waving at her to attract her attention, his face shining in the bright moonlight.

How had he known she would be out on the roof? But that was Moshe.

She saw he still had the same bloodstained clothes on, his hair unkempt and matted. Miryam guessed that he'd stayed on the hills by the graves all the day before.

He came onto the roof and reached for her hand, gently but urgently pulling her to her feet and beckoning her to follow. She heard a murmur from inside the room as she slipped quietly down the stairs. Moshe moved swiftly and silently down the deserted city streets, waiting at each corner for Miryam to catch up.

She guessed he was going to one of the graves, but this wasn't the way she knew. That route would cross the city, go through a gate and then back along the outside of the walls. This must be a shortcut. Presently they arrived at a walled garden into which Moshe crept, pulling himself up onto the boundary wall and sure enough, when Miriam scrambled up after him, she saw that they were directly above the new garden where Yeshua's tomb was, but it was a long way down the other side. Moshe climbed down the wall quickly and expertly. Miryam tried to follow, kicking off her sandals to get a better foothold, but her tunic impeded her and when she was halfway down, she felt herself slipping. Scrabbling for a foothold, she fell into the arms of Moshe who broke her fall and they ended up in a heap on the ground. In a jumble of arms and legs, she lay still in sheer relief for a few seconds, getting her breath back. Moshe held her tightly in his arms until she made to move, and they rolled apart. She adjusted her clothes, dusting off the dirt and the chalky streaks from the crumbling wall.

But Moshe was now even more urgent. Holding her hand unashamedly, he led her down through the garden terraces. They were still on a higher level and some distance away from the tomb but could see it clearly.

There was no longer an armed guard! Not only that, but the stone was no longer over the tomb entrance!

Miriam grabbed Moshe's arm.

What was happening?

Where were the soldiers?

What had the authorities done?

As they had not entered the garden through the proper entrance, Miryam was wary. They may have problems explaining themselves if they met the guard. Moshe was trying to tell her something, gesticulating and signing earnestly, but Miryam had never been good at understanding his signs.

He was still desperately trying to explain when Miryam heard footsteps and shook her hand in warning, dropping down low against another tomb to keep out of sight. Some women came on the main path to the garden. Dropping their bundles they cried in dismay and ran to the tomb.

Miryam recognised them immediately as friends, other women-followers of Yeshua. She ran down the zigzag terrace paths, catching up with them as they came out of the tomb.

"An angel! He told us… he told us… he's not here!"

"He has risen from the dead!" they exclaimed, wide-eyed and incredulous, looking at one another in amazement.

The first edge of the sun appeared over the hillside opposite.

The Sabbath had ended.

A new day was dawning.

Miryam turned to Moshe.

But Moshe was no longer there.

Chapter 47

Miryam sat on the women's side. The men were chanting the psalms and everyone was rather subdued. It had been ten days since Yeshua had left.

Left for good.

The days after Passover, or rather, after the day Yeshua had come back from the dead – a date that must surely eclipse even the greatest Jewish festival of all – had been heady times.

Yeshua would appear in different places and to different people, and though no one could tie him down, there was no doubt in anyone's mind.

Sadly, some of his followers couldn't tie it all together. They had been expecting at the resurgence of Israel as a nation and questioned where this was all leading. Incredibly, Yeshua coming back from the dead didn't shift their political agenda. For her part, Miryam had seen Yeshua along with a large crowd of several hundred. She was desperate to talk to him, to explain about Issa and about her confusion. She tried to push to the front to get to him, but everyone was so excited that she just couldn't get near. But then, suddenly it was as if he knew she was trying to reach him, and he turned towards her. Everything else faded and he had eyes for only her. She wanted to explain, to tell him about Issa, to ask what it all meant, but the look from Yeshua made her fall to her knees. As his gaze penetrated deep into her soul, she heard his voice from the past.

"Her sins, which are many, have been forgiven."

There were no words spoken aloud, yet she had no doubt about what he was telling her: "Don't think about others. It's all about you. You follow me."

Yeshua had moved among the crowd. She spoke to many afterwards who had experienced the same intimate look that made them feel that they were the only person in the world at that moment.

After singing with her at the cross, Miryam had made a new friend in Mary, Yeshua's mother. Whenever she could, Miryam would seek her out and listen to stories of her life with Yeshua. Sometimes John had been there too. He was Mary's nephew, the son of her niece, Salome, with whom she had always been close. Mary had now moved in to live with Salome's son, John, in the big family house in Jerusalem. Salome's husband, Zebedee, had a salted fish business and traded in Jerusalem, being well connected with the authorities. Miryam had always held John in high regard as one of those closest to Yeshua, though he tended to be quite aloof and distant. Somehow he had changed. He was no longer arrogant and angry as he had once been, wanting to be in control. Miryam had spoken to him about the look she and so many others had received from the risen Yeshua.

"Yes," he said, pondering. "I know that look. I might have missed it though. I so wanted to be the most important of the disciples. Then Yeshua washed our feet in that room above the inn. He said that if we wanted to be first, we must be the servant of all and wash each other's feet. Then he looked at me, and that look said, 'You are the disciple I love.' If he had told me in one of the earlier periods of my life, I would have thought it was because I was the best among the rest. But now I know now that it's because that's the way he wants me to feel about myself, not the way he wants others to regard me."

Miryam remembered the look in Yeshua's eye and thought back to that night in the Pharisee's house. That was her secret.

"Washing feet might bring ridicule and make you feel an idiot, but it made a bond of love that was wider deeper and higher than anyone can imagine," she thought.

But that had been while Yeshua was here. Now he had gone, the followers weren't exactly sure what to do next.

They remembered that Yeshua had said he would send a spirit on them, but she wasn't sure what that meant. Hopefully, it didn't mean what was happening now.

While Yeshua had been alive she had often sung psalms for the group, but now they'd reverted to the synagogue ways, so only the men took part.

There were long silences and heavy prayers.

They had tried to do something with bread and wine but got into complex discussions about who was allowed to administer it, or even who could take part. They were slipping back into the legalism that they'd known before Yeshua liberated them with his teaching about the kingdom.

The only highlight had been the choosing of a twelfth apostle to replace Judas who'd betrayed Yeshua, but even that was a formal affair with dice and straws, long discussions and heavy prayers.

And Moshe had gone, too.

Her brief, though forever memorable encounter with the risen Yeshua, had given her closure on Issa. She so wanted to see Moshe to try to explain about his friend! But Moshe had disappeared. He had obviously been deeply affected by the Yeshua's death, and had clearly seen something in the garden that had made him search her out. She had never understood what he was trying to tell her. Did he understand anything about what was happening? How could she ever explain to him how things were? His deafness was a barrier between them.

It was now the Feast of Weeks. They were reading the law, as the tradition demanded, and it was taking a long time. No one was sure what part they were supposed to take in the celebrations, or if the celebrations were still even part of the new kingdom.

The group of believers were now down to just over a hundred. They were sitting formally in rows, listening to the law, smelling the food that was cooking ready for the street parties, hearing the hubbub from the crowds assembling for the procession to Jerusalem.

Miryam's mind went back to her childhood in Bethlehem. She wondered if they would recount the story of Ruth and if she would be allowed to join the feast once their formal meeting was over. Was dancing allowed? Could they drink wine?

Miryam's mind was drifting when she heard another sound in the street. In the early summer months the local hot and cold differentials created small whirlwinds, which would whip up dust and small debris. The one she could now hear seemed bigger than normal, such that the congregation all turned to look at the windows, expecting street rubbish to blow in.

The speaker at the front droned on, oblivious to the lack of attention from the listeners, when suddenly, with a roar the wind blew into the room and the whirlwind was among them! But instead of dust, there was fire, and flames danced around everyone's heads! Spontaneous joyful singing broke out and Miryam, losing all inhibitions, leapt up with her hands in the air, singing at the top of her voice. The others around her joined in, but many in languages she had never heard. Everyone was on their feet, laughing and hugging each other. The speaker at the front looked up from the scroll he had been laboriously reading, perplexed, but only for a second. Holding the scroll above his head, he joined in the dance around the room, his formal rabbinical skirts swinging with the rhythm. People were now bursting out of the door onto the street, and the gathering street party outside were impressed at the eruption of praise and joy.

"Drunk already!" muttered some in the astonished crowd.

"But they're speaking our languages!" exclaimed some foreign pilgrims.

Everyone was dancing, singing, leaning out of the windows. Miryam led a group dancing in a line out of the room.

Unlike some of the others, she was singing in her own language, but found she just couldn't keep her arms and hands still! She was waving and gesticulating in time with the music, which swelled and broke into complex harmonies as others joined in. The people outside were clapping and swaying in time to the music. At the back of the crowd she caught sight of someone waving arms in harmony with hers. She stared as the words she was singing came back to her in the movement and gesticulations and she made complex gestures in reply. A dancing, smiling, gesticulating figure emerged and swung towards her, hips swaying, feet kicking up the dust, arms above his head.

It was Moshe.

"We're not drunk. It's only ten in the morning!" came the booming fisherman's voice of Peter. "The Spirit of God has come upon us. The prophet Joel said:

'Your women and children will prophecy.
your young men will see visions
and your old men will dream dreams.'"

Even as she heard it, Miryam was signing what he said and Moshe signed back:

"Yes, yes, yes!"

They could understand each other! She was full of joy and delight at this newfound gift. She could hear others proclaiming the message Peter was shouting in many languages, which the Spirit had given them.

And she could talk with Moshe!

They were heady days. Many thousands joined them. Gone were the grey formal days! They met together in each other's homes; they broke

339

bread together simply and easily; they shared all they had. No one was in want.

Miryam never lost the gift she had been given of signing with Moshe. Sometimes complex ideas and sermons took longer than the speaker allowed, but the slower repetitive psalms were easier, and she added dance, which also became part of her signing, much to the obvious delight of Moshe.

But the authorities were not pleased.

They had conspired to have Yeshua executed and were furious that his followers had grown more than ever. They had been relieved when they'd heard that Yeshua had 'gone to his father'.

Maybe that marked the end of it. That had put a stop to it!

But now this!

They tried ordering them to stop. They tried locking them up and they tried beating them, but whatever they did, it just made the group grow and grow. Many priests were joining them and haemorrhaging the ranks of temple workers.

One of the last commissions given by Yeshua was to take the good news to all nations. As persecution was growing in Jerusalem, and they remembered the words of Yeshua, the leaders encouraged those who came from other parts to return home, carrying the good news with them.

Miryam thought of her little home in Tiberias. She was reluctant to leave the bigger group of believers in Jerusalem, but she could see the good sense of the leader's suggestions. But she was fearful. She sought out Moshe to tell him that she would be leaving Jerusalem. He received the information with his usual inscrutable smile. She had enjoyed his company over the last few weeks, but she always knew it would not last. One day, true to form, he would just melt away. So on this occasion, Miryam mused, it would be she who left.

Chapter 48

Miryam arranged to join a caravan of believers heading up to Lake Galilee. Most of them were pilgrims who had recently come to follow the way of Yeshua and were now heading to the villages around the lake. As she swung her pack onto her back, adjusting the head strap, she felt it being lifted. It was Moshe. She smiled at him warmly, wondering if, just maybe, he was planning to travel with them; he had his own blanket and bedroll with him. As if it was the most natural thing to do, he quickly took some of the heavier items from Miryam's pack, giving her a lighter load to manage on the hot descent to the Jordan. Miryam's spirits lifted. Moshe was coming too! She would have at least one old friend among the travellers; someone she could rely on to look out for her.

As they set off, as well as carrying his own load, Moshe hoisted a small fretful child onto his shoulders as the caravan made its slow progress down the dusty Jericho road to the valley of the Jordan. The long descent over, everyone was pleased to be by the river, away from the threatening atmosphere in Jerusalem. Some remembered the days of John the Baptiser, and each evening there would be singing, dancing and sharing of food. They would pray and break bread together. This was particularly poignant for Moshe, being so clear, symbolic; not dependent on words. He was still wearing Issa's old tunic. The bloodstains from Issa's beatings and from carrying the bodies, though fading, were still quite noticeable. No one else, except Miryam, knew the significance.

The journey up the Jordan valley was leisurely. They would start early and walk until the heat of the day, then rest in the shade. The women would busy themselves with the food or washing; the older men would dangle their legs in the water, while the young men and children went off to find somewhere to play, making swings or mud slides wherever they could.

Miryam would have loved to join them. As a child she had always envied the freedom of boys and had exulted in the thrill of her illicit adventures on the hill when she could escape through her secret hole in the wall.

In Tiberias, with the other dancing girls, she would often go to a secluded spot by the lake in the early hours of the morning, to bathe after their dancing sessions; to wash off the greasepaint and ease the memories of their sordid job. She had watched the lake children playing in the water, swimming and diving like fishes. Having been brought up in the arid hills of Bethlehem, swimming was not a skill she had learnt. At the lake, women usually bathed discretely in the shallows, but one of the other girls had been a child by the lake and persuaded Miryam into deeper waters, teaching her to swim. On hot nights, when they had no dancing engagements, they would go to the lake, swimming way out into the cool waters, even diving from one of the rocky promontories if they thought no-one else was around. But, she had mused, as she was already regarded as a lost soul, if she was seen diving naked into the lake in the early hours of the morning, it would only confirm what the people thought of her anyway.

Now she sat with the other women, rinsing her clothes in the muddy waters of the river and beating them against a rock. She had persuaded Moshe to let her wash some of his scant wardrobe, to which he had reluctantly agreed, heading off in his loin cloth with the fathers and children who had come to adore him. She carried the wet clothes up the bank to hang on a tree, choosing one in the full sun, as Moshe would be needing his clothes immediately since he had few others to change into among his meagre possessions.

From her vantage point way above the river, she could see that the children's group had made a mud slide down a bank, splashing water onto it to make it all the more slippery. With great whoops of delight, they slid and slipped into the river. It was a noisy affair and looked great fun. The men, returning to boyhood, had shed their loin cloths to be able to slide more effectively. Miriam stood watching for some time and saw Moshe sliding down, arms and legs in the air as he hit the water. The children splashed him as he emerged and he chased them playfully. Miriam admired his bronzed strong body and the freedom he clearly felt with the other men. After a lifetime of rejection in Bethlehem, he had found acceptance as a follower of the way of Yeshua. The sun felt hotter and her clothes heavier as, hidden by the branches of the tree, she watched them enviously. It would be such fun to do the same with the women, but she doubted that any would join her; their husbands would certainly not approve.

As they walked the next day, Miryam fell into step with an older woman whom she had previously noticed. Very warm and chatty, she seemed keen to get to know the other women in the caravan.

"And for how long have you and your husband been married?" she asked Miryam who, only half listening, was taken aback, realising with consternation that she meant Moshe!

It was a preposterous assumption, but instead of disabusing her of her mistake about their relationship, Miryam found herself replying, "Oh, we grew up in the same village, Bethlehem in Judea."

"Childhood sweethearts!" cried the other, delighted. "And do you have any children?"

Miryam thought for a minute, but she was tired, fearful about the future and there were still scars from her past. She was old for a single woman and she didn't want to say why she was unmarried. It was all so complicated, and it would be easier to fend off questions than to explain. They would go their separate ways in a couple of days anyway.

The particular circumstances of Miryam's childhood made her an expert at living by her wits, but she still liked to tell the truth, or at least a version of it. And if the hearers jumped to wrong conclusions, so be it, especially if it worked in her favour.

She shook her head.

"No, we can't have children as things stand. But I would love a baby one day," she added quite truthfully.

"Oh my dear, I'm so sorry. That is so hard." Then she leaned over, whispering confidentially, "Your husband… Well, you know, he is deaf and dumb… Does he have… I mean, has he…?"

Miryam coloured. She was cross that, like so many other people, this woman assumed that just because Moshe was deaf, he was might be lacking elsewhere.

"No, he's got all that's necessary, if that's what you mean," she retorted sharply, blushing still more because she had spent some time admiring his naked, manly body rather than embarrassment at the turn of the conversation.

The older woman stuttered. "Oh, my dear! I didn't mean…!" They were quiet for a while. Miryam searched for a way to change the subject, but the older woman went on. "Tell me about your family."

"I haven't seen my family for years. My parents are both dead. I was brought up by my grandparents."

"My dear, it's so hard when family disapprove of your marriage," she clucked, assuming marriage was the cause of the estrangement.

In a sense it was, so Miryam went on. "The family wanted me to marry an old man, but my grandfather stepped in for me. But he's dead now. He died about 14 years ago."

"Oh, I am sorry. Just as well he was there in time to bless your marriage. So where do you live now?"

"We've been around different places," she replied, thinking of the years apart when she'd thought that Issa and Moshe were both dead.

"We've never really had what you might call a home together."

"My poor child, it's no wonder you couldn't conceive. A stable home is essential."

Miryam smiled at the thought of Moshe's 'stable' home in Bethlehem. Not sure you would conceive in that sort of stable home! Though of course Mary had given birth to Yeshua there, she thought to herself.

"But where are you going to now?"

"There's a little house I know of in Tiberias."

"Tiberias! But that's wonderful. My husband wants us to move to Tiberias. If we do, then we can be friends! Now we've become followers of Yeshua, he's really excited. We live in a small village high above the lake, but he has decided that we should move to Tiberias to tell people there about Yeshua. You know there are some really lost people in Tiberias. I'm sure a lovely girl like you would have no idea about some of the things they do." She leaned towards Miryam, continuing in a confidential tone. "There are these dreadful dancing girls who make men wild with desire. Some of them are even Jewish girls! Would you believe it? They go to these orgies and do all sorts of terrible things. It's true!" she ended, moving away for effect.

Miryam was thinking fast. It had never occurred to her that this saintly old couple would be likely to live in hedonistic Tiberias!

The old woman was still talking and Miryam, absorbed in her own train of thought, was suddenly startled to hear the story about herself.

"...and then apparently one of these dreadful dancing girls burst into the feast and poured all this perfume over Yeshua's feet! My dear! Can you imagine? But Yeshua didn't seem to mind at all! She even became a follower. Yeshua just accepted her and forgave her for her old life. They say she sings beautifully. Just like you!"

"Well I never," Miryam replied faintly.

The old lady turned to her husband and said in a loud voice so that he could hear, "My dear, this is Miryam. She and her husband Moshe are going to live in Tiberias. Isn't that wonderful?"

345

He looked around, a bit perplexed.

"You said the Lord would provide the way for us to live there," she shouted in his ear. "So maybe Miryam can help us find somewhere to live. Maybe she is the angel you were expecting to meet!" She turned and said in a loud whisper to Miryam, "He does have these strange ideas. An angel! I ask you!"

Several of the others in the caravan listened in on the conversation, a little bemused. As it was being shouted loud enough for the old man to hear, everyone else could not help hearing in as well. Miryam was relieved that she'd not really known any of the other travellers before this journey, so hopefully none knew the true state of affairs between her and Moshe. More importantly, nor of her past life in Tiberias.

The old lady continued in a quieter tone, much to Miryam's relief. "You know, my dear, that my husband is a priest. He would like to pray for people for healing as Yeshua has said. I'm sure he would pray for you and your husband to have children."

Pleased with her idea, she turned to shout this to her husband, but Miryam pulled her cloak to stop her. This was about to become a debacle and she must stall for time.

"No, please! I mean, thank you! I... I will need to talk to Moshe first. It might be difficult to make him understand," she said by way of understatement.

Looking round for Moshe, she was relieved to see he was some distance away, playing with a group of children as they walked along, and she could excuse herself to go over to him. She shrugged and spread her hands, smiling weakly, whilst heading over to Moshe.

"Think about it and let me know," the old lady called after her kindly.

Miryam did think about it. She was heading back to Tiberias and didn't really have any plans in mind. She suspected that the town would still be suspicious of her. It was one thing to come and go as she had when Yeshua was travelling around Galilee, but she now had to build a new life. How much better it would be if she did have a husband! Moshe was such a hard worker and he would be able to earn honest money. For her part, she could provide him with a home. Although she had been sharp with the old woman about Moshe's fecundity, she really had no idea what Moshe thought about women. He was so servile, so retiring, never showing any disrespect, lustful looks or inappropriate interest in women. Or any interest at all, for that matter.

She knew she had little chance marrying at her age and with her history, so maybe such an arrangement could be a practical solution for them both? In any case, he seemed to have rather attached himself to her and it would never do for her to have a man living with her in a one-room house who was neither family nor spouse. The gossip would say that she'd gone back to her old ways. Besides, she really did like having him around. He was healthy, strong and a good worker. She could care for him. What would he do without her anyway?

That evening after the worship time, when Miryam had led the singing and dancing with the other believers, they returned to the campfire. Miriam wondered how to make Moshe understand. Best to ask him straight, first off, and then go round the subject in different ways till he understood what she meant.

Once they were relatively alone, she hesitantly broached the subject, signing, "Will... you... be my husband?"

She had expected the grin which meant 'please explain again in another way', but she had not expected him look at the ground and quickly get to his feet, turning his back.

She thought she must have offended him. Maybe he had misunderstood what she was saying. Maybe he thought she was making a pass at him. Troubled, she went after him to explain. She touched his shoulder anxiously, but when he turned back to her, she saw his kind, gentle eyes were moist, and he took her hands, smiling.

He dropped them to sign. "How?"

She was a bit taken aback. She'd expected more discussion, not absolute surrender. She regrouped quickly.

"There is a priest," she signed, pointing in the direction of the camp of the old priest and his wife. "He could marry us."

Moshe seemed relieved, signing, "Go ahead. Please." He obviously had no idea what was involved.

They returned to looking at the fire and no more was said, though when their eyes met Moshe would smile a little sheepishly.

Miryam thought fast. She had committed herself now. But what had she done? Would this work? Had she rushed into something foolish? Was he going to disappear again? She looked over to Moshe. The smile on his face showed that at least he was not harbouring doubts. That was definitely an encouragement.

First thing in the morning, she went over to the old couple. Miryam would have to choose her words carefully to achieve what they wanted while keeping the old couple on side. Maybe a little in the shade or, to be truthful, completely in the dark.

"Oh my dear, there you are!" welcomed the old lady, beaming as Miryam approached. "I've told my husband your story. It's so romantic! I also told him about 'you know what' and he will be very pleased to pray for you."

"You're very kind," replied Miryam, desperately searching for the right words. "I have spoken to Moshe and we would like you to pray for us to have babies. But we also have a special favour to ask. You see, we have never had the priestly blessing that you would normally expect at a betrothal. We wondered if your husband would say that for us?" She was red-faced from guilty feelings about the deception but hoped the other would think it was her modesty causing her some embarrassment.

The old lady took her hand kindly and turned to her husband.

"They would like the priestly prayers you use at a betrothal," she shouted to the old man, who looked puzzled. "The family didn't approve of their marriage so obviously didn't arrange things properly. Poor things! For all these years they've waited for the blessing," she shouted.

"My, my," responded the old man, concerned. "How long have you been betrothed?"

"14 years," put in the old lady before Miryam could answer, but as she rather hoped she would.

"But it only seems like yesterday," Miryam added truthfully.

"Little sister, which prayers were omitted?" asked the old priest with some concern.

"It was so long ago, how can you expect them to remember?" chided the old lady, and in a flash of inspiration Miryam seized the opportunity that had fortuitously presented itself.

"Maybe you could say the whole thing for us? That way we could be sure everything had been done properly. They are such beautiful prayers, it would bless us to hear them as if for the first time."

And so it was arranged, more easily than Miryam could have hoped!

That evening, after the worship time, Moshe and Miryam went to the old couple's camp. Some of the others in the caravan had overheard the morning's bellowed conversation so news had spread, and a good crowd gathered round.

Miryam hoped she wouldn't have to explain anything, but she needn't have worried – the old lady took charge, embroidering their story, elaborating on what she thought Miryam had said, making the tale into a romantic love saga, though in truth it was barely 24 hours old!

The old priest said his prayers beautifully, and as prayers for children were part of this, Miryam felt she was not being entirely untruthful before the Lord, though she did have a pang of conscience about it all.

"Please Lord, forgive me. He is a good man. I will care for him," she prayed in her heart.

Tradition had it that there should be a period between betrothal and moving in as man and wife. Although everyone in the caravan assumed they were already married, living in such close proximity, husbands and wives were discreet with each other. Miryam was glad that she could conform at least to one tradition, albeit in this rather roundabout way.

That night Miryam lay by the fire, her mind racing over what to do tomorrow when they would arrive at Tiberias. Moshe sat leaning against a tree beside her. Eventually she dropped into a fitful sleep, but whenever she woke Moshe was still there, sitting alert and attentive, ready to do her bidding with his kind, ready smile to reassure her.

They had camped that night close to the southern end of the lake where the Jordan made its exit, and the next day, in a state of excitement everyone rose in the predawn light to prepare for the last stage of their journey together.

As the caravan made off, heading along the road that would lead up the Western shore, Moshe indicated that they should cross the river at the ferry and head to the eastern shore. Miryam pointed after the caravan, trying to make Moshe understand, but he was determined, insisting they go on the ferry. The caravan was moving off without them while they argued, Miryam becoming more and more irritated, waving wildly in frustration. She was taking on a huge responsibility and he wasn't making it easy for her. But he would not be swayed and made off towards the river crossing point, stopping at the water's edge.

The old couple were waiting for them and Miryam was perplexed, beginning to panic. What could she do? Was this going to be the shortest marriage in history? How could she ever explain if they separated now? Miriam looked from Moshe to the departing security of the caravan and back to Moshe. What was he thinking of? Throughout his life, he'd had this habit of disappearing then reappearing when needed. Was this going to happen again? He would have to choose. If he didn't want to come with her he would have to fend for himself. As she wrestled in her mind, a sharp pain stabbed her heart at the very thought of losing him; a growing longing to be with him welling up inside her. Her mind flashed back over the past few weeks, remembering the comfort and close bond they had shared at the Issa's grave. The safe strong arms catching her as she fell from the wall of the garden. How she had lain for longer than really necessary, enjoying the warmth of his body in the cool of the morning. She recalled how much she had missed him after he had left her in the garden; how she'd been constantly looking out for him, wanting to share the joy and excitement of the days after the resurrection; and the joy of their reunion at the Feast of Weeks when the Spirit had gifted them with the ability to sign together. How she loved dancing, especially when he was there, as if she was doing it just for him. While everyone else could join in the singing, they would worship in sign and dance. And she had felt a deep warm security as he sat by her side last night, watching over her while she lay curled up in her blanket by the fire, such a security as she had not felt in years.

In the jumble of thoughts that flashed though her mind, she realised now that she'd been manipulating Moshe for her own ends. She was relying on the security of her little house in Tiberias in case things didn't work out for them together. She had assumed Moshe would be there to do her bidding, her guard dog, her slave. This was decision time. All at once, she had no doubt that she couldn't live without Moshe. It was as if she'd woken up to find the one she had always so missed all her life. As a shiver ran through her at the thought of losing him, she looked round desperately in case he had disappeared again, but he was there, waiting for her, and made every sign that he intended to sit it out. She would have to trust his commitment to her. But how could she doubt anything of faithful loyal Moshe? Now it dawned on her that it was all or nothing. The loss of the precarious security of a life in Tiberias was of nothing compared to the loss of the care and protection of Moshe.

She ran over to him, taking off her pack and cloak, which she put down beside him so there would be no doubt that she intended to return. She knelt submissively before him so she could hold his hands and look up into his eyes. There was no time for more complex explanations. For his part Moshe was used to patiently waiting while those with hearing went through an elaborate mouthing ritual, trying to work out amongst themselves what was all so obvious if anyone bothered to look and think.

She signed, "I'll come back... Wait." Then she rose and turned, running back to the old couple, conscious that a woman of her age should not be covering the ground quite so fast with her skirts hitched up quite so high.

She had been wrestling with an uneasy conscience about deceiving them, and now with this new resolve and change of plans, she knew she needed to set the record straight. Miryam arrived at the couple breathless and unsure how to start. Everything she had led the old lady to believe was really not true.

"We are going the other side of the lake. There's a change of plan," she started wildly, turning to look back at Moshe, searching for the words to unravel the web of intrigue.

"Please God, help me tell the truth as it is for once in my life!" she murmured to herself, dropping her eyes and saying as loudly as she dared, hoping the old man could hear, "I haven't been straight with you." She looked up desperately from one to the other. "You see, we weren't married... weren't at all married... before yesterday. I don't know why I didn't tell you straight off. But then you asked so many questions and I got into it deeper and deeper until I didn't know how to find a way out."

She paused, looking at the ground then looking up, trying to compose herself. "Moshe was not my husband. I had hoped to marry his best friend, Issa, but he was imprisoned and executed by the Romans. Moshe had always just been there. He and Issa were so similar that people took them for brothers. When they used to come back together over the hills, leaping from crag to crag like in the Song of Songs, you couldn't tell them apart until they were close. Like everyone else, I took Moshe for granted. Worse than that, like everyone throughout his life, I felt he was a little lacking as he couldn't speak."

The old lady coloured just a little.

"But he helped everyone he could. He was always there when you needed him, then he would fade away into the shadows and wait till he was needed again. He came with me when we left Jerusalem. I was pleased to have company on the journey and someone to carry my heavy baggage but hadn't really thought about him and what there was for him next. I never thought of his needs, no one ever does. But your questions made me think. Why not? Why should we not be married? You see, I'm too old to marry now and..." She paused, looking away over the waters of the lake, in the direction of Tiberias. "I have a past. The family *did* want me to marry an old man. It was just like I told you. But when my grandfather died, I ran away. Moshe and Issa had long since disappeared. We all thought they were dead. I needed to find some way to support myself and when I got to Tiberias I became one of those 'dreadful dancing girls' I think you called them."

"Oh, my dear!" The old lady laid a loving hand on Miryam's arm. "I'm so sorry I said those things!"

"No. I was in an awful trade. Ostensibly making people happy, but really causing so much misery. I deserve that condemnation. Then I met Yeshua. I was the woman who poured the perfume over his feet. Caused quite a fuss. So I'm sorry I deceived you. But I must thank you for opening my eyes to Moshe."

The old man was having difficulty following and looked at his wife perplexed, much to Miryam's relief. She was desperately worried that when he heard the truth, he would declare the marriage ceremony null and void.

"My dear, let the girl finish. I'll explain later," she told him a little sharply.

"I had thought we would go and live in Tiberias. I do have a little house there which my friend gave me when she moved away with her soldier husband. I'd assumed that Moshe would fetch and carry for me, but he is set to go the other side of the lake, and I must go with him. I know that now. But that is all I know. We won't be going to Tiberias. Moshe has other plans."

Suddenly it became clear to Miryam what she must do. With a sense of joy and relief she put her hand down the front of her tunic and pulled out a large key on a red cord.

"Please will you do something for me? It's not payment for your kindness to us, but rather another kindness I am asking of you. Something I know Yeshua would want me to do. This is the key to my home in Tiberias. It's up the street opposite the harbour with a baker's on the corner. The house is near the top, just before the open hill. Just ask for Miryam's house. I'm afraid it's in the poorer part of the town and isn't much to look at. It's only one room, but it will give you a little home in Tiberias. Please go and use it! No! Have it, it's yours! You must tell the people… especially 'the dreadful dancing girls'…" Here she smiled at the old lady, "…about Yeshua. Tell them the good news about the Kingdom and about forgiveness and a new and full life."

"But my dear, what if you need the home?"

"Please understand. I am going with Moshe. I thought I would provide for him, but I realise that I must give up everything for him and let him provide for me. He doesn't know about the home in Tiberias so he's not counting on it. In fact, you must also have this." She reached into her tunic again and pulled out a small leather purse. "It's not much, but you must take it. I want to take nothing with me. I want him to be my security. I'm so sorry I deceived you. Please, do this for me? Do this so I can depend on his care and learn to love him for who he is."

The old lady's face was shining.

"But my dear! This is so romantic! More romantic than the Shulammite in the Song of Songs! Just wait till I tell my friends!"

Miryam looked over at Moshe, waiting patiently. She knew in her heart that as surely as he had always disappeared when not needed, he would now always be there for her.

"Goodbye, my kind friends. Maybe we will meet again." She hugged the old woman warmly.

The old man still did not understand and bowed more formally when Miryam turned to him. She hurried back along the rough path towards Moshe, the shouted explanations of the old lady to her husband echoing across the ground. As Moshe helped her shoulder her pack, there was a deep sonorous shout and Miryam looked up and saw the old man waving and hobbling towards them.

Help, thought Miryam, he's coming to tell us we aren't really married! She waited with some trepidation, but when he arrived, breathless, to her surprise he clasped her in a fatherly embrace, and turning to Moshe, hugged him too, warmly.

"I have never hugged angels before. And I certainly have never married them." He shook his head, muttering to himself. "I need to rethink what I know of angels. I thought they didn't marry." He looked at his feet, puzzling this out, and then turned back to Moshe and to Miryam, who was trying to suppress a nervous giggle.

"God bless you! And thank you! The Lord told me he would provide. Jehovah Jireh!" he shouted as he returned to his beaming wife.

"But my dear, this is so romantic!" mimicked Miryam, laughing with relief and waving to the old lady as she awaited her saintly old husband.

Chapter 49

Miryam had no idea where Moshe was taking them as the first rays of sun appeared over the lake. She wondered if they would head into the hills to one of the Ten Towns, as they were called in these parts. The eastern side of the lake was more pagan than Jewish, and she was a little apprehensive of how they would manage. But Moshe chose the narrow tracks on the floodplain. They were mostly fisherman's paths, and from time to time they would come upon small clearings where the locals would clean their fish and cook their breakfast after a night on the lake. Fishing styles varied around the lake and in the shallower southern end, they fished from the shore with throw nets or hook and line. There was a strong smell of stale fish everywhere, and sometimes the path was muddy underfoot. The sun was climbing in the sky when eventually she could see the end of the floodplain, where the mountains came closer to the lake. The hilly shore to their right had numerous caves visible, which Miryam pointed out to Moshe, who signed that they were tombs. She shuddered, but was relieved that Moshe didn't seem to be heading towards them. For a moment she had thought that maybe he was thinking of making one of these into a home, like the one he had in Bethlehem.

As they trudged on, the tough grass and coarse bushes scratching her bare legs, the hot sun with no shade, the constant smell of fish, and no obvious dwellings apart from the caves of the dead made that morning's resolve to follow wherever he led wear thin.

"This is so romantic!" she muttered to herself sardonically.

But now a small clump of trees on a rocky promontory came into view and she looked forward to being able at least to rest in the shade. Maybe there would be a spring, for the water they had with them was lukewarm, and she certainly didn't relish drinking the brackish water at the edge of the lake.

Moshe turned and grinned back at her, pointing happily to the first outcrop. A well-worn track led up from the shore and as they reached the top of the rise, they came upon a small meadow in front of a house, smoke rising from a fire beside which two older men sat looking out over the lake. Moshe waved, but they didn't notice, and it was only when they were a dozen metres away that the men saw them, leapt to their feet shouting a joyful greeting, and turning, called to the house.

"Rachel! Rachel! They've come! They're here!" A portly woman appeared in the doorway, and the men called out, "It's Moshe and he's brought his bride!"

"Moshe! Moshe! Welcome home, my boy!" called the older of the two, walking stiffly, leaning on his stick and embracing Moshe warmly, then turning to Miryam.

"And you must be his bride! He was so excited when he left to fetch you. He told us, in his own way of course, that he was going to Jerusalem to bring you back. You are welcome! Most welcome!" he said, taking both her hands in his and beaming at her, his kind old eyes moist with joy as the woman called Rachel arrived from the house, smiling radiantly and folding Miryam in a capacious hug.

Miryam looked from Moshe to the others, completely at a loss. She thought she had engineered the whole thing, that she had more or less tricked Moshe into marrying her, but these people were expecting them.

It had never occurred to her that he might have had a similar plan!

The other man was a little more shy and awkward, but greeted Miryam just as warmly, proffering her a bench in the shade of a tree.

"You must be tired after your journey," he said, scooping a gourd of water out of a pot. It was cool and sweet, obviously from a spring and not the lake. Miryam accepted it gratefully.

"But your feet are so muddy!" he noticed, jumping to his feet, enthusiastically fetching a bowl of water for Miryam to put her feet in.

Miriam was a bit taken aback, and Rachel took the old man's arm to restrain him.

"I'll look after her!" she said, shooing him away as he stood back, looking a little crestfallen.

"I thought we'd heard that Yeshua said we should wash each other's feet?"

"Stick to the men, Silas. Ladies have delicate feet. Your hands are much too coarse!" laughed the older man, while Moshe looked on grinning, proudly standing behind Miryam with his hands on her shoulders. Rachel busied herself with a sponge and towel, while Miryam felt totally bewildered.

She looked at the older of the two men. There was something about him that was familiar. She was searching her memory. Suddenly she had it! It was Daniel!

She sat up with a start. "Are you Daniel? From Bethlehem?"

"Do I know you?" he asked, looking into her face.

"You were at the grave of Sarah, Issa's mother. I was the girl who sang."

The old man got to his feet and came over to her again, searching her face with his kind old eyes as Rachel withdrew to the house with the pail and sponge.

"You are Miryam? Oh my dear, my dear! What a joy that you are safe! Everything was so sad, so sad. Sarah first, then Issa and Moshe disappeared and then you…"

"Ran away," put in Miryam, as Daniel searched for a delicate way of putting it tactfully.

"Yes. Yes. But I would say escaped. And now poor misguided Issa is dead too. So much sadness. But now, God has forgiven this selfish old man and allowed him to have joy in his old age," he said, his voice trembling.

Miryam looked puzzled.

"But Daniel, what are you doing here in Galilee? So far from Bethlehem!"

He sat back against the tree, looking out over the lake.

"After Issa disappeared I couldn't carry on with shepherding. My eyes were failing and my legs were stiff. Then miraculously Issa came back. But he was so bitter and angry. He got mixed up with the Zealots and came to a bad end. You maybe know more than we do about that?"

Miryam nodded sadly. "Moshe and I were there when he died. We buried him together."

"Poor, poor boy. He wanted to marry you. Did you know?"

His familiar voice quavering with emotion, as it had at the Sarah's grave, stirred memories of Miryam's life in Bethlehem. Her grandmother had always scorned her prospects of marriage, saying that no good man would marry the daughter of a whore. But she had sensed a kindred spirit in Issa, not least because her grandmother referred to him as 'that bastard-child next door'. From the time she had caught his eye at the feast, he would seek her out, and she made sure she was alert to his advances. Having gained her grandfather's sympathy over Sarah's death, Miryam knew that if she waited patiently she might yet one day be his wife. But then…

"Yes, I knew," she replied simply.

Daniel sat quietly for a few minutes deep in thought. "Did he ever find you? He said he wanted to search for you."

"We met by chance just before he was captured. But…" She shrugged.

Daniel looked up and nodded sadly.

Miryam continued. "So much death and destruction. He was no longer the young shepherd boy I had loved. I wept at his cross, but it was really for the lost love of my youth." "If only he had met Yeshua. I told him there was another way!" Daniel cried in frustration, banging his stick on the ground.

"Daniel, he did meet Yeshua. At the end he did," replied Miryam quietly but emphatically, recalling the few gasped, barely intelligible words that had passed between the two as they hung dying. She hadn't grasped the full significance of those words in the pain, barbarity and hopelessness of that day. But Yeshua had risen to new life and now there was a bright, dawning hope. She knew in her heart that this hope reached even to Issa and he too was now safe. And out of the ashes of that tragedy, she and Moshe, the two who had loved him most, were starting a new life together.

"I am pleased that I have been trusted to marry his best and truest friend."

"You have found a good man, my dear girl." Daniel looked over to where Moshe stood casting a fishing line into the lake. He had wandered off to fish, not being able to join in the conversation, and already had a small catch in a wicker basket.

"So how did you get here, Daniel?" prompted Miryam gently after they had watched him in silence for some time.

Daniel looked up, clearing his throat and spitting discreetly. "I was in Bethlehem hearing stories about John the Baptiser. The people were getting excited, saying the Messiah was coming. Then there were amazing accounts about Yeshua and the things he was doing. The poor spoke well of him, but the religious weren't so sure. Hostile even. I had known Yeshua when he was a baby. They stayed in my house while they lived in Bethlehem. I was desperate to go and see him, to hear his teaching, but how could I? My legs were frail and I was almost blind. I prayed and prayed for a way to open up. Then Moshe came. He was so excited and somehow explained that he wanted to take me to see Yeshua. I don't know how I understood. I find him so hard to comprehend even now when I can see. It was a long difficult journey for us, me being almost blind and Moshe deaf. But we managed with lots of bumps and scrapes, especially crossing Jerusalem." Daniel laughed at the memory. "It wasn't amusing at the time, though. I was always anxious lest we got separated in the busy streets, but we held each end of a short stick and somehow got through the crowds. Then I worried about the Jericho road, which is notorious for vagabonds, but we went through Samaria. That was little better for me as the people there can be so hostile! We stopped at Rachel's home and she could see that we were struggling, so she offered to come with us."

Rachel had just arrived back as he got to this part of the story and smiled.

"I knew Moshe from a while before, when he and Issa got into problems with some outlaws and hid in my house. I was pleased to go with them as I so much wanted to go to hear more of Yeshua. I didn't dare go as a lone Samaritan woman. It was good that we could help each other."

Daniel nodded, looking out over the water as a hot east wind gusted and rippled the surface.

"It's going to be a hot day," he observed. "But it was even hotter that day when we arrived at the lake and the last of my eyesight failed in the bright sunlight shimmering off the water. Eventually Moshe found out where Yeshua was staying, and he and Rachel took me to him. It was evening, and there were many people with all sorts of problems, but Yeshua and his disciples attended them all. When it was our turn, Yeshua laid his hands on my eyes, and suddenly it was as if a mist lifted and I could see again! Perfectly! I'm still old and shaky and do get a bit confused at times, but now I can see! There before me was the lake, and the sun setting behind the hills, the gold of the sunset reflecting off the water. It was so calm and beautiful. So green after the arid Bethlehem area. It was like I imagined heaven to be.

"We stayed a while near Yeshua, hearing more about the kingdom. But then he went on one of his journeys and we couldn't easily follow. I didn't know when or how I would make the journey home, but Moshe had other plans for me. A lot of Yeshua's followers were fishermen, so Moshe arranged for some of them to bring us here by boat. Yeshua often used boats to get about so it was no problem, especially as they might do a bit of fishing on the return trip. And here I met this grumpy old man!" He slapped Silas on the knee affectionately. "And here I am, and here I will be buried."

Silas looked at his feet, smiling shyly, so Miryam prompted him. "And you, Silas?"

He looked up, starting diffidently.

"I used to live in the cave tombs. I wasn't in my right mind for many years, tormented by spirits... many spirits." He pulled up a sleeve, revealing disfigured forearms. "My whole body is covered with the scars of those years. The spirits tried to destroy me." He stared at the ground for a few moments, recalling the horror. Then, looking up, his face transformed.

"Yeshua came!" he took Miryam's hand, eyes shining. "Yeshua came, and I was free! The people here weren't pleased and told Yeshua to go. I wanted to go with him, but he said no. He wanted me stay and tell the people what he'd done for me. It was then Moshe turned up. I think Yeshua must have sent him so we could go around, two together, as he used to send his followers. But what good would a dumb preacher be? But you know Moshe! We set up home together here. Together we built this little place and cleared some little plots for a garden. He knows a lot about animals, and we got some goats and hens. Then he told me he was going to fetch Daniel. I'd expected a man, but not a woman as well!"

"But they even let me stay," added Rachel, "which was just as well, as the house was a bit of a shambles. I am their housekeeper."

"No you're not, and anyway less of the 'let you'. You fussed around like an old hen and took over the house!" cried Silas, laughing, more confident now. "The locals think we're all one crazy family, which we are, of course. Yeshua has brought us all together."

Miryam looked around, taking in the house and its paddocks, the meadow and the small headland jutting out into the lake.

"It's so beautiful on this side. I used to live over there in Tiberias and would see these hills from my home. Do a lot of other people live nearby?"

Silas laughed. "The local people are superstitious and afraid of the ancient cave-tombs. The Jews don't like it much because the people this side of the lake keep pigs."

Miryam wrinkled her nose. Some of the pagans in Tiberias had kept pigs and she could never bear the smell.

"Are there pig-herders living around here?"

"Not close by. The pig people keep away from me. They think I'm bad luck. So we mostly have the place to ourselves."

Daniel looked over to Moshe, who was now raking the coals of a fire to grill the fish, and back to Miryam.

"But you two. When is your betrothal ceremony?"

Miriam was a little embarrassed.

"We... we had that yesterday," she said hesitantly. "A priest, a follower of The Way, did it for us. Sort of. It seemed too good an opportunity to miss," she continued more quietly, conscious she was slipping back into her old habit of adapting the truth. Not knowing what else to say, she added lamely, "He said all the prayers."

"And did you have a marriage feast?"

"Well, no. You see..." started Miryam, wondering how to explain.

"Wonderful! We can have it here!" Rachel clapped her hands with joy. "Everything is prepared and ready. It took us a long time to understand why he was so excited. It was not until he made a big bed that we understood that he had been trying to tell us he was going to bring a bride home."

Miriam coloured. She hadn't really thought about the practicalities of a marriage bed. Certainly not in a shared house. She looked over at the small house, trying to work out the domestic arrangements.

"Is this Moshe's house too, then? Do you all live together?"

"Oh, no. The three of us old ones live here. Moshe has built his own house just over the hill in the next cove. He's been whitewashing it and making it into a lovely home for two. He'll take you there later, after we've celebrated this happy day. Won't you, Moshe?" she said brightly, as Moshe appeared with a platter of small grilled fish he had just caught, smiling uncomprehending, but enjoying the fun and jollity while looking for a space to put the food. Rachel briskly waved Silas off the bench, setting it before Miryam, on which Moshe placed the fish.

"You must be hungry, my dear. Sit and eat some breakfast while we prepare. I have made Moshe a bridegroom's jacket, and we'll all dress in our best for the occasion," she laughed happily, bustling off, organising the three men.

Miryam's mind was in a whirl. There was so much to take in. Just two days ago she had vague plans of eking out some sort of hand-to-mouth existence with Moshe, in the hostile pagan community of Tiberias and her sparsely furnished one roomed house in a squalid part of the town. Now she found a house lovingly prepared for her in a little homestead with livestock and fruit trees and gardens, set in the sort of wild hills in which she had always dreamed of living. And all with a loving family waiting to joyfully welcome her in!

She was overwhelmed, her eyes brimming with tears, partly from the abundance but also because she was supposed to be the bride and she had not prepared at all for her wedding. She didn't even have a festival dress, let alone a bridal gown or any jewellery. Everyone else would be in their finery and she would have just her travelling clothes. True, her under-tunic was of fine linen, well cut with fuller skirts, appropriate for wearing when she danced at the worship times, but it was still plain and modest and would be dusty and stained after the journey.

She remembered the wedding celebrations she used to go to in the Bethlehem area. Her grandfather would often volunteer her to sing for the bridal party in the certainty of getting an invitation as her chaperone. He did love a lively celebration with rich food and particularly, abundant, good strong wine to drink. Miryam had always admired the finery of the bride and her attendants and dreamt that one day she might be the happy bride; beautifully attired and bedecked in jewels, even though her grandmother made sure she was under no illusions that there would ever be such a celebration for the likes of her. And now, suddenly, it was her wedding day. But it was more like one of those awful, recurring dreams where everything is wrong, out of place and unprepared.

Rachel returned with some water for her to drink and, noticing Miryam's tears, knelt beside her, taking her hand. "My dear, what is it? Have we upset you?"

Miryam looked into Rachel's kind eyes, trying to compose herself, rubbing her eyes with her knuckles and wiping her nose on her sleeve.

"It's nothing. I was just feeling sorry for myself." She tried to sound bright and cheerful, but then her lip quivered, and she blurted out, "But I haven't prepared! I have no bridal gown, or anything to wear at all. Moshe has done so much, and you are all so happy, and making a feast and are going to dress for the occasion. And me? I've brought nothing." With an effort, she tried to pull herself together. "Look, I'm sorry. I should be grateful for all you are doing."

Rachel stroked her head, thoughtful.

"But maybe..." she said, a little hesitantly. "Maybe I have something you could wear. Come. Come and see if it will do."

She helped Miryam to her feet and led her into the house. The main room was simply furnished but neat and tasteful. Rachel went through into a small back bedroom, obviously hers, and pulled a wooden trunk from under the bed. Rummaging through the top layers, she eventually found what she was looking for and smiled as she carefully pulled out a garment protected in a linen sleeve. Gently unwrapping and tenderly opening it on the bed, she straightened the folds, smoothing the creases with her hands, looking at it and smiling, her mind far away. It was long and full, with clear sequins in the way of Samaritan garments. The whole was sheer, cream-coloured, to be worn over the shoulders and sleeveless. The skirts were sown in strips of the same fabric, flowing full and wide. Low at the collar, a fine veil was loosely attached that could be worn over the head or dropped as a train. Miryam looked at her questioningly.

"It was my mother's and her mother's before that. It was passed down the family, but..." She sighed long and sadly. "I never had the sort of wedding you could wear this for. I was just passed around between the men. But..." She brightened, though her voice trembled. "If you like it... At last someone worthy will again be able to wear it."

Miryam reached over and gently stroked the delicate weave, running her hand over the sequinned skirts.

"It is quite beautiful," she said in hushed tones.

Rachel looked at it thoughtfully. "It's quite revealing and made to be worn over a light undergarment, so we will have to find something suitable."

"I have my dancing tunic! Look!" Miryam pulled up her skirts. "This is quite respectable. I used to dance every night, so it was easier to wear it underneath than try to find somewhere to change," she chattered excitedly, her voice muffled as she pulled her outer clothes over her head.

"That's so lovely!" cried Rachel, clapping her hands. "Then it's settled. But you must try it on; you are so delicate… You may have noticed that Samaritan women are of a fuller figure."

Miryam put on the bridal gown, standing erect, while Rachel quickly and expertly folded the hem up until it was the right length for Miryam, pinning it back with some large pins. "The skirts are full and billowing and the hem won't notice. I'll get it stitched in no time."

"Oh, but let me, I can do it," insisted Miryam ."Let me. You have much to do." She hoped she sounded convincing, for the truth was she was not particularly good at sewing. But surely a hem would be within her capabilities?

Rachel smiled and handed Miryam a needle and found some thread. It was almost the right colour, but the stitches would be hidden.

"My girl!" Rachel then exclaimed, noticing Miryam's dancing tunic stained with mud and dust from the Jordan valley. "We must wash this. It's so light, and with the hot east wind blowing it will dry in no time. But first you must bathe."

She led Miryam into a small enclosed courtyard and pulled a curtain across the doorway to the house.

"And how shall we arrange your hair?" she wondered, running Miryam's long wavy locks through her hands and leaning back to admire Miryam's slender figure. "You will be quite beautiful for Moshe!"

In a rather full tunic that Rachel had lent her, and sitting under a tree sewing her bridal gown, Miryam had time to think.

"No more feeling sorry for myself. They have done so much and I… I am a bride!" She laughed happily to herself, thinking of the double horror for her grandmother if she was alive to see her now. Not only to be dressed as a bride, but as a Samaritan bride! She determined to throw off any reserve, give her all, and revel in the festivities, blotting out any traces her grandmother's disapproval, joining with high spirits in exuberant, joyful celebration that would have made her grandfather roar with approval. She sang as she sewed, joy welling up inside her in anticipation.

Daniel soon came and joined her with his clean white tunic and shepherds' ceremonial headscarf. He sat down stiffly on his bench, wiping the sweat from his forehead. Silas was basting a whole goat kid, split and spread open, spiked on wooden skewers leaning over the coals to roast, while round the fire were half pumpkins, slow-cooking in their skins. Satisfying himself that the meat was firmly staked and at the right angle to cook adequately, he came and joined them in the shade, away from the hot embers, keeping watch from a cooler distance.

Daniel made a space for Silas to join him on the bench and turned to Miryam.

"So, you have been in Jerusalem during all that has happened?"

Miryam recounted what had happened to Yeshua. She still wasn't ready to explain about Issa and Barabbas and the part she and Moshe had played. Maybe later. Maybe never. Alongside what happened to Yeshua, it was not important. Maybe sometime, somewhere, someone would tell their story. Maybe their story might help others understand better. Maybe no one would believe it anyway.

"We heard from some returning pilgrims that Yeshua had been crucified," Daniel continued. "They'd returned early. They said the city was in turmoil and they feared an uprising and reprisals, so they came home quickly."

"And did you hear that Yeshua had risen from the dead?"

"We heard rumours. Moshe arrived and tried to explain, but then…" Daniel leaned forward. "He came here."

"Here? To this house?"

"Yes! It was early in the morning. Rachel always gets up really early to make bread. We love our bread fresh and hot. Suddenly, a man appeared. He seemed familiar, but there was something different about him We have no idea how he got here. We offered him some bread, and when he gave thanks for the bread, we knew it was Yeshua by the way he said the prayer…"

"And the scars on his hands," added Silas.

"He told us he was meeting some friends and wanted to prepare breakfast for them, so could we let him have some of the bread. We said they were welcome here, but he needed to meet them further along the coast. Moshe was with us, and he and Yeshua went down to the lake with some hooks and line and they spent an hour fishing together and caught many fish. Just like Moshe was earlier. Though they caught many fish from the shore, there was a fishing boat from the other side, way out in the lake, having no success. We could tell from the way they threw their nets out again and again that they weren't catching anything. Moshe strung the fish he and Yeshua had caught on a line, which he slung round his waist, and the last we saw of Yeshua, he was heading off over the hill with the fish and bread and some burning embers to make a fire to cook the fish on. Yeshua had his hand on Moshe's shoulder and it looked as if they were deep in conversation. But of course, they couldn't have been. Soon Moshe was back. His face was shining. The fishing boat headed for the shore and we didn't see any more of them, so we reckoned that's who Yeshua was meeting. From then on, Moshe started making the house ready for you."

A thought started to trouble Miryam.

"Do you think Yeshua told Moshe he was to marry me?" She was touched that Yeshua might care so much for her, if this was so, but she was a little disappointed that she might just be a project for Moshe to fulfil rather than a beloved.

Daniel was quiet for a while.

"I don't think God ever tells anyone who they should marry, except in extra-special circumstances. And when he does, it tends to be a tough call. I think we would always blame him when things got difficult if that was the way he did it normally. But God is pleased when we make a good choice and if we walk with him humbly and prayerfully we can avoid problems. No. I think for the first time Moshe understood that he could be loved… that he was allowed to be loved. Moshe's had a hard life. He's never known a mother's or a father's love. He's always been ready to help, but in the village we treated him as an imbecile and would drive him away. I've known him from when he was a small boy. I was grieving for my lost wife and child and failed to see the poor lost boy who needed love and care."

"I'm sure Sarah loved him dearly," put in Miryam quietly.

"Oh, there's no doubt about that. But he was just beginning to respond to that love when she was so cruelly taken. It need not have been. If I hadn't been so proud and worried about my status, I could have married Sarah. God made our paths cross, but I was stubborn. I could have been a father to both Issa and Moshe. Things might have been different for all of us. But God in his mercy brought back Moshe, late in my life. He was more willing to be a loving son to me than I had been willing to be his father. Now I have him as a son, I'm so proud of him." He looked tenderly at the bronzed figure, busily helping Rachel prepare the wedding feast.

"I'm sorry if I'm taking him from you."

"My dear, you'll be my daughter, and God willing, you will bear us grandchildren, eh Silas?" Silas grinned, looking a little embarrassed.

"But one thing I don't understand. Why did Yeshua not make Moshe able to hear and speak?" puzzled Miryam.

"There are things we don't understand. But then, maybe there are things that Moshe understands that are hidden from us. He can't hear what you say but he seems to know what you're thinking; what's in your heart. And he seems to know when he's needed from many miles away. We need to see people for what they have, not what they lack. But so often, what they have to offer doesn't fit our narrow view of life.

In any case, speech often causes the problems in life. Love, joy, peace, goodness, kindness and patience don't need speech. Talking often starts the difficulties."

Miryam looked at Moshe again. "But I'm so glad the Lord gave us the ability to sign together."

"Yes. It is very important for a married couple to have a way to misunderstand each other!" He roared with laughter at his own joke as Moshe arrived, and Daniel slapped him on the back. Sensing the good-natured spirit of the joke, Moshe joined in, happily signing that they should all prepare for the feast that was now ready.

Chapter 50

Miryam sat on a bench while Rachel attended to her hair, braiding in flowers she had gathered from the hillside. They had decided to leave it as long flowing locks, which suited Miryam as she had an aversion to the elaborate hair creations that reminded her of the dancing days. Rachel was making the final adjustments to her gown when there was a timid knock at the door. It was Silas, dressed in a Greek cloak with a small hat perched on his head. He leapt back, startled, as Rachel forced the barred door open with a sudden jerk. He was clutching a small silver chain, which he nervously twisted round his fingers.

"I have this..." he started, looking at the chain for inspiration as he struggled to express himself. "Once I had a wife... Well, she made it... rather, she wore it..."

By now Miryam was in the doorway and, sensing his confusion, smiled encouragingly.

"She wore it at your wedding?" she prompted.

Silas nodded, relieved. "It's one of the few things I have to remember her by."

He held it up, searching for what to say next. Miryam took it from him, gently laying it in her hand. It was a silver headpiece, a circlet of a delicate chain with coins worked into it, the larger one in the centre designed to lie in the middle of the forehead.

"She made it over the years from when she was a small girl. There was a story behind each coin; how she had come across it, or had earned it, or been given it. Each one was very precious. She wore it on her wedding day." He looked at it, remembering that day years before. "She would have passed it on to her daughter but we had no children." He looked up hopefully. "When I heard Rachel mention you were wearing her bridal gown as her daughter would have, I remembered it. I thought, maybe… you see… like my daughter perhaps?" His voice trailed off and he turned away, looking over the lake, fearful of rejection.

"But that's so beautiful!" Miryam was quite moved. "It will be a privilege to wear it."

She held it out to Rachel. "Rachel, please set it in place for me?" she asked, leaning forward, holding her head still. Silas looked on, smiling happily as Rachel adjusted the bridal veil to accommodate the headpiece.

Once again moved by the generous love she was being shown as she was welcomed into this extended family, she found herself saying quite naturally, "Silas, I never knew my father. Would you do me the honour of being my father and leading me to the feast? Rachel has become a mother to me. You are all my family now."

A beaming Silas, with Miryam on his arm, walked together slowly down the gentle slope to where Moshe, bedecked in his brightly-coloured bridegroom's jacket, waited for his bride; his adopted father Daniel clapping and chortling with delight while Rachel strewed flowers and greenery onto the path, being simultaneously mother and flower girl. They were only five, and the feast was simple fare, but in Miryam's mind it was the feast of feasts, with singers and dancers and tables laden with food. She could hear her grandfather's inebriated cheers, and the cries of joy from her nephews and nieces and her childhood friends. Her dancing friends were there too, dressed fittingly for the occasion, happily singing and swaying in dance for her. And moving among the guests and family was the unseen but tangible presence of Yeshua himself, delighting in the joy of the occasion.

Moshe took her by the hand and led her to the place of honour, a bench bedecked in an embroidered cloth. Such joy, such peace, such a celebration! There was bread and olives; curds, raisins and roasted grain; a melon and some sweetmeats made from nuts and wild honey, and soon the roast kid and vegetables arrived.

The old men had saved a whole skin of wine ready to celebrate when Moshe returned with his bride, and they all sat and ate and drank and laughed away the afternoon.

Later Daniel noticed Moshe signing to Miryam, who shook her head, a little embarrassed, but he persisted.

"You do understand each other so well. What does he want?"

"He wants me to dance," she answered, tossing her head in embarrassment and looking away.

The old men clapped their hands.

"But of course you must dance!" Daniel turned to Silas and Rachel. "If this girl dances as well as she sings it will be wonderful!"

The old men were quite tipsy now.

"We'll all dance!" And they got unsteadily to their feet while Miryam, still a little self-conscious, cleared her throat and got ready to sing.

"It's a wedding song from the Psalms," she explained hurriedly by way of introduction.

She slipped off her bridal gown, borrowed a bright coloured scarf that Rachel was wearing and hitched up her skirts to avoid tripping on them, revealing shapely calves. Daniel picked up a wooden bucket and stick to use as a drum while Rachel ran to the house and returned with a tambourine.

My heart is full, moved by the joy of the moment.
a song, a poem for my king.
It flows like verses from a poet's pen.

You are the most handsome of men
and your hands bless us with grace and goodness

since God has blessed you for ever!
Gird your sling and staff, O strong one!
Clothe yourself with glory.
In splendour, stride out to claim your prize.

Miryam slid and pirouetted, moving fast around Moshe, waving her scarf alluringly over his head, adapting the words to apply to Moshe and signing them for him. Daniel beat time and stomped as well as his old legs would allow while Rachel waved her tambourine, wobbling her rather large figure, swaying in time with the music. She didn't know the words but added a pleasing harmony in her slightly cracked older voice while Daniel added the bass notes. Moshe, taking his cue from the beats he could see from Daniel's drumming, swayed and clapped in time, turning slowly as Miryam danced around him, bowing and arching in harmony with her graceful movements.

Silas, clearly not a dancer and a little embarrassed, nevertheless managed a few steps. The song finished, the old men cheering delightedly, Moshe proudly beaming as Miryam curtsied before him.

Rachel squealed with delight. "My dear, where did you learn to dance so beautifully?"

"Oh, you know. I used to dance, but... I stopped when I followed Yeshua." She looked up, smiling confidently. "Then the Spirit came and gave me a new dance." Joyfully, she pirouetted, flaring her skirts and dropping to her knees, looking lovingly at Moshe.

"You must dance for me later, just for me," he signed in response, in as much of a secret whisper as signing allows. But no one else understood. Only Miryam.

Miryam looked down shyly. Inside, she was troubled for just a second. Maybe one day she would tell them all of her shabby dancing days, but this was her wedding day! Did Moshe know of her previous life? Probably not in detail but, yes, he would know. She would dance for

Moshe later, but in no way would it even hint of any erotic dance from her past.

They sang and danced again, this time some popular wedding songs that her grandfather would have loved. Soon they were spent, with the food and the wine taking their toll. This was so special. Miryam was used to men becoming lurid and coarse at weddings as the wine flowed, but Daniel and Silas were gentle, happy old men. They all sat in the shade for the rest of the hot afternoon, except for Rachel, who was busy somewhere.

Sometime later Rachel returned from her errand, flushed from the heat of the sun but obviously very pleased with herself.

"Now you must be going to the lovely home Moshe has prepared for you," she said excitedly, picking up Miryam's bridal gown and holding it up for her to put on. She clicked her tongue as she looked her up and down. Miryam's hair was undone, her face streaked with sweat, and she was quite dusty from her exuberant dancing.

"My dear, you do look a state," she clucked with motherly concern, adding in a whisper as she adjusted the silver headpiece, "There's a secluded bathing place by the lake. Tonight will be hot with this east wind blowing. Make sure you bathe!"

Daniel stood a little unsteadily. "Today has been such a joy. And we'll have so much more to enjoy now you have come home. You can tell us more of the teaching of Yeshua. You know so much more of it than we do. You've spent so much time with him."

"Me?" exclaimed Miryam, horrified. "But I'm a woman! I can't even read!"

"Then I will teach you," settled Daniel. "And then if you get a chance, you can learn the scriptures and teach us those too!"

Daniel became more serious. He took their hands and joined them together, holding them in his gnarled old shepherd's hands.

"That wedding psalm you sang. It goes on:

Listen, O daughter. Consider. Give ear.
Forget your people and the home that raised you.
Your lover is captivated by your beauty;
Honour him alone. He is now your king."

He took Moshe by the shoulders while the couple still held hands, and looked deeply into his eyes.

"My boy, you can't hear my words, but you know what is in my heart. Care for this precious girl, your bride. Love her and give yourself for her."

Chapter 51

As they all stepped apart, the three old people cheered while the younger couple went slowly up the path, turning at the crest of the hill to wave. As soon as they were out of sight Miryam turned to Moshe, laughing and spinning round, her hair flying in the wind. How she loved the hills! She was free! She hitched up her skirts and bridal gown and ran along the path, laughing with joy, full of the excited anticipation at seeing her new home for the first time. Moshe bounded after her and swept her up in his arms, carrying her the last few steps to the next crest and held her up high so that she could take it all in.

There was another cove, smaller than the first. The hillside sloped steeply down to the lake, where it terminated abruptly in a ledge rather than a beach. A path from the water's edge led up to a small, whitewashed cottage with a latticed courtyard covered with a vine. Smoke curled lazily up from a fire and the door to the house was open, welcoming, beckoning. Behind the house, the hillside was levelled in terraces, the first partly fenced to make a small corral where two milking goats stood chewing the cud and, on seeing their arrival, bleating for their attention. Some chickens were pecking around under a tree, where they would shortly roost for the night. The other terraces were cultivated with vegetables and shrubs.

The sun was dropping in the sky over the hills of the western shore of the lake. Miryam could see Tiberias, still brightly lit by the sun across the lake, and further round, the other Galilean villages. Moshe put Miryam down and led her into the house. The one-roomed cottage was neat and simply furnished with some chests and, in the far corner, a large bed discreetly hidden behind a beaded curtain, a multicoloured braided cover pulled back and to one side, welcoming, inviting: 'Come and pull me over you and be safe'. It was the braided cover Moshe had hidden under two years earlier. Now she would hide under it herself, safe in his arms.

Their bundles were inside the door against a wall and Miryam supposed that Rachel had brought them over, prepared the house and started the fire.

They went back outside and stood looking over the lake. She pointed out Tiberias and signed that it was her old home. Moshe grinned his 'I know' grin and a cold hand gripped her heart. What did he know about her life there? She took his hands and looked deeply into his eyes. There must be no secrets now.

"There were other men," she signed and dropped her eyes, fearing.

He gently held her face in his hands, coaxing her head up so that she would look again into his eyes. They were so full of love that she felt the fear evaporating. She had seen such a smile before. It had so much of the look Yeshua had given her, the look that John said made him feel that 'he was *the* disciple Yeshua loved', and she felt that love reflected now in the face of Moshe. Blended into the searching soft brown eyes that gazed into hers was a joyful incredulity. What was it Daniel had said? 'He understood for the first time that he could be… was allowed to be loved.'

"And I am loved by you! It is just us now!" his loving gaze expressed as clearly as if he had spoken.

Joy welled up inside her, banishing the fear. She looked again to the far shore. The bright setting sun was just above the western hills. Tiberias was now in shadow, fading from view as the sky flamed, orange, red, and azure; a searing, purifying flame of fire shimmering across the lake to where she stood, seeking her out, dazzling her with light, purifying her mind of the pain and memories, burning up the dross of her past life. And as the sun dipped below the peaks, Tiberias was visible no more.

Her past life was gone forever, buried in the depths of the sea before her.

She turned back to Moshe, who dropped her hands, swinging, signing a dance.

"You will dance? For me? Later?" he queried.

"A dance! I must have a special dance for him!" she whispered to herself. She would need to be alone to get this just right.

"I must bathe first," she indicated, pointing to the lake.

He smiled and gestured that there were things that he too must do. He signed that the lake was deep here, and she should be careful, but she indicated that she could swim and he laughed and left her. She hurried back to her bundle and found some rough soap and a towel and headed towards the lake.

The house and the terrace were hidden behind the outcrop and the bathing place was quite secluded. The evening was warm as the hot, easterly breeze was blowing. She stood for some time looking out over the lake, thinking of how she might dance for Moshe. She struggled to remember the words of the Song of Songs that she used to sing when she lived in Bethlehem. She hadn't sung the words since then, and they were a little muddled in her mind. They would be the basis of her dance, a song of pure love. She must banish all the memories of the erotic dances of her past life from her mind. She left her bridal gown and headpiece some way up the path to keep them safe from the water, and stepped down to the lakeside.

She hitched up her tunic as she stepped off the ledge, but the water was even deeper than she had imagined for the lake side fell away rapidly, as Moshe had warned. She had to hold onto the ledge to avoid slipping in.

But how inviting the water looked! She remembered her night swims in the lake in Tiberias after the dancing orgies. That was the one good memory she had, for she had enjoyed the cool cleansing of the water and the freedom she had felt as she swam. Free of all the memory of sordid, drunken, vomit-strewn orgies in the villas where she had danced. She was ever grateful to her friend who had taught her to swim and dive, just like the lake children. She would swim now!

She climbed back out, slipping off her clothes, and pushed off from the ledge into the deep, swimming underwater, breaking the surface with a cry of joy and throwing her arms high into the sky. She struck out, dipping and diving as she had seen the children do in their exuberance. She swam to the far side of the cove and pulled herself out onto the rock, still warm from the heat of the sun. Hugging her legs, with her chin resting on her knees, she basked in the warmth of the rock as she looked out over the water. She must try and remember the song, how did it go? But it escaped her. A light twinkled, distracting her as the gathering darkness allowed the lamps of the towns across the lake be seen.

A light in Tiberias!

She thought of the old priestly couple. God bless them as they lit a light in Tiberias! She prayed that they would soon have a group of other followers of Yeshua around them, maybe other dancing girls or some of the pitiful young sex slaves.

Soon other lights appeared around the lake, and she imagined the other returning pilgrims setting up small communities of followers of The Way, unlikely as such groups might be in Tiberias. As they were here. A healed pagan, an old shepherd, a Samaritan woman, an ex-dancing girl and a deaf-mute outcast, whose servant heart had drawn them all together.

She must try and think of a dance for Moshe! He wouldn't be able to hear the song, so she must dance it for him. She must recall the words so that she could make its meaning clear. It was getting darker now and she needed to get back. She stood on the rock, arms outstretched to the evening star over the hills of Galilee, then throwing her head back face upturned to the twinkling stars in the sky above her; she held her pose before springing neatly into the water and swimming slowly back to the ledge.

With still no dance planned she deftly slipped back onto the rock, wrapping her towel around her shoulders, heading back up the path to find her bridal gown.

But Moshe had found it first!

He stood in the twilight, smiling at her. His hair was brushed and oiled. He was wearing his bridegroom's jacket with a clean linen loin cloth wrapped around his waist. She quickly pulled her towel off her shoulders, holding it in front of her to cover her embarrassment. Moshe stepped forward and tenderly wrapped the bridal gown around her shoulders and placed the headpiece gently on her head, then stood back smiling, signing "Thank you... for the dance."

She looked at him puzzled, and he signed: "I watched you... dive... swim... beautiful!"

She lifted her the towel to her face in horror, her eyes expressing her shock. She'd assumed he was busy with the animals, but he had been watching her!

He shrugged, grinning. "You watched me... when I was swimming with the children... not married then."

So he had known. The infuriating man saw everything and had known she had dallied, watching, admiring his naked body as he'd played on the mud slide! She beat her clenched fists on his chest in frustration and as she did so, he pulled her into his arms, stroking her glistening hair and gently kissing her forehead as she let the towel fall to the ground. His chest and neck were loaded with the scent of spices; manly spices. She turned her face to him and their lips met, kissing tenderly. The exhilaration of the swim, the warmth of his body, the kisses, the spices, all made her dizzy with love. Couplets tumbled through her mind, unlocking the song she had been searching for:

Kiss me, full on the mouth!
Your love is better than wine, than spices.

382

Take me with you, let us run off together,
We'll celebrate, we will make music together!

He swung her slender body up into his arms, carrying her back towards the cottage, her head thrown back, arms stretched out behind her as she looked up at the myriad watching stars who became the friends in the song. Her friends from the past. But look at me now!

I am weathered but still elegant.
Darkened, they ridiculed me,
Made me work.

With his lips, with his face, Moshe was sensing the vibration of her voice, laying his cheek against her throat. The song burst through her head as the aroma of the spices and aromatic oils in his hair burst over her:

With his head between my breasts
my lover was a sachet of myrrh.

As if on cue, he straightened and looked into her eyes:

You are so beautiful.
Your eyes are so beautiful, like doves.

In amazement, she realised her singing was following his actions. Yet she thought she was supposed to be dancing for him!

The song had become a duet, Moshe leading in dance and she following in song.

And as he led with swaying, dancing steps, delicate manoeuvres and intricate signs, the words of the song wafted into her mind on the zephyr-like breeze. They moved and spun over the ground as she dangled in his arms, and he swung her in an effortless lilt and perfect rhythm. Words she had long forgotten came back, fresh and pure:

> Come north wind, blow south wind,
>   blow on my garden. Let its fragrance spread abroad!

He carried her through the trees, the moon flitting through the branches, and under the vine and into the cottage, until finally he laid her gently onto the bed, springing back with a flourish, his bridegroom's jacket slipping off his shoulders onto the floor.

> And you, dear lover, are so handsome!
> And the bed we share is a forest glen.

She took in the rough beams of the roof above her, rough acacia wood but, to her, boughs of cedar in the forest of Lebanon:

> A canopy of cedars.
> Cypresses, fragrant and green.

He knelt by her side and looked lovingly into her eyes. She looked from one dark soft gentle brown eye to the other and back again.

He, incredulous that after years of rejection by others she would want him for her lover.

She, faint with the joy of the beloved.

She sang for him.

> Like a delicate lily among the briers
> is my beloved among women,
>   And then

He carried me into his banqueting hall,
 Love, the banner over me.
Bring me passion fruit, raisins, apples,
for I am delirious with love.

And as deep called to deep, resonating with, responding to a love that filled his whole being, she saw again the echo of that look of love they had both known in the eyes of their Lord Yeshua:

I am my now only beloved's! And he is mine!

She took him in her arms, pressing his head to her breast so he could feel the vibrations of her voice.

Yes! The winter is past!
The storms have passed, the rains have gone.
Arise, my lover,
 Come my handsome one.
Come away with me!

Bible Links

Mary's songs
Chapter 4:   Luke 2
Chapter 9:   Numbers 6:24-26
Chapter 13:   Psalm 27, Psalm 36

Sarah's songs
Chapter 14:   Psalm 27, Psalm 36, Psalm 136
Chapter 16:   Psalm 91
Chapter 19:   Luke 2

Daniel's songs
Chapter 17:   Micah 6:6-8
Chapter 19:   Psalm 119:105, Psalm 15
Chapter 23:   Psalm 22, Lamentations 3, Psalm 23

John's songs
Chapter 21:   Psalm 32, Psalm 51

Miryam's songs
Chapter 27:   Psalm 91, Psalm 27
Chapter 28:   Psalm 23

Daniel's farewell song to Issa
Chapter 32:   Psalm 121

Love songs
Chapters 4, 22, 51: Song of Songs

Love story of Ruth and Boaz

Chapters 2, 5, 19: Ruth

Wedding song

Chapter 50:   Psalm 45

Prophecy quotes

Chapter 19:   Micah 7

Chapter 47:   Joel 2

Acknowledgements

I would like to thank the friends and family who have encouraged me in my writing over the years. Particular thanks to my wife Tricia, for her loving support, and to Mike Snook, whose brotherly chiding and coaxing eventually saw the text of Ramah completed. My thanks to Chris Orme, Rachel Maurice and Lindsay Sharpe and granddaughter Izzy who also read the first draft, giving me a critical appraisal and encouraging me to try for publication. I am grateful to Chris and my ever patient Tricia, who then spent many hours rereading the manuscript, making corrections and detailed suggestions, in particular teaching me what the buttons adorned with various squiggles, which I had often noticed at the bottom right hand corner of my keyboard, were actually for.

Special thanks to Malcolm Down and Chloe Evans for their patient encouragement and careful and critical editing in getting Ramah published.

I am ever grateful to the children's groups, both leaders and young people, of King's Church Reading, who indulged me in my early creative writing as we explored the many stories of the Bible, and where I started writing the first chapters of Ramah.

And last but not least, my thanks to the Wichí Indian young people of the Gran Chaco, whose contextualisation and often hilarious dramatic renderings of Bible stories inspired me and made me look at Bible times through the eyes of a culture far removed from my own.